this shattered promise

Born in Kalgoorlie in 1982, Sharada loves poetry, nature, reading, writing, electricity, hot running water, petrichor, a certain degree of cliché, and circumstances that ensure young people can enjoy basic human rights, be nurtured, and grow old happily and healthily. She feels strongly that people of all ages deserve a wider variety of stories and storytellers. Sharada grew up in Australia and Canada, with parents from Guyana and Yorkshire – influences that still shape her writing. She studied agricultural economics in university, and has spent many years working in the third sector. Sharada now lives with her partner, two young children, and ancient old cat in London, UK.

In memory of Shirley and John Dixon

1

MORA

vivisection

I take a lungful of muggy air and count my blessings.

Once I thought the Skøl invasion had swept away everyone I loved. I've since discovered families grow in the stoniest ground and love can endure even the end of the world.

I'm alive. Kit's safe. So is my brother, Zako. And Ruzi – my father, as it turned out. *I'm lucky*, I tell myself. I've got a new job. I get to live in the Castle Hotel, no less, in Rundvaer Square – the beating heart of Portcaye town. The downside is my boss is a nightmare and I am basically a prisoner.

I've been up here, sleeping in a room annexed off Nezza's, for nearly four weeks. Nezza Sculpin, the six-year-old ward of my new boss. She looks sweet, but with me she's pure vinegar.

I can hear her in the next room.

"Minty, up. Minty, Minty, Minty boy! Up!"

Minty is her pet spotted devil – brown-furred with black markings and a tufted black tail. He's the size of a rat, with the same vicious teeth, but he's half fluff and half bones, light as anything. Devils are common garden pests down south, not usually tame. We don't get them this far north.

On top of my main duties, I'm supposed to help with Nezza. Help her dress, keep an eye on her, fetch her meals, look after her when she's sickly, do her hair. Sting's assistants say her nurse and her father both died on the journey up here to Portcaye, though they won't say how it happened beyond a tragic accident at sea.

Nezza doesn't like me, and her hair doesn't like anyone. True to her, it won't be governed. *No, no, no! You can't tell me what to do.* Tantrums like a child half her age. *I don't want that!* Throwing her food on the floor, getting crumbs everywhere so I have more to clean up. *Mora, read to me. Mora, play with me. Mora, I'll tell if you don't…* Minty has better manners. And he isn't a snitch.

Nezza Sculpin's not what you'd expect. She's got that nose-in-the-air attitude of most rich Skøl, but not the matching set of ice-pale features. Her father was Skøl, so her mother must have been mixed – both Crozoni and Xan. Perhaps she had the round face and curly hair of many of my own people, the Crozoni. I wonder if her eyes were a vivid violet like Kit's or the muddy violet that Nezza's are. Nezza's Skøl half is most evident in the colour of her skin and hair – both lighter than mine, apart from a birthmark over part of her neck and a smattering of freckles.

The personal sketchbooks that survived her father, Mister Ardent Sculpin, expedition scientist and artist, are full of elektrical diagrams and animals – elektric eels and fancy catfish, knifefish, torpedo rays. All animals somehow connected to elektricity – an interest of his. No drawings of Nezza. He must have knocked up her mother the minute they invaded. I'm not naive – I'm sure a lot of that happened. More unusual is that he kept the child after her mother's death and raised her like his own, gave her his last name. A child his people think is half scum.

And now his former boss and my current one, Sciencemaster Sacrifice Sting, the most prominent scientist in all of Skøland, is raising her as his ward. Sting must have been very close with her father to take her in.

Nezza's not allowed outside either, but she's so young she just accepts it.

Flap, flap, thud… One of Rundvaer Square's pretty pigeons lands beside the window, flaunting its freedom. The glass only opens a crack, and it's so warped that everything on the other side swims. The heat of the Sevenmonth is as trapped up here as Nezza and Minty and me, cooking up smells of pencil shavings, charcoal, paper and glue. The kind of smells I used to love – when drawing was my choice. Not any more.

With a scrabble against the roof's metal edging and a soft feathery snap of wings, my visitor departs. I pretend it's me flying over Portcaye this afternoon, looking down at the markets, the docks, the big trade ships at anchor, the slow River Rin spilling into the dark swells of summer sea, curving away to the edge of the world.

I can smell my own stale unease mixed with pencil and spotted devil. Behind it is the clinging taint of the Sciencemaster General's laboratory work – his preserved specimens and gruesome boiled concoctions. My clothes feel grubby with it, though he keeps a tidy enough lab – everything squared away in the dedicated space he's commandeered up on the fifth floor.

That night a month ago, when the branders dragged me away from Kit and threw me in the filthy drunk tank, I'd thought that was it. That they'd somehow figured out it was me who'd killed Venor – the man about to be sworn in as Governor of the New West. Deputy to the High Governor, Clarion Lovemore.

But no. It seemed Lovemore herself had bought me – for her famed Sciencemaster General. Lovemore is passionate about scientific discovery – some say to a fault. She pours money like water into developments in elektricity, physical science, feats of engineering – anything to prop up her own power.

Twenty-seven days ago today – I am counting – the first thing Sting said to me was, "Mora Dezil. You draw."

"Y-yes?" My voice cracked.

"I have heard of your recall and depiction skills," Sting explained. His bushy and mostly white moustache grew right into his sideburns, which faded into the thinner and even whiter hair on his head.

We were standing in the brand-spanking-new Hexagon Hall exhibition centre, another of Lovemore's pet projects – to display the latest advances in scientific discovery. I'd never set foot inside before. The sun shone beautifully, oblivious to my miserable mood, through the pitched glass roof, bathing the carvings, crates, display cases and sundries stacked around in multicolour tinted light. "I require a demonstration," Sting said. The sideburn-moustache monstrosity bristled in the light.

I nodded, trying to forget that I'd come straight from a night in jail without so much as a bite to eat or a splash of water on my face. How had a man like him heard about someone like me?

He placed a shallow brown cardboard box with a dead beetle inside it before me at a marble table. Pencils and blank paper of exceptional quality followed. I noticed his fingers were sunburnt, blunt and stubby.

"You may commence with this sculpin weevil. Magnify it – to the size of my fist." His squat fingers curled until the smallest was strangled by its panelled gold ring. I noticed some scabs on a few of his outsized knuckles, trailing up the back of his sun-weathered, reddish hand. Not elegant hands. Not how I might have imagined the hands of an eminent Skøl man of science to look.

The beetle was roughly the size of my thumbnail, a miniature riot of colour to rival the glass roof, pinned between its head and body to a cushion lining the box. The wing cases were open, transparent wings exposed.

I picked up its little coffin to examine it more closely, my hands shaking, from hunger as much as anything. After a brief moment, he plucked it away and placed it out of sight.

"Draw exactly what you remember, down to the finest detail. And be sure to do your best, or I may do my worst."

My fingers clutched the pencil and stopped shaking as the pretty weevil took shape beneath my hand, larger than life, although drained of colour. I drew the spidery lace pattern of its wings, its dull eyes and strange mouthparts. Larger than death. *No.*

Sting came closer. "What is this? Your embellishment?"

"There are small pits in the wing cases."

He retrieved the box, swung a pocket magnifying lens from its leather case and peered through it. "Hmm. Your eyes function well."

I breathed a little easier. "And if I could ask, wh—"

"Conceivably you *could*, but you may not."

He repeated the test with a water beetle and a dusty moon moth – still beautiful – and then a carved amber figurine of a kine, roughly done, only a few inches high. I'm fond of kine – the thick-bodied, long-nosed, four-horned beasts the Skøl brought with them when they invaded nearly seven years ago.

I perched the figurine on one palm and lifted it to the light.

"This looks Xan," I ventured. The Xan people are known to mine and craft with amber still, out in the Badlands, their last refuge.

"It is Xan in origin," Sting confirmed. "An ancient piece, I believe, fashioned around three to four millennia past, when the desert was not the barrier it is today."

The desert was what kept us separate, before the Skøl invasion. They came anyway – from the west by boat and across the northeastern sands, over the Mala mountains, riding their kine. Kine are hardier than horses.

"Now." One of his big hands snatched the piece away. "Make haste. Draw it true to size, schematic view."

I reflected on the amber's lightness, its hair-thin interior crackles and imperfections. Sting nodded, then handed me another item.

It was a cube of wood the size of his fist, strange symbols carved into each side. Xan again.

"Don't rush with this specimen. I want a *complete* depiction." He left the item on the marble table and went across the room to supervise an assistant opening one of the crates.

I focused on the cube. Odd he had left me this to study, when it seemed much simpler than the other objects. *A complete depiction.* The Xan symbols looked familiar, but I wasn't sure why. Dust drifting in the morning light danced with my breath, and memory struck like a sail boom.

One late summer evening the year I turned nine, I was in the shed with my baby brother, Char. He was around two. The sun was setting, and he was trying to catch the dust motes fired up by its glow as they floated in the still air of the shed. *Ooh! Ooh!* He was all raw delight and I was filled up with it, joyful. He was only five when they killed him.

Taking a breath, I picked up the wooden cube and something moved inside.

It was hollow, the corners bevelled. A pleasant shape, meant to be held. No obvious lid or opening. I knew what it was now though. A trick box.

Trick boxes, like amber, are more Xan than Crozoni. Grandpa was keen on them though, and Pa had two that he'd inherited from him. They needed different knacks to open them. A panel would pop open from one of Pa's if you squeezed the ends. The other had a secret piece that needed sliding out before the lid would pivot.

I tried both techniques on this box, but it didn't give. Then I realized the symbols carved into the faces were part of separate joined panels – subtly constructed from the same piece of wood to give a uniform look. Pressing only those smaller sections on two parallel sides opened a crack in one of the perpendicular faces, allowing me to tease out a drawer.

Inside, I found polished amber again, with – surprise – another dead bug. A bee this time. A trap within a trap.

The Sciencemaster General gave a ghastly smile when he came to see my work.

"Your talents have not been exaggerated," he said. "You will join me at the Castle Hotel. I think you will prove useful indeed."

After that, I was dragged up here: not eighteen years old and the official new expedition artist attached to Clarion Lovemore's first-ever tour of the New Western Counties. Sketching away under the watchful eye of Sciencemaster Sacrifice Sting himself. Plus, unofficially, Nezza Sculpin's replacement nursemaid – two for the price of one.

Sting's two assistants – one man and one woman, Mister Glor Stanwin and Miz Hunter Vinslar, are both in their twenties. They consider themselves far above me and we barely speak, though they hang off Sting's every word.

The other day when I asked one of them what all this experimentation was supposed to add up to, he deigned to tell me a little – in hushed tones.

"We are on the cusp of a scientific breakthrough that will change everything." His whisper was fervent. "It will shape the future of Skøland. It is the secret to extending life."

"Really?" I'd said, sceptical.

But Glor had nodded eagerly.

No wonder Lovemore is interested. The Skøl treat life like land – something you must buy, own. Something you can sell. Why not try to acquire more – for those who can afford it?

Butterflies seem to be key to these experiments. Sting's

upstairs all hours, and when he isn't desecrating Xan bones, he's jabbing hollow metal needles into defenceless caterpillars and sucking their insides out into little glass vials. Grinding up butterflies by the boatload. And then there's what he does to the spotted devils. There's a word he calls it – means cutting things open while they're still alive. He made me sketch that the first week I started working for him.

Vivisection.

2

MORA

shipway town

The Castle Hotel is Lovemore's now. She came to Portcaye to appoint one of the three colonial magistrates as a new deputy, a Governor of the New West. I murdered the man she wanted – Valour Venor.

But she's sticking around, leaving the post vacant for the time being. Rumour from the kitchens is she grew keen to tour the colonies after rumblings of dissent in the homeland. We don't get much news of such rumblings out here. But they say she's desperate to prop up her reputation as *still powerful, still in control.*

You can only grind people down for so long before they expire or explode. The cost of life is too high. Her decision to invade and hold Makaia and the Crozon Isles has been expensive. She needs branders to keep the peace. New Life Registries. Administration, guns, elektricity. It hasn't been smooth sailing, taking over the known world.

Lovemore's up for a vote this Tenmonth – the Council of Magistrates only votes every decade. The election is usually a formality – Lovemore has ruled for nearly thirty years and no one has dared oppose her. But now, a real rival has emerged – a challenger from the Council of Magistrates in Skøland called Temper Wilforn. Instead of proposals that affect a few, he promises change for all. It's easy to see why his campaign has caught fire. Rumour has it that Lovemore is worried.

"She bought half the votes the first time and all of them the last time," I overheard one of the assistant cooks telling another. "Temper Wilforn isn't going to sit on his heels another ten years, trembling every time she barks. He's nearly sixty now … says he wants change."

"Pity *Long Live Wilforn* doesn't have the same ring as *Long Live Lovemore*," the other one joked. "He'll never pull it off."

"Never say never. Maybe Lovemore is right to be scared. Did you hear what they're saying about the old magistrate that killed himself?" The other assistant pushed a copy of the *Portcaye Post* across the table, with its headline reading:

MAGISTRATE'S SUSPECTED SUICIDE

Did Valour Venor end own life? Or was death a political assassination?

"Who knows, eh, who knows with these high folks?"

I'd had a sudden vision of Venor after I poisoned him, smashing up his desk, his face contorted with anger. I'd turned away. *Venor is dead*, I'd reminded myself. He's not coming back.

Yesterday evening, Nezza barged in as I was drawing at my desk. It was the first day of the Sevenmonth.

"I'm hungry," she said.

It was early. I could tell by the light – well before anyone might reasonably expect an evening meal. "Nice to see you too. Dinner won't be for a while yet."

"I need food." She rubbed her stomach. "I had my treatment this morning, remember?"

Sting was treating Nezza for fits that she'd apparently had since birth. These weekly doses of medicine always left her feeling fragile.

"It's too early," I told her.

"What time is it?"

I sighed and pulled the timepiece from my pocket to show her. It was the one Goldie Reedstone had given me. I'd only kept it because I hadn't had time to try and sell it. It didn't look too out of place among the frills and flourishes of the stuffy outfits I'd been made to wear as one of Sting's servants. I had on my jet-black trousers and a pale-purple blouse with a ridiculous number of rounded fabric buttons, on top of grey undergarments. Half of me was covered up with a crisp white artist's pinny. It had gold thread round its rectangular front pocket, framing a silhouetted face, also picked out in gold thread – Clarion Lovemore's, of course. You'd think she'd get sick of seeing her profile everywhere.

Even more irritatingly, I'd been obliged to replace my favourite hair wraps with ineffective white beribboned caps in Skøl design. They didn't keep my hair secure. They were more like old Crozoni cloth jam-jar covers.

"It's only half past five." I interpreted the dials on the pocket timepiece for her. "Why don't you pop down to the kitchen and ask them for a snack?" I knew Nezza was more than capable of storming into the kitchen to demand food herself. I'd seen her do it.

"I don't feel good. I'm all shaky." Her annoying whine.

"All right. Give me two minutes."

"Go *now*!"

The old injury in my right hip was stiff from sitting so long at the table, sketching and labelling, and in truth I wanted a break from drawing the items Sting's team had removed from a Xan grave for an upcoming exhibition.

"Fine," I told Nezza. "I'll go find you something."

I stripped off my white pinny and went down the servants' stairs.

And there was Kit, where he absolutely shouldn't have been, on the lower-ground floor of the Castle Hotel – the servants' domain, but still not safe.

How many times had I daydreamed just this?

"Mora." He spoke so softly I thought I was hearing

things again. His voice, low and husky with emotion, absolutely sent my heart galloping off.

He was dressed like one of the Castle Hotel kitchen staff – the yellow-gold jacket fitted well, but the grey trousers were an inch too short – and he bore a tray peppered with empty dishes. He took in my new outfit with a sympathetic look before his beautiful smile stretched out and tripped my racing heart.

A thousand feelings united to ambush me. Thrill to see him, terror he'd put himself in harm's way, a stupid shyness, quickly strangled by my irritation at that shyness, joy fizzing like salt in one of Nezza's fancy baths, plain relief.

When I snapped back to myself, he was five paces ahead down the corridor. I followed.

"You'll get caught!" I hissed, instead of the ten thousand other things I'd imagined saying to him over our weeks apart. *I love you. I miss you.*

The familiar, obvious affection in his dark-violet eyes grounded me. A blink. That smile again. We reached the storage room at the opposite end of the corridor. The elektric light in the centre of the ceiling, softened behind a frosted-glass sconce, was already on. Clean linen and other supplies were stacked on the shelves – I think, I didn't pay much attention as I hastened to shut the door. Kit clattered the tray down on a rare bit of empty shelf even as he reached for me. One hand tangled with one of mine, the other gathered me close. The ghost of a laugh built like something elektric behind his smile.

"Here you are," he murmured, hoarse with emotion, probably a similar soup of feelings to mine. I breathed in the warm scent of him, nuzzling my face into his neck before the desire ratcheted up another notch and I kissed him, right where skin met collar.

Only when he turned his head and found my lips was I sure it wasn't a daydream. It was real – beyond fantasy or memory. I'd forgotten how good it was to kiss him – I who never forget anything. We'd kissed before, but not like this. I tangled my fingers with his, even as I pulled his waist closer with my free hand. His other hand moved feather-light over my back before cupping my head. My spine was singing. I wanted to burrow into him, under his skin, and never let go. I wanted to wear him like a costume, without all these layers of fabric between us – jackets, shirts, trousers.

Everything else – the fear and frustration of the last few weeks – dropped away. We drifted back against one of the shelves, thigh to thigh, chest to chest, lips to tongues to teeth to lips. I wanted to stay right where I was, to hell with escaping.

Captivity was good.

Too soon though, reason began to insert itself into the tiny spaces between us. There is only so far you can go in a cramped lower-ground storage room in Portcaye's fanciest hotel before someone walks in on you. Time was not on our side.

With an effort of heroic magnitude, I put a few inches

of space between our chests and turned a serious eye on him. His tousled, stung-lipped expression nearly undid me, but at least my stupid shyness had evaporated.

"What are you doing here? How'd you get in?" I was still short of breath, my mouth hovering near his, our shared desire roaring so loud I could hardly hear myself. He kissed me again. Stubborn and reckless and exactly what I wanted.

I untangled my fingers from his and moved my hands to his hips, huffing a little laugh. "Kit, we have to talk."

"Uh-huh, okay," he agreed immediately, at the same time closing the tiny gap for another kiss he knew full well I had no will to oppose.

After a minute or two, I slid gently away again.

"Kit."

"Okay, okay."

Another kiss, on the corner of my mouth. Then my neck. I gathered myself and managed, "*Kalqitlan*."

His sigh sent a warm shiver through me. He leaned back and brushed my bottom lip with the soft edge of his thumb. "What I'm doing here is seeing you. Glister got me in. But I can't get you out." His confession sounded miserable. "Her security's tight as a…"

I'd suspected it wouldn't be safe to try and leave with him, but I still fought to keep my disappointment at bay. Lovemore's guards never relaxed. Vigilance always, whether she was in the hotel or out on a visit.

"At least you got in."

"I don't have long."

Kit was looking at me in an overly serious way, like he was trying to memorize my face.

"You never got my note?" he said.

"I got nothing."

"Thought so."

"Did anything happen? Is it... Is Zako...?"

"No. Everyone's fine. It's nothing bad. I just had to see you." His gaze broke from mine. "I'm going away for a bit. With the Reedstones. I promised them I'd do one more job..."

My heart started to bang hard, fire and fury. "Another job for those—?" I spluttered. "I wouldn't be stuck in here if it weren't for them! They owe *us*!"

He winced, winding some of my curls around two of his fingers then stroking the back of my neck so tenderly I began to calm despite everything.

"They didn't have much choice," he murmured, and I knew he was right. No one can openly refuse High Governor Clarion Lovemore or her Sciencemaster General anything.

It's my fault as much as anyone's that Sting found out about my drawing abilities. I wanted to make a name for myself with my sketches. To draw attention and make money.

Still, I don't trust the Reedstones. I certainly don't like Kit working for them. "What have you promised them this time?"

His eyes flitted over to the door.

"Someone's coming," he whispered. I strained to hear and caught footsteps growing louder. Kit reclaimed his abandoned tray, balancing it on one arm. Less gracefully, I gathered a stack of clean linen, piling it high enough to cover half my face, praying all the while the footsteps would continue past us.

The feet in question, belonging to a Skøl maid, did not oblige. She wasn't young, but we discovered she was timid when she let out a shriek of surprise to find two people – repayers at that – inside with the door closed.

"Sorry!" I dropped her a deferential bob, before her startlement could melt to anger. "Sciencemaster General sent us. Needs more of these—" I moved my face closer to the pile of linens in my arms and edged round her.

Plausible, I thought to myself.

When we were out of earshot, Kit gave me a look and whispered, "Have I taught you nothing?" His grin was infectious.

The secret to being somewhere you don't belong, as he's told me more than once, is to act like you do belong. The secret to breaking in. To staying in. To breaking out. Perhaps to a lot more.

Our flight from the storage room had taken us close to the narrower, less popular one of the two servants' stairwells.

"I have a room on the fourth floor," I told him.

I led the way. I wanted his clever hands running over

my ribs again, playing me like a musical instrument. The thrill of his mouth on mine.

We mounted the steep stairs, squeezing into the wall to let a harried servant with a bucket and mop pass us on the way down. He didn't spare us a second glance.

"The Reedstones have done their best," Kit said. "They've bought Ruzi out of the Glassworks – he's staying with us at the Lugger. And they're paying his passage, and Zako's, out to the Isles. Blithe has done all the paperwork. It's flawless. Their ship sails Endweek after next – on the tenth of the month."

The tenth! Nine days.

"It's all arranged. They'll be safe, Mor, with Missus Scarlet's friend."

My little brother, Zako. And my father, Ruzi. Finally leaving Portcaye to start anew, with new identities, out in the Crozon Isles. It's what we'd always planned for Zako, if we could get the money together and find a good forger for his papers. Blithe Even Ronbor, or "the Artist" as he so humbly calls himself, is the best forger there is. We'd risked our necks for him only a month before and I suppose he was paying us back.

"Speaking of Ruzi—" Kit pulled on a thin bit of black ribbon that went round the back of his neck and disappeared down his shirt. It was a pendant. A lozenge of green glass dangled at the bottom, swaying with his steps. "He sent this for you. With his love – for your birthday."

"Ruzi got that? For me?" It wasn't a normal thing for

the Glassworks to sell. He must have asked someone we knew to make it specially. I was touched, especially since I'd done nothing to mark my birthday, my eighteenth, the week before.

"Yeah. Here." Kit took it off and we paused as he eased it over my cap, over my head. My high collar hid the ribbon so no one would know it was there.

"We'll celebrate properly when you're out of here. But I got you something small," Kit said, digging in his breast pocket.

"Really?" I thought for an absurd minute he was about to give me jewellery as well.

He fished out three lock picks, and I gave a short laugh. Kit's idea of romance.

"I know you're not about to escape with these, but you never know when they might come in handy." His unguarded, open expression melted my heart and I felt cruel for laughing. Lock picks were far more useful than decorative glass.

Ruzi and Zako, nearly safe. It was the best outcome I could have hoped for, and my heart swelled to know Kit had arranged it. But I had to consider the catch – that Kit must have promised the Reedstones something in exchange.

"And you told Goldie and Glister you'd go with them," I said. "For one last job. Where, exactly?"

"Shipway town."

3

MORA

feverish sleep

I stubbed a toe, already pinched painfully in the silly shoes my uniform required, into one of the risers and stumbled gracelessly up the stairs before Kit steadied me.

County Shipway is so far south they say winter's breath barely reaches it.

"*Ship*way?" I moaned. "Ten thousand miles away? But..."

"Three thousand, at the most," Kit corrected.

He might have been going to Skøland, or the moon, or to whatever lay beyond the impassable shallow sea. It was an unthinkable journey, doubly so for people like us – weeks and weeks by train, if it was a day.

"It's three weeks by one of their fast ships," he reminded me, reading my mind. "I'll be back before you know it."

I frowned. The sea route would be faster than going by train – and *much* faster than taking a carriage or a kine overland. The expense of such a passage wouldn't be prohibitive for the Reedstones.

"What do they want you doing in Shipway?" I asked.

"It's an easy job. Goldie and Glister are attending a fancy fundraiser for Temper Wilforn's campaign. Shaking hands and greasing palms. They seem to think this Wilforn's worth going out on a limb for. And while they're doing that, me and Blithe will be liberating and copying some documents. The usual."

The Reedstone's *usual* was not as reassuring as Kit tried to make it sound. *Liberating documents* usually meant breaking into a private property, one secured with the newest elektric locks, to steal something the Reedstones could use to blackmail the owners. They moved in high society circles, coming from an influential family, but they made their own fortune selling elektric locks and were politically motivated to boot, with an axe to grind against Lovemore.

"What's the paperwork?" I asked as we hurried towards the door to Nezza's room.

"I don't know."

Was his answer too quick? I couldn't tell if it was truth or evasion, but I knew the Reedstones weren't ones to go for small fry. Especially not if they were going three thousand miles for it.

"Ooh! Finally!" Nezza bounced on her toes, oblivious to our agitation. She saw Kit's tray first – though she couldn't see its plates were empty – and looked hopeful.

I remembered too late, with a dreadful sinking feeling, her promised snack.

"Hello, there." Kit flashed her a toothy grin before he turned his bemused expression my way. Nezza was a surprise to him too – her obvious mixture of Xan, Crozoni and Skøl.

Some of the more unruly edges of her hair caught the sun as she cocked her head at Kit. I was struck again by how sweet she looked, and how entirely deceptive that was.

"You're brown!" she blurted. "Like – like my friend. Who are you?"

"He's … no one special," I tried to keep my voice steady. "He's a servant here."

No one special? Kit narrowed his eyes at me until I felt it in my bones, but I held my neutral expression in front of Nezza and she accepted it well enough.

"All right Mister No-one-special. Is that my food?" She wasn't letting that go. "I'm starving!"

I improvised rapidly. "No. It's – it's for drawing. Your guardian needs us to do this right away. This man is helping me. Give us five minutes."

"I feel yucky," she said. "I had a new treatment today. Minty's hungry too!" She slurped a string of dribble back up through the gap in her front teeth, another disgusting habit of hers.

"I'll find you something soon," I soothed, shutting the door to my annex room in her face.

“Uhnngggh!” Her wordless outrage penetrated the wood, followed by a series of Minty’s chittering calls.

“Her treatment?” Kit whispered.

“She’s fine. She’s Sting’s ward, but she’s—”

“Five minutes!” Her shrill reminder sounded on the other side of the door. “Looking after me is also your job, not just drawing. All. Day.”

“She’s a pain,” I finished.

I blew out an exasperated breath and joined Kit by the desk. He wrapped an arm around me as he took in the works in progress I’d brought down from the laboratory to complete here. He picked out a nearly finished drawing of a palm-sized Xan sculpture taken from the last desecrated grave we’d been documenting.

“Haven’t seen one of these in years.” It was made of red clay, shaped like an armadillo, with an artistic pattern on the shell.

“You know what it is?”

“It’s an ocarina. See the holes? It’s a big whistle – you blow in this one in the tail. Put your fingers over these ones –” he pointed at the body of the creature – “to change the note.”

“Oh.” Sting had it catalogued as a decorative figurine. All the time I’d spent drawing it, I hadn’t realized it was an instrument.

Kit put the page down and tightened his arm around me. I recognized the wicked glint in his eyes as he leaned into me and whispered, “Five minutes, hmm?”

"She doesn't have a timepiece. We might get ten before she hammers the door down."

"Ten minutes..." His lips were a feather's breadth from mine.

We had spent several of our limited minutes engaged in pleasurable explorations, when a seagull's mournful cry jolted my thoughts back to Kit's upcoming sea voyage. I extracted my limbs from his and put some air between our mouths.

"When are you leaving?"

He sighed and consulted his timepiece. "I should be meeting Glister now."

"No ... I meant, to Shipway."

"The boat sails at the Endweek."

This Endweek? I flicked my eyes away so he wouldn't see my mental wailing. *In two days!*

"Passage is booked. Blithe's grown a moustache, forged his papers. He's calling himself Trusty Telholt."

I swallowed and looked out of the window, like I could see more than fleecy clouds wavering in the distorted glass – like it wasn't my own tears pitching the view around like water.

"It's a massive trader ship, Mor. Already at anchor. Wish you could see it. Worse name than Trusty Telholt, though – *Toothsea Tear* – or *Tear*, I don't know how they say it... Mor, look at me. The job's less than eight weeks, travel and all. They're not getting me for longer. Goldie's secured the return passage. *Toothsea Tear*'s running that route up and down all summer. We'll be back this way in no time."

I sniffed back my own treacherous tears. In two more days, he'd be off on a big boat with a stupid name with his stupid friends and I'd still be stuck in the stupid Castle Hotel even more alone than before.

His hand massaged my neck and I spent another precious minute squashing my feelings away. "How did Glister get you into the Castle?" I said, finally.

"He agreed to pay a visit to his beloved cousin, Sacrifice Sting."

"Ugh."

"He mentioned another man here on Sting's staff. Name of Praiseworth Cob. You know him?"

"The silverprinter." I nodded.

Mister Cob and I were acquainted enough to exchange polite greetings – not bad for a Skøl.

A slightly older vintage than the Sciencemaster, Cob's shoulders were stooped and his fingers stained yellow rather than sunburnt pink. The silverprints he crafted – pictures made with light and chemicals – were an impressive science, but didn't deliver the kind of fine detail Sting needed. Silverprinting wasn't about to put me out of work just yet.

"Cob knows Glister and Goldie," Kit said. "Goldie says you can rely on him in a pinch."

"Interesting," I murmured, quietly contemplating the dreamlike way his long, dark eyelashes fanned up and down. *Dark drifting seaweed*, I thought. *Those tall thin trees, combed by the wind. Long grasses all bending the same way, purple evening sky you could fall into.*

"Interesting," he repeated, tracing the line of buttons set ridiculously close together down the front of my blouse. "I shouldn't like this outfit on you. And yet." His fingers moved up to caress my face, sending tingling sensations everywhere.

"I hate the buttons," I told him, sinking back and pulling him down with me on to the narrow bed for another kiss.

"Despicable," Kit agreed when he came up for air, giving me a wink before he plucked my pocket timepiece deftly from its nest and frowned.

"What's the time?" I sat up.

"I'm a bit late." He traced three fingers gently across my cheek and lip and I bit one gently before leaning into his touch. Then I saw the time. We'd been fifteen minutes in my annex and Nezza hadn't beaten the door down.

I straightened Kit's jacket as all the emotions I'd barely succeeded in battening down pulled free again and started swirling like a cyclone.

"Please promise you'll take care on this job," I choked out. My voice cracked. He'd only just arrived, and it was already time for him to leave.

Nezza gave a high-pitched wail next door, setting off Minty, whose soft trills built to a squeaky alarm call.

Another whine from Nezza followed, punctuated by a distinct sob.

"She loves drama," I said over my shoulder to Kit as I opened the door. *Fight fire with fire.* One of Ruzi's sayings clattered into my mind.

I walked over to her, injecting some steel into my voice. "What *is* the meaning of this?" Not a tone I used much, if ever. Even as I spoke, I realized I sounded like Ma – the way she told off the little ones, told me off, when I was naughty – years ago.

I felt suitably ridiculous, but Nezza hunched on her bed, chastised.

I felt her forehead – hot and clammy. Her skin, paler than mine, looked paler still, her lips a very odd shade.

"I feel bad," she moaned, genuine tears in her eyes. "And you don't care." A shiver shook her small shoulders. I reached down to try and hug her, but she pushed me away. Minty sniffed her neck, then directed his pointy nose my way with an angry chitter. He was shivering too.

"Okay, let's lie down." I helped her horizontal. She was limp and floppy. "Are you cold?" I asked, channelling Ma's soft, concerned voice now. I pulled her blanket up, though I felt more annoyed than guilty.

"She all right?" Kit murmured behind me.

"Sting's treating her for fits." I pushed back her hair and tried to meet her eye.

"He cut my arm today." She sniffed and touched a lump

in her sleeve I hadn't noticed. A thin bandage was wrapped around her forearm.

"Bleeding her to make her better," Kit scoffed. "Sounds like Skøl medicine."

I leaned over Nezza. "I'll ask them to make some of that hot ginger soup you like. Back in two minutes." She nodded and closed her eyes.

Kit reached for my hand as we started down the servants' stairs.

"When I'm back, I'm getting you out of here. We can run away together – three thousand miles if you want to. Ten thousand."

"If we run ten thousand miles, we might end up in Skøland." I shuddered.

"I don't care where we end up as long as we're together," he said, squeezing my hand.

My throat felt too tight to answer him. At that moment, I would have run anywhere with him too. If I could have waltzed out with Glister Reedstone, past Lovemore's awful guards, I would have left Nezza shivering in her bed without a backward glance.

"Where could we run to?" I whisper.

"There's Hunger Canyons." He pointed as if the Badlands were down by the kitchen.

I knew Hunger Canyons only by name – the last Xan refuge, the oldest and the most remote, deep in the Badlands, bordering the blighted desert. Xan from all over Makaia ended up there, after my forebears forced them off the rest of their lands about a hundred years ago. They were sent to the Badlands, and allowed to keep them only because they're barren, dry and rocky: only good for a bit of clay mining or for finding semi-precious stones. Amber, jasper, greenstone.

The Skøl have left them be – for now. Too remote, poor and undesirable compared to the rest of Makaia.

"I thought the living was desperate in Hunger Canyons," I said as we reached the lowest stair.

"Maybe. But I aim to see it for myself. I can travel there after the Reedstones' job and still come back on time. It's my people there, Mor." Strong emotion made his voice huskier.

Once I was blessed with a big family – two sisters, a little brother, four lovely cousins, aunts, uncles, grandparents. Kit never had that. He was the only Xan person in our whole school. He lived with just his mum and dad – until they died. No sisters or brother or cousins.

"Wish I could come and see it with you," I told him as we rounded the corner into the kitchen. Glister was there already, finishing a bowl of pudding he'd charmed out of the staff – or helped himself to.

"Right!" He spotted Kit and pounced. "Let's go. We're late."

Kit pulled me to a gentle stop beyond the threshold. It was getting busier, but the staff milling around paid us no heed. He dipped his forehead to mine and I felt him breathing me in, even as I tried to memorize his face anew. I knew it already. Every line of laughter. How deep the dent above the centre of his top lip was. The old scar on his cheek. His perfect earlobes, the stubbled skin at his jaw.

"How will I bear it with you three thousand miles away?" I whispered.

"Well, I can't bear it now and you're right here," he replied.

"Bit cruel," I sniffed and poked him, but it didn't lift either of us.

"I mean… I can't bear it more than you can't bear it," he tried to clarify.

"Come on!" Glister's bark shattered my already fracturing composure. I shot him a glare. He looked away.

Kit raised my hand, my drawing hand that was still covered from the edge of my little finger down the edge of my palm in silver pencil lead, and planted a kiss on it.

"Be careful," I said. *I love you*, I didn't say.

With a last slow nod at me, Kit went.

I watched them turn up the corridor to the wider staircase and tried to switch off the clamour in my head. *Work now, cry later*, I told myself.

One of the cooks set to work directly on a quick ginger soup for Nezza while I cut some bread and cheese to go with it and prepared a pot of milky fikka.

"Have you any fruit to tempt her?"

They gave me some pears and two small oranges, and I rushed back up to my young charge with the tray, almost glad for once of the distraction of looking after her. She then refused to eat a single bite before collapsing back into a feverish sleep.

4

MORA

everything beautiful

The air felt cool when I woke. I'd overslept. I'd been up in the night with Nezza, who had burned hot then cold. She was gone from her room though, which I took for a good sign. If she was up and about, the illness must have run its course quickly.

Her room smelled sweetly herbal. It was cold, much colder than mine, though the large windows let in more light and were wedged firmly closed to trap any heat. A thin layer of frost had even spread its tiny talons up the edges of the glass. It was melting, but it was still there, past eight on a summer morning.

Minty was curled on her pillow, breathing slowly. Nezza usually took him out with her – all over the hotel – but not when she went upstairs to Sting's laboratory, being well aware of the things he did to spotted devils up there.

I dressed in a hurry, misbuttoned the unforgiving blouse and had to do it over. I still reached the laboratory on the heels of Sting's two snooty assistants who'd both made it down for breakfast.

Sting was heading out the back of the big main room as I entered, muttering angrily to himself. He often talked to himself as he worked – another indication, I thought, of how much he liked the sound of his own voice.

Nezza wasn't with him. I spotted Praiseworth Cob, the silverprinter, watching Sting with a frown, even as he decanted chemicals from a large jug to a smaller one at one of the window benches. He did most of his silverprinting in a different room he could keep dark, downstairs, but some of his supplies lived in the big laboratory.

As I approached, Cob caught my eye. "Watch out! The Sciencemaster's in a terrible mood today," he said in a low voice.

"More terrible than usual?"

"Oh, yes. It's Lovemore. Threatening to pull the plug on his research. This new candidate has rattled her, and she's scared she might need to do more than buy votes and twist arms this time. People want practical, solid things like roads and railways, not *research*. Of course, we'd never have those things without the other … but no one ever sees it that way. The purse strings are tightening, and this research of his with the butterflies hasn't delivered. She wants his full attention on another project of hers."

Sting was, I had gleaned, leading two science flagships

for Lovemore. One was his pet project, his pursuit of eternal life no less – which involved research into a Xan ritual and a treatment made from butterflies. The other was to do with a new generation of tall ship – a literal flagship – being built somewhere down south.

I filled a jug of water to take to the spotted devils in the smaller lab at the back. That was also the way to Sting's office.

Twenty-two spotted devils lived in the back lab, kept two to a cage, stacked along the windowless wall. They were all meeker and paler than Minty. The room was also home to caterpillars in glass tanks and the butterflies Sting used in his experiments. They were all the same kind, Glor had told me – amber Glass Butterflies – slightly bigger than the ones I was used to seeing outside. They're common all over Makaia, but Sting brought these ones from Xan territory down south.

I noted a new crop coming – a row of cocoons bursting open. Some had fully emerged, their wings still unfolding. Soon they'd be fluttering behind the net frames.

I was drawn to one, its cocoon smaller than the rest and just being breached. The butterfly was still wing-wrapped like a gift, only one leg waving. I'd seen animals born before, well, kine – a bloody but breathtaking entry to the world. This was different. Butterflies were like crawling things that had died and transcended, as if angels or spirits could get stuck down here in the mud with the rest of us.

Poor things.

His office door at the other end of the room was ajar, and I could hear him in there, snapping at someone. Nezza.

Approaching from the side, I tried to listen.

"Tell me again. What happened immediately after the treatment?" Sting demanded. I bent closer.

"I felt sick," Nezza whispered. "But later it was cold and then when I woke up in the night I felt like … something was coming out of my head…" Her voice tailed off.

"Something was coming out of your head? How so?" Sting's voice had grown a little softer.

"I – I don't know. Out of my eyes. And I was dizzy."

"Show me your arm again. Hmm. It's nearly healed. The elixir must be working."

"I don't like the treatment."

"You have to ignore the fear. You have to be brave."

"I'm not," Nezza choked out, sounding close to tears.

"You're not an infant," Sting said sharply. "Your father was a great scientist. Your mother was a scientist's daughter. They would want you to do this."

What was Sting up to? This didn't sound like treating her for fits.

I moved into the doorway and gave the low bob they like their servants to do.

"You! What time do you call this, girl? Come here!"

"Sorry, Sciencemaster, I was—"

"Promiscuous slut!" Specks of saliva flew from his lips as I stood before him.

What? His fingers dug into my arm as he dragged me to stand inches in front of him.

"What's this I hear? You invited a man into your bedchamber for a private assignation yesterday?"

"No! I—" But he cut through my protest.

"I count that a gross misuse of the time you are obliged to dedicate towards the advancement of science." He looked at Nezza. "Or indeed the care of my young ward." His fingers squeezed deeper into my arm. "You ought to be punished."

He gave me a sharp shake but let me go. I couldn't believe it. Nezza had told him about Kit. Why in the world had I stayed up caring for the loathsome little toad?

I narrowed my eyes at her and she looked right back, her expression traitorous, the sour-faced snitch.

"She will be more attentive, Nezza," he turned to her, "or I will give her work to fill her nights as well as her days, so she cannot stray into the arms of servants. Go and rest, child."

Nezza scurried away.

By a stroke of luck, before Sting could lay into me again, one of the assistants, Hunter, appeared in the doorway with her notebook. Sting dismissed me with a curt nod.

"Any news on the coffin, Sciencemaster?" she said.

"It will arrive this morning. We must hope it yields some answers. Lovemore's patience has nearly worn through," I heard him tell her as I went back into the smaller lab. I peered through the mesh to the butterflies, still crouched stickily, as if stunned by their own transformation. *People like Sting*, I thought, *just have to spoil everything beautiful.*

5

KIT

about love

Once upon a time I had a family. Then they were gone.

Mora's tried to tell me how her memory works. It's not like everyone else's. Most people remember fragments. She remembers *everything*. She has every detail packed away in her head and gets it out when she wants to.

She said her memory was like a cave. I can't help thinking of the Life Registry – rows of cabinets holding everyone's records, arranged by name, by date. How much life they've paid for.

My memories aren't orderly like that. Childhood's mostly a blur, and just as well.

I can count on one hand the memories that stick from back then. It was only ever the three of us. Mum's heart gave out when I was nine and she was not even forty. Dad made it another three years before he followed her.

She used to complain he never let her do anything on her own.

When the Skøl came with their Cull, I was fourteen. Can't believe it's been six long years – nearly seven. Gods, but I was an angry fourteen. When they shot me with their fancy elektric guns it's like they did something to that anger. Gave it an escape route, maybe.

I lived. Three years before, Dad made me do a Xan ritual to please the gods. Maybe it was the ritual that saved me.

Through the vocifer's feathers tattooed over my back like an ink cloak, with my solemn promise and the rest of it – the elders' secrets, the spoken and unspoken things – I won the gods' favour.

Look, Dad … it worked. Now my heart is strong enough to survive even the Skøl's deadly elektric weapons.

They sent survivors deemed capable of heavy labour south. Not me. I was fourteen, but still small. My spurt came after.

They put me in repay labour there in Portcaye. Mister and Missus Scarlet bought my life debt so I could work in their public house. The Lugger. A real job, more food than I could eat, a soft bed and decent bosses. I fell into a routine there so easily it spooks me. But I was just a kid (until I wasn't).

Sure, it meant lots of Skøl looking down their pointy noses at me. Little digs. Big digs. I was used to that from the Crozoni, but I still got angry. I'm no angel.

Dad never liked me losing my temper.

Don't talk so loud, Kalqitlan. Don't stomp around. That's what he used to say. *If you feel your anger growing, take a deep breath. Breathe. In. Out. Slowly. Don't let it take over.*

There was something else, always, under the anger. A feeling something bad was going to happen. *It's not real,* Dad would say. *I used to get worries like you. Little sparks, little fires. Blow them out before they grow. Don't start a wildfire. Imagine you're blowing out a flame. Blow it out with me, come on.*

I still use that trick when I'm feeling anything too deeply.

Dad hid any joy he felt so deep no one could see him feeling it (could he even feel it?). He thought I should do the same – stay quiet for my own good, go through life as unnoticed as possible. Blow out every flame, good or bad.

He had a point. Being noticed was bad. When I found the biggest oyster of the summer and won a prize for it, when I was eleven years old, the other kids noticed that, didn't they? Pummelled me to shit over it.

"It's okay," Dad told me that day. "There's no need to cry. You'll laugh about this one day. Be strong, Kalqitlan."

And a year later, when he was pretending he wasn't dying, when Nena-Okuma was inking the vocifer into my skin as part of the ritual, he said, "I'm sorry. It's for your own good." After the inking I had to promise to sacrifice something – and it had to be something I really cared about. I had to choose it myself.

"Think of Mum," he said.

Mum who never tried to diminish herself.

And so I made my choice. My promise. My sacrifice. It seems a small thing, from the outside, perhaps, but it wasn't. Giving that up meant so much to me.

They were both right, Mum and Dad, in their own ways. And I did laugh about that oyster. I laughed about it with Mora.

Endweek, Sevenmonth 24th. Shipway town. Afternoon.

"Goldie's had a bowl of soup but Glister's still on hunger strike," Blithe tells me, joining me on the sofa in front of the open back doors. One spot of breeze in the house.

The Reedstones were both sick as dogs on the journey. Caruq (an actual dog) wasn't sick at all. Bit hot, perhaps, but after he moulted half his shaggy pelt, he couldn't have been happier (even made friends with the ship's hound, an unlikely Makaian mutt with short legs and a round barrel for a body called Cinbar).

I spent the journey trying to soak up the sights – sea, a bit of coast, more sea. It was freeing. The speed of it. The distance. I've always wanted to travel. See more of the world.

Not like this though. Not with all that distance stretching between me and Mora like something set to snap.

Now we're here, in Shipway town, in the accommodation the Reedstones secured for us (a cavernous, tiled bungalow belonging to one of their absent rich friends – nice to have connections). I just want my part of the job done. Then I'll have time to see Hunger Canyons.

"How long until they perk up?" I ask Blithe. "We're on a deadline." It's the middle of the afternoon already.

He spent the whole trip down fussing over Glister – more mother hen than lover – but now we're off the boat, his worries have shrunk. "Relax," he orders with an easy smile. "They've got two days to recuperate before the fundraiser for Temper Wilforn. They'll be right as rain by then."

"Hmm." Temper Wilforn, currently a member of the Council of Magistrates in Skøland – and the only one with any chance of unseating Lovemore at the election. "What do you make of Wilforn, then?" I don't trust magistrates – they all have the look of snakes from the same snakepit to me.

"He's good. I mean, he's better than Lovemore. Worth our support at any rate. Come on," Blithe goes on. "Let's get out. Take a look at this place."

Blithe Ronbor was wanted for many things, chiefly for falsifying Life Registry documents for elicit sale.

Lovemore wanted him publicly executed, so I suppose he would favour her main opponent. Outside, the heat seems to bounce off his mood like everything else. He might look pink and sweaty as a cooked crab, but he's flourishing.

I don't enjoy it and neither does Caruq, moult or no.

We stroll together past the Harbour-master's office

where the familiar wanted posters are pasted up like oyster shell, layers thick. They're loose at the bottoms, wafting in a warm breeze smelling of honey, sea, dry grass.

"Any sign of me?" Blithe murmurs.

"Not yet. Maybe you're not wanted any longer."

"I'm always wanted," he huffs quietly, smiling. Pirates, not forgers, are the order of the day in County Shipway.

PIRACY! MURDER! PIRACY!! PIRACY!!!
Debt-of-life Avoidance!
Absconding from Justice!
REWARD ₭10,000! REWARD!
PIRACY!

"Lot of piracy," I say.

"Yes..." Blithe muses. "Lovemore's embarrassed by them – can't seem to stamp them out. But they only target big trade ships."

"Like *Toothsea Tear*?"

"Like her, yes." He grins. "Don't look so worried. They prefer to go for the traders set for Skøland full of ragleaf fuel or other juicy goods—"

His grin drops and I follow his gaze.

BLITHE EVEN RONBOR! "THE ARTIST", WANTED FOR TREASON, THEFT, EVASION OF JUSTICE. REWARD ₭10,000.

A big bounty, by anyone's standards. "They got your nose all wrong," I say before I remember the reason it's bigger now is that the branders broke it for him.

It's not a good likeness, and it's not just the nose that's wrong. His disguise is good – Trusty Telholt wears prominent glasses and has a shocking moustache and hat. He's also thinner round the jowls. Blithe lost a lot of weight when he was locked up, although he's been eating every waking hour since they let him out trying to make up for it. Still, no one is going to be recognizing him from that poster.

We keep walking. It's not at all like County Portcaye here – the streets, the buildings, the people. Nearly as much as half of them must be Crozoni. Crozoni in Portcaye are rare. And there's even a few Crozoni here who look like they've got Xan in them.

I'd never seen anyone with mixed blood before that girl Mora's looking after. Half Skøl, she must have been, and quarter Crozoni, quarter Xan. *Halfling*, Mum would have said, or *self-hater*, something like that. Oil and water. Our people were few and not much for mixing up north. I sometimes wonder what she'd think of my feelings for Mora. She wanted me to travel when I was older, meet a nice Xan girl. That was because she wanted me to be happy though. If she could have met Mora, she'd have changed her mind.

We head at an easy pace down one of the wide streets, packed dirt and stone, over to the southern side of town.

The look of this place is something else. Far less stone, sprawling buildings built of brick and wood, raised up off the ground. People's houses, rung with verandas with neatly turned railings are all mixed up with businesses and empty plots. Everyone seems to walk slowly in this heat, or to pedal by at a leisurely pace on bicycles. Bicycles are rare up in Portcaye, and usually haring around. Here they're everywhere, but like the pedestrians, more sedate. Never realized it before, how much folk up north rush around.

This place has a warmth. Not just the weather, but the feeling underneath. There's clearly a degree of poverty – tatty clothes, dirty faces – but people don't seem as ill and ground-down as they do up north. Those in charge here do things differently.

People sit in the shade outside the houses on raised wooden verandas, drinking strong fikka in tiny cups. Kine carriages roll along at walking pace, the kine more suited to the heat than they are up north, tall and slender, their wool sheared close, some with decorations or charms to keep the flies away, hanging from their horns and harnesses.

We stop at a fikka house. Everyone's dressed for the hot weather. Skøl men favour flowing trousers of light materials, loose in the crotch and tight around the calves. Their feet are dusty in leather sandals.

Their women wear the baggy trousers, small differences in the tailoring, and sandals with higher heels. Some also wear dresses – plain coloured like the ones up north (white, sandy, grey, black), but not thick and woollen, more like blouses stacked on blouses, impractical-looking tiered skirts puffing out at the bottom like one of Renny's pastries, nearly to the floor, but cinched at the waist with braided belts. I wonder what Mora would look like in a dress like that. The kind of face she'd make if she saw one. And I'm grinning at nothing again.

There's more Skøl than Crozoni in the fikka house and not much mingling. That's the same as up north.

Crozoni men and women wear simpler clothes. Some look like cheap uniforms, but others have pieces tailored from Crozoni cloth. I recognize the telltale patterns, the embroidery. All this Crozoni cloth can't have come from seven years ago. They must be making it new.

Up north, traditional dress like that gets you heckled. Here it's run-of-the-mill.

I blow on my fikka and take a sip. "Fuck me," I cringe.

Blithe laughs.

It's thick and sweet as syrup. I feel cooler when we've finished, but I don't think the taste will grow on me.

We carry on, sticking to the shaded roadsides, emerging on the shorefront. There's a boardwalk that runs a quarter mile along the beach that they say the Shipway magistrate, Clemency Rosclaw – one of Temper Wilforn's biggest supporters – had built with his own funds. It's all pristine and pretty.

"Is this heat melting my muscles or does everything feel … relaxed here?"

"Probably a combination," Blithe decides.

The sun slams into us but the sea looks almost black. It was greener up north. The same sea and the same sun, even if it's ten times brighter and swollen as an infected wound.

Caruq lies down on the boards while we stand and stare, the breeze hitting like some great animal's breath.

The ocean – it must be warm as blood – has little clusters of yellow-haired Skøl children bobbing up and down in the shallows. No school on the Endweek. I spot a few dark heads playing some distance from the others. They're young. Children with Crozoni or Xan in them who were born post-Cull.

"Repayers can't afford to have children in County Portcaye," I say, gesturing at the swimming children. "Do they put them to work?" I think of little fingers picking in the orchards or the farms.

"They go to school," Blithe says. "Magistrate Rosclaw insists." Then he nudges me, redirecting my gaze.

"That's it," he whispers.

This is the place we came to rob. Like its neighbours, it's clad in white-painted wood. Two tall storeys with small windows and a windowless attic in the pitched roof space. Its main door at the front, up three whitewashed wooden stairs, overlooks the ocean. A second one at the side looks disused, dusty and cobwebbed. SELFLOWERS, the sign reads. There's a frosted panel in the top half of the door with one of the fast Skøl cargo ships in full sail etched into it. Selflowers makes sails.

"What are you doing?" Blithe hisses as I peer through the unetched glass. It's not illegal. And besides, I need to case the joint.

There's a short entryway into a big open space with a high ceiling and sanded wooden floors that remind me of the Lugger after hours.

Huge bolts of fabric (black, white, red) lean against the side door, but more striking is the amount of sailcloth on the floor. Great reams of canvas are left folded into waves across the wide-open space, tall as my waist, a still sea of black, like a painting. I note a clear pathway through it to the stairs. That's probably where the office is.

Black sails. Don't see those much.

The sails being sewn here are for a special kind of boat, for Lovemore – a boat like no other. All the Reedstones know is that it's called *Dominion* and that Lovemore has poured a huge amount of money into it. The question is, why? What makes it so special? They're here to find out more.

I rejoin Blithe, who's moved to loiter on the shingle, and we crunch down the beach.

"Why would Lovemore want black sails?" I ask. The three tall ships Lovemore sailed into Portcaye on all had red sails.

"That's what we're here to find out." Blithe looks back at Selflowers. "This will be a doddle for you, won't it?"

Could we be so lucky?

The lock on the front door looked simple. Suppose it

depends on whether the paperwork the Reedstones are after is in a high-security safe.

I don't answer him. I ride a scree of shingle down to the shoreline where there's more sand, a dark grey. The water, this light. Both hard. Both soft. Two old rivals rehearsing some well-worn argument neither one ever wins.

This stretch of shore is quiet, but we can still hear the children. Caruq plunges in, snapping and pouncing at the foam like a pup.

I envy him. A swim would be lovely.

But I don't swim. I haven't since the ritual and my promise, when I was twelve. I had to choose to sacrifice something I loved, and swimming was the thing I loved the most.

I try not to remember how good it was to be in the sea on a hot day, lifting and dropping in the great breath of it. It's not a sacrifice if it's not about love.

6

KIT

courting bad luck

Back at the bungalow, Glister and Goldie are up (progress!) and sitting side by side on one of the big sofas.

"Hello, you two!" Blithe calls when he sees them. "We should have brought you some Shipway fikka…"

"No, thank you," Glister says. "I'm still taking it easy."

Goldie shakes her head. "What I wouldn't give for some ice," she sighs.

"Good idea!" Blithe agrees. "I'm sure I saw a place not too far. We can go and look later."

"Are you going to be better for your fancy event Seconday night?" I ask.

"We can't miss it." Goldie looks fierce. "Magistrate Rosclaw is counting on us being there. I hope people are brave enough to come. Lovemore's had her branders warning everyone away in rather bleak terms." She meets my eyes. "We go to this thing, we're raising our flag against Lovemore and telling the world we're for Wilforn. Rosclaw's poised to be Wilforn's right-hand man. He'll play the deputy role Lovemore wanted for Venor, before Mora got so…" Her voice lowers: "involved. As long as he prevails, he'll be a powerful ally for us. But supporting Wilforn from the shadows is one thing – coming out publicly quite another." She sighs. "We'll be under much more scrutiny than normal. It will be harder to make the kind of inquiries we usually do from a position of neutrality. I wish we knew whatever it is Lovemore's plotting with this damn ship."

"We will uncover her secrets," Glister rumbles reassuringly, but I catch a hint of worry on his face too.

Goldie takes a deep breath and sighs it out, nodding.

"We saw Selflowers," I say. "Front door looks easy. No obvious guards. Simple lock. You think they've got an elektric safe?"

"Probably," Goldie says.

"It should be a quick job," Glister says, emphasis on *should*, accepting a glass of water from Blithe.

I know that appearances can be deceptive. All the same, we rushed thousands of miles down here for this, and now that I've seen Selflowers – a small, unassuming, ordinary trade operation – I'm confused. It's not ringing the usual Reedstone bells.

"Your source, they're *sure* this ship is important?" I ask.

"Well, that's just it, we don't know … exactly. But our

source is reliable. He thinks Lovemore plans to unveil it before the election to give herself some kind of advantage. She's been pumping money into this. We're talking ten times what a tall ship like *Toothsea* cost."

"Really?" I say. "Are they making this ship out of gold? And how's it going to win her the election?"

Goldie and Glister swap looks.

"Maybe this ship has something special about it," Goldie says slowly. "An engine, perhaps."

An engine. I laugh but they're not smiling. They're serious. "An engine for a boat that size? That's… Is that possible?"

"Let's say it is. What could she use it for? Piracy is a serious problem here," suggests Glister. "Tackling that would make Lovemore very popular with wealthy people in Skøland."

"Which would damage Temper Wilforn's chances. So, you're here for a spot of sabotage on the new ship."

Glister sighs as he finishes his last sip of water. He looks better for it. "First we need to find the ship itself."

I look at them. They're serious about costing Lovemore the election. The Reedstones don't stick their necks out for anyone. Not, it seems, till now.

"Are you sure Temper Wilforn is worth it?" I ask quietly.

"You've got to pick a side, sometimes," Blithe says. "Even if what they offer isn't perfect. It's the only way to change things."

Are they trying to convince me or themselves? I'm not sure, but I let it lie.

"All right," I say. "But if this ship is so top tier, why have they got a backwater sailmaker like Selflowers on the job?"

"Because Lovemore's keeping it a secret," says Goldie. "And she's arrogant. She doesn't think anyone would dare sabotage her."

"I'm here for a fortnight and I'm out," I remind them firmly. "You know the deal."

"We know." Goldie wafts my words away like flies. "Don't go wishing yourself gone, yet. It's courting bad luck."

7

MORA

scratch

"Delivery! Fresh off the boat."

Two porters entered the lab, a wooden crate between them. I put my sketchbook down and steeled myself. This was presumably the discovery Sting was pinning his hopes on.

"It's here!" Glor whispered. He hurried back to Sting's office to let him know. They soon emerged, all enthusiasm.

"This is it! A Xan coffin from the Badlands, from a disused site," Sting announced. "I received a telegram about it weeks ago. Most irregular. Most intriguing!"

A child's coffin, then. It was too small to be anything else.

They soon had the crate open and the coffin lifted out. It was fashioned of three different colours of hardwood – pale green, black and cream – traced with delicate patterns in copper. An intricate design, with an especially ornate lid inscribed with Xan script. They placed it on the long, high, marble-topped bench that commanded the centre of the big laboratory.

"What does this say?" Sting mused, drawing a blunt finger along the two shortest lines of script on the front. "Name and dates, I think." He looked over at Glor, his eyes shining with excitement. "This word looks familiar. Could it be *Hiramlan*?"

Glor looked up sharply. "Spinda's son, Hiramlan? The one they performed the ritual on?"

"Yes, of course."

"Umm…" The assistant's voice wavered as he peered at the script. "Yes. I think you're right."

Glor wasn't strong on translation – something even I'd noticed in my few weeks with them.

"And what does the date say?" Sting snapped.

"It … says… I'd have to check what this Xan date corresponds to. But … yes, it's probably about a century old. Which would fit with Hiramlan's death and the attempted resurrection."

"Go and check the exact date with your reference books, then. Quickly!" Sting turned to Hunter. "Fetch the crowbar! Let's open it up!"

The lid, lined inside with hammered copper, yielded with a scent of resin and old wood, but nothing foul. They placed it at the furthest end of the bench, near the door.

"Get these things out quickly," Sting ordered, peering in. Some items had been arranged on top of the child's body and tucked in beside it. Grave goods. The body itself was still wrapped in a shroud. Glor and Hunter passed the dead child's things to me. Ceramic jars, a rounded figurine I dimly recognized as another ocarina – like the one I'd been drawing the night before, but more simply shaped – a book-sized wooden box, intricately decorated, some copper jewellery, an ornate jewelled dagger, a blanket and some clothes – stiff with age. I set them down carefully further along the bench.

"Hold that end!" Between them, Sting and Hunter lifted out the body wrapped in a brittle shroud. They put it down on the other side of the coffin.

Sting had some shears ready. He cut away through the end of the material closest to the head. The look on his face was unsettling – like a child eager for a gift. But when he'd removed enough cloth to expose the top of the skull, he gave a sound of great exasperation.

Not the gift he'd wanted, then.

His fingers prodded at the patch of white bone and straggles of black hair – the only visible parts of the poor body.

He groaned, his fist thudding into the bench. "Not amber..." he muttered, massaging his forehead as he paced to the door and back. "It may still be the Hiramlan from the book," he decided loudly. "We will finish the examination in a few minutes. I ... need another fikka."

He pointed at Glor on his way out. "Get that translated!"

Hunter gazed after him while Glor continued to scour the reference books, looking ill.

I began to lay out the grave goods along the bench, wondering what Sting had hoped to find on the dead boy's head. Amber? A carving in place of a skull, perhaps?

Hunter looked over Glor's shoulder. "Do you need my help?"

"No!" he snapped.

The wooden box was a puzzle, but an easy one. I opened it to find a handful of glass marbles – Crozoni toys. Odd to see them buried with a Xan child.

I studied the child's ocarina, noticing it was shaped like a bee. It was more worn than the one I'd been drawing the night before. I gave a soft blow into the slit in its body, to hear it whistle. The sound it gave was husky and hollow.

"How's that?!" Hunter grabbed it off me. "A musical toy!"

I pointed out the holes to change the notes and she laughed like a girl. "Imagine burying this for a hundred years?"

Ruzi said to me once, *the Skøl have no imagination.*

"I can imagine burying it for ever," I told Hunter testily. "I can imagine never digging up a child's final resting place and stealing his toys."

She wasn't ashamed. "Well, you're a makkie. Naturally your opinion is … coloured." If anything, her smirk grew. "There's no sense in it – you must see that. Burying perfectly good toys. And food, jewels? Weapons?" She blew a few notes on the ocarina, low and melancholy. "These things are expensive. The dead don't use them, do they?"

"Don't they?"

"You needn't be deliberately obtuse." She flung a pitying look at me and shook her head.

Praiseworth Cob coughed. He was back, refilling more chemical bottles. "The living do it for the living," the old silverprinter said, over his shoulder. "It's not for the dead."

Hunter picked up the dead boy's blanket and snapped it open. Its colours were still bright.

"He died ninety … seven years ago," Glor announced from where he stood beside the coffin lid, wrinkling his nose in concentration. "Sting will be happy… The dates match and the name is definitely Hiramlan. It's the boy they tried to bring back to life."

"He's real, then!" Hunter left the blanket in a rumpled heap. "The boy they performed the ritual on, posthumously." She walked over to his shroud and placed a hand over the middle of it. "I was starting to think it was all a story."

"What *is* the story?" My voice fell into the silence. Glor and Hunter both turned to look at me.

But before they could explain – or tell me to shut up, which was more likely – Sting came back. His black cloud seemed to have lifted somewhat.

"Well, do the dates correspond?" He clapped Glor on the back.

"Yes, Sciencemaster General," Glor said, pleased to be bearing good news. "They correspond roughly with the Tenmonth, Golden Era 86 and the Fivemonth, GE 92, so this Hiramlan here died ninety-seven years ago."

"Perfect," Sting said. "The dates match. Our Hiramlan was five and a half."

"Yes." Glor nodded triumphantly. "As you suspected."

Mollified, Sting pointed at Hunter. "Was there any written material among the grave goods?"

"No, Sciencemaster."

"Very well. Unwrap him!"

His heavy head swung round to me.

"Get your pencil! I want a sketch of the process." Turning back to Glor, he said, "Keep on with the translation. There may well be valuable information in these inscriptions."

I stood beside Hunter as her keen scalpel sawed through the slightly yellowed outer layers of fabric to the inner ones, eaten with age and rot, swaddling a pitiful heap of bones.

"Sciencemaster!" she shrieked when the fabric fell aside. I paused my pencilling.

Sting and Glor barrelled over. Sting picked up the two-toned skull of the dead child.

"As I live and breathe!" he murmured. He turned to Hunter. Every hair on his face seemed to quiver.

Moustache, mutton chops, eyebrows. "Are you seeing what I'm seeing?"

She nodded, awestruck. We could all see it, clear as day. Large sections at the sides of the skull weren't white bone – they looked like strange, polished amber. The same went for several of the other bones. They weren't bones at all, but that glassy, orange rock-like material in shifting shades that seemed to catch and throw the light, even to shine, a bit like water, or a coloured mirror. The strangeness set off goosebumps across my skin.

No trick of the light, nor the shroud nor age had discoloured them.

Various rib, finger and wrist bones were amber too, but the half-changed skull excited them the most. Two bottom and two top teeth, part of the lower jaw, and a segment at each side at the temple, close to the eye sockets – curved shapes, not geometrical – had gone amber. The joins between the white bone and amber on the outside of the skull were perfect, seamless as a master-crafted musical instrument.

Sting studied some of the knuckles through a glass. "Even the hands," he murmured.

"Incredible," Hunter agreed, turning the small skull over in her hands. "You were right, Sciencemaster. Amberfication. An amber skull… It exists! Almost."

"Almost." Sting's deeper voice echoed as he plucked it from her grip. He ran a finger over the amber-bone interface on the outside of the skull. "A partial transformation. Dewilder never mentioned it."

Dewilder, I thought. A common Crozoni name.

Sting moved his calipers to measure the boy's skull diameter while Hunter and Glor bent their heads over the bones. "No obvious trauma," Hunter said. "But there's no soft tissue."

"Dewilder states that he drowned," Sting told her. He held the delicate-looking jawbone up to the elektric light where the amber parts flickered as if with firelight. "It may only be a *partial* transformation, but it's a great leap forward. It proves that such a thing is indeed possible. That the process worked – to an extent."

"I should like to read the story myself," Hunter said. "It's in the same source book... Dewilder's *Sacred Secrets*, is it not?"

"It is. But remember, these stories about primitive rites are not reproduceable science. It is our duty to untangle the science from the nonsense. Hiramlan's story has both. He suffered an accidental death and his mother, Spinda – who was herself a rare, amber-skulled individual – attempted to resurrect him with the same ingredients that drove her transformation years before. The Xan bone-altering rituals were usually enacted for health, healing and long life, but in Hiramlan's case, they put his body through the ritual after death. Very taboo. Probably because the outcome they sought was not possible..." Sting tapped the amber section of the jaw with a fingernail.

Hunter watched, we all did, waiting for him to go on.

"Dewilder contended the resurrection failed because the boy had been dead too long before their attempt. But there was a passage relating to those events that led Sculpin and I to hypothesize that Hiramlan's skull might have amberfied posthumously."

He smiled at the little jaw in his hand.

"What was the passage?" Hunter prompted.

"I don't recall exactly," Sting told her. "But it was something about him joining the amber brethren in the Burial Circle."

"So all this … it's like petrification, isn't it?" Glor held up one of the amber bones to the late-morning sunlight. "Happened just after he died?"

"I believe so," Sting said with his characteristic confidence. "During a ritual – the work of minutes, not geologic ages." He put the jawbone down. "I must inform Lovemore. If anything can convince her to continue funding this line of research, here it is. But she will have questions. We must anticipate them. I want those inscriptions translated." He narrowed his eyes at Glor. "That's your only task today."

The younger man fled back to the end of the high bench where the coffin lid rested.

"Dezil." Sting turned to me as he bit out my last name, so simple and yet so strangely stretched by the Skøl tongue. "This man you were with last night…" He scratched one palm with the fingernails of his other hand. "Nezza said he was very brown. Was he Xan?"

"He was only here delivering something," I stammered. "He's gone."

"Gone? Repayers don't just go. Sounds like a tale to tell witless girls."

"No … he left with his owners," I said. "He only came to say goodbye." *Leave Kit out of this.* "If it's about the translation, I can help."

"What do you know of Xan language?"

"About as much as most Xan from round these parts," I lied. "I'm a fast study. My memory for images helps."

"Very well. Assist Mister—" He waved in Glor's direction. "After you have completed the required sketches."

Hunter had laid the bones on a fresh linen. Neat queues of ribs and backbones. She started taking and recording measurements like length and weight of individual bones.

"Here." Sting lifted the skull and the lower jawbone from their place of prominence. "Draw these articulated. Jaw agape and jaw closed. I want the view from this angle. Focus on the temple. Use colour. True to size."

He paused to contemplate the inside of the skull again – like a man mesmerized by some magic trick. Then he brought it under my nose, turned round so I could see what he saw.

My breath caught and I stepped back. *Away*, screamed my muscles, as if they had brains and mouths and were appalled. *Get away.* On the inside, each amber temple patch was surrounded by tendrils of amber growing over or into the bone, several dozen vines of them radiating out. On the outside, it might have been sculpture.

On the inside, it was clearly not craftwork. The joins between bone and amber were grown, looking like two substances fused naturally. Or unnaturally.

Amber and bone interlaced in intricate but wild patterns that overlapped and merged into each other. Some of the bone edges nearest the joins were black as charcoal. In places it had the look of moss, then ferns, then leaf veins. Here it resembled the growth of frost, there the pits of an emptied seed pod, there a spray of petals becoming the many frames of insect wings, rippling into the pattern of a puddle pelted with pebbles – on and on. A few long, lacy threads of black-lined amber even webbed over the top of the skull. They didn't show on the outside. The more I studied it, the more my horror blossomed, deep under my skin.

Hunter watched us. "It's uncanny," she offered with feeling.

"It is *proof*," Sting said, recovering himself. "That confirms years of digging – literally." He sucked in a breath. "I will tell Lovemore it's abhorrent. But captivating nonetheless."

It was more than that. It made my skin crawl and my blood cry out and my stomach try to seek both exits. I was dreading the thought of copying it out with pencil and paper, even while part of me was desperate to peek again.

I began on the sketches of the skull's outside, the small jaw with its four amber teeth, to give my wayward guts time to adjust.

"These amber bones are dense," Hunter was saying to Sting. "As heavy as stone or glass." She touched one of the white ones. "These ones appear as ordinary bone, do they not?"

"To the naked eye."

"They are almost one point five times as dense. Even these have undergone a transformation."

Hunter continued her measurements while Sting set one of the amber rib bones on the big wooden chopping block at the far end of the marble bench and sawed back and forth across it with a fine-toothed file.

"Not a single deformation!" he reported. "This is the substance Dewilder writes of… A phenomenon unto itself." His eyes gleamed. "Imagine a person with such bones. A person of incredible vitality, living twice the natural span."

He sawed on. An awful half-metal squeal pierced the room and seemed to reverberate down the full length of the bench.

Sting's file lost its edge, but the amber rib remained unmarked. He took a rock hammer to it next, light taps at first, then stronger, ringing blows. It didn't even scratch.

8

MORA

swearing

Hunter laid the last of the child's bones on a fresh linen, with anatomical precision. His amber ribs formed a fragile-looking spider-like shape at the centre, while the fingers and wrist bones – even the skull – seemed so distant from that core.

I'd finished my sketches of the skull, inside and out, killing my hunger. I'd no desire to eat, though I hadn't had a bite since the night before and the midday mealtime was marching past.

With only the outside of his skull visible, the small boy's remains looked much more like, well, just what they were. Stolen bones of a boy who was once loved enough to be buried in an ornate coffin with his toys and treasures.

Ninety-seven years later. Everyone who loved him must be dead.

"The last sketch, Sciencemaster General," I said, passing it over.

"Good." Sting added the page to a folder under his arm then straightened some of the grave goods that were laid out near the coffin.

"Help Mister Stanwin and … you too," he told Hunter. "Get those translations done. I will hasten to apprise Lovemore." His voice was filled with fire and suspense.

I watched him collect my sketches and a boxed-up sample of amber finger bones before he hurried out.

"What have you got, then?" Hunter asked Glor.

Glor indicated the text that sat below the boy's name and dates, separated by a prominent figure-of-eight toppled on its side.

"This word means *Spinda*," he told us. "She's Hiramlan's mother. The one who carried out the ritual."

"Is that all?"

He shot her a murderous look and we worked in silence for a while, leafing through the reference books, until Hunter broke it again.

"This could be *bird* or *glass*." She pointed at another word. "The Xan words for *glass* and *bird* are homographs – spelled the same, but pronounced differently," she told me.

"Well, this is *butterfly*…" Glor said. "So that's most likely *glass* – in reference to Spinda."

"Of course," Hunter agreed.

I tried to focus on the curious text, but my head was heavy with fatigue. I studied the pattern of inlaid wooden squares around the edge of the coffin lid instead. Dimly, I noticed one of the squares at the corner was the wrong colour. A tiny error, breaking the pattern.

"Definitely *son*, here." Glor tapped on another word and I went back to the books.

We had the working translation for the first part.

Here lie the sacred and adored bones of the first son of Spinda the Glass Butterfly.

"So they called her *Butterfly*?" I asked – but they ignored me, moving swiftly to the longer line of text around the rim. I thought of the amber Glass Butterflies emerging in the back room.

A long while later, Glor sighed. "This is what we have so far."

Great One, Macotl. True Naqramaree. Merciful Seff: Curse those who move these bones. Bless and thank the elderly(?) kin — — in Seff's Burial Circle.

He frowned and ran a pale hand through his staticky hair. "Would it kill them to use punctuation?" he moaned.

Voices began to reach us from the corridor.

"Be prepared to be astonished," Sting was saying. "This is the promised land on the horizon we've been sailing towards!"

"Speaking of sailing – what news of *Dominion* have

you?" Another, higher voice that I didn't recognize interrupted.

"Your ship continues to schedule. The gold-beater's skin is proving sufficiently impermeable as a lining for the sail... All is progressing well, High Governor."

The High Governor herself, Clarion Lovemore. I'd seen her face pictured a thousand times but only seen her in the flesh from a distance. And I'd never heard her speak before. Glor and Hunter both shot to their feet, and I stood too.

She entered, following a huge, heavy-booted guard, and then Sting. Her attendant came next – a beautiful young woman bearing a fan. Two further guards brought up the rear.

Lovemore. All this time, I'd never seen her close-up. I forgot not to stare, but so did Glor and Hunter.

She wore dark-green trousers in an unusual, billowy style, made of a shiny fabric that seemed to puff out around her thighs and hug her calves. Her blouse was similarly flowing, but not shiny. It was fastened with ties of the same material – no buttons in sight.

"Please, step this way, High Governor," Sting said in a servile sing-song voice I'd never heard him use before.

They stood side by side before Hiramlan's bones. Sting was a head taller. He fetched the skull for her. We watched in silence as she examined it.

"So you must be feeling vindicated, Sacrifice. Amber bones, just as you said." Lovemore sounded caring, almost motherly. I had never heard Sting called by his first name before.

"Yes, High Governor," he replied warmly, his eyes following Lovemore to the window. She held the skull in a thick beam of sunlight. Her face betrayed nothing. She returned to the skeleton and swapped the skull for a rib bone, one of the longest amberfied ones, which she then struck lightly against the side of the marble bench. *Thunk.* The dull sound it produced hung overlong, as though resonating around a room ten times larger.

"That sound is like…" Lovemore mused. She struck it repeatedly, with force. "Not like metal … or glass…" she said between blows. A chip of marble went flying and hit Hunter on the cheek. She flinched and held a hand over the small trickle of blood.

"Most curious," Lovemore said, setting the rib down. She turned to Sting. "And so, can you use this amber for your research?"

"I will try, High Governor … though I believe we need several fully transformed skulls to act as elektrical amplifiers of the…" He stopped talking as she drew away, bored of his speech, and reached for the skull anew.

Sting edged closer, his forearms hovering like a worried hen. Lovemore took a moment to examine the skull's insides before she dashed it to the floor.

Sting's jaw hit the floor along with it, shards of shattered bone flying in all directions. No one moved, except for Lovemore's attendant, still waving her fan in a slow, one-armed motion. We could hear the spotted devils in their cages next door, shuffling and scratching. Sting tried and failed to recover his composure.

"Give me that." Lovemore addressed the nearest guard, and he stooped to retrieve the surprisingly large section of skull that remained intact. The opposing amber temple patches were held together by a network of veiny amber thread-work stretching over the top of the skull – a web that had been invisible on the outside and only hinted at on the inside.

"Beautiful," murmured Lovemore.

Was it beautiful? I didn't think the feeling it gave me was admiration. Awe, maybe. Awe lacing its fingers with horror.

"Your scientific mind as ever, High Governor, does not disappoint," Sting said finally, regaining his composure. "Let me show you the coffin itself. We are working on a translation of the inscription."

Lovemore put the horror down and turned to Glor. "Your name?"

Glor managed a strangled "Glor Stanwin, High Governor," before he fell into a coughing fit.

"And you?" Lovemore inquired. Her voice was still soft, but it carried over Glor's noise easily.

"Hunter Vinslar, High Governor."

"Of course. Of the Fellridge Vinslars. So, this is the text you are interpreting?" Lovemore prompted Hunter.

"Yes, High Governor. We think this reads: *Here lie*

the sacred and adored bones of the first son of Spinda the Glass Butterfly," Hunter said.

"Spinda the Glass Butterfly!" Sting repeated. "We have the same boy Dewilder spoke of then, no shadow of a doubt."

"But this body was not found at the peculiar burial location you seek?" said Lovemore slowly.

"No. He was dug from a disused but marked graveyard, High Governor," Sting informed her. "We have explored every inch of it and found a handful of Xan, but we are digging wider in hopes of discovering the Burial Circle itself."

"The *Burial Circle*..." Lovemore murmured. "Yes."

"All reports suggest it must be very near Hunger Canyons."

Hunger Canyons, I thought with a start. *Kit wants to go there. Isn't it a sanctuary?* I felt uneasy, like some pattern was weaving around us with amber-thin threads.

Foolish of me to think somewhere would be safe from the Skøl. If they're not robbing old graves, they're putting good people in new ones.

"Hunger Canyons, the outlaw settlement on the edge of the desert?" Lovemore asked.

"Yes, High Governor."

"So let me be clear. You still need the Burial Circle to obtain the amber for your experiment, and this find delivers no clues as to the whereabouts of said circle, is that right?"

Sting opened his mouth but said nothing, uncharacteristically lost for words.

"The Burial Circle is mentioned in the coffin's inscription though," Glor broke in.

"Go on," Sting urged him, and Glor began to translate the longer piece of text around the side of the lid.

"*Great One, Macotl. True Naqramaree. Merciful Seff,*" he started. "Those are the three uppermost Xan gods."

"Savage races always have so many." Lovemore's thin smile didn't reach her eyes.

"You're right, High Governor." Glor nodded. "Macotl they call the Mother Goddess. Then Naqramaree and Seff sit directly below her … so, Naqramaree is associated with Beginnings, while Seff is the Lord of the Gods of Endings."

"Naqramaree and Seff take a human, or mostly human form, while Macotl is almost always depicted as a giant serpent," finished Sting.

The pair of them, vying for Lovemore's approval.

"Naqramaree is strongly associated with the longevity ritual. And with butterflies. Which, as we know, are crucial to the catalytic elixir."

Of the three gods they were discussing, Macotl was the only one I'd heard Kit mention. *Macotl – mother of creation and destruction, of making and decay.* He occasionally evoked her when he was swearing.

9

MORA

hidden

"Where is the Burial Circle mentioned, then?" Lovemore brought their attention back to the coffin lid.

Hunter pointed.

"Here, High Governor. This section begins, *Curse those who move these bones.* Then it finishes, *Bless and thank the elderly kin* for something – we haven't managed to translate this in full – *in Seff's Burial Circle.*" She cleared her throat. "So, there we go. The Burial Circle is clearly mentioned."

Lovemore's brow furrowed in a definite frown. She directed a sharp look at Sting. "Not much of a clue."

"No," Sting hedged. "But this is merely a preliminary translation. They may have missed something." His moustache quivered. "The amberfication ritual took place within the Burial Circle, even if the boy was later removed. It must be nearby. Which means we are close…"

Lovemore laid a hand on her fan-waving assistant's arm and pinched it, hard. I noticed how the fingernail crescents and blotches she left sat among fading bruises and previous marks. The assistant didn't flinch, but she stopped waving the fan.

Lovemore whispered, "You're close. But you can't dig up the whole desert."

One of Sting's eyes twitched. "High Governor, we can now experiment with the amber bone material for the first time. And this translation is incomplete. It may yet deliver a clue if we consult a native speaker. When I suspected the significance of this find, I sent for my Xan assistant—"

"When will he arrive?" she cut across him.

"He follows just days behind."

She walked to the doorway of the smaller laboratory where the spotted devils languished in their cages.

"Have any more of these creatures exhibited advanced health and healing?" she asked.

"Not yet, High Governor. But the human subject is showing promise."

She smiled coldly. "*Promise* simply isn't enough, Sacrifice. If you can't find this Burial Circle, then all you have to show for years of research is a handful of strange bones and a half-cocked hypothesis. You promised me the secret to everlasting life." She pivoted for the exit. "Let us hope your native speaker can work miracles."

Then she swished out, orbited by three huge, silent

guards. Her beautiful fanning attendant hastened to add herself to the moons of Lovemore.

Sting took a deep, steadying breath as their footsteps faded. Hunter's stomach rumbled into the silence. Sting turned to her and Glor.

"You've done good work today. Get some dinner. Daruunlis will be here any day now. We will have the translation straight from the savage's mouth. We're close, I can feel it." With one final glance at the bones, he left.

A light volley of tired laughter ricocheted between Glor and Hunter.

"She's a hard nut," Glor said with a grin.

Hunter cursed softly. "I can see why she wants more than a little half-cooked skeleton though."

"It *is* more!" Glor chided. "It's what the skeleton means, Hunter. Immortality, well, extending life… It's possible. Hiramlan was real. Spinda must have been too. And the Burial Circle of legend. The legends are real."

One of Hunter's fingers flicked out at the coffin lid, then she stretched her back until it cracked. "I'm starving."

Glor clapped his hands together. "We've earned a drink or two."

I should have thought of filling my belly, but Sting's words echoed in my mind … *the human subject is showing promise*. I thought of the odd conversation I'd overheard between him and Nezza earlier. *The elixir must be working…*

They seemed relaxed enough that I dared ask, "Who did Sting mean … the *human subject*?"

Glor was busy washing his hands, but Hunter held up a rib bone beside my head and squinted at me oddly. She came to lean on the bench just inches away.

"Never you mind. Look at me," she said. She yanked at my bonnet without a by-your-leave and pulled it clean off. "Your eyes are the same colour as these bones."

She peered at me like I was an artefact she'd never seen before, not a person. Her eyes were small and blue and mean.

"You're not ugly," she decided after a few overlong moments. "But your hair is awful."

I was tempted to agree with her, but resisted. *You are ugly*, I thought, *on the inside.* Hunter Vinslar of the Fellridge Vinslars, family links to Lovemore, shoo-in for a cushy assistant's job under the Sciencemaster General.

I looked away instead. "All these experiments, then," I continued. "What do amber bones have to do with butterflies and long life?"

Hunter let out a yawn and rolled her eyes like I was the world's dimmest dolt. "You wouldn't understand. Cover up everything before you finish, including that stuff you call hair." She tossed the bonnet back to me. "Bye, Glor." She walked out.

Glor looked about to follow. I touched his sleeve. He shook his arm like I was a spider crawling up it, but at least he paused.

"Sorry," I said quickly. "I just wanted to know – who is this Dewilder you're all talking about?"

I could see Glor's warring desires. Show off how clever he was, or ignore me.

His know-it-all side won. "Dewilder was a scientist. He wrote a book about secret Xan rituals – a seminal reference text. Handwritten. The Sciencemaster and Mister Sculpin discovered it years ago. It's in Crozoni – easier to follow than this Xan gibberish."

Dewilder. It was a common enough Crozoni name, but it felt familiar for another reason. I tried to remember if I'd known any Dewilders in my childhood. "A Crozoni scientist?"

"Yes … primitive methods, poorly explained, of course. He focused on ancient Xan religious rituals – to do with health and healing, blessings and curses. He wrote at length about the case of Spinda the Glass Butterfly and her first child, Hiramlan."

"This boy." I gestured to the empty coffin.

"That's right. Spinda was ageless, they said, thanks to a ritual she carried out that involved butterflies and amber skulls … skulls from a special Burial Circle. That's what Sting is trying to track down. She tried to use a similar ritual on her son after he drowned – to resurrect him. That failed. As you can see."

"And so the butterflies are like her emblem?"

"Exactly. The Xan love a title. She ate amber Glass Butterflies as part of the ritual to extend her life. To *receive the gods' favour*, they call it – becoming their servant. Health and healing, long life. Amber bones. The Sciencemaster was never sure if the term *amber skull* was just Xan poetics, or if it was an actual phenomenon. Now we know for certain."

To receive the gods' favour. A vision of Kit flashed into my mind. He undertook a ritual when he was twelve. Nothing to do with amber skulls – or not that he told me. He did tell me it was about attracting the gods' favour.

He thought that's what had protected him from the Skøl's elektric weaponry. And it sharpened his senses, helped him heal, stopped him falling sick.

Recalling what he'd said about the ritual itself, I realized it was very little. Nothing about eating butterflies. He'd told me he had to give up something precious to him. And that was when he got his vocifer tattoo – part of a promise to carry an image beloved by the gods on his skin.

I'd asked him, *What precious thing did you give up?*

And he'd said, *Swimming.* Twelve-year-old Kit had loved swimming in the ocean near Portcaye more than anything.

I looked back at Glor. "So the amber Glass Butterflies he's breeding back there…" I gestured to the back lab, beginning to wish that I'd spent more of the past four weeks paying attention to Sting's work. "They're supposed to turn people's bones *amber*? And somehow make them ageless?"

"Well, Sting thinks the butterflies are *necessary but insufficient*. They're special. Only found in Makaia." He was still showing off. "The Xan say if you cut one of the caterpillars in half, you get two new ones. If you squeeze the cocoon, it gives milk that can cure blindness. If a Glass Butterfly dances for you, you'll have good luck for three moons."

"Really?"

He shrugged. "Not the one about cutting the caterpillar in half. Tried that, didn't I? Stories don't spring from nowhere though. And the Xan approach isn't scientific. So we have to experiment. But whatever process made Spinda powerful and long-lived – that can be recreated. With a combination of butterflies, amber skulls and a few other components. The skulls are key. Once we find the Burial Circle, Sting will crack it. He's a genius."

He certainly thinks he is.

My eyes slid again to the small skeleton. Glor followed my gaze.

"They say this boy's mother was old enough to be a great-great-grandmother and looked fifty. A kind of immortality. She died in the Cull – still full of vigour at a hundred and eighteen."

"And her body is … in the Burial Circle?"

"Sting thinks so."

It occurred to me for the first time that the Sciencemaster General was a secretive man. He kept a very small, discreet lab for someone so prominent. Just two young, biddable assistants, and Cob. His main partner, Nezza's father, was dead.

"What happened to Nezza's father – Mister Sculpin?" I asked.

Glor frowned, looking past me to the door. "That's not a topic the Sciencemaster wants us discussing. Ask him yourself if you want a hiding." He had turned mean at the drop of a hat, as I found Skøl of his class often could.

"Oh." I stepped back as he brushed past me on a beeline for the door. He'd told me more than I thought he would.

I walked past the glinting bones, back to the smaller lab to tidy the devils' cages.

My mind returned to the boy as I worked. Hiramlan. His intricately inlaid coffin lid with its neatly engraved script. *Curse those who move these bones.* I must be counted in that curse, now.

This book they were using – Dewilder's book, *Sacred Secrets*. I wanted to see it for myself.

My eyes snagged on the door to Sting's office. It was locked, of course. But now I noticed the lock was a simple single catch, of the type Kit had taught me to pick. The lock picks he'd brought me the day before were in my room, hidden.

10

KIT

mysterious project

Thirday, Sevenmonth 27th. Shipway town. Morning.

"Tonight's your night to shine," Goldie announces in the morning, sipping her tiny, blood-thick cup of fikka. I've tried it twice more since we arrived. It's still not for me.

She and Glister were out shining the night before – hobnobbing into the wee hours at the fundraiser held by County Shipway's Life Registry Magistrate, Clemency Rosclaw.

"A good man," she tells me. "I'm sure of it. I'd never seen him work a crowd until last night. A true man of the people. Grounded."

"Handsome and single too," Glister jokes. "A man of many qualities."

Goldie smirks.

"Any policies you fancy, or just him?" I tease her.

"Minimum wages," she shoots back. "Sensible hours and acceptable working conditions. For everyone. A real chance for repayers to actually dig themselves out of their life debts."

"What's the catch?"

"Oh, you would say that," she groans. "You're a cynic, Kit. Change has to start sometime, doesn't it?" The earnest note to her voice surprises me.

Thirday, Sevenmonth 27th. Shipway town. Afternoon.

I push thoughts of this morning out of my mind and go over the plan for tonight. I can't see this job posing any serious challenge given what Blithe and I have seen in our stake-out of Selflowers over the past two days.

We've set up a simple artist's stand with an umbrella to shade the worst of the sun, there beside the boardwalk. Blithe – as Trusty Telholt – paints seascapes on pebbles and offers quick portraits of passers-by done on bits of thick paper. I pretend to be his assistant, and we both pretend to be drinking a light ale. Our faux-drunkenness keeps potential buyers away. It's given us an excuse to loiter near the front of Selflowers and observe.

We've seen enough. Workers arrive early, from half past seven, and begin trickling off from half past six. By eight the place is empty. Not out of the ordinary for this type of Skøl business.

Our modest artist's stand is doing its best (only) business

today. Sales so far include two pebbles with seascapes (five krunan for the pair, to an old lady early in the morning), two pebbles with faces and legs looking like frogs (traded for four plain pebbles – okay, not technically a sale – to two Skøl children who stopped to talk to us on their way home from school), and one paper portrait (ten krunan).

The portrait commission comes later in the afternoon. A couple, out courting, stop by our stall and ask Blithe to do the woman.

"How do you like it?" he asks her when it's done.

She's part Xan and part Crozoni. Her eyes are purple like mine (well, I assume they both are – I can only see one as the other's hidden behind a patch).

Her glance at the paper is self-deprecating. "Not bad, given I'm not sure I'm at my best."

"What happened to your eye?" Blithe asks bluntly.

"Injury at work."

"What kind of work's that?"

"We're at the fruit cannery, yonder." She gestures vaguely to the other side of town. "It'll heal."

Her long hair floats around her face in the breeze. I'm not sure if that made Blithe's task harder or easier, but I think he captured her piercing eye nicely.

"Is it worth ten krunan?" she asks the man walking out with her.

"Well, you're worth *more*, obviously, but yes. I shall cherish it," he says in his nasal voice.

He's full Crozoni, with deep-set, big brown eyes and

longish hair tied back. Didn't want his portrait done (probably for the best). His face lacks balance. One edge of his smile (he smiles a lot more than her) seems higher than the other. He's not ugly, exactly, but he is odd-looking.

"Trusty Telholt – affordable portraits – tell your friends!" Blithe waves them off. An unlikely couple, I think, as they link arms and wander down the boardwalk, chuckling at her portrait.

I wonder what Mora's doing now.

"Sales are going to soar." Blithe waves his new ten krunan at me with a wink. "The whole cannery will be down here before you know it."

And we'll be gone. It's all going to plan.

Tonight, well after midnight, Glister will wait with the kine and carriage he's rented down the road. When the coast is clear, I'll walk up the white steps to Selflowers' front door like I own the place, and crack the lock. Blithe and Goldie will join me inside.

We'll find the safe and liberate the plans. A quick getaway in the carriage. Blithe will copy the plans, and then we'll have them back (same night or the next, depending on how slow Blithe is) before anyone misses them.

I decide to ignore the bad feeling brewing in my gut.

I'll have time to visit Hunger Canyons while the Reedstones finish up their political meetings here. And then it's home to Mora. The next time I come back this way could be with her.

Five o'clock rolls around. Some ships new-docked from

Rundvaer have livened up the sleepy pace we've been enjoying the last three days. It's the sort of liveliness we can blend into (though it might mean more witnesses).

But at ten past five, an extra-long, open-backed wagon – looking like it belongs on a farm field rather than in the middle of town, pulled by no less than four draught kine – stops in front of Selflowers. The kine are sheared close, but their height and power are obvious. What is this doing here?

I look at Blithe. His moustache is drooping in the heat.

"Oh dear," he says, dropping the half-drunk tone he's been putting on all day.

Workers emerge from Selflowers carrying a dark train of canvas to the wagon bed.

"They're finished already?" I groan. "They were still sewing this morning..."

Blithe grimaces. "You keep an eye here. I'll go and tell the others. If we can find out where the sails are being sent, we can use this to our advantage. They must be going to the special shipyard."

He sets off. It's not a quick job, loading the folded piles of canvas into the wagon. If I hadn't seen them through the window the other day, I wouldn't have believed the extent of them.

As they bear the river of folded canvas out the door, all I can think of is a Crozoni clown I saw once (years before the invasion), pulling a fake handkerchief from his pocket – one of those never-ending ones. His face went from *I don't believe this*, to *I'm pissed off*, to *I'm exhausted*, and all the while yanking out armfuls of the stuff.

The black fabric's still flowing on to the wagon-bed when Blithe returns, Goldie and Glister in tow. I watch them approach – three beautiful, wealthy people out for a stroll. No hint of criminal intent.

Goldie stops in front of the draught kine paired at the head of the wagon. She pats a nose. "Aren't you a darling, my beauty," I hear her sing-song.

I know the look she's giving the driver – that soft smile, a shy peep from under her eyelashes. *I'm the darling*, it says. *I'm the beauty.* I've seen many a man fall under her spell.

"What have they got you dragging around in this heat?" she asks the kine.

"It's a decent load," the driver agrees, looking back at the last of the black canvas finally topping the pile.

"She's in!" one of the workers announces, slinging a length of rope across the wagon to his counterpart. They tie it all down with neat seafarers' knots.

"Have you got far to go?" I hear Goldie ask the driver.

"Up to the station. It's catching the evening train," he answers, just as the foreman calls over to him.

"All ready to go, Prudy!"

"Evening." The driver tips his hat to Goldie and the kine walk on.

We regroup by the artist's stand as the wagon trundles away.

Glister turns from his contemplation of it. "Selflowers'

foreman is watching us," he murmurs to Blithe. "Start painting Goldie and laugh like I'm obnoxiously rich but you want my money."

Blithe complies with a loud laugh and, "Certainly! It will be a pleasure."

We arrange Goldie on the wall to pose while Blithe selects some brushes.

The foreman retreats inside Selflowers.

"If they're taking the sails to the ship," I say, "don't you need to follow them?"

"We do." Glister looks at his sister. "We need to be on that train."

"And we need to be here." Goldie meets his eye. "You love trains."

"I loved trains when I was five," Glister grumbles.

Goldie's gaze moves back to Selflowers. "They might have already torched the blueprints or whatever they had to work with. But it's possible they still have sensitive paperwork on site."

"You rob Selflowers, I follow the sail." Glister starts to nod.

Goldie smiles like she's posing prettily and talks through her forced grin. "You travel with the sails and telegram word when they reach their destination. We'll regroup and" – she glances at me then looks back to Glister, her jaw hardening – "set the whole bloody thing on fire."

Set … on fire? I stare at Goldie. This isn't like the Reedstones. They're about political manoeuvring, delicate blackmail. But what they're talking about now is sabotage. I'm used to secrets – but this is uncharted territory.

"I'm only here until *Toothsea Tear* sails back," I remind them.

I haven't told them my other plans. That I want to get out to Hunger Canyons. I want to see the place where my people sought refuge. The heart of the homeland, or what it shrunk to. The little piece the Crozoni let us keep when they pushed my ancestors out over a hundred years ago.

Somewhere I could make a home with Mora.

"Pack lightly and hurry," Goldie says to Glister. "We'll be along to the house soon, to avoid suspicion."

Glister leaves. His mind must already be racing ahead, to the station, to the train, to *Dominion* missing its black sails, the secret dry dock where they're building it.

Lovemore's mysterious project.

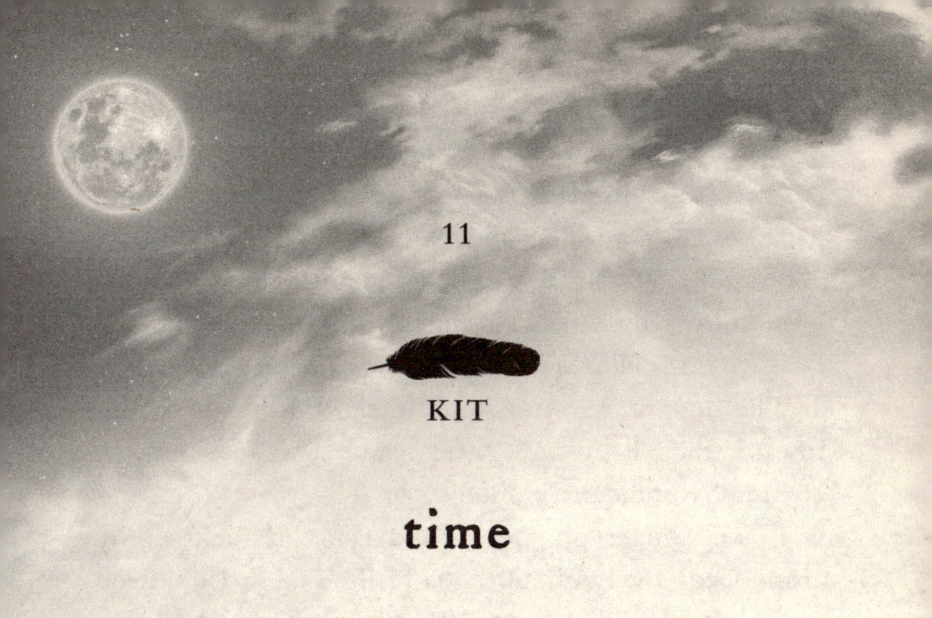

11

KIT

time

Thirday, Sevenmonth 27th. Shipway town. Night.
After midnight, we head back to Selflowers. Town's been rowdier with the crews from the Skøl traders in, but they're mostly settled near the docks further west, in the fikka houses and pubs there. The seafront here (and helpfully, the street with Selflowers) is deserted.

I've got the pick in before I realize the front door mechanism is busted.

I raise a hand to push some hair back from my forehead – so Goldie and Blithe, watching from a safe distance, will interpret the sign as *something's wrong*, but not *abort*. Then I go in. Like a man with a key, like I belong here, like it's not forbidden.

This is the good part. It's not the challenge of cracking a tricky lock. Not the money, though it's good. Not even that shiver of knowing I could be helping to relieve complete brickheads of stacks of cash or compromising paperwork. No. The good part is simply breaking in. Getting myself someplace where I'm not welcome. I don't even know why I like it so much, why that thrill doesn't fade. *Fuck you all, I'm welcome. You're welcome.*

The door sticks on a stone in the floor as it swings inward, then it gives. I notice the glass panel with its etching has some dirty smudges on it.

I don't linger on the ground floor. It looks eerily abandoned now, without the sail filling the space. I need to find the safe. The sinking feeling in my gut is back. It's darker upstairs. I light a lantern. The office door has a glass panel with a design etched in it too (*SELFLOWERS* in fancy lettering). This door isn't locked either. I can't tell if it's been busted.

Inside it's clear we're too late. Not because the documents have been destroyed. Not because the safe's hanging open. Because the safe is gone. There's a gaping hole in the wall where it used to be.

"What the fuck?" Goldie hisses as she and Blithe join me.

"Someone just … took it? But those things weigh a ton," Blithe murmurs.

"Let's get out of here," Goldie says, already heading for the stairs."

"Has your man got other people on this?" I ask her.

"Not that he's told me about."

"Would he tell you?"

Her jaw hardens. "He will if he knows what's good for him."

Fourday, Sevenmonth 28th. Shipway town. Morning.
Goldie and Glister adorn the cover of the local paper, smiling in a smudgy silverprint, along with a dozen other brave souls sticking their necks out to support Temper Wilforn, Lovemore's only opposition.

SHIPWAY SHOWS SUPPORT FOR WILFORN

Magistrate Clemency Rosclaw Secures Funds

"Prominent dignitaries, socialites, business owners and donors back Magistrate Wilforn for next High Governor, including Glister and Golden Reedstone of G&R Locks..." Blithe reads out to me, before taking a bite of buttery toast and shuffling to a different newspaper folded over on the other side of his plate. "But look at this!"

It's the latest available *Evening Gazette* – the Endweek edition they ship all the way from Skøland with news of the capital. This one's from four weeks ago, and the story he wants to show me isn't front page. There's no silverprint, but an artist's sketch shows a view down over a large crowd, stood before a makeshift stage where a man in a light jacket and trousers stands with no paper or lectern, his arms spread wide.

Clashes Erupt in Unruly Crowd Gathered for Temper Wilforn; 20 Casualties Result

—

Supporters Gather as Wilforn Unveils Pledges to the People

—

Wilforn Vows to Tackle Soaring COST of Life, Root Out Corruption

—

Estimates of 7,000-Strong Rally Marred by Violence and Rioting: 2 Dead, 18 Seriously Injured

"Is this in the middle of Rundvaer?"

Blithe nods, sipping fikka. "Yes. Lovemore tried to scaremonger people into staying away, but it didn't work. Sounds like her goons turned up too. *Clashes Erupt… Casualties!* No prizes for guessing who killed them!"

"Branders?"

"Of course. They'll try to paint Wilforn's camp as violent rioters. Don't believe a word!"

"Will people fall for that?"

"*Gazette* readers? Probably." Blithe frowns. He flips back to the front page. "This paper's in her pocket. Lovemore propaganda front and centre."

High Governor Continues Triumphant Tour

—

Clarion Lovemore Charms the New West Counties

"Charming us, is she?" I roll my eyes and look back at the local paper, picking it up to examine the silverprint. The Reedstones have pride of place among the dignitaries, flanking a broad-shouldered man in a waistcoat, his shirtsleeves rolled. He's clean-shaven with a hawkish nose and sharp jaw. "Is that the magistrate? Clem Rosclaw?"

"The man himself!"

"Does Goldie actually fancy him? I mean, is she serious?"

"Well, you could ask her, but she left ten minutes ago to see him."

"To see Rosclaw?"

"Yes."

"Wait." I have that feeling, like a lock clicking open. "*He's* the one you're working for, isn't he? The one who told you to steal the blueprints?"

"Maybe," Blithe confirms. "He's convinced this *Dominion* is something big."

"I didn't realize your source was quite so elite."

Blithe sighs. "It's just their world." Goldie's and Glister's, he means.

It certainly is, I can't help thinking. *Even if their preferred candidate loses later this year, it'll still be their world.*

Won't it? Perhaps that depends on how far and how publicly they align with her enemy.

"I'm going out," I tell Blithe. "Caruq needs to run."

I head with Caruq to the train station. He's got his tongue out like he's tasting the salt air.

There's a man outside the Harbour-master's office hanging up some new wanted posters. More **PIRACY!!!** I buy a few pieces of corn to eat on the way to the train station. A girl calls the local news.

The station is buzzing. Two men in a dedicated booth transcribe telegrams. A youngster outside waters troughs full of pretty plants, and two women in the office dispense tickets and information. I can hear the hum of the telegraph lines singing their coded messages up and down the wires.

Incredible technology. The kind of science you have to admire. The Skøl are evil, but they get things done.

I give my head a shake. It's never something I thought I'd have to guard against – coming to admire these cold people.

"Let's see your paperwork." The woman in the office stretches out a hand. She glances down at Caruq. "What are you doing with a hound like that?" There's always a reminder.

"He belongs to my owners." I tell her what she wants to hear. "I'm down here working."

Her colleague, an older woman, finishes helping someone else and joins in questioning me.

"You a runaway, boy?"

"I look like a runaway?" I'm neat. Hair trimmed, shirt tucked. Shoes shining.

"You look exactly the type to high-tail it to Hunger Canyons through Ridmouth, I'm sorry to say." She raises her pale brows setting off a ripple of wrinkles in her forehead. "Your hound, mind you, he's a shade too pale."

"Well, as it happens—" I pull out my immaculate paperwork: travel documents, copy of the Life Record I'm obliged to carry as proof of payment, special permissions from my owners Mister and Missus Scarlet, and a note from the Reedstones. Their name carries weight everywhere.

Only not here, it seems.

"I can't sell you a ticket to Ridmouth. If one of your bosses were to buy it for you, we could let you have it. Otherwise, you're a runaway risk."

I draw in a breath and try one more time. "But my documentation is all in order—"

She cuts me off. "We're not allowed to sell to you. We don't make the rules."

Frustration's rolling off me in waves, but I hide it, nodding serenely before walking away. I'm getting on that train, whether Goldie buys me a ticket or no. They won't *allow* it? I allow it.

Thankfully the train I need leaves in the evening. I relax my jaw. I need to cool down.

"Come on, Caruq." I let him piss up the edge of their pretty plant trough. Then we head beyond the station to the northern side of the town. I spot signs to the cannery and think of that odd couple, the woman with the eye injury who said she worked there.

When I reach the gates, it's clearly closed. Looks like it's been that way a while, judging by the bits of old newspaper blown round the door and the unloved patina speckling the gate's padlock.

"This place running?" I ask a passer-by.

"Not the season, yet. Starts in … another month."

So she lied. The half-Crozoni, half-Xan woman with her eyepatch. And the man, with his face like a mean dog. I think of them chuckling, walking away from us. Did they use our stake-out to stake out bloody Selflowers?

"What news from Rosclaw?" I ask Goldie, back at the bungalow. She glares at Blithe, who shrugs.

"He guessed," he said.

Goldie turns back to me. "Well, the fundraiser got him a good sum. And everyone's talking about Wilforn's *Pledges* rally back in Rundvaer. Clem is thinking about holding a rally here too."

"*Clem*, is it?"

She rolls her eyes at my teasing and continues. "To celebrate Temper Wilforn's sixtieth birthday – Eightmonth the eighteenth. It's a fourday – a workday. Perfect for a spontaneous public holiday. Shipway doesn't have much of a town square, but he's thinking to close the central thoroughfare. A street festival. Food, speeches, games, activities for the children, drinks! A show of support."

"But what did he say about the sails? The job? The missing safe?" I ask.

"He swears up and down he hasn't asked anyone else to look into *Dominion*. Says he prefers things simple, and I believe him. One team, one task."

"Whoever did it must be after the same thing we are," Blithe says. "Lovemore's secret. Perhaps we're on the same team?"

"I think it was opportunistic," Goldie counters. "Someone saw a big job shipping and assumed a great deal of money had changed hands. That safe might have been stuffed with coin."

"I think we saw them. The thieves." I look at Blithe. "I think you painted their portrait."

"What do you mean?" Goldie looks between us.

I tell her about the woman with the eyepatch and the cannery standing disused for months.

"It's not much to go on." Blithe frowns.

"There was something off about them," I insist, thinking of the man's foxy eyes.

"Maybe," Blithe admits, just as a rap at the door disturbs us – four taps, the middle two quicker. Caruq rushes over like he's expecting someone. The rest of us file behind.

It's a telegram runner. A Crozoni child, born before the Skøl invasion. A survivor. Don't see many of those. She's maybe twelve or thirteen, with an accent of the south. Child survivors weren't shipped around. They only moved the grown-ups south for the extra labour. She's a girl, but something about her makes me think of Zako. Her neatly trimmed hair, or her copper-rimmed glasses.

Thinking of Zako makes me think of Mora. Gods. Is this what love does? Hijack your brain so every turn your thoughts take lead to the same destination? My mind tips back to her like it's trying to wear a rut. I've seen brains. They're full of grooves and my grooves are all channelling into thoughts of Mora. Her name. Her smile. The whole shape of her mouth.

Caruq gives me a look with his liquid-yellow eyes like he knows what I'm thinking. *Do you miss her too?* I think, but I don't ask it out loud, because Blithe will take the piss.

The telegram runner sticks the toe of her boot forward when Goldie makes to shut the door. "Nothing for my troubles?" she's bold enough to ask.

"Come back in half an hour. I'll have a reply for you, and a treat," Goldie promises.

I can see the type, bleeding at the edges into the soft fibre of the paper as she unfolds it.

PKG DELIVER RIDMOUTH. REACH ME AT RM/2. G.

RM/2 being the telegram code for the property he's staying at. So we have a location for Lovemore's ship. Ridmouth – the first stop northbound. The same place I need a ticket to. Goldie's keen to join her brother, naturally. I could laugh. A small stroke of luck to resolve my problem with the ticket sellers. Sometimes I do feel favoured by the gods.

Goldie spreads her map of County Shipway on the dining table.

"Looks tiny," says Blithe.

"I hear there's not much to it," I say. "There's another train heading that way tonight."

Goldie turns sharply to look at me. "Are you sticking with us, then?"

"I'll come to Ridmouth with you. That's the way to Hunger Canyons, up Red River. I've a yearning to see it. It's the last refuge of my people."

Goldie pouts at this. "You've always got to have a side quest, don't you? You sly thing."

"Shall we buy the tickets now?" I suggest. My chest feels tight. I remind myself to breathe. I could be walking around Hunger Canyons in two days' time.

12

MORA

guilt

Nezza ignored me when I came in, so I went directly to our shared washroom to splash my face in the basin and then to stand for a while at my tiny window, gathering up the ragged threads of myself, tucking them away.

When I return to her room, she's sitting on the floor, back to me, sharpening one of her coloured pencils. "You didn't come at lunch."

"Sciencemaster didn't allow it." I'm still furious she told on me to Sting.

A huff. Her pencil snaps. She puts her back to me and resumes sharpening it.

I pick up the book she's been drawing in. It's one of her father's sketchbooks – only part filled. She's using the pages at the end he didn't get to. Sting let her keep several of Sculpin's books that he said were *without scientific merit*.

This isn't one with sea animals. It seems to be mostly technical drawings of elektrical plans. An elektrical cage? Some part for an engine? I realize I haven't seen these figures before, but they don't mean much to me. Flipping through, I find a spread with something non-technical – a young woman's face on one side and the same woman, sitting in a chair on the other, dressed very informally. *Jafalla* reads the label.

"Nezza – do you know who this is?" I hold it where she can see it.

"My mother, of course." She tries to grab it back but I'm still looking. Jafalla might be my age, or a little older.

"I'm using that." Nezza snatches successfully this time. "You lost my page."

I peer over her shoulder while she finds her place. Her drawings are naive, but they have an undeniable charm, and I feel my anger defrosting. "What's happening here?" I ask, pointing to a dramatic scene – some sort of massacre.

"Pirates," Nezza tells me shortly.

I realize there's quite a lot of gore. A man with a sharp blood-covered blade and a comically glaring expression stands beside a tall thin woman holding a kind of long club. There's something at their feet… *Are those dismembered limbs?*

"What a lovely imagination you have."

"It's not imagination."

"Oh? You know a lot of pirates, do you?"

She doesn't reply.

She's only six, I think. *I could be kinder to her. She's lost her dad and her nurse.*

I sit in front of her, trying and failing to catch her eye. "How are you feeling?" I ask. "I heard you talking to Sting this morning about your treatment. You had nightmares."

She sighs, sounding more like a teenager than a six-year-old. "The medicine isn't good for me," she says.

Sting's words echo in my skull. *But the human subject is showing promise.*

"Nezza, can I see the place you bled from in your treatment yesterday?" I put a gentle hand on her shoulder. She twists her arm gamely enough, hand up to her shoulder and points at a thin dark line on her forearm about two inches above her elbow.

I stare at it, my heart beating faster. There's no way this cut was from yesterday – or rather, no way I can think of that's not tied up in Sting's experiments with Xan rituals. The mark is barely there – it looks at least a month old.

"That's definitely the place he cut you?"

"Yes. With one of those nasty scalpels."

"And that medicine he gives you … is it made from butterflies?" She pulls a face and nods. "He eats it too. We eat it together."

"He eats the butterfly medicine?"

Another nod. "His cut didn't heal like mine though." *So he's experimenting on himself as well.*

"Do you always heal so quickly?"

"I don't know." She examines her arm, then the other one. I can't see any more marks. "It hurt. A lot."

"When you were talking with the Sciencemaster this morning—" I start to ask, but she interrupts me, her cheeks glowing red.

"I didn't mean to," she blurts out.

"You didn't mean to what?"

"To get you in trouble."

"Oh. Well, you did."

A scowl.

I take a deep breath and so does she, mimicking me without realizing. I soften my voice.

"Nezza. Enough. Let's put it behind us. The medicine Sting gives you … does he say what it's for?"

"To stop my fits. You know that."

"When did you last have a fit?"

"When I was a baby."

"You don't remember them?"

"Course not."

"And he's been treating you the same way every week since you were a baby?"

She shrugs. "Him or Father."

"And last night," I go on, "you told the Sciencemaster your head hurt. Where did it hurt?"

She touches her temples. I think of the child's skull, turning amber from the temples, the teeth, the jaw.

I feel a rage climbing up my throat like I haven't felt in weeks. They're experimenting on Nezza like one of their spotted devils. Is there no depth these people won't stoop to? Has she ever been a child to them? To her own father? Or was he just like Sting – dosing her and hoping for *results*? Why do they feel no qualms hurting anyone, child or no, whenever they please? My rage still simmers, but something else is boiling over.

Feels a lot like guilt.

13

MORA

finally gives

Nezza insists on finishing her drawing before we head down together to find a corner of the kitchen to sit in. I dish up some food. Yellow-gold liveried waitstaff carry Skølcakes, pots of jam and carved fruit out on tiered plates – destined for the fancy wing, Lovemore's domain. For the likes of us there's still sweet grist pudding, at least.

"Is there more?" Nezza asks hopefully, scraping the last smears from her bowl and turning to scowl at me.

"There is."

"Then get me some. Please." She gives me a fake, gap-toothed smile. I think of the boy upstairs with the amber molars.

"Have you been cleaning your teeth properly?" I ask her, refilling her bowl.

"Yes."

"Open up, then. Let me look."

She narrows her eyes, pursing her lips shut mulishly, but I hold the filled bowl out of her reach until she gives in with a snarl.

Her teeth all look normal, small and sharp and milk-white. My relief surprises me. *I can't start caring about this little witch. I have more than enough to be dealing with.*

Back in our rooms, Nezza settles cross-legged on her bed, cradling her sketchbook. She talks to herself and occasionally pauses to pat Minty as he curls around her neck and shoulders like a furry scrap of scarf.

"You could try to get to sleep early," I tell her. "You had a rough time last night with your fever."

She ignores me.

"Nezza," I sigh.

"I don't want to," she says, still not looking at me.

"You know, you don't have to fight everything I say. I'm here to look after you."

"You're cack at it." No hesitation that time.

"Cack? Excuse me? Don't say things like *cack*."

"You say *fucks ache*. I heard you."

I blink. *Fuck's sake.* When did she hear me say that? Must be Kit rubbing off on me.

"Nezza, I'm much older than you."

"So?"

"So … young people listen to their elders and do what they say."

She finally looks over at me. "That's stupid," she

decides. *You're stupid*, she means. She picks snot out of her nose and rolls it into a ball between her thumb and forefinger. "Do you listen to your elders?"

A neat trap. My high ground just crumbled. I listen to Sting because I'm a repayer, and if I don't, I'll be in a world of trouble. I don't want her listening to me for reasons like that.

"Okay. Bath time." When in doubt, change the subject.

"Neh neh bath time!" she retorts in an exaggerated Crozoni accent, pointing a snotty finger at me. "I'm just a chore to you. You don't care about me."

"I care *for* you. Every day."

"That's … different."

"Not really," I lie. I'm sick of this. *Fuck's sake.*

"You *don't* care." She sniffs angrily. "Leave me alone!"

I comply, going to retrieve Kit's lock picks from my room. It is a bit early for bath time. When I walk out again, she's watching me.

"Where are you going?"

"Upstairs. And you can't come."

"Ugh. You're so boring!"

"That's me. I won't be long, I promise. You won't miss me."

"Of course I won't miss you."

"Don't forget your bath, Nezza. Or at least wash your face and clean your teeth." Her sulky glower stabs me in the back as I leave, fiddling nervously with the lock picks in my pocket.

There's an unusual whiff of stale sweat when I reach the fifth floor. The door to the laboratory has a guard standing in it. This is new.

"Name?" The guard asks.

"Mora Dezil."

He consults a list he has clipped to a board.

"You … may enter," he says. "You may not remove anything from these rooms."

So Sting has set a guard for the boy's sacred and adored bones. They're precious, to be sure, but no one could break through the outer guard on the Castle Hotel to take them. *Well, Kit could do it*, I think, immediately contradicting myself.

I can't seem to go five minutes without thinking of Kit.

"Did the Sciencemaster General say if he'd be returning tonight?"

The guard shrugs.

I straighten my silly bonnet with only slightly shaky hands. I want to see that book. *Now or never*, Mora. *No time like the present. Seize the moment.* I reach for every platitude Ruzi ever spouted. *Don't be backward in coming forward* – Ruzi never said that one though. That was Ma.

I'm jabbing two lock picks with more desperation than art into Sting's office keyhole when I hear the guard's gruff voice again.

"Name?"

Shit. Someone's here. It isn't Sting – the guard would hardly ask his name.

"Praiseworth Cob."

I stuff the picks in my pocket and stand near one of the devil's cages so I can pretend to be cleaning it while I listen.

"You're not on my list. Sorry."

"What's going on?"

"No one who's not on the list goes in, and no human remains are to leave the room."

I hear Cob sigh. "It's those bones, then," he mutters. "I've nothing to do with those."

"Take it up with the Sciencemaster," the guard offers.

"I'll get it sorted tomorrow," Praiseworth says and leaves.

I edge back over to Sting's study door with my picks. Moments later, the lock finally gives.

14

MORA

filling the world

I've been in here dozens of times – delivering sketches, receiving instructions, listening with half an ear to Sting's rants. He keeps it tidy, though he doesn't have a clerk to help him.

I get the feeling he likes managing things himself. And that he doesn't want anyone knowing his secrets. His desk is home to a stuffed black songbird mounted on a bit of wood. It has a yellow beak, yellow feet and shiny black glass eyes. It perches beside his fancy hourglass. The ornament has an odd, sharp-edged construction, evoking the two nestled triangles of the Life Registry. The Registry motto, *Life Is Golden*, is painted on one of its black wooden ends. The stuff inside isn't sand, but beads of gold. I flip it over and watch it run, silken and warm in the lantern light, then put it back to rights.

There are books stacked on the windowsill – I spot titles about biology, chemistry, alchemy and occultism, mixed with tomes on health foods, medicine and tonics. There's a compendium of butterflies open on his desk and more titles lining a low shelf along one wall. *Inflammable Air and its Applications*, *Dynamical Elektrical Systems* and *The Science of Materials* sit side by side with *Stamina for Long Life*.

His official portrait of Clarion Lovemore – the only art outside the books – has been accidentally toppled. It gives my heart a peculiar lurch to stand over it. I've seen the same version in Valour Venor's old office at the Life Registry. It's twenty years old at least, so she looks much younger, less jowly and droopy, full of a vitality she lacks in her older age. I move to his desk drawer. More glinting metal. He seems to have several medals on ribbons for athleticism. Long jump, jogging distance, marching, lifting weights. Dates inscribed on them range from GE 145 to 148. He must have been a child of around ten when he collected these. I push them aside to find the book I'm after.

Sacred Secrets of the Ancient Xan and *Lume Dewilder* it says on the blue cloth cover in neat type, filled in gold foil. I frown. Glor said it was handwritten, and this is a printed book. I flick through and see it's a Skøl translation.

I search for the original on the shelves – Sting must have it somewhere. When I can't find it, I return to the translation.

Sacred Secrets of the Ancient Xan is a slim work. A short

note on the first, otherwise blank page reads: *Written in year corresponding to Skøl GE 171.*

That's eighteen years ago. The year I was born. Eleven years before the Skøl invasion.

Sacred Secrets has just seven main chapters, the first of which is a preface. I flip through the beginning quickly on the hunt for images, finding several, all in black and white.

The thick outlining and soft, confident shading – and other peculiarities to the style that perhaps only a fellow illustrator would notice – convince me this is Sculpin's work. He must have drawn the copies from the source.

I skim Chapter One – a dedication and preface.

> I have compiled these findings over several years and dedicate this work to my half-Xan children Crimona Dewilder, Jafalla Dewilder and their forthcoming sibling.
>
> Equal dedication is due to their loving mother, my devoted wife Raqmalis, who, in joining her life with mine, was forced to leave so much behind…

So, Dewilder had a Xan wife and children. That explained his interest in their culture. The name of his second child – *Jafalla*. Not uncommon, but still. I think of Nezza clutching Sculpin's old sketchbooks. Her mother was called Jafalla, and she must have been mixed – Crozoni and Xan.

I flip to Chapter Two, which describes the Xan gods. Macotl is listed first, drawn as a huge snake coiling around a craggy mountain for scale.

> Figure 1. *Macotl, Goddess of Making and Decay; in her serpent form.*

Naqramaree comes next, Lord of the Gods of Beginnings.

Affinity with Butterflies, his caption says. He's attractive, more human-looking than most of the others – a young and rather soft-looking man, eyes downcast, with a light fuzz of stubble enhancing gorgeous dimpled cheeks. They're pulled up in a smile. There's something completely arresting about it. Four wings arranged at his back are the only animal aspect, though they look too small to carry him. There's a note in the margin here, in pen – in what I recognize as Sculpin's hand. Bee wings? it says. That's exactly the animal they evoke. The stubble on his face is like bee fuzz too. *Naqramaree*, I whisper the four syllables of his name, wanting to hear it out loud.

Then comes Seff. Lord of the Gods of Endings. Seff's portrait is rather shadowy, his feet hard to see, his face gaunt. He wears a crown of feathers. A tufted tail curls up behind him, a bit like a spotted devil's. *Affinity with Dogs, Cats and Vultures.*

I continue to look through. Someone – Sting, probably – has folded the edge of the page to mark the beginning of Chapter Five.

The Rites of the Ralkalit: Seeking the Favour of the Gods

A Rare and Dangerous Ritual

Foremost among Xan religious rituals of health and power are the Ralkalit Rites, otherwise known as the ritual of the gods-favoured.

A successful appeal to the Xan gods under the Ralkalit Rites is said to manifest as heightened health and well-being, as well as heavenly cures for illness or injuries encountered. Successful aspirants are known as Ralkalit. Xan practise the Ralkalit Rites with great secrecy in both northern and southern Makaia.

Known Components of the Ralkalit Rites

The intimate details are guarded by elders who maintain and pass down the ways of their people. Oral histories support five central requirements:

1) A personal sacrificial oath;
2) An ingesting into the body of a creature beloved by the Xan gods;
3) The letting or pouring of blood;
4) The singing of sacred incantations; and
5) Lightning strike.

NOTE: Some sources indicate the use of artefacts of spiritual power, known as Amber Skulls, to channel or direct the aforementioned lighting.

Ralkalit are favoured by the gods until they or their oath should perish.

This sounds something like Kit's ritual, I think. *The personal oath at least.* I read on, intrigued.

Ralkalit to Alit-fel: Consequences of Oath-Breaking
Should a Ralkalit break their sacrificial oath they are said to be cursed, rather than favoured by the gods. The Xan term for this is Alit-fel.

The likeliest outcome in such cases is immediate death.

Death? Is this really what Kit has done? If he swims he'll die? *No*, I tell myself. *It's only a myth.*

The Xan believe that in most cases Macotl, the Mother Goddess, returns oath-breakers to her cycle of making and decay.

Any Alit-fel not cut down by Macotl faces one of two outcomes in the living world:

1) Undeath Eternal, in service to Seff; or
2) A Greater Life, in service to Naqramaree.

Naqramaree accepts fewer servants than Seff, and the oath-breaker must undergo a mysterious ritual. The patronage of Naqramaree is more desirable, though Seff's servants are said to be called upon less frequently. Both types of servitude begin with the amberfication of the skull.

Amber skulls again, like Hiramlan. I flip the page.

Chapter Seven
Spinda, Alit-fel: A Case Study

The words seem to spiral, and I look up through the open doorway. *Spinda*, the mother of the boy whose remains lie next door.

I turn the page to find a portrait.

Figure 48. *Spinda as an Alit-fel, age 106.*

Piercing eyes in an unsmiling face. One hundred and six years old. At supposedly over a hundred, Spinda looks no older than a woman in her mid-forties.

The history of Spinda, who came to be known as the Builder, the Glass Butterfly – after the sacred emblem of her ritual – and later, Grandmother of Hunger Canyons, is as fascinating as it is unusual.

In [year corresponding to GE 83], at the age of

eighteen, Spinda underwent the Ralkalit Rites to beg the favour of the gods. She was successful.

Her sacrificial oath was one of celibacy, and her sacred emblem is an animal adored by Naqramaree. She ingested Glass Butterfly as part of the ritual.

So, Spinda ate butterflies. Kit had a bird tattooed across his back, a vocifer.

Three years later, in [year corresponding to GE 86], Spinda's sacrificial promise was forcibly broken.

Rape. That's what it means. I stretch my sore neck and hip. I've been bending over the desk to read, not daring to sit down in case someone comes. My pocket timepiece says it's already five minutes past nine o'clock. I should leave – I'm pushing my luck.

Spared by Macotl, she survived her oath-breaking and undertook to join Naqramaree's service. Her broken oath was dissolved. She bore three children, though her first son died at a young age.

That's him, I think. *The bones. Hiramlan.*

Spinda's second-born came over a year after the death of her firstborn. He still lives and is—

The devils start piping to each other. Sometimes they wake more with sundown. I skim further down the page.

> Spinda's children and grandchildren have never undertaken the Ralkalit Rites and age naturally. She alone among the Xan of Hunger Canyons serves Naqramaree, and her duties and devotion to her people mean she does not stray far from that territory—

The guard's voice breaks across the devils' chittering.

"Evening, Sciencemaster General."

I'm closing the book, putting it back where I found it, spreading his collection of medals out over it.

"All quiet, I presume?" Sting asks. I'm shutting the drawer, dashing for the office door, my heart pounding.

"There's been no trouble, Sciencemaster General," the guard confirms. "A Mister Cob was seeking entrance earlier. Seemed to think he should be on the list."

I'm shutting the office door behind me. It locks by itself.

"An oversight. You may add him."

I'm pretending to shove new bedding into the nearest devil's cage when Sting appears. His steps falter when he spots me.

"Why are you seeing to your duties so late? Has Nezza eaten?"

"Yes, Sciencemaster."

"Good. Now out with you. Cover the artefacts before you leave. I want no disturbances."

"Yes, Sciencemaster."

Back in the main lab, I begin the careful task of placing cloth covers over the coffin and bones and other items laid out on the central table.

Dewilder's book scampers all over my mind.

Favours and curses. Blood and lightning. Gods and butterflies. Rape. *Spinda's sacrificial promise was forcibly broken.* Macotl spared her. She joined Naqramaree's service through a mysterious ritual. There was nothing explaining what that involved. And I didn't get a chance to read about the resurrection she tried to perform on her son, Hiramlan.

I wish I could see the original *Sacred Secrets of the Ancient Xan* – the one Glor said was handwritten in Crozoni. Sense or detail is often lost in translation. Perhaps there's more.

Back at our rooms, Nezza is fast asleep. I look at her, curled around Minty, and imagine the gold droplets in Sting's hourglass piling up over each other like the folds of a blanket, spilling out of the glass, filling the world.

15

MORA

fall silent

The hollow note of the dead child's ocarina wakes me. But am I awake? I'm in my annex room at the Castle Hotel, lying on my back, and there's an old woman standing next to the bed, leaning over me. She looks eerily familiar.

Her eyes glow like tiny violet lanterns. I'm sure I would scream at the shock of it, if I was able to move an inch or utter any sound at all.

She doesn't introduce herself and yet I'm so sure she knows me. And I think I know her. The mother of the boy upstairs. She looks older than the portrait I've seen, grown old without her child, come back from beyond the grave to curse me for disturbing his bones, just like the coffin lid said. Curse those who move these bones. *Spinda.*

Her hair is short and white-grey, her features hard to make out in the light – coming as it does mostly from her eyes. Weird shadows play up and down her face, prickly forests cast by her eyelashes.

The wrinkles in her upper lip look like stitches in the flesh.

I wonder how old she was when she died. Her mouth is puckered with displeasure, but the skin on her cheeks is smooth. She looks younger than Missus Scarlet. Her eyes are old though, when I see to the depths of them. Perhaps she doesn't look that old, but the description old woman *sits well on her.*

She puts the bee ocarina down. A bracelet on one of her wrists tinkles. Her head tilts my way.

"You moved his bones from the copper shroud."

Oh, her voice is beautiful. I want to hear her sing.

"You took him out and rifled through him like a sack of kindling. You played with his toys. You looked into the wound of him, and I felt it, fresh. What fire are you trying to start, girl?" She's not speaking Crozoni. She's speaking Xan, but I understand her. How can I?

I find I'm able to move again – and speak. "I'm sorry." I start to sit up.

The ocarina is back at her lips though she hasn't moved. Suddenly. Impossibly. I freeze again.

"You will be," she says as she disappears.

I sit up and peel back the curtain to peer out of the window, half expecting the view to be some alien dreamscape. But it's Rundvaer Square at night. I'm awake, heart thumping with dread, and the ghost is gone.

*

It's Endweek, but I have to spend the day working on more drawings of the awful inner skull for Sting. My mind keeps trying to revisit Spinda's visitation, and imagining Kit and the Reedstones setting sail on *Toothsea Tear*, floating away from me with every passing second.

Every pulse in my ears pounds its reminder, *away, away, away.*

Sting is full of furious energy, scribbling away, urging me to work faster. Glor and Hunter have the Endweek off. So does Mister Cob, but he's been in and out all day, mixing up chemicals by the window to carry back to his station downstairs.

I take my drawings of the inner skull to the doorway of Sting's office. He's writing. I wait until he looks up. "Finally." He gestures me over, reaching for the papers. "You're a dawdler. Makkie traits will out. Tendency to laziness. Poor work ethic, fecklessness, philandering. Look at your cap – hopelessly askew. Were you caught in a windstorm? Tie the ribbons properly. You look slovenly."

I just nod and turn away. It's easier to let them think what they want.

"Wait a minute. Did I say you could go?"

I shake my head.

"As a reward for finally finishing this simple task, I have one other."

I keep my expression flat.

"I require visuals of the spotted devil Nezza keeps."

"Minty?"

"Indeed." He clears his throat proudly, shuffling papers on his desk. "I am to make a formal presentation to Lovemore. She must be impressed enough to grant us more time and resources. You will work with Cob for a few days on transferring the required images to lantern slides and colouring them. We'll include these bones, and a sketch of the girl's pet too."

"Minty is one of your … subjects, then?"

I shouldn't have asked. His eyes snap up from his task and red blotches of angry colour creep over his neck and cheeks.

"I give you tasks. You perform them. Nowhere in your list of duties is it written: *Question, incessantly*! Is a simple order too much?"

I step back, giving a shallow bend at the knees.

"My apologies, Sciencemaster. I only thought—"

"Don't think, slug-brain. You were not made for thinking," Sting hisses. "What can you conceive of the pressures? Skøland's very future depends on this type of scientific advancement!"

He bangs the desk, jolting the gold in his hourglass.

"DRAW THE RAT!" He shouts his last command and flaps one of his big red hands in a clear gesture of *get out*, then calls, "Mister Cob!" at a more measured volume.

I flee past the silverprinter, somewhat reassured by the raised eyebrow he offers as we pass in the smaller laboratory. The devils caged there chitter, roused by the noise, then fall silent.

16

MORA

darkened room

No dreams last night. Small mercies. Another week dawns sticky and slow inside the Castle Hotel's suffocating, carpeted halls. I hate the framed depictions of Clarion Lovemore absolutely everywhere. On prominent walls. Propped on furniture. In the water closets, even. Is that someone's idea of a joke? I can't tell. The yellow-gold outfits on the fancier servants make them look light and fun – but light and fun couldn't be further from the order of the day in this place. And half the light is elektric. I want to see the sun, and *not* through poxy glass.

Firstday, Sevenmonth the fourth, and here I still am.

I escort Nezza to the fancy room in the other wing where she sometimes dines with Sting and whichever of Lovemore's advisors and bureaucrats happen to be breakfasting. There's no carpet near the table. The wooden flooring is arranged in chevrons, all pointing like arrows *away, out, elsewhere.*

I wish.

Back in the other wing, up in the lab, I see to the devils – fresh water and feed. By the time I'm done, Glor has arrived and uncovered the child's bones.

I show him my sketches of Minty. "Nezza's pet," I tell him. "I didn't realize he was one of the test subjects."

"An early success," Glor confirms, before he frowns. "And something of a sore point."

"What do you mean?"

"This animal is the first evidence of the longevity science working. Sculpin fed it a weekly elixir made from amber Glass Butterflies – from the time it was about a year old, five years back, and it still lives."

I frown. "You think the butterflies have made him live longer?"

"I don't think, I *know*."

How? I shake my head.

"He's been with the girl since she was an infant, they say."

"Yes."

"And she's six years old now. They're about the same age."

"Okay." *Spit it out, man.*

Glor strokes his chin. "The thing about these devils is, they run hot. Fast heartbeats, fast burn-through rate, fast runners, fast breathers. High temperatures."

He's more like his irritating mentor every day, I reflect, waiting.

"It means they're short-lived. Two years at most – in captivity. But that one –" he prods at my drawing – "is *six*. So, he's three times as old as any spotted devil has ever been."

I stare at the image. Minty, an immortal? How amazing. How ridiculous. Three times a full natural lifespan – it's like a person living past two hundred and fifty.

"Besides, we've cut the rat open and it heals again," Glor says as though it's nothing. "No amber bones though—"

He stops, realizing Sting's arriving.

"Today, Mister Stanwin, we ascertain the amber's elektrical properties," Sting announces. "Bring the portable generator and the box of elektrical leads. And there's a roll of copper wire on my desk."

"Right away," Glor says.

"Dezil." Sting walks past me to the bones. "Have you finished the sketches I asked for?"

I hold them out. He flicks them a bare glance before handing them back. A flushed excitement stains his cheeks – under the mutton chops. "Good. Take these down to Mister Cob. You are to help with the lantern-slide preparation." He hands me a note. "Tell him they must be in that order *precisely*. No deviations. Much is riding on this."

I edge past the guard and head downstairs to Mister Cob's workroom, perusing the list of items on my way.

He wants a picture of himself, a butterfly, figures from

Dewilder's *Sacred Secrets* and my drawings – of Minty and of Hiramlan's remains. Twelve items in total.

Mister Cob is expecting me. His workrooms on the third floor are narrow and windowless.

I hand Sting's list over and watch as he reads it.

"Good … good." His voice rumbles. "Let's start, shall we?"

Mister Cob's not bad. He doesn't treat me like I'm stupid. He doesn't snap or smirk. Working with him reminds me of the days I spent with Ruzi and the other deliverers at the Glassworks. I feel some tension sliding off my shoulders.

To begin, he gives me five black-and-white lantern slides with images on them to colour, and another two he's already coloured poorly, to fix up. Each slide is a delicate piece of glass, about four inches square, framed with wooden strips.

"Whatever you do, don't break them. They're incredibly fragile."

"I used to work with glass," I tell him. Now I work with paper and pencils. And Nezza – she's like glass, the sharp little thing. Liable to cut you open. Or to shatter into a thousand-piece tantrum.

I notice that one of the uncoloured glass slides is a silverprint of the cover of Lume Dewilder's book. Not the version I've seen – the original Crozoni. I lift it to the light.

It's plainer than I imagined, but perhaps the slide doesn't do it justice. The typewritten translation in Sting's office had gold lettering on its clothbound cover. This looks to be bound more simply, its title in large and looping ink. Still, the Crozoni script is exceptionally neat.

"I've heard of this," I say cautiously, though my heart swoops. "Glor told me about it. It's in my language."

"Oh, yes. A seminal work on Xan ritual. The Sciencemaster has based his research on it."

"I'd love to see it in real life – to get the colours right."

"I have it back there." He points to the door that leads to the darkspace where he works on the silverprints. "I'm using it for one final image today, then you're welcome to look tomorrow morning, how does that sound?"

I nod eagerly. "This talk for Lovemore … it seems very important to him."

"Oh, it is." He lowers his voice. "Lovemore's patience with this research is low. The Sciencemaster is desperate to go south and dig up the Badlands with his bare hands. Well…" He clears his throat. "Now they've evidence amberfication is real. It's the first proof *any* of this might pay off. And the Burial Circle was even mentioned on the coffin…" His voice trails off thoughtfully.

"So he's hoping Lovemore lets him go south to find the Burial Circle? Full of amber skulls?"

I think of the book.

> Some sources indicate the use of artefacts of spiritual power, known as Amber Skulls, to channel or direct the aforementioned lighting.

"He's hoping she doesn't stop the funding. But you're right. He wants to emulate the ritual of the primitives – or the scientific aspects of it. Eternal life, don't you know? Lovemore was taken by the idea at first – but like I say, she's lost patience." He laughs. "Shame, I rather like the idea of squeezing another few decades out of these old bones." He cracks his knuckles theatrically. Then he walks off, closing the door to his darkspace. Question time is over.

I look over the slides, marvelling at the tiny black lines. I'll need a brush like a hair to paint some of this. Two are more complicated than the others and I hold them closer to the lantern to examine the fine detail. They must be images from Dewilder – from the part of the book I didn't have a chance to read.

One shows a woman, hooded but rather Spinda-like in profile. She stands part-ringed by an arc of five human skulls. A slice of the Burial Circle.

With one hand she holds a skull aloft on the end of a pole. A bolt of lightning shoots from the sky, hitting the skull. Her other hand is thrust out, fingers splayed. Lesser lightning strikes travel between her fingers and the skulls arrayed near her. I can't tell if the skull she holds or those on the ground are amber, since the slide has no colour, but I strongly suspect they are.

The image on the other slide is equally striking. Here the central woman is smaller, fully circled by twelve skulls arranged like the hours on a clock. The way they're drawn suggests it's dark and they're glowing like lanterns.

Something glows close to her feet – a thirteenth skull. The one she was holding aloft in the other picture, probably. The illuminated figure still looks like Spinda, though it's harder to tell with her so tiny. She has both hands raised. One holds a knife touching the palm of the other – cutting it.

I lower the slide, a shiver running down my back. This, then, is the ritual of legend Sting's keen to capture with his science. To transform into a commodity, as the Skøl do everything. Whether it's a miracle of the gods or one of science remains to be seen.

It turns out colouring slides is incredibly fiddly. Hours later, I'm two-thirds frustration, one-third headache.

What would help is a long walk outside. To see the ocean. To look up into endless sky, a real blue sky, so I can feel small and insubstantial – in a good way. Instead, I'm giant, hunched and sore, my big nose two inches from this sliver of glass like something a mouse would hang on its wall.

When I've coloured two of the simpler slides as well as I ever will, I pick up the shrunken image with the circle of skulls again. That must be blood dripping from Spinda's hand and down the knife, pouring over the skull at her feet, flowing on to the ground. There seems to be an awful lot of it. But what's blood and what's shadow?

"How are we doing out here?" Mister Cob has come out of his darkspace and caught me not painting.

"Not bad," I hedge. "Though I'm not sure what colours to use on this one. It's from Dewilder, is it not?"

Cob squints over my shoulder.

"Ah, yes. Skulls are orange, blood is red. Make it bright, but don't lay it on too thick," he says. "How many of the others have you done?"

"Um … three," I lie, wetting one of the paintbrushes.

"Splendid. On track." He gives me an encouraging smile and heads back into the darkened room.

17

MORA

save us

My stomach grumbles. Cob still hasn't emerged, and my head is swimming with spots of wet colour.

"I'm going to get Nezza's dinner," I call through his closed door.

"Very good," His muffled voice comes back. "See you tomorrow."

Marbles are scattered all over her floor like death traps, but Nezza's playing with her spinning top. She throws a scowl at me when the top falls.

"You hungry?"

"Yes. Obviously. You're late."

"Let's go and eat, then."

"I'm playing."

"Eat now, play after." I try to take her hand, but she slaps me away.

"Come on, Minty – dinner." I've nothing to tempt him but the sound of the word is enough. He scurries over from his spot on Nezza's pillow then wrinkles his nose at me with a shrill *tsk*.

He doesn't look old. He doesn't move like an old animal. No joint pain, no drooling. Sharp white teeth. Glossy brown fur with pretty black spots.

Nezza deigns to join us. On the stairs down to the kitchen, we disturb a man and woman whispering fiercely to each other in a corner of the lowest landing. Or rather, we fail to disturb them, despite Nezza sniffing loudly and stomping. They're standing very close. The man has his hands on the wall behind the woman, bracketing her head with his arms. They're completely absorbed in whatever it is they're discussing. I look back at them when we're past. He's moving one of his hands to touch her hair. "I'll look after you…" I hear him murmur. The rest of the world might as well not exist.

I can't see much more than the man's back – tall and broad, in the garb of a guard. The woman's dress is familiar. I don't like to stare, but I'd put good money on her being Lovemore's attendant. The fan-waver. Whatever they're whispering about, it looks intense.

I'm reminded of Kit, of kissing him in that storage room, how everything around us fell away.

Downstairs in the bustling kitchen, Nezza and I sit at a table in the corner to make a start on some garlicky red-lentil stew. The day's been hot as anything, but the kitchen staff will make stew regardless. It must be a favourite of Lovemore's, though it's simple fare. Most of the dishes destined for her dining table in the other wing are rich and elaborate – not for sharing with the likes of us.

I'm blowing on a spoonful when Nezza lets out a high squeal. "Eeeee!" It's a noise I've never heard her make in over four weeks, more like some awful stringed instrument than a girl. The glasses on several shelves actually ring. *A fine balladeer*, I imagine Ruzi saying. Several of the staff turn to glare at us.

"Pipe down, piglet," says one, holding a hand to her chest over her apron. But Nezza isn't listening.

She's flinging her arms around the waist of a tall Xan man who's just come in. "Daruunlis!" she cries.

Sting's translator, arrived at last.

"My favourite Benezza," Daruunlis says. "Here you are, *Ruahee*." A Xan endearment I don't know, though I've heard Kit use something similar.

"What are you doing here?" Nezza squeaks. Minty, perched on her shoulder, adds his chitters of excitement to the reunion.

"Looking for you, of course. I've been all over this place – patted down by so many guards I'm tender as a fish steak." His eyes crinkle. "Should have known to check near the food, shouldn't I?" He has a voice like smoke, soft and penetrating, with a pleasant undercurrent.

He must have crossed paths with Kit, I think, sailing north while *Toothsea Tear* was bound south.

I've seen so few Xan people, most of them in books. This man is older than Kit, in his late twenties, I would guess. He's half a foot taller, nearly as tall as one of Lovemore's guards – but he's leaner. His face is craggy and there's something underfed about him, but his arms, lifting and swinging Nezza in a hug, are roped with muscle. So she *does* do hugs. Daruunlis kisses her cheek too. He gives me a short nod and turns back to Nezza.

He wears strange clothes – trousers tight near the shins and billowing above, and a square-necked shirt. Perhaps it's the style in the south.

"I heard about your father," he says softly. She hugs him tighter, then releases him.

"Why didn't you come before?" she asks as they slide on to the bench beside each other, opposite me.

"I wasn't invited before, was I?"

"But you go where you please. Father always told me you do."

"You go where you please?" I blurt.

"Well." He smiles at me. "I still need papers, but probably not as many as you. The patronage of Sacrifice Sting opens many doors." He ruffles Nezza's hair. "I can't go everywhere I want, can I? But I'm not a repayer. We live unregistered up in Hunger Canyons."

So he's from Hunger Canyons – where Kit thought we might make a life, where his people have a refuge.

"I don't know much of Hunger Canyons," I admit, hoping he'll tell me more. But he turns back to Nezza.

"How are you holding up?"

Nezza looks at her food, then at Minty. "Minty missed you," she says. "Have some stew. It's good."

He looks at me, slurping stew, so I put down my spoon and extend a hand. "I'm Mora, by the way. Nezza's new..." I don't want to say nurse.

"She's supposed to look after me," Nezza says. "But she mostly just draws, like Father did, for the Sciencemaster. Mora's better at it."

Her rare praise tightens my throat for some reason. Daruunlis nods slowly.

"You hungry?" I ask in Crozoni.

"I could eat," he replies in the same. "But I can't stay. I've a job already." His chin tips to Nezza. "How is she?"

Nezza looks daggers at us. She hates it when I speak Crozoni.

"She is..." My voice peters out. What can I tell him? She's trapped here – Sting's human subject.

I need someone to trust. But is it him?

"She could be better," I say at last with a frown.

He stands. "Let's talk later." He switches back to Skøl to tell Nezza he'll see her tomorrow.

"Tomorrow?" she whines as he leaves.

"Eat your food," I say, dipping my spoon back in my lentils and doing a quick inventory.

Kit is gone, the Reedstones are gone. My only allies, somewhere at sea. I'm as trapped as Nezza, stuck indoors painting tiny glass slides for a maniac who's searching for the secret to long life by digging up old bones and torturing butterflies.

It doesn't sound real, but Minty lives beyond his natural lifespan. Nezza's wounds heal. Sting is dissecting old Xan belief, exposing some scientific process at the heart of it. He's intent on finding the things that unite the rituals. The smallest common denominators he can believe in – amber bone, butterflies … but not prayers or promises or incantations. When he has the parts, he will build the impossible whole. The most powerful scientist in the land believes in creating an elixir of life. A potion or a treatment regime to bring the Skøl closer to immortality. Power to heal. Power over death, power to sell more life. It's bigger than cruel experiments and dusty theories.

If such power is really within his grasp, within Lovemore's – gods save us.

18

KIT

the river

Fourday, Sevenmonth 28th. Shipway town. Night.

My private cabin is narrow but plush. The train pushes into the night, its movement smooth – nothing like a horse- or kine-drawn carriage (something about it soothes), and its roar is not even that bad with the window closed.

I pull the plate of glass down (moon's full) and stick my head out above Caruq's. He wants to taste the dry southern wind. Stars wink like they know something we don't, out here, far from the places people stain with their lanterns and elektric lights.

I sleep eventually with the window open, letting in the noise and the night.

Fiveday, Sevenmonth 29th. Ridmouth. Morning.

When I wake, it's past dawn (my cabin for this jaunt has a sunrise view) and the wheels sound subtly different. It's because we're going over a bridge (metal cables, great metal pillars secured with rounded rivets), already halfway over the Red River (which turns out to be more orange). The bridge is high and redder than the river.

I slide open my cabin door and find a window opposite. The sea is a wink in the distance – this crossing's miles inland, where the banks of the river are already steep, though the span is wide and the smell seasoned by the sea. I head with Caruq into the common carriage where Goldie and Blithe are already sitting with empty cups of fikka.

"Impressive, isn't it?" Goldie says. "It's called a suspension bridge."

We can see the whole hamlet of Ridmouth from up here. It sits on a plateau that looks man-made, halfway down to the river on the north bank, lining either side of a laterite road that starts beside the train tracks and runs in a shallow incline all the way down to what look like steps leading to a dock (for small boats) at the riverside. I could count the little vessels there: less than a dozen. A lone pair float beyond the bridge on the other side – early fishers. Certainly no sign of anything that might be *Dominion*. No big dry dock of the kind you'd need to build a Skøl tall ship. Ridmouth must be a temporary stop for the sail.

"Not much to it, is there?" I summarise.

"It's what's left of the workers' accommodation when they were building the bridge … five years ago." Blithe says.

Scraggly trees, twisted and out of place, grow between the sparse buildings which are all simple in structure. I spot a solitary veranda in the style of Shipway town. On the edge of town, a large building stands out like a hammered thumb. Its grey-brown metal roof winks in the morning light.

A single-storey building like the rest, but it must be close to a hundred yards long.

Train brakes squeal as we pull in to the station. There's no platform to speak of, not like there was in Shipway town. No planters or sheltered spaces or signs declaring us welcome. A low black building sits quiet, locked up.

No other passengers disembark, though a stack of newspapers tied with twine is tossed down to one of the only two people waiting – he puts them in a crate on the back of his bicycle and pedals off.

The other person is here for us – Glister.

Caruq bounces up to him and wins half a biscuit for his troubles, before Glister's hugging Blithe, then his sister. "Welcome," he says in his deep, jovial voice. "Thought when I set off I wouldn't see you for an age."

He hands round a paper bag of savoury biscuits while Goldie fills him in on the missing safe and lack of boat blueprints. "And Kit's not stopping with us. He's going upriver to Hunger Canyons," she tells him.

"I need to see it," I add.

Glister contemplates me. "The heart of Xan territory, I hear. Very good. In fact, that serves our cover story. I told a local brander I was here to meet traders of native artefacts. We can say you're going to help up at the enclave while we wait here in … comfort." He gestures ironically at the small town and begins to lead us down the road.

"What will you do while I'm gone?"

"More meeting and greeting, I think," Glister says. "This place is pocket-sized. The telegram operators must be privy to a great deal. We should make progress by making some friends."

"And the sails?"

"They took them over to a building at the end of town. Hopefully we won't have to wait too long before they move them on."

"Where have you found for us to stay, then?" Goldie asks.

"Rooms in the branders' outpost. There is a guest house, apparently, but it's being renovated – not open for business."

Goldie gives her brother a sharp glare. "We're rooming with branders? Really?"

Branders keep the Skøl law. They're as brash and brutal as the Crozoni police used to be, packing heavier arms that they're quick to deploy.

"It's not like you think," Glister placates her. "There are no extra branders staying at present. The peace keeps itself here."

"What do Ridmouthers do for a living, then?" Blithe asks as we walk in the middle of the empty street. "Ridmouthians? Ridmouthites?" Only a smattering of locals are out and about.

"Not enough to warrant a collective noun," Glister says. "Some trade with those upriver – special clay from the canyons mostly. It's a sleepy town."

"It's a stinky town." Blithe wrinkles his nose as the breeze changes, and we catch a whiff of something gone beyond stinky, flying past putrid.

Goldie curses and shields her nose. "What is that? Smells like … ugh." Words escape her.

Glister laughs without humour. "Yes, rotten, isn't it? Ridmouth is home to a gas processing plant – they say the smell's a by-product." He points down the road in the direction of the oddly outsized metal-roofed building I noticed earlier.

"It's that place," he says. "And you'll never guess where our sails ended up."

Goldie gives an annoyed groan.

"What are our sails doing in a gas processing plant?"

"Indeed," Glister murmurs with a baffled shrug.

We've reached the building where they're staying. It's opposite the only one with a veranda. Someone's sitting on a rocking chair there, dressed in a brander's uniform with a paper resting on his knee.

"Good luck with the quest," I tell Goldie. "Caruq – we'd better be off."

But before I can finish taking my leave, the brander unfolds from his chair and comes to meet us.

"Good morning. These your friends, Mister Reedstone?" He peers unhurriedly at each of us in turn.

"Brack," says Glister. "This is my sister, Goldie, and one of our colleagues, Mister Telholt. Kalqitlan here is on our staff. Helps us appraise the art."

"Ah, so you're all artistic types?" His eyes land on Glister. "My missus has just seen you in the papers. You were at that fundraiser of Rosclaw's."

"We were." Glister winks. "Guilty."

"You hoping Temper Wilforn topples her?" Brack sounds genial, but I wonder if there's threat behind it. Branders all love Lovemore – she's been good for those in the business of keeping her laws. Generous. And very encouraging of overzealous enforcement under the guise of keeping the peace.

Glister said the locals swallowed his cover story, but I wouldn't be so sure. Goldie sees it too, I think. She narrows her eyes at Brack playfully and says, "Time for some fresh blood."

"Hmm." Brack adjusts his hat. His eyes flick towards the big building at the edge of the hamlet. "Lovemore has another term in her – she's full of surprises, that one. Her opponents underestimate her at their peril." There's an edge to his voice that makes me wonder again. Does he know something?

Goldie spots her cue. "You think Lovemore has

something up her sleeve that we'll see before Tenmonth?" She puts a bit of scepticism into her voice.

"Oh, you'll see," the brander says, goaded. He smiles. "Enjoy your morning."

"Enjoy yours," Goldie sing-songs after him, before turning her thoughtful face to the rest of us.

"Intriguing," I summarise in a low voice, "but perhaps not the man to befriend for secrets."

Blithe chuckles in agreement.

"If I'm not back in a few days…" A sudden fear grips me – that old anxiety I used to have as a child, that something bad was coming. "Well, no, I will be." I laugh it off.

"Take care," Goldie says.

Glister clasps my hand. "Come back in one piece," he orders. Blithe pats me on the shoulder.

Unfortunately, Caruq and I have to pass closer to the source of the stench so we can get round the bend and down to the docks where I've been told I'll be able to find a boat travelling on to Hunger Canyons.

There's a sign on the way leading up to the big building declaring it: RIDMOUTH GAS PROCESSING CENTRE. DANGER. HIGHLY FLAMMABLE CHEMICAL MANUFACTORY. NO ENTRY.

Caruq whines like he'd like to go up there to roll around in whatever it is. "Don't be disgusting, you awful hound," I say as I urge him on down to the river.

19

KIT

old crone

Fiveday, Sevenmonth 29th. Red River.

A sailor called Oden Fisher takes us upriver in his boat, *Clara*, along with a cabinful of things to trade and a trail of timber banging along behind. *Clara*'s narrow but long, easily fitting the two of us and Caruq. On the water, again. This river's a trickle compared to the sea, but I still worry. There's no sense to it, but I feel more vulnerable here than I did on the tall ship, for whatever reason.

"The big boats can't make it to Ridmouth, let alone up here." Oden gestures upriver. "They sit too deep in the water."

His craft is powered by some kind of solid, dried-ragleaf-burning generator hooked up to a propeller at the back. Never seen anything like it. "Xan tinkers' design. They call it a powerbox," he tells me.

The thing's hot as a furnace. Oden has to keep feeding it pellets of ragleaf waste and pouring ladles of river water over it (so it doesn't, in his words, explode). Caruq sits at the front of the boat, as far away from it as he can get, occasionally giving me looks over his shoulder like I've betrayed him. Of course, he'd happily explore a mystery building that smells like the spawn of death and rot, but sitting on this boat is too much for him.

"It's not one of the good ones, but it does the job," Oden apologizes. He's Crozoni. Looks like Mora's father, though he's at least ten years Ruzi's junior, and his forehead, one eyebrow and part of his cheek are marked by a deep burn scar.

He survived the Cull near Coppertown, two thousand miles north of here, though when he was unconscious after they shot him, something burned his face. He doesn't know what. He got sent into repay down here, worked laying track.

He's been a runaway going on five years. The rumours are true – repayers who run to Hunger Canyons are afforded a kind of unofficial amnesty. Branders don't go there. And they don't usually detain workers like Oden who travel to and fro between Hunger Canyons and Ridmouth.

"They need us up there mining the clay and ferrying it out," Oden tells me. "So they turn a blind eye. That and there's hardly any of us who manage it, especially these days. Less runaways every year."

"Why's that?"

"Runaways from the northern counties get caught and killed." He doesn't mince his words. "Rosclaw down in Shipway's doing things different – improving conditions in the orchards and the farms so fewer people risk running."

"Really? And it's working?"

"For now." He smacks his hot, hissing generator with the dripping ladle and we chug on.

"Are you also in the clay business, then?" I ask him.

"*Clara* and I float it down sometimes."

I have to ask. "Is *Clara* named after your … sweetheart?"

"My wife – as was."

"I'm sorry."

"Everyone's got someone. Not your sin to be sorry for."

"I'm still sorry," I tell him.

The canyon walls get higher and more layered. Most of the layers are the rusty orange-red of the banks downriver, but lighter and darker strips run through it. It's slipped in places to reveal pale greens and blues.

"Canyon clay, ten o'clock." Oden points as we approach a pale patch near the waterline. "Thick and sticky."

"Oh, right." I don't know the first thing about clay. "Good, is it?"

Oden nods. "Hunger Canyons clay is the best. The Skøl can't get enough. They use it in their elektrics. And for the wires, you know, for the graph, what do you call it?"

"The telegraph?"

"That's the one."

"I can't believe they let you get on with it," I tell him. "No paperwork. No Life Registry. Like old times."

Oden laughs bitterly. "Think about it. They round us up today –" he gestures upriver in the direction of Hunger Canyons – "no one digging clay tomorrow."

"Because everyone would die."

"Because we'd die."

We chug upriver past nightfall, colour bleeding out of everything with the growing dark. The land goes grey, the water black. Red River starts to wind, narrowing to half, then a quarter of its former width. It's still wide.

For a while, rapids form white water and our tied-on-timber tail dances a jig, but we stick to the centre and *Clara*'s propeller does the work of two kine.

The stars out here are as thick as the light off the sea on a sunny day. Has the world moved closer to the Haymaker's Way when I wasn't looking? Feels like it. I don't recognize the constellations of my childhood. As if they've been swallowed by something greater.

Past the rapids, on a straight stretch, we tie up to sleep – on the boat. There's no way off, short of swimming through deep water (breaking my promise to the gods). Even if swimming was an option, I'd have to scale ten yards of vertical riverbank to really get away. Perhaps I'd find handholds in the day, but at night – starlit or no – I wouldn't fancy my chances.

The temperature plummets and seems to take all my

energy with it. I shiver despite the blanket Oden tosses my way. *Clara*'s rickety powerbox keeps cooking for ages after we stop, but Caruq's lost his fear of it just in time to hog all the heat.

Above us at the top of the sheer banks, I spot a creature prowling, predatory. It's eyes shine silver-green. It isn't the cold or the beast that keeps me awake though. Oden could slit my throat, empty my pockets and dump me in the Red River. Who would know? Only Caruq.

Suppose I could do the same, though, and Oden snores like an old man.

Sixday, Sevenmonth 30th. Hunger Canyons.

We fry eggs in a pan on top of the powerbox when we get going again.

"Is the river the only way in?" I ask.

"They tried building a road in the beginning—" The Skøl tried, he means. "But it collapsed in a sinkhole a few miles in. No one passes that way. The land won't have roads and rails, bit and bridle. Won't wear them. When they had me working on laying rails – Thea's wounds, times I nearly died. That was graft like no other. First rains of the season and it was all for naught." He pats the side of his boat. "We don't mind the rains, do we, my darling?" He looks back at the land we've passed, at the great shining ribbon of the river we're rippling through. "The Skøl can't take this patch. They know better than to try now."

Before noon, the land opens out to the north (though the river doesn't widen, southern bank still steep). The township sprawls on the northern bank, over an area five times the size of Ridmouth. The buildings are smaller though, and weathered. Back over the river I see bridges strung across, like green webs, trailing vines.

Hunger Canyons.

When we're closer I note the bridges are a network (grown, not built). They're vines, not vine-covered. Must have been trained over years to grow that way. It has a lush feel I didn't expect from the Badlands. The Xan here must have put the river to good use with some sort of irrigation.

The vine bridges reach between raised platforms of parched-looking wood on the north side and yawning black holes in the rock opposite. Caves. Children climb and play. This place has more children than Shipway. Sleepy dogs and slinking cats. Fat pigeons and even bigger birds – I don't know them – perch on the rooftops. It feels alive in an old way, like Portcaye when I was a child. Lovemore's influence feels far away.

Oden ties up and takes me to meet a woman called Neema with some floor going spare. I can sleep at hers for as long as I'm looking to stay, for a fee.

"You running away?" She takes the payment in advance before she asks, pausing in her work. She's watering a thin vegetable patch outside her low-roofed house. She's Crozoni, like Oden, a similar age. A baby sleeps on her front, cradled in a shoulder sling of traditional Crozoni cloth.

"Not yet."

She considers me a moment. "You here for an audience with the crone, then?"

"With the who now?"

"Oh, so you've not come to see her? Perhaps you will, all the same." She gives me a pensive look. "You've come far."

It's obvious from my accent. "I wanted to see what it was like here. I thought … maybe I could come back someday, with my … with my friend. Mora."

"Oh, I see. Mora. Good Crozoni name. At least she's not Skøl!"

I scoff.

"Well, she won't be welcome on the east side." Neema points in the direction I thought of as the river's southern bank. "The caves and yonder are for Xan." The baby begins to wake up and fuss. "Some won't welcome her, but there will be a place for you. Have a look round."

Badlands seems an unfair name. I explore, admiring the hills and gullies heaped with orange- and red-banded sediment, some brown, some blue-green. Two big rocks shaped like mushrooms catch my eye in the distance (they're like stacked boulders). They must be enormous as they're quite far away. They look unreal.

Low bushes, some grassland. And is that barley grist? A copse of those same thin trees they had in Ridmouth stand still as death in the mid-distance.

Past the edge of town, over towards the mushroom rocks, a corral. Delicate horses graze on thin grasses. Also a handful of kine with broken horns, a pair of stocky donkeys, and another animal I don't recognize – long-necked, ears like cupped palms, pointing up.

Hang on. Horses. I look back at them, shock catching me up. I'm so accustomed to seeing kine that they look small.

I haven't seen horses alive since the Skøl invasion. These Hunger Canyons ones are raw-boned, like the dogs (like the children too), but not starving. Lean but not unhealthy. *Mora would love to see this*, I think. Her family kept horses – and a pony – before they were all killed.

The people here do more than trade clay, I learn. Fossils, jewels, amber. Bit of gold.

"Is Badlands amber still cursed with bad luck?" I ask a seller. She's part Xan, part Crozoni.

"Not by me," she says with a wink.

I think of walking out to the big mushroom boulders, but they're further than they look.

The sun sinks between them, confirming how the river's wound us around. The north bank faces westerly, the south one east.

There's a semi-permanent camp over to the southwest, where some men, all Crozoni, are digging around.

One of them greets me when I walk over, with a polite, "Hello, stranger." He takes his hat off. I'm not used to being on the receiving end of Crozoni manners – Mora and her family aside.

"What work are you doing here?" I ask him.

"Just trying to make a living," he mutters, defensive. Another man comes up to him, leans on his spade. "We're searching for ancient graves," he tells me. The Skøl scientists and collectors pay top dollar if you strike the right kind."

Xan, he means.

"Are you striking them?" I ask.

They're reluctant to tell me, but in the end they can't help bragging about a recent coffin – just a small one – they sold for a fortune to an eminent scientist. *Vultures*, I think, but I'm not here to fight. I head back to the town proper, my feelings all over the place.

There's no escaping the obvious fact of how few fully Xan people seem to live in Hunger Canyons. I've seen the odd child, playing with the Crozoni and mixed-origin kids by the vine bridges and the riverside. I count only two Xan women at the market with vegetables to trade. This was supposed to be our refuge.

I head back to Neema. Her husband Jevlan, who is Xan, is back from the clay pits.

"Where have all the Xan gone?" I ask them.

"They stay in the caves." Jevlan gestures to the east, where the river is. "It's plush living, everyone says so. And they've got land out beyond, I hear. Never been there myself, of course."

"Why 'of course'?"

"Only pure Xan are allowed to enter the caves. Only pure Xan can set foot in their territory in the Badlands beyond."

"Really? That sounds like…" I don't say it. It sounds like a Skøl kind of rule.

Neema nods.

I look at Jevlan, at their children waiting for the simple meal Neema's putting on, at the baby tucked in Jevlan's arms.

"But you're Xan," I say to him.

"We're Xan tainted by Crozoni blood." Jevlan shrugs. "I've got a Crozoni grandfather, though it hides well, doesn't it?" His features are all Xan. "And so we're not allowed in the caves."

"Who enforces it?"

"The old bird keeps the old ways," Jevlan says. "She's the boss."

"Only one? No circle of elders?" Xan elders always governed as a group, I was taught, in the old days.

"Just one old crone. She's not bad but she's … rigid."

"We do all right where we are." Neema squeezes his upper arm affectionately. "Better than many."

Dinner's ready and I can tell they're ready to discuss other things.

I sit, feeling uneasy. I came here looking for refuge, but this place is as divided as any other.

Endweek, Sevenmonth 31st. Hunger Canyons.
I've been sleeping on Neema's kitchen floor with only Caruq and a thin blanket for warmth.

I wake in the middle of the night to a strange booming noise. Temperature's lower than it was on the boat last night. Caruq gets up and goes out. The booming again. I follow.

This is a land of extremes. Baking hot in the day and now this ball-shrivelling night air.

Everything's quiet, including the woman in Neema's vegetable patch, turning a critical eye on her aguatos and carrot tops.

"Like weeds," she murmurs in a musical voice that's older than her face. She looks about fifty and speaks in Xan. It's been a while since I heard this language out loud.

"The gods used to smile on this place," she says. "Not any more. Well, Seff still likes it here, but his presence isn't always … uplifting." *Seff*, I think. *God of Downfall.*

She looks up, takes me in. She looks as fully Xan as Jevlan, but what do I know? Could this be the one they mentioned, the old crone?

"Hello, young vocifer. Where's your voice, then?"

"Mine?" I ask her, in Xan too. Does she know about my tattoo? My voice is crackly. I feel foolish. Who else could she be talking to?

The noise booms again. I step closer to her. "What is that?"

"Little fellow talking like the gods, trying to impress

someone." It's hard to see in this light, but there's something weird about her teeth – like they're stained, like she's eaten some glowing plant. Still, her voice has a rare, quiet authority.

"Doesn't sound like any little fellows I've met."

"Oh, you must meet him, then. If you see a Butterfly Bird dance you'll have three moons of good luck. He's down by the river. Come." Her enthusiasm is catching. She pinches my arm between her thumb and two fingers. A bracelet on her wrist jingles with small bells. "I felt you," she says, leading the way. "Not many walk the path these days. Where did you make your promise, boy?"

I know the promise she means. The ritual my dad put me through, when I was a child, to beg the gods' favour. "In the north, near Portcaye," I tell her.

"Well, the gods like you, don't they?"

"If you say so."

"We don't do those rites here any more. The risk is too great."

Caruq's not with us. We've reached one of the platforms to the vine bridges.

"We'll see him from up there," she says, and climbs (fast for an older lady). I follow her.

In the centre of the swaying bridge, she stops and turns to me. Her short grey hair catches the breeze and sticks up in tufts. "Did you come looking for sanctuary?"

"Perhaps, one day. Not just for myself," I tell her.

Her deep-set eyes seem to look right inside me for what feels like a minute but must be about five seconds.

The booming noise comes again, and she turns towards it, leaning over the edge of the bridge so far I fear the vines will snap. She points out not one, but two birds in the shallow water by the bank. They look like short herons. Their colour is different too. One lowers its head before the other.

"He dances for her. Do you think she'll have him?"

The bird lowers his long neck and spreads his wings wide. They're resplendent in the starlight, barred, each with a bright circle at the top. From up here on the bridge, with the bird's head lost in shadow, he looks like a huge moth. Like a butterfly with wing spots. More insect than bird.

"Butterfly Birds," I murmur, suddenly understanding the name. He takes his legs out of the river in a slow, purposeful strut, then he shakes his wings at her, snakes his head, and booms his strange call again. She backs away a few steps.

"Well. He's a stunner. I'm impressed even if she isn't," I say.

"And what will you do with your three moons of good luck?" the old lady asks.

I don't tell her I already feel lucky to be seeing this dance. It feels like something god-sent.

"They're a rare sight in these parts now," she tells me, like she sees what I'm thinking.

"Are the females too picky?"

She ignores me. "But the gods still love them well."

The female accepts the male's advances, and he mounts her to mate.

"Now you've seen more than you bargained for." The old lady has a smile in her voice.

I smile back at her.

"Perhaps some privacy is in order?" She gestures to the cave at the end of the bridge. A dim light seeps out. It looks inviting (warm).

"Why do the gods love them so well?" I ask. I was always taught the gods love predators best.

"The gods painted them. They speak with a god's voice." The male lets go of his mate, finished already. "They fish like the gods," she goes on. "You've seen. You've heard. Naqramaree loves beauty and surprise, life and growth. It's not all pain and violence and decay – even with Seff. You will find the gods love many things best and all at once. Their love is not a cup that runs out and needs to be portioned. It is eternal as them. Come, now." She turns away to the cave entrance.

I've a strong compulsion to follow her, but I feel, absurdly, like a starveling boy in some old Xan tale, about to chase a song and get lost. At the edge of something I don't understand.

She turns to look at me again.

"I'll come in another time," I tell her.

"Be sure to keep your promise now, boy," she says

before she turns away. "Your promise to the gods, I mean. If you struggle, for any reason … you must come and find me. It's important."

My lungs haven't got enough air. I suck in a breath before letting it trickle out, blowing on a flame and watching it flicker, flicker, fail.

Sure thing, old crone.

20

KIT

suffer

Firstday, Eightmonth 1st. Ridmouth.
Oden and *Clara* take me, Caruq and two young women (mixed Xan-Crozoni) with a bag of amber back downriver the next morning. I stayed long enough to know Hunger Canyons isn't what I was hoping for. It wasn't a wasted trip. I learned we could run there if we had to. But I want to do better than that – to find a place where it doesn't feel like we don't belong (or don't belong together).

When we dock in Ridmouth there's a pair of branders checking papers. The girls are squeezed for a few choice pieces of amber, but the branders recognize Oden and don't tax him.

They ask me about Caruq, who's hot and bothered. He growls at them. Eventually they have to let us pass. No cracks in my paperwork.

I find the Reedstones – they're staying in the same place.

"Let's walk up to the lookout beyond the station," Goldie suggests. Then, more quietly, "To ensure privacy."

They've learned the awful smell coming from the RIDMOUTH GAS PROCESSING CENTRE. DANGER. HIGHLY FLAMMABLE CHEMICAL MANUFACTORY is actually not gas (which they do make but which doesn't smell), but kine intestines.

"They're being shipped to the place in bulk from what smells like every slaughtered kine in all of Skøland proper and its colonies in the New West," Blithe tells me with a grimace.

"What? Why?"

"To be turned into something called gold-beater's skin."

"Gold-beater's what?"

"It's a thin membrane applied to fabric to make it air- or water-tight. We artists use it for gold leaf." He leaned closer to me. "I was thinking you could use it for sails. If you treated them, they'd be waterproof. They could harness the wind better."

I think about it. Those vast black sails, being brought out here for treatment. A mysterious ship, being assembled in secret. We reach the lookout. From here we can see Ridmouth to one side, the bridge, the river and even the distant sea.

I stare back at the large factory building. Its roof glints dully. "What kind of metal is that roof?"

"Copper," Glister tells me.

I can see it's weathering. It's no longer shiny, but it hasn't had time to go green as old copper does. "Copper roofing on a factory?" It's unexpected. Copper's expensive – usually reserved for fancier locations. Important civic buildings. Luxury hotels. Houses of the well-to-do. Museums.

"It's the fire credentials, apparently," Blithe says. "And see those treads? They can open it up, let the fresh air in – or the stink out."

I follow Goldie's gaze in the other direction, out to sea.

"So where is the rest of the boat?" I ask.

"Where, indeed?" She glances at me. "We did hear an interesting rumour."

"How's that?"

"Word is *Dominion* will be *here* by the middle of the Eightmonth. With Lovemore herself. It's supposed to be a secret … and it doesn't make sense."

"Surely they'll bring the sails to the ship, not the other way around."

Glister nods. "Exactly. It may not be true … or it may be a major development taking place in just two weeks. At any rate, they're renovating the only guest house in town for a person of importance. It's a lot of tarting up. Could well be for Lovemore."

Goldie leans closer to me. "We need to investigate further. Clem – Magistrate Rosclaw – is counting on us."

"They've got a raft of repayers in there working for them – who don't come out," Glister adds. "And another thing we know is that Sacrifice Sting, our esteemed cousin, is definitely involved. He's been sending and receiving regular telegrams through Ridmouth Telegraph Office directed to that place."

My heart lurches. Sacrifice Sting is the High Governor's chief scientist. Mora's boss. She downplayed how scared she was, stuck working for him in the Castle Hotel. But I have a bad feeling about this.

"It stinks to high heaven." Goldie gives words to my feeling. "Like everything he touches. To be sure, if he's had a hand in it, it'll be worse than we thought. Our cousin is not a man of scruples."

"And he hasn't improved with age," Glister cuts in. "There are too many moving parts. We don't know what they add up to."

"I'll eat my hat if this *Dominion* project isn't something very sinister," Goldie says. "We must discover more." She turns to me. "We need you, Kit. To help us infiltrate the building. We'll pay double. You'll be back in boring Portcaye soon enough."

She's trying to pick me open like a lock. I almost give in to her. But they don't *need* me. "Exciting as this is," I say cautiously, "I promised Mora I'd be back on the next boat."

Blithe gives me an indulgent look. He thinks he understands, but it's not just that I miss Mora. I'm worried about her.

"If you stay, you'll be helping make sure Lovemore's defeated in the Tenmonth vote. Imagine that feeling.

Wouldn't it be worth some … delayed gratification?" Goldie persists.

"A few more weeks won't hurt Mora. She's made of tough stuff," Glister puts in.

What does he know? The trip down here took so long that I haven't seen her in nearly four weeks – his cousin has her trapped. No. I can't ignore the dread that's been clinging to my ribs for days.

"Temper Wilforn will bring change. We need to do all we can to ensure he gets in," Goldie goes on. "The first magistrate with the guts to go up against Lovemore in years. Decades. And Rosclaw's his man. He genuinely wants to make things better. Shipway town was different, wasn't it? It's freer down south. A girl can breathe."

"A girl still has to pay to live," I remind her.

"But wages are good. Corruption isn't rampant. The branders are in check. The jails aren't simply there to generate bribes. How many heads on spikes have you seen since we got here?"

"Zero."

"There you go!" Goldie insists.

"That's not quite a standard," Blithe chips in awkwardly.

"Then think of it like this," Glister says. "Those who take serious positions against Lovemore have a nasty tendency of disappearing without a trace. It means people like Wilforn and Rosclaw don't come around often, and when they do, we have to get behind them, so they have a fighting chance."

“Are you not afraid of disappearing without a trace, too?” I ask them.

“Of course,” Goldie says. “And I shouldn’t have to be. I resent that.”

Glister places a big hand on one of her shoulders.

“Look, I tell you what,” I say. “I’ll carry a message about what you’ve found and the mid-Eightmonth … rumours … to Rosclaw. In person. Write him a letter and I’ll see it reaches his eyes only. If this is as big as you say, surely he’ll step up. He can send you some backup to further the investigation.”

Goldie’s lips twist thoughtfully. “That’s not a bad idea.”

“I don’t trust the telegraph office with this,” Glister adds.

“Then let’s get on with it,” I say.

We head down from the lookout in silence. Change but gentle has always been the Reedstones game. Small change, bit by bit, adding up to something meaningful. They’re certainly getting more ambitious. They think if Temper Wilforn makes High Governor *everything* could change.

Are they right this time? Or is this just … more games where the Reedstones flourish? Where the powerful pieces move around the board and the pawns all suffer?

21

MORA

darkspace

I head up to the fifth floor early. There's a smash as I reach the landing. The guard with the heavy breathing has knocked over his cup of fikka, breaking the ceramic into three sharp pieces. I help him sponge it up, then offer to fetch him a fresh cup. He agrees with a nod but doesn't offer a smile or a word of thanks.

The scientists are still at their breakfasts. I go to top up the devils' vittles. They rattle their cages when they hear me. I talk to them as I work. When one tries to clamber over my hands, I gently place it back. "I can't help you, little one."

Tears prickle. When was it people first held creatures in cages? A thousand years ago? Ten thousand? My emotions are all over the place. Perhaps, more joy, it's my time of the month coming.

I finish and find Daruunlis in the main lab. He's uncovered the grave items and the coffin lid, but not the bones. He stands with his craggy head bent over the dead boy's things, one of Glor's notebooks in hand, just looking. He has a fountain pen, but it's clinging by its lid to his breast pocket.

"Early riser," he says when he hears my footsteps – speaking Crozoni like he did last night.

"Needs must," I say, walking to his side. "I hope you slept well?"

"Well enough." He looks at me.

"Daruunlis," I try out pronouncing his name. "You've known Nezza a while, then?"

"Her whole life."

"What happened on the way up here? To her nurse? Her father? No one will tell me."

He leans closer, though he's still speaking Crozoni. "Pirates."

"What?" *Is he serious?*

"Sailors of questionable virtue. Brigands of the seas. Highwaymen of the waves. You know, most pirates are your people – and mine."

I curse softly. "They went for Lovemore's ships? I had no idea they were so bold." Pride wells up in me. *My people*, taking on the High Governor.

He's nodding. "Indeed. You won't hear it in the papers. They like to keep quiet about genuine threats. Think it makes them look weak – which it does. Pirates cut down a dozen of her keepers." He looks at the door where the burly guard still stands with his back to us and smiles fully. I'm starting to think it's more of a sly smile than a shy one.

The guard can hear us plain as day, but we're still speaking in Crozoni, and I'd bet my life he doesn't understand.

"Rumour is they tried to take Nezza with them," Daruunlis adds.

"To take her? Why?"

"Good question. And you didn't hear any of this from me, remember? No one is permitted to know. Lovemore's not keen on all and sundry finding out some ragtag crew of sea prowlers nearly killed her, just like that." He snaps his fingers.

"So they killed Sculpin, and the nurse."

"Yes. And Nezza saw it all. She didn't tell you?"

"She doesn't like me."

That draws a short laugh from him. "She's not the best judge of character."

"She loves you."

"Well. She has her moments."

"She doesn't seem that cut up about losing her father, or her nurse."

"No?"

"Did you know them well?"

He twists his mouth. "Sculpin I knew, well as I cared to… Well as you know a slug or a snake."

What game is he playing? He wants me to trust him. Speaking Crozoni. Confiding in me. He's already told me more in five minutes than I manged to learn in four weeks.

But he's Sting's man. He's not a repayer. He doesn't have to, but he aids Sting in a pursuit that dishonours his own people, rips open their wounds, their graves, their traditions and pours corruption over everything. Does he do that for money?

"Good morning!" Glor's entry cuts my line of thought.

"Did you fix the translations?" I ask Daruunlis, reverting to Skøl.

"I did. First thing yesterday," he replies in the same, with an affable smile. "Here, I'll show you."

He leads me over to the coffin and points. "You translated this as, *Here lie the sacred and adored bones of the first son of Spinda the Glass Butterfly.* It's not a bad translation. Pretty close."

I frown, then indicate the longer bit of text running around the outside of the lid. "What about this?"

"Yes, this one stumped you, didn't it?" Daruunlis flips open the notebook to the page where his translation stands opposite our meagre attempts.

Great One, Macotl. True Naqramaree. Merciful Seff. Curse those who move these bones. Bless and thank the elderly kin — — in Seff's Burial Circle.

∞

Almighty Macotl, True Nagramaree, Merciful Seff. Your curse on those who would disturb these remains. We thank the Kin [aunts/uncles] for their work of love in Seff's Burial Circle.

Their work of love. The text near Seff's Burial Circle we didn't know doesn't sound like much of a clue for how to find it.

I read over Daruunlis's looping writing slowly.

"What was the work of love in the Burial Circle?"

"It's a reference to the ritual they tried to use to resurrect him."

"How so?"

"It was a joint attempt – Spinda and some … relatives. This part of the message acknowledges their efforts, even if they ultimately failed." He looks back at the coffin lid with a sad expression and I'm loath to ask more questions about that episode.

"Does this mean something?" I point instead to the sideways figure-of-eight he's drawn above his translation. Same as the symbol on the coffin directly below Hiramlan's name and dates.

He moves the pen from his pocket and turns to a blank page in the notebook to draw another sideways figure-of-eight, tracing over it until the symbol is thick and neat.

"Macotl exists between and around and above the Gods of Beginnings and the Gods of Endings. This outline is her," he says as he traces over the eight one last time. "Making and decaying. And here –" he points with the nib inside the left-hand circle – "live the Gods of Beginnings, led by Naqramaree, God of Uprising, and here –" he moves the nib to the right circle – "the Gods of Endings, led by Seff, God of Downfall."

He closes the notebook abruptly, but I can still see the figure-of-eight on Hiramlan's coffin, like a round-edged Life Registry symbol, turned on its side. Two shapes connecting in the middle. I touch the short line of text above the symbol, and sound it out slowly. "Hiramlan."

"His name." Daruunlis nods.

"I know some Xan names have other meanings…" I prompt him. Kit's full name, Kalqitlan, means thunderstorm, or growling bear.

"Hiramlan means…" He pauses, searching for the Skøl word. "Lichen. It grows in the Badlands. It also means *a kind of green*. Half grey, half green."

"Oh." It's not what I expected. "So, how long have you been translating for Sting?"

"Since they first invaded, just about. Soon as I learned enough of the Skøl language. Six years or so."

He walks back the length of the high workbench, looking at the items from the grave again. The boy's ocarina, some sticks scratched with markings, a collection of pretty pebbles, a copper bracelet hung with copper bells, that trick box of Crozoni glass marbles that must have felt big in the boy's small hands.

I think again of Dewilder's *Sacred Secrets* – someone must have translated that from Crozoni to Skøl for Sting and Sculpin. I glance at Daruunlis. Was it him?

"Are you familiar with an old Crozoni scientist called Lume Dewilder?" I begin.

He turns to me quickly, mouth opening fish-like. No words come out. But Glor interrupts, coming to stand beside him at the bench, not bothering with a greeting. "All this copper," he says, picking up the copper bracelet.

"What about it?" Daruunlis asks equably, his bored composure back.

"There is an unusual amount adorning the coffin. Inside the lid. And this. Is it purely decorative? Do the patterns have meaning?"

"The patterns are decorative," Daruunlis says. "The metal itself… well, the elders say copper shines in the spirit realm. It gives light to those who have passed so that they are not left in darkness…"

He looks up just as I hear Sting's shoes tapping down the hall.

"Good morning, Sciencemaster!" Glor's cheerful greeting sets my teeth on edge.

"Let us hope so," Sting replies. He looks at me. "Why are you here? Is your work with Mister Cob complete?"

"No, Sciencemaster. I've been seeing to the devils. I'm going down to paint the slides now."

He waves an irritated hand. "Ignore the creatures. If our funding goes, we'll have to cull them all. Helping Cob is your priority. The High Governor's patronage for our continued research hinges on this presentation."

I turn to go. "Oh, wait!" He seems to remember something, heading back to his office muttering to himself. He emerges a moment later with a book, gold glinting on its clothbound cover. I fight not to show my astonishment.

Dewilder's *Sacred Secrets*. He opens it to a page near the end – further into the book than I managed to look – and I realize a piece of paper, thinner than the other pages, a bit translucent, has been added, glued in near the seam so that it floats over one of the figures.

"Now, pay attention." His tone is sharp. I meet his eyes over the book. "We have a slide of this already." He indicates the image underneath the thin paper – it's the woman surrounded by twelve skulls – at Hiramlan's failed resurrection. "But I require one of this schematic. Tell Cob it is to come at the end of the sequence. The final slide."

He flattens the thin paper, and I see dots and lines – an elektrical circuit diagram. I recognize the type and some of the symbols from Sculpin's sketchbooks. I think they signify wires and elektric currents and things like light bulbs, but I don't know.

"Yes, Sciencemaster."

"The paper is fragile. Tell him to be gentle with it." He shuts the cover carefully. "Now go."

I nod and dash for the door.

"And if you get paint near it, I'll have your head," he calls after me.

*

The old silverprinter is already in the back room.

"Morning, Mister Cob!" I call through the door.

"Don't come in!" he shoots back. "I'll be out in ten minutes. I've left a slide out there for you. And that book you were keen on."

I put Sting's book on the desk as I spot the slide first. It's the face of Spinda, taken from the original *Sacred Secrets.* Spinda at over a hundred years old looking forty-five.

Then my eyes land on the other book. The Crozoni version, just off to the side. My heart swoops. I've seen the silverprint of the handwritten cover of course, but to have it before me in real life is different.

Sacred Secrets of the Ancient Xan. Lume Dewilder.

I touch the impossibly neat script of its title with my fingertips before I call through the inner door.

"Found them. Thank you."

I snatch up the book and crack it open, smelling its slight sweetness. It's in good condition – no annotations or wrinkles – and it's not so faded as Cob suggested.

I want to look for the strange scenes I've only seen as tiny slides, and I begin to flip through, but the illustrations in the earlier chapters catch my attention. I have to pause. *How well did Sculpin do?*

Not too bad, it turns out. Naqramaree is even more striking, his beeishness more obvious. His big eyes are downcast, but I imagine them snapping up to mine, black as a bee's, night black. His stubble looks like it could graze my fingers. I imagine it against my cheek, like Kit's stubble. I think I can smell Kit, warm from cooking something in the Lugger kitchen, savoury and peppery. The Crozoni caption reads *Affinity with Bees and Memory.* Not *Butterflies* like the Skøl copy said. That's a bit odd.

I flip fast to the image of Spinda's face. Sculpin's copy of this was more faithful. The image is coloured here, but the colours have faded. Her eyes, the brightest part, are a pale, watery violet.

The two strange images with the skulls and the central standing figure of a woman come later, following a subheading titled *Resurrection at Seff's Burial Circle.*

It's certainly Spinda in the pictures again. The one where she holds the skull aloft is the brightest, the skull distinctly amber coloured. The lightning zigzagging out of the black above it is white with purple edges. The caption on the right reads:

> Here in Seff's domain, the Alit-fel in service to Naqramaree, those who have broken their sacrificial promise and been redeemed, can channel the raw power of the gods and of nature, including lightning, into the miracle of life and healing.

On the overleaf is the second image featuring Spinda cutting her palm, standing ringed by skulls. There appears to be an awful lot of blood dripping and pooling. This image is faded, the blood more orange than red, more like the skulls.

The caption reads:

Inside Seff's Burial Circle, one with the blood of an Alit-fel in service to Naqramaree can rouse and wield the power of Seff's eternal undead.

Wield the power of the undead.

Something makes me put the book down and flip through the translation until I find the right page.

In Skøl, the description reads:

Within Seff's Burial Circle, the blood of an Alit-Fel can rouse and wield the power of life, healing and preservation of youth.

Wield the power of the undead sounds different to *wield the power of life*. Or does it? I'm frowning at the discrepancy when Cob comes out.

"The Sciencemaster wanted me to give you this." I flip quickly to locate the thin page with its elektric schematic. "He said to tell you … it would be the final slide in the presentation. Number thirteen."

Cob frowns at the image. "It's based on the circle of skulls."

I peer sheepishly over his shoulder. I hadn't realized the

elektrical schematic was based on the twelve skulls arrayed in a circle. Of course it is.

Cob closes the book, keeping one finger in the page he needs. “All right. You’d better speed up. You’ve seen the colours now, haven’t you?”

“Yes.”

“Then carry on. Let me move this distraction.” He plucks the original book from the desk and retreats with both copies of Dewilder’s *Sacred Secrets* back to the darkspace.

22

MORA

Daruunlis

My head is aching by the time Cob finishes for the day – earlier than me this time. I help myself to the books he left behind – both versions of *Sacred Secrets*, and dash as quickly as I can back to my room. I'll replace them early tomorrow, before I see to the devils. He'll never know they were gone, and I can read through carefully tonight.

I leave them on my desk and take Nezza down for a quick dinner of salted fish and steamed greens. Later, while she splashes in her bath, I return to a close side-by-side study of them. I want to see how the rest of the translation matches up.

It's good to read in my own language, like slipping on comfortable shoes. I turn to the section on Spinda the Butterfly Bird—

I stop. That's not right. In the translation, she's

called Spinda the Glass Butterfly. After the amber Glass Butterflies. *What's a Butterfly Bird?*

On the pages about the Ralkalit Rite and the five requirements, there's another discrepancy. Instead of:

> 2) An ingesting into the body of a creature beloved by the Xan gods

The original reads:

> 2) A displaying on the body of a creature beloved by the Xan gods

Are these errors a coincidence? I flick between the two books. The translation reads:

> Spinda ingested the Glass Butterfly as part of her ritual.

But the original says:

> As part of this ritual, she promised to carry on her body the image of a creature beloved by Naqramaree. She chose to ink a Butterfly Bird on her body...

A tattoo, like Kit. Of a Butterfly Bird. Not a Glass Butterfly. Seemingly no butterflies were eaten. No Butterfly Birds either.

But Sting's research is all about butterflies – ground up into various medicines. He's been dosing his subjects with butterflies. And it seems to be working, on Nezza and Minty at least. I read on. Spinda the Butterfly Bird in the original. Spinda the Glass Butterfly in the translation.

Hunter told me *glass* and *bird* are homographs in Xan – spelled the same, for all that they sound different. They aren't at all the same in Crozoni. This translation of Dewilder's Crozoni to Skøl – it can't be an error. A *Glass Butterfly* and a *Butterfly Bird* can't be confused. Someone has made a deliberate mistranslation.

Who? I flick through, but no translators are named. I do know one, of course. Daruunlis. Sting and Sculpin's pet translator. Is he behind this?

Did he change Butterfly Bird to Glass Butterfly? And why?

I can't puzzle it out. It's undeniable that, even if it's based on an error, Sting's butterfly elixir works on Nezza and her pet.

I get up to check on her in the next room. She's in her nightdress, still wet-haired, steadfastly ignoring me. I can see she's playing one of her fantasy games, acting out voices – pirates again. With her pencils, her book, her spinning top. I look over her shoulder, remembering what Daruunlis told me. I see her games differently now. She's not just drawing imaginary pirates. She encountered them. They killed her father and her nurse. The people who were supposed to care for her, before me.

Her picture boasts the same pirate pair she drew before – a tall woman with a long club, and a shorter man with a blade. They're squaring up to a guard in Lovemore's colours who's brandishing a Skøl weapon – gun or prod, I can't tell.

"Aaah!" Nezza murmurs to herself, flicking her spinning top away and picking out her red pencil to scrawl blood all over one of the woman's eyes and half her face. Then, "I'll save you!" She adds blood to the guard's neck, then the man's blade. More noises follow that I think are supposed to sound like Skøl weaponry, before she starts stabbing the paper with her pencil.

"What's happening here?" I ask.

"Pirates," Nezza says with another strangled cry. The red pencil lead snaps.

"Did you see these pirates?" I quiz her as she sharpens it.

"Aaah! Die, promiscuous fiend!" She stabs the air with the pencil and ignores me.

"Do you know what promiscuous means?"

She turns to me. "Yes."

"What?"

"Evil."

"Not quite."

She's back to ignoring me.

"They're in love." She tells me, abandoning the red and turning her page.

"Who? The pirates?"

"Yes."

"It's late," I say. "You'll give yourself bad dreams. Put that away now and into bed."

I try to tuck some curls back from her face, behind one of her ears, but she flinches away. "Ugh. Stop it." She curls a lip at me, then, still locking gazes, flings her book on the floor. She brushes her lap full of pencils and pencil shavings after it, before ducking under her covers, careful not to disturb Minty, who's already sleeping near her pillow. She faces the wall.

I don't have the energy to fight her to clean up. She knows it. I gather her things and put them on the windowsill, before switching off her elektric light and retreating to my room.

My mind's going like a butter churn but nothing's coming together. Because if the amber Glass Butterflies are a misdirection, why have Sting's elixirs changed Nezza and Minty? Is *Butterfly Bird* just an odd way of saying *Glass Butterfly*? In a dialect of the south, perhaps? But then, why the replacement of tattooing with eating?

Some time later, I think I hear a creaking sound and look in on Nezza. She's asleep on her back. Minty's curled on top of her chest now. He raises his nose at me and sniffs, then tucks it back under his paws.

I can't stand by while Sting experiments on her like she's a spotted devil.

I need to find out more. And I know who I must ask.

Daruunlis.

23

MORA

drop of grace

A soft knock sounds on Nezza's door before I can retreat to my room again.

"Nezza?" Daruunlis's friendly voice calls from the hallway, as if I've just conjured him by thinking of him.

Minty wakes up and jumps off Nezza, who wakes up too.

"Nezza?" Daruunlis knocks again.

She launches out of bed and yanks open the heavy door.

"Sorry to come at bedtime," Daruunlis says, looking over Nezza to me. "I have something for Nezza."

"It's nearly ten," I scold, but I fumble for the lever to turn on her elektric light.

"Keep your hat on."

"Yeah, keep your hat on, Mora," Nezza echoes, her voice decidedly sleepy.

I realize I'm still wearing my work clothes and the stupid bonnet. I rip it off. Then I look at Nezza's face and have to give in.

"Fine," I say. She's so happy he's come to see her.

"I brought this for you," he tells her, producing a small ceramic jar from his pocket.

"What is it?"

"Honey. Hunger Canyons honey. We've got the best bees in the world."

She pops the cork and sniffs, her nose touching the honey. She sticks a finger in it and licks it. "Oooh." Her face spreads into a sleepy smile. "Mora. Try this." She holds it out to me.

"Let me smell it, then," I say, taking the jar. I'm touched she wants to share it, but not sure I want honey that's had her nose in.

It does smell lovely though – sweet and floral.

"Try it," Daruunlis urges, looking at me like it's some sort of test. I think of how I brought fikka to that guard and he just drank it. I think about Venor, eating an orange, the poison twisting his mind. I shake the thought away and dip a finger into the honey. *Don't be absurd, Mora.*

It *is* delicious. Desperately sweet, with an undertone I can't place. Some kind of flower I don't know.

"Good, right?" Daruunlis asks.

"Very."

"Give it back." Nezza reaches for it.

I pretend I'm going to drink it. She snatches it from me with a scowl.

"So, what have you been doing today, *Ruahee*?" Daruunlis asks her.

"She was sleeping when you got here," I mutter crossly.

Nezza looks at the floor, as if expecting her sketchbook and pencils to still be lying there. She looks at me and demands them.

The pair of them sit on the rug and begin discussing Nezza's sketchbook and her imaginary games.

He tries to ask her about the weekly treatment for her fits.

"I don't want to talk about it. Can you tell me a story?"

He gives her a serious look and nods. "I should tell you Xan stories. They're my people, and yours. Should I tell you about Spinda?"

Nezza's book of drawings thuds to the floor. "Spinda!? Spinda's not real," she whispers, then louder and panicked, "Spinda's not real!"

I go to sit beside her. "What do you know about Spinda?" I ask. Daruunlis glances at me.

"My nurse said she was just a dream. She came to my dreams. She scared me."

Daruunlis takes her hands and gives them a little squeeze. "What did she do?"

Nezza's lip wobbles. "She said Father was a … a bad man."

"When was the last time you dreamed about her?" Daruunlis asks softly.

"I don't remember. When Nurse Prowess was new, I think."

"But you were only three."

"Yes."

"But you still remember Spinda?"

"Of course." Nezza pouts. "She scared me."

"I'm sorry." He sighs. "They were just dreams."

Nezza looks unconvinced and I feel sorry for her. Dreaming of Spinda unsettled me too. *Was mine only a dream, or does Spinda's ghost walk past the veil a lot?*

Nezza yawns.

"It's late," I remind Daruunlis.

He makes a show of looking at his timepiece and then pulls a face at Nezza. "Oh. She's right this time. I'll tell you about Spinda in the daylight, perhaps."

Nezza doesn't argue.

He tucks her covers tight around her and kisses her cheek.

She closes her eyes, then whispers, "Don't go yet."

He sits on the bed beyond her feet, leaning against the wall, his long legs stretched out, waiting for her to fall asleep. Nezza's so affectionate with him. She never asks me to keep her company. A pang of jealousy takes me by surprise. I retreat back to my annex to study the books.

I'm looking at the section about Spinda's attempted resurrection of Hiramlan – in the last chapter of the original.

The two images with the amber-coloured skulls are the final ones. The original doesn't have the extra piece of thin paper pasted in with the elektric circuit. But it has plenty of blood, lightning, glowing skulls. I've propped the books open side by side and am still comparing the text closely.

Broadly the accounts match. Both state the resurrection must be conducted in the Burial Circle. That Spinda began the ritual to return her boy to life too late.

Dewilder's original text makes more reference to *Seff's servants* than the translation does though:

> Seff's servants answered the call, but were unable to fulfil the request to restore the child to life...

The translation just says *Spinda's ritual was unsuccessful in restoring life to the child…*

Seff's servants aren't pictured in either version, only Spinda as a lone figure, with her knife, her blood, the skulls and the lightning.

Details of the ritual itself are sparse in both. Blood of the Alit-fel is required. As is lightning. Neither version mentions Glass Butterflies – or Butterfly Birds.

> ... and the request to the gods is made through the singing or chanting of a set of sacred verses called Kol-Koldia's Song.

I tear my eyes from the text as the door creaks behind me.

"She's asleep." Daruunlis pops his head round the opening. I wave him in and gesture to the books. His expression when he sees them is hard to read – but it's certainly not bored. He shuts the door behind him quietly.

"Lume Dewilder's *Sacred Secrets of the Ancient Xan.*" I speak in soft Crozoni, so at least if Nezza wakes up she won't understand us. I pause, but his look is still unreadable. "You translated this, didn't you?"

His eyes narrow. "How'd you get hold of those?"

"I borrowed them from Mister Cob. He's making silverprints from them." I can almost see the cogs whirring in Daruunlis's head. "I noticed some small discrepancies between the original and the translation," I say.

"Does Sting know you're so … fond of reading?"

"He does not," I reassure him.

He smiles. I smile back.

"How long have you been interested in languages?" I ask him.

"Oh, since I was a boy."

"How old are you now?"

He rubs his temples. "Twenty-eight." Clears his throat. "And you?"

"Eighteen."

"Sting told me you have a young man. Wants me to keep an eye out. I hear he's Xan." He peers at me in a way that reminds me of Ruzi, my father, but his sudden shift of subject throws me – perhaps that's his intention.

"Yes," I say after a few beats. "He's called Kalqitlan."

Daruunlis just nods.

"He's…" I shake my head. "He's not in town right now."

"Where's he gone?"

"To Shipway, actually."

Daruunlis blows out a breath. "Bit of a jaunt. He in repay?"

"Yes."

I pick up *Sacred Secrets* and wave it his way. "You translated this didn't you?"

He nods. "Some of it. Jafalla had already begun when I joined the team."

"Jafalla… Nezza's mum?" I ask and, as he nods, I wonder aloud, "So was she Jafalla Dewilder, the author's daughter?"

"He had three. She was the second," Daruunlis confirms gruffly.

"What happened to her?"

"She died when Nezza was a baby. Complications after the birth." His face turns half away, like he can see Nezza sleeping, through the wall.

"I'm sorry."

He nods.

"She was your friend," I say, because he's stopped talking.

"She was." His voice is thick.

"Is Nezza like her?"

"Hah." His face takes on a faraway quality. "Yes."

"Then I think her mother would probably be mad

about the Sciencemaster experimenting on her because of some nonsense translation you two concocted about ingesting butterflies."

His eyes swing round to mine. His expression a mix of alarmed and impressed. "You noticed that, did you?"

I say nothing, just wait.

"I went to work for Sting and Sculpin on the order of an elder," he says at last. "The elders thought I should keep an eye on them – that Sting might be about to stumble across something he shouldn't. Jafalla was just a girl. Eighteen. Her head was turned. Sculpin manipulated her into translating Dewilder's words … said she was special. Unique. She wanted to believe him. She was." He clears his throat again. "He promised her the moon and the stars. She told him our people's secrets, but it wasn't her fault. They knew what they were doing. Putting her on a pedestal and then knocking her down for the fun of it." His hand swipes his lips again. "It wasn't her fault. Lume had no right to make that gods-cursed book in the first place. You people, always coming in and mucking with stuff you can't hope to understand. Jafalla didn't deserve any of it. But she saw through Sculpin before the end."

"And so you – what? Decided to tweak the translation?"

"Jafalla helped. It was all we could think of, to keep some secrets hidden. A bit of harmless misdirection. Bird … in Xan we say *mash*, and glass – *mahsh*. We write them the same way. We were worried he would learn too much – or go after the Butterfly Birds."

"What *is* a Butterfly Bird?" I interrupt. I've never heard of them, outside Dewilder's book.

"Kind of bird," Daruunlis says – so bluntly I'm reminded of Kit. Sometimes he has that same plain way of speaking.

"Why's it called that though?"

"Ah." Daruunlis cocks his eyebrows. "Very pretty bird. River bird, yea tall." He holds his hands apart, one level with his chin, the other by his waist. "Likes to spread its wings out, like so." He indicates this with his arms and hands too, stretching them comically wide, out to the sides this time. "Guess what kind of markings the males have on their wing feathers?"

"Butterfly markings?" I realize.

"Top marks for the young lady."

"Butterfly Birds," I murmur. "I've never heard of them. But why did you and Jafalla encourage Sting—"

"Encourage Sting?!" He cuts me off. "You can stop right there. You think he needs my encouragement?" His anger gushes like a fall of water, fast and fierce. "He saw that picture of Spinda – looking barely half her age… He saw it, and he was obsessed. I've never met someone more afraid of death. Not Sculpin. Not anyone. Every person has a fear bigger than death. He has none. He feels his age crawling up his neck like a spider. He knows he'll end like every other and he can't bear it. All we could do was misdirect him. I didn't realize he would feed Nezza butterflies."

I take a deep breath. "But here's the thing I don't understand. *It's working.* She's healing – faster than she should do. So, if the butterflies are a con, how does that work?"

We look at each other for a long moment.

"It's a sacred secret," he says at last, straight-faced.

I snort. "Her pet has lived three times his natural lifespan. He's another experiment. If that's not Sting's butterfly elixir, what is it?" I wave an arm at the wall, past its peeling wallpaper, in Nezza and Minty's direction.

"Secret."

"Oh, come on."

"No. Sting has already learned too much."

He stalks over to my tiny, distorted window and looks out.

"He won't stop now," I whisper. "He thinks he's nearly found…" I can barely bring myself to say it. It's so absurd. "*Immortality.*"

"And what would he do with it if he did?" Daruunlis says softly. "He's the worm who eats the seeds. Eats the future. We will stop him."

"We?"

"Not you. Me and mine. We made the mistakes and we'll set them right. All you have to do is stay out of it. Keep your –" he gestures at the books still propped open on my table – "discoveries to yourself. *We* will fix it."

"What are you going to do?"

"What I should've done a long time ago." He turns to leave, opening the door to Nezza's room.

I bite my lip and follow. He's nearly at the outer door, nearly away. Nezza still sleeps soundly.

"Spinda," I say when he's half in, half out. I keep my voice low. "The boy's mother. What happened to her, in the end?"

"She was killed in the Cull."

"Her powers didn't protect her?"

"No."

"Why not?"

He shrugs.

"I think she… I think her ghost…"

"Her ghost, what?" His eyes bore into me, violet like Kit's, but not warm. Not kind.

"I dreamed about her, that's all. Like Nezza said she did. She looked like her picture, but older."

"She visited you?"

I nod. "Did you know her?"

"Everyone knew her. Every Xan person. People used to travel for miles to see her – for her medicine. She was a great healer. She cared a lot."

"She said I moved his bones. Something about the copper shroud. She said I would be sorry."

He shakes his head with a genuine smile. "Ghosts can't hurt you," he tells me.

Well, that's not true, I think. *My ghosts hurt more than anything.*

"So, Spinda died in the Cull and was buried in the Burial Circle? And no one knows where that is?" I ask.

"Its location was always a great secret – guarded by the elders. And everyone who held that secret died in the Cull, when she did."

"I don't believe that," I say. "Someone must know where that circle is."

"Listen." Daruunlis leans closer. "As far as Sting's concerned, I work for him, and him alone. I've said there's no way to locate the circle. Everyone he's asked and bribed and threatened has told him the same. Are we staying on the same page, Mora?"

"Can you just speak plainly?"

He leans towards me on the balls of his feet. "The dead don't tell tales," he whispers. I flinch, but he goes on, less creepily. "I don't know where the Burial Circle is, and neither do you." His eyes flick to Nezza sleeping behind me, then back to me. "Plain enough?" *No more Mister Forthcoming.*

I nod.

"Can you keep your nose out and your head down? If it means helping her?"

"Yes."

"Good."

He shuts the door on us and leaves. I feel a strange wash of fatigue and excitement and go to stand over Nezza's sleeping form. Her breath barely moves her, but I can hear its light sigh through her nose. When she's like this, I can forget how bothersome she is. I think of those bones sleeping upstairs, tall as her. Spinda's firstborn's adored bones.

Did Hiramlan have a little pet like Minty? Perhaps a pony he liked to barrel around with, like Char? Was he anything like my sisters? Enca, soft and kind, and Eben, cheeky but gentle. Loving girls, always laughing and cuddling. So unlike Nezza in every way.

Where are *their* bones? Their three white skulls? In which mass grave? In which out-of-the-way, unmarked mound do they rot, without rite or sacrament or a single drop of grace?

24

MORA

bait the trap

It's Thirday, Sevenmonth the sixth. Only four more days until the remainder of my family – Ruzi and Zako Taler – set sail for the Crozon Isles. Unlike Kit, they don't have a return voyage already planned. How long before I see them again? If ever?

I replace both copies of Dewilder's *Sacred Secrets* in Cob's lab before I go upstairs – even earlier than normal. Sting wants his slides, but I can't just leave the spotted devils hungry in their cages. The guard isn't at his post. When I go in, he's inside, looking at the bones. He sees me and tilts his head at the coffin lid.

"That piece –" he points – "the wood is different – the colour. Why'd they do that?"

He points at a small rectangle inlaid near the top end. Similar rectangles form a pattern that runs all the way around – dark wood, light wood. And he's right – that piece breaks the pattern. I noticed it earlier, but gave it no thought.

Why is *he* giving it thought? I suppose he has nothing to do all day but stare out into the hallway.

"It might mark the start of the written passage," I tell him. The longer text running around the outside begins just after that oddity in the inlay.

I look at his broad shoulders, the way he hunches slightly, and I'm sure it's him – the same guard I saw in the hallway, cosying up to Lovemore's attendant.

"Why would they mark that?" His eyes meet mine and I almost startle. They're the palest blue I've ever seen. "It's their language."

"I… You're right. I don't know why it's there."

He's still holding my gaze, like I'm another pattern he can't decipher. His irises are beautiful, full of needles of frost or ice, his short eyelashes darker than his pale hair. Blue veins in his eyelids stand out.

I feed and water the devils, and hurry out before Sting finds me here. If I don't finish colouring the slides, there'll be hell to pay.

Cob isn't in yet, but I pick up my brushes and begin. The revelations from last night and Daruunlis's caginess have left a bad taste. So Jafalla Dewilder, Lume Dewilder's daughter and Nezza's mother, helped to reveal her father's book for Sting and Sculpin – while falling for Sculpin. Even if she was young, so am I, and that seems idiotic.

Daruunlis is lying to Sting about the Burial Circle. He says he'll protect Nezza. But how?

The odd exchange with the guard plays over in my mind as I paint another layer, pale blue like his eyes. Something about that coffin lid itches the back of my mind like a stick tapping on a window.

Cob comes in, bearing chemicals from upstairs.

He carries on into the back room with his grin and his jar of chemicals while I return to my dabbing.

At midday, I head up to the lab. I've no reason to be here, but that tapping at the back of my brain won't stop. All I can think about is the broken pattern on the coffin lid.

It's quiet inside. Empty, in fact – well, aside from a different guard, standing like a statue surveying the hall. I vaguely recognize him from an earlier shift. He's about thirty, round-faced and owl-eyed, but not as large as some of them.

I edge over to the lid, focusing on the miscoloured rectangle that stands out like a sore thumb. It reminds me of a huge trick box.

Trick boxes are Xan, I think. Designed to be difficult to solve.

I try pressing and prodding, but nothing moves. *It could simply be how they constructed it*, I tell myself. This off-coloured piece might be correcting a fault, like some knot or crack in the wood. But surely for Spinda's son they'd make a flawless coffin.

I find a crack that my fingernail fits into. Push up. Pull out. My nail bends and breaks. *Am I barking up the wrong tree?*

You moved his bones from the copper shroud, Spinda's dream voice slinks into my mind. Then Nezza's panicked one, *Spinda's not real! Spinda's not real!*

I drag the lid towards me and run my fingers along the bottom of the rim until they touch the oddly-coloured piece. I tug down until something clicks – a soft, metallic sound. The piece moves like an oiled cog, leaving a space behind.

The guard's still oblivious, facing away.

I bend to peer into the now-exposed gap. It runs along one of the coffin lid's shorter sides. Not a large cavity. Just big enough for a small scroll. I'm teasing the old paper out gently when Daruunlis enters. He sees right away what I'm doing and a distinct look of shock, and something else – anger – flits across his features.

He takes in the empty lab, then looks back over his shoulder towards the guard, who's still facing the hall.

He doesn't speak, but his eyes say enough.

Still holding the scroll in one hand, I slide the secret door back neatly, and then try to replace the piece that holds it in place. It won't stay. It keeps dropping back out into my hand.

Daruunlis shakes his head.

"You going down to Nezza?" he asks me. It's an instruction.

He takes the piece of coffin lid from me and slips it back

so it's propped back in place. If someone moves it, it'll fall out again and they'll see.

I nod and turn slightly away, still with my back to the door, to put the small scroll gently down my top, nestled near the pendant from Ruzi. The warm oval of glass isn't any bigger than one of those boiled mint sweets Ruzi favours. It's so light, I usually forget it's there.

Daruunlis catches up with me before I reach Nezza's room.

"Give it to me," he tells me.

"No," I say quickly, shaking my head.

He looks taken aback so I say it again, softer.

"You always this good at putting spokes in people's wheels?" Daruunlis grumbles. "I can read it, you can't. Come on." He pulls me into Nezza's room. She's not there – she must have gone down for lunch.

I pull the scroll out of its hiding place and he snatches it from me, though the paper crackles. I'm worried it'll crumble to bits as he unrolls it, it's so stiff. It cracks in several places but holds firm. It's covered in Xan script.

I hand it to him. "What does it say?"

He examines it. "It's a letter from the boy's mother."

I give him time to read it. When he looks up, I see a strange expression stretching across his face. He leaves it there, for once.

"Well?" I prompt softly.

"It's private. Her grief and her guilt. It's for him to read in the next life. I shouldn't have read it."

"Her guilt?"

"That she wasn't there to save him. And that she was burying him … outside."

"Outside where?"

"Outside the main refuge, away from the places they were making into real homes … never mind. You wouldn't understand."

"What happened to him?"

"He drowned. It was an accident. Playing in the river."

Daruunlis rubs the side of his face and one eye with the hand not holding the scroll. He looks set to crumple it up.

"Don't damage it." I lay a hand on his arm.

"No one can find out we have this."

"I'll hide it." I stretch out my arm. "I'll keep it secret. Don't destroy it," I plead, and he gives it to me. I don't know why – why I wanted it, why he gave in.

I don't know enough Xan to read it, but I can't bear the thought of all those words from a grieving mother crumbling away.

"Why did she hide it in the coffin and not leave it with the other goods?"

"It's an old tradition. For privacy. Some of our coffins have a niche like that on each corner so loved ones can leave last words or secret gifts with the dead that no one else will ever see. The Skøl haven't *discovered* them yet."

The paper's light as air in my hand, but I feel guilt settling on me like sediment. Prodding and poking at that boy's coffin lid like Glor, or Hunter, just like one of them.

Like some dead boy's final resting place is a puzzle box. He's already been exhumed, unwrapped, his bones pored over, his skull smashed on the floor, his toys played with.

Daruunlis goes on. "It was kind of you to find the trick compartment for me though. I was sure it was there somewhere, but I can never open those things." His mouth twists shrewdly. "Keep that hidden, whatever you do. And stay away, and don't touch anything upstairs for a few hours. Can you manage that?"

"What will you do?"

He's nearly out the door, but I can see his sly smile forming. "Bait the trap."

25

MORA

bows his head

I paint all day, until my hip is sore from crouching. Daruunlis only said to stay away *for a few hours*, which have certainly passed. I'm itching to go up there, see if he's made his move.

I launch myself up the stairs at a trot, stretching my uncooperative muscles – then I hear Sting's loud voice booming down the stairwell. *Is he angry?*

I pick up the pace and dash down to the open door, only to see Hiramlan's coffin and its lid lying in wooden splinters and curls of copper on the central table.

Sting, Glor, Hunter and Daruunlis are beside the mess, sharing a loud but distinctly cheerful toast with cordial glasses of flavoured schinn.

"What happened?" I ask the guard. It's the one who was

curious about the coffin. His ice-pale eyes watch from the door as the liquor disappears down four gullets.

"Turn up for the books," he says. "Box had a hidden compartment. They found something good inside. Smashed up the rest looking for more."

I nod at him and slip into the room. Daruunlis spots me, holding my eye briefly before directing his full attention back to the scientists.

"Imagine!" Sting is enthusing. "We could soon be ushering the first generation of a new kind of human! A new class of superhumans living twice the natural time." He raises his glass, and they follow him like a class of children mirroring the teacher.

"To the superhumans!" Hunter responds as their glasses clink.

"I knew this find would be a turning point, though I'd almost given up hope of finding this wretched Burial Circle." Sting sniffs and pats Daruunlis on the shoulder. "The key has been here, under our noses!"

Glor pours another round into each of their glasses. "To a loooong and brilliant future!"

Sting is flushed with triumph – and probably schinn. "The amber skulls at the Burial Circle are the final piece. Lovemore will see the merits now, I am certain."

They all beam at each other, until Sting puts his glass down.

"Daruunlis, come," he says, gently collecting some aged-looking pieces of paper from the bench near him.

"We must write down everything this says." He looks around and finally spots me.

"Dezil!" he barks. "Have you and Cob finished my slides?"

"Nearly, Sciencemaster," I say cautiously.

"Very good." He and Daruunlis disappear into the back office.

Hunter sighs. "I'm going out," she tells Glor, nipping past me. Before Glor can do the same, I grab his arm.

"What did you find?" I ask.

"A map. And not just a map," Glor enthuses, tongue considerably loosened by schinn. "A map to the Burial Circle. There's a scroll too."

"Is there?" I think of the scroll I found, still hidden in my room, covered in rather messy Xan script I've not made head nor tail of.

"Daruunlis did a quick translation. It describes Seff's Burial Circle holding a great well of *life-altering power*, triggered by lightning and ritual. That's the amber skulls. They're the key. We've discovered the boy's bones have unusual elektrical properties. The skull curvature – in a fully transformed sample – will amplify those. Sting thinks once the nodes are linked together in an array, they'll concentrate the charge of healing elektrons and amplify and channel them to the subject."

"They'll do what?"

"Irradiate the subject with healing light, accelerating the changes catalysed by the butterfly treatment."

"Have you tried … that … with Hiramlan's bones?"

"We performed some experiments. But those little bones aren't enough. They're not pure either. But now we can go directly to the very place where all the skulls of legend lie. Spinda's remains will be there, and the bones of all the great Xan healers who came before her! Each a repository or amplifier of incredible power that the Xan are too dim – or superstitious – to exploit." He shakes his head. "Astonishing those people stumbled across science like this with primitive practices."

"So, where exactly does this map say the Burial Circle is?"

"We weren't far off the mark – it's near Hunger Canyons."

Next morning, while I'm stretching a stiff paintbrush back to life, Cob comes in and tells me to hurry.

"Sting wants to present his case to Lovemore early – today at noon."

Thea's wounds. I rush through the last two slides, using lighter colours than Cob would like, and sit them in the sun on the window ledge to dry. They'll have to do.

Cob carefully arranges the materials, slotting slides into purpose-built trays, making sure the order corresponds to Sting's list. He'll have to load them into the lantern projector one at a time.

"You can help, can't you?" he asks. "Afraid you'll have to sit still as a mouse. And the Sciencemaster isn't one for short speeches. Are you able?"

It feels strange to be asked, instead of directed. "Of course," I tell him.

The presentation is being held in Lovemore's high-security wing. I've never ventured far into this side of the hotel – only escorted Nezza to the fancy breakfast room.

This wing is kept to higher standards. The room Sting's using for his presentation is a level above and deeper in than the breakfast room. The wood panel and flock wallpaper feel fussy in a room this small. Its wooden floor is mostly hidden under patterned rugs. The back of the main piece of furniture – a commanding button-tufted sofa piled with tasselled cushions, faces the windows. Spindly-legged side tables flank it.

Cob sets up the lantern slide projector on a high table behind the sofa. There's a movable silk screen opposite to catch the light. Sting has arranged for a lectern beside the screen. Cob and I are to perch on each side of the projector, a stool apiece.

Sting paces, his agitation thinly veiled. His shoes shine like mirrors, and he's wearing a paler jacket than usual, with a fancier collar. He comes over as we draw the heavy curtains to test the lantern projector.

"I see you've taken your lessons in colour from Mister Cob." He frowns at me.

"He suggested stronger colours would work best."

"Naturally.," Sting sighs.

The door opens.

Lovemore arrives, wreathed in floral, sugary perfume.

She settles in, her guards at their posts and her fan-bearing attendant stood in place of one of the side tables, wafting perfume everywhere. That woman's arms must be made of steel.

"Do proceed, Sacrifice." Lovemore gives him his cue. "You have an hour to convince me. If you fail, this study ends today."

Sting nods and walks swiftly to the lectern.

Silence. Not even a creak from the fan.

He begins with a paeon to Lovemore and the indomitable spirit of the Skøl settlers who, like him, have spent seven long years civilizing these savage Western Colonies.

"Our gains have been hard-won. They have cost friends and allies. Here in this great town, we remember the late Registry Magistrate, Valour Venor. My own team, as you know, was violently divested of a committed scientist, Ardent Sculpin, who was my trusted colleague for many years. This territory – land and sea – is brutal. It tries to claim us. But civilization will ascend savagery. We say to wildness, to nature: submit! We will tame you for your treasure and unlock your promise with modern industry and science.

"Every month brings new discoveries of scientific merit to my attention. We truly live in a Golden Era of Science! Lucrative elektric technology brings illumination, weaponry, transportation, communication. Our domination over land and sea is unconquerable.

And soon we'll conquer more." He pauses. "One enemy remains. One enemy still defeats us all."

Another pause.

"Death." He raises both arms in the air, his hands curled. "Even those of us with wealth enough to buy many lifetimes grow old and pass away. A gross injustice! We who can afford to live for ever age and wither, betrayed by our own bodies."

Lovemore sits stiff as a board, her hair gently wafting in the fan's breeze.

"We are injured in accidents and life drains from us, whether it be paid or not. Must all lethal injuries truly be so? Age, injury and infirmity are the most formidable challenges facing humanity today."

He's getting more generous with his pauses for effect. Lovemore is nodding ever so slightly now.

"Death must come for us all," she says.

"But it need not arrive so promptly," Sting counters swiftly. "As we uncover and master more secrets of science, we will bring nature to heel. I believe we stand on the cusp of knocking death down for a round or two."

He draws in a deep breath and scans the room, holding Lovemore's eyes for a few beats. She gestures for her attendant to pause. "You have had years to perfect this life-prolonging procedure, Sacrifice."

Sting clears his throat. "And they have not been spent in vain! They paved the way to our recent breakthrough. Now we are firmly on track. For those who can pay. I have already proven that great potential lies in the butterfly elixir. And now we have proof that a remarkable new substance exists. We have called this Clarion Amber." She nods at this tribute to her name. "It is proof that people can transform. As a caterpillar turns into a butterfly, so too can ordinary humans transform into superhumans, with vastly extended lifespans."

His eyes are shining.

"Through the correct process of elektrical amplification using nodes of Clarion Amber, a subject's inherent life energy can be stimulated to achieve healing and longevity. This is the ultimate promise of Life Registration and our Golden Era – life that is paid for is valued and lived well. And we will pioneer a process to allow, for a price, people to live vigorous, youthful and triumphant over nature's tyranny!"

Lovemore gives another gentle nod. "Hear, hear," she says. It would seem she's being won over – unless she is only playing with him.

Sting stands taller. "Let me demonstrate my findings. Mister Cob, lights. First slide!"

Thea's wounds, I curse internally. *He's just getting started.*

While Cob cuts the room's elektric lights, I insert the lantern slide and power up the machine. Its internal light glows yellowish behind a bubble of glass.

We show the first few slides while Sting talks through his introduction. Sting and Sculpin standing side by side holding shovels. Their first expedition to the Badlands. Dewilder's book. A butterfly.

Spinda's face at one hundred and six years old, looking less than half that, fills the silk screen.

"More than fifty years ago, the savages achieved this with a combination of primitive medicine and even more primitive belief. With science, we will go further."

I stare at Spinda's glowing eyes.

"As well as long life, it is told she developed…" Sting is saying, "certain rare abilities as a healer. These powers are not god-given as the primitives supposed, but linked to a bodily process we term *amberfication.* The bones themselves change. As you know, I have already had tremendous success with two subjects who were fed butterfly elixir—"

One of the guards shuffles. Lovemore's fan-waving attendant glances at him. He stops shuffling. It was definitely them that evening on the stairs, locked in intense conversation. Now they seem like strangers again. I know better…

"Your election is in a few short months," Sting segues neatly. "You could be sharing the news of a proven, reproducible process before then. Imagine what an extraordinary boost that would bring. No one will talk of anything else."

"Not quite so hasty," Lovemore interrupts, a smile in her voice. "They will talk of my other triumph as well. My *Dominion*."

"Yes, of course," Sting hastens to agree. "I meant to say that you will have *two* victories to boast about. Dominion over everything – and even death!"

Lovemore's murmur of assent seems pleased.

Sting discusses the slides dealing with Spinda's attempt to resurrect her son, and my sketches of Hiramlan's remains. The attendant and the frost-eyed guard keep sneaking looks at one another.

"The butterfly elixir is one step in the process, but we must go further. I am more convinced than ever of the need to reach the Burial Circle. There we will find a rich deposit of Clarion Amber that will provide the second vital step in the process."

Sting's arm movements are becoming more effusive.

"Cob, show the final slide," he orders. The elektric schematic leaps on to the wall.

"These circles –" Sting indicates the ones I've painted orange – "represent nodes of Clarion Amber, while this –" he points at a white box off to one side – "is an elektrical source we propose to use to power them. The subject stands in the middle of the circle, holding another node, through which he or she is irradiated. The subject undergoing irradiation must have taken the butterfly treatment. That is the catalyst."

"But you don't know where this precious Burial Circle is," says Lovemore, sounding bored.

"Cob, lights!" Sting calls, rubbing his hands together. "You –" he points at me – "open the curtains. And now, High Governor…" His hands clap once, loudly, daylight streaming into the room for the first time since the talk began. "The best for last. We have made a most compelling discovery. We have found a map hidden for nearly a hundred years in the walls of the coffin of Spinda's dead child that details – irrefutably – the precise location of this long-sought Burial Circle."

Lovemore leans forward, directing her attendant to begin fanning again as Sting carries on. "It lies very close to the outlaw settlement of Hunger Canyons. A day's journey from the site of *Dominion*'s construction at Ridmouth. With your blessing, I would like to travel south to witness the birth of each of these critical projects. To secure these golden achievements for the glory of Skøland. Your scientific legacy will be unassailable!"

He has made his pitch. He watches her, breathing hard.

Lovemore relaxes into the cushions. The mesmerizing arm of her attendant drifts through the warm air like a languid water creature. "Very good, Sacrifice," Lovemore says. I can't see her face, and I don't know her well enough to read her dry tone. "I will admit, I was reaching the end of my patience on this project. But your latest discovery is so timely, it almost feels fated. I think … you must undertake this expedition."

She pauses as Sting's mouth stretches into a wide smile of sheer relief.

"This could completely transform our nation," she says quietly. "Enhance it. For the financially deserving, of course. It could reinforce the natural upper class with great distinction."

"Indeed, High Governor."

"I will make sure you have the required resources at your disposal… But remember … this kind of research has its detractors."

"We will keep our explorations discreet, High Governor," Sting is quick to assure her, bobbing his head. "Not a soul will know. Not before time."

"Temper Wilforn has eyes everywhere."

"Exactly so. His supporters are like rats. Scientifically illiterate but beady-eyed—"

"You will go," she cuts him off. "And you will see that all is in order with *Dominion* first."

"Yes, High Governor."

"Too many disturbing rumblings have emerged from Rosclaw's county. I will journey there myself and attend *Dominion*'s maiden voyage," Lovemore muses. "We will make it a trip to the site of the Clarion Amber deposit. A visit to Hunger Canyons."

Sting looks startled, but recovers. "A capital prospect, High Governor."

Maiden voyage … Hunger Canyons – the river there must accommodate tall ships, then.

"Splendid," Lovemore says sweetly. "It is my dearest wish to return to Rundvaer ahead of the vote in the Tenmonth with *two* scientific victories!" Her voice tells him to grant her wish. If he can't, he will have failed.

"You will have both these jewels, High Governor," Sting promises. "The team assures me your magnificent

Dominion will be fully operational by the middle of Eightmonth, at the latest."

"Then I will be in Ridmouth for Eightmonth the fifteenth." She raises a finger. "Keep these plans to yourself."

He nods. "High Governor, I will be silent as the grave."

Lovemore stands to leave. Sting bows his head.

26

MORA

pass in the night

So begins the whirlwind of preparation.

We are all to go, sailing south on one of the tall ships from Lovemore's escort. Later that afternoon, as soon as I can extricate myself from the chaos Sting's triumphant presentation has created, I go to find Daruunlis. His room is on the same floor in the same wing as Nezza's, but looks over the back.

His door is open and what I can see of his room looks sparse and empty. Did he bring anything with him but a few changes of clothes and … more pots of honey?

He has a visitor – and her pet. They're sitting on his floor, eating honey spread on bits of bread this time. Minty holds the small pinched-off pieces Nezza gives him very delicately in his front paws, then shoves them in his mouth. His pink tongue licks neatly at his furry jaws and his little black eyes glint. Both Nezza and Daruunlis are half turned from the door, and they don't hear me coming – the carpet back here is thick.

"Are people very hungry in Hunger Canyons?" Nezza asks.

"No. It's just a name. People in Coppertown aren't made of copper, are they? Hunger Canyons is full of food. I can make you a soup with the tastiest vegetables you've ever eaten in your life. Fresh as the dawn. I grow them myself. You can visit the bees who made this honey."

"Okay," she says, her voice small.

"You'll like them. They're clever bees. Gorgeous things. So fluffy."

"Do we have to go there?"

"You don't want to stay here. Nothing happens here."

"Yes, but…" She shoves another bit of honey bread in her mouth.

"What's the matter?"

"Do we have to go by … by sea again," she says round her mouthful, dropping crumbs. Minty eats more tidily.

"Sea's fastest. And we'll be on a plush boat. And it's not pirate season. It'll be plain sailing, all the way."

"It's not pirate season?" Nezza looks up.

"Even if it was," he says, "can I tell you a secret?"

She leans closer.

"I know the pirates," he says. "They're a lovely bunch, once you get to know them."

"*Lovely?*" Nezza echoes, incredulous.

Daruunlis looks at her and sighs. "Your mum knew some of them. She … really got on well with some of them."

"She did?"

"Your beautiful mum, Jafalla… She didn't like just anyone. There's a lot you don't know about her. Did you know she had two beautiful sisters?"

Nezza scowls. "Beautiful as her?"

"Well. Those girls were all different – but yes, all beautiful in their souls and their reflections. Jafalla was … my favourite. But her youngest sister still lives. She's a bit impulsive, but she's big now. Grown. Mora's age – or older."

Gods alive, I wish I felt big and grown. Nezza doesn't comment.

"And…" Daruunlis holds up a finger. "This is a secret I'm about to tell you, Nezza. You mustn't tell your guardian. Or anyone."

"I won't tell."

"Your aunt wants to see you. Very much. She wants you to live with her, and I think you two could have some adventures."

"I want to live with you," she says softly, looking up at his face.

He pauses. "Well, your Auntie Pony, she's family," he says at last. "She's got her heart set on you, and she's got a home and everything ready, just waiting. She's got horses. You remember those?"

Pony? It must be a nickname. Pony Dewilder. Something about it rings a bell. Why does it sound familiar?

Nezza's shaking her head.

"Horses are great. Like kine, but prettier and cleverer and don't they know it. Bit like the Dewilder sisters. And Pony's got plenty of space for Minty."

Nezza looks at Minty, tucking in for a nap on her lap. She scratches his ear. "He doesn't need space."

"Well, this aunt of yours will come and fetch you, after we get to Hunger Canyons—"

I hear dim voices behind me. Staff from the hotel are approaching. I slip a few paces down the hall and come back, letting my feet fall louder.

Daruunlis's eyes are on the door when I reach it.

"Mora!" cries Nezza.

"I see someone sniffed out another pot of honey," I say, walking in and closing the door.

"Daruunlis says he knows pirates."

"Does he?" I look at him.

"Get to meet all sorts, my line of work." He gives me a grin and offers some bread and honey.

I sit with them and eat. There's no denying it's good honey, smooth and flowery and sweet as potted summer. I haven't been outside in weeks but this at least feels like a bit of outside coming in.

"Convenient you found the map to the Burial Circle," I say in Crozoni, raising my eyebrows at Daruunlis.

"I thought the location was a sacred secret. I thought you didn't want Sting to find it."

"I don't make the decisions. And now it's in the hands of the gods."

I lower my voice, though I know Nezza can't understand. "But is it real?"

His grunt could be interpreted either way.

"And no one wonders why there might be a map to this long-sought location in that particular coffin?"

He shrugs. "Sting's more than ready to believe. I suggested that Spinda was so mad with grief she drew a map for her dead son – to where she knew she'd end up once she died – so they could reunite in the afterlife."

I blink. Memory like a black wave drops over me. Ma's funeral. Our little brother Char refusing to look, his stony face fixed on his shoes.

Daruunlis is still talking. "He swallowed it whole."

"I hope you know what you're doing," I say with a shake in my voice. My mood is bouncing like a ball. I feel low, then giddy. Naughty as a child playing truant from school. I feel light.

"Hope makes a powerful wine," he says. Thea's wounds, he sounds like Ruzi.

Nezza yanks my sleeve with honey-sticky fingers. "You're not allowed to speak that language."

"Who's going to find out?" I ask her. "You going to tell on me again?" I turn back to Daruunlis to demand, still in Crozoni, "Who sent you here? Who are you really working with?"

"That I can't divulge. For your own safety."

I'm fed up with roundabout talk. At least it's clear as day how much he cares about Nezza. He's here to help her. And right now I don't want to quiz him too much. I need a favour.

"You're allowed to leave the hotel, aren't you?"

He nods, looking bemused.

"I'm not. And … I want to get a letter to someone. Could you carry one out for me tomorrow? To a public house? It's not far from here."

"Be happy to. Might have to hide it in my shoe. Sting doesn't want any communications leaving the Castle."

"If you have to. Thank you. I'll bring it first thing."

Nezza hugs him goodnight. I've never seen her hug anyone but him.

"Clean your teeth and into bed," I tell her back at our rooms. Should I hug her? I'd better not try.

When she's abed, I retreat to my room. I leave the elektric light off and use the softer glow of a lantern to write a short letter to Ruzi and Zako. Just one page. I may never see them again, but it has to fit in a shoe. They sail on the Endweek. I fold it up small and seal it.

Then I start on one for Kit. There are so many things I want to say to him. Or rather, I long to just hold his face in my hands and say nothing.

In the end, I keep it neutral, in case a guard discovers it.

Fourday, Sevenmonth 7th

Dearest Kit,

I hope you are well and returned in good spirits.

How I wish it was me, not just this letter, here to meet you. I am forced to leave with Sting's party – travelling to Hunger Canyons. I will try to send more news by telegram. There is much to tell you that I cannot write.

I love you.

With all my heart,
Mora

I kiss the paper, fold and seal it. I address both courtesy of Mister and Missus Scarlet at the Lugger. They'll make sure my letters reach the right hands.

Kit will still be sailing south today. His ship only left four days ago. The journey takes three weeks. But if he keeps to the Reedstones' schedule – and he promised he would – he'll be sailing back on that same ship ten days after it arrives – in the first week of Eightmonth. It means he'll be back on the water even as our party arrives in Shipway town.

Our ships might pass in the night.

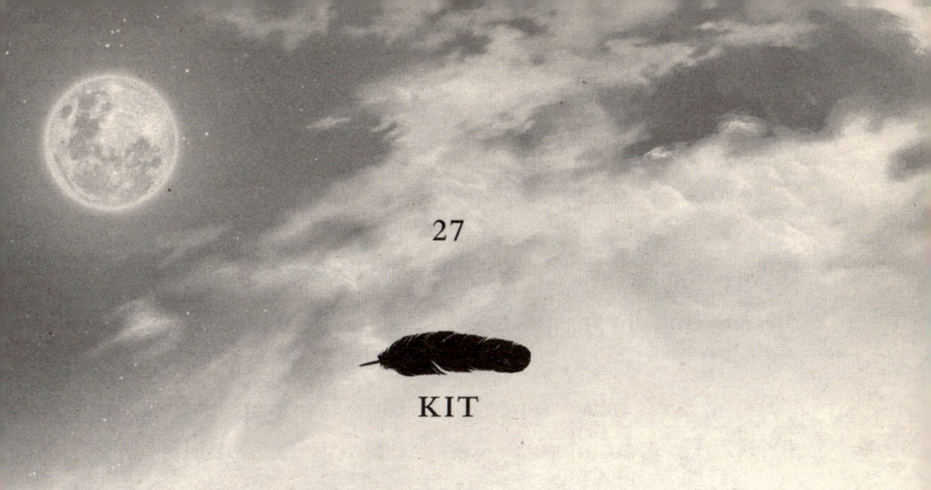

27

KIT

some god's hammer

Sixday, Eightmonth 6th. At Sea.

It's just me and Caruq again. Night's new-fallen, moon aglow and stars beginning their crawl across the purple sky. Third night of our journey back to Portcaye on the same *Toothsea Tear*, under full sail, clipping along at a pace. Back to Mora. Home.

We set off days ago following the coast, staying in sight of land, but now I can't see a thing out there. No telltale lights (no lighthouses, villages, towns). Black water everywhere, too warm for the bloodsucking kraits you find in northern reaches, though it has its own creatures. Some glow soft and strange, below. Not the reflection of the stars, but deeper. Do elektric creatures down there use lights to find their friends? To find their prey, perhaps.

Everyone's at supper, except the watch – and me.

Without my buffer of Skøl travelling companions (the Reedstones and Blithe) there's a distinct new flavour to this leg.

I'm not welcome to eat with the others. The Reedstones' coin has bought my passage and a sliver of tolerance. Not goodwill.

I took their news in person to the Magistrate of Shipway Life Registry, like I promised – Clem Rosclaw. His clerks there didn't wear robes, for obvious reasons. Their uniforms were practical for the heat. Rosclaw's office was light and clean, free of portraits. A collection of pebbles (shingle from Shipway beach) lined one windowsill. He had a watering can and a spreading potted plant with tiny, delicate leaves branching from a forest of fragile stems on his desk.

"It's a feather fern," he said when he saw me looking. "Do you like plants?"

"I've never seen one like this."

"It's from Skøland. Come, let me show you something." I followed his broad back to a partly shaded glasshouse behind the building, stuffed with more plants, from tiny seedlings to big, lush things with enormous leaves. The place was stifling as a steam bath, though it smelled lovely (like life feeding life, nourishing). The glass made me think of Mora.

"You can't grow them outside?"

"Not many would survive out there. Mind you, some would surprise you and thrive. We can't let them become invasive."

“The plants?” My eyebrows lifted by themselves.

Back at his office, someone had left two cups of that thick, awful fikka.

“And Golden and Glister are sure it’s Lovemore herself, heading to Ridmouth?” He held his cup and looked at me, really studied me, more than most people do.

“They heard she’s due in two weeks. Staying at a guest house that’s being gutted and redone.”

“Sounds like Lovemore.”

“They’re sure it’s to do with *Dominion*.”

I told him where the Reedstones were staying. He said he’d send someone to help them. Honestly, I wasn’t sure what to make of him. Perhaps he felt the same way about me.

Now, Caruq and I are quiet, under the stars, sharing biscuits. He sets a paw on my knee and his throat rumbles. I follow his pointing snout. Lanterns, maybe a dozen, buoyed up with small flames, over to the southwest. Tall ships carry those lanterns. Their cloth’s like silk, coloured red to stand out in the day and specially treated so it doesn’t catch fire. From here they look like red jellyfish. Gives me an eerie turn, imagining us underwater, below them, like there’s no air, all the way up to the stars.

Those lanterns are distress beacons, meant to call in aid if a ship finds itself falling afoul of unseen rocks or sea brigands or sea monsters (they don’t work in a storm). Tonight there’s no hint of a storm. The wind is low and the few clouds are high and spaced out like the rib bones of some giant creature.

"*SHIP IN DISTRESS!*" The sailor on watch – he's over by the helm – spots them just after Caruq. His cries rouse the rest of the crew, and with barely a grumble, *Toothsea Tear* swings to follow the lanterns down a shallower, calmer sea road.

A mist seems to have sprung up from nowhere and I can't make out any details of the ship that loosed the beacons (too distant, too shadowed).

"Can you see it?" One of the younger sailors comes to stand beside me. Some of them noticed on the way down how the dark doesn't slow me like it does them. They think I see like a cat. Truth is, they're all half night-blind from living on bad ship fare (stale biscuit, pea stew) and staring into the sun glancing off the sea all day. Sailing's hell on the eyes.

"No," I tell him. But something winks at me out of the black like a flame off glass and a darker shape looms in the distance that's nothing like a Skøl tall ship – in distress or otherwise.

Dominion? I wonder. What if it's already made? Could the High Governor's monstrous ship be plying the waves already?

It's not a Skøl ship. We draw closer. No. I think *they* draw closer to *us*. The wind's fallen out of *Toothsea Tear*'s sails like a rock dropped from a torn pocket. The odd mist that wasn't here moments before starts to climb up around us.

The other ship is an enormous outrigger, like a Xan ship of yore grown out of all proportion. Huge, fifty times the size of a little canoe with a float on each side. The main hull, sitting above the central float could fit half *Toothsea*'s cargo. And then each of the pair of outrigs are nearly boats in their own right, by volume perhaps a quarter of *Toothsea* each, trailing ropes and floats and a veritable mat of unidentifiable hangers-on. It's very much neither a Skøl tall ship, nor in distress.

I hear a small sound and spot through the lighter mist near the water a straight line of bubbles popping towards us. The distress beacons – or now I'm thinking lures, float off beyond the fog, higher and further, star distant and forgotten.

Then an almighty crunch rips *Toothsea Tear*'s wooden hull open like it's been hit with some god's hammer.

28

KIT

in its throat

"PIRATES! We're under attack! To weapons!" the captain shouts. "Mercy, with me! Vallie, look to the launch!"

The strange outrigger has fired an explosive – something like a huge old Crozoni gun, underwater. *Toothsea* starts to fold like a toy boat, shuddering and squealing.

After the hull breach, the attacking ship lights up and start screaming like a demon.

WAKKA WAKKA WAKKA WAKKA.

It seems to breathe like one too, giving out great streams of smoke. It bears down on the already-listing *Toothsea Tear* with incredible speed.

While the Skøl's deadliest guns are usually reserved for the thickest-headed (guards and branders), the bigger, faster, more expensive trading ships like *Toothsea Tear* are allowed to carry elektric weapons for protection. *Toothsea*'s complement isn't half bad: several elektric, heart-stopping guns, and elektric prods – almost one to each crew member. The captain and the pilot also carry long, curved blades (a Skøl seafaring tradition their land folk don't go in for).

I lead Caruq and his friend Cinbar (the barrel-bodied ship's dog we met on the way down has come above deck to see what all the commotion is) up to the high bit of the helm, furthest from the attacking boat. A quiet, forgotten perch – for now. I'm not delusional enough to think we'll get a space on the launch, given the number of crew crowding on to it. *One thing at a time*, I tell myself. *You've weathered worse than this. You have to live to get back to Mora.* I can't leave her wondering. What if I die here and she never hears news of it? Would she think I just left her and never tried to get back?

The pirates board, leaping over from the nearest float of their extraordinary vessel, swinging on ropes and dropping down to the foundering *Toothsea*'s deck. I think of my promise, the one that's always there, just under my skin, the one I made for the gods' favour. I can't forget it, especially when I'm this close to the water. *I promise not to swim.*

The pirates are a mostly Crozoni crew, but I recognize with a jolt that some of them include Xan. Men and women, with the balance probably tipping to women. They carry no guns – Crozoni or Skøl. Long blades flash. And one woman has a traditional Xan fighting staff, almost as tall as her. The fizz of *Toothsea*'s quota of elektric guns greets them as they arrive. They dodge and swing and weave to make difficult targets of themselves.

The fog is everywhere, but one thing's clear – these pirates have experience. *Toothsea Tear* is not their first catch.

They move like dancers and kill like the deadly jellyfish their lures echo. Graceful (almost floating with it) as if there's music behind the melee that only they can hear. It's horror and craft at the same time. I'm not doing it justice.

Imagine. Clattering blades, thudding bone. Splintered wood and frothing water. Screaming. Floundering. Mist meeting smoke meeting spray. *Toothsea*'s rigging is on fire and its crew, like the ship, well and truly outmatched. Awful. Violent. Unreal. I feel like I'm not here. The calm blanket of denial. I'm going to die here, but I don't believe it.

The elektric weaponry of *Toothsea*'s crew doesn't slow their attackers. The pirates are so confident, some ignore the sailors and go straight for the goods. They unfasten crates roped to the deck and even make their way down tween decks, coming up shouldering bales of kine wool they toss overboard, easy as they do any sailor who gets in their way.

I stand with Caruq and Cinbar by the shadow of the tilting wheel (observing, so far unobserved).

"What have they got?" The pirates speak Crozoni. I hear one, a tall woman, hair back in a long plait, who caught my eye earlier for her brutal facility with her Xan two-sectioned staff, stopping to quiz another.

"Not much fuel. Some wool. Some grains, looks like maybe sugar and fikka. Brick ballast."

A nod from the staff-bearing woman. "Get what you can over – I'll see to the men."

Her staff is a living thing, now extended at a diagonal angle, swiping, stabbing, singing. Now it's vertical, now horizontal, gripped in both her hands and upending sailors like skittles.

Three of *Toothsea*'s crew face up to her, one with a blade, two brandishing prods. The first bleeds out on the deck, his neck ripped open by something jutting from her staff… A spike? I can't see from this distance. It seems to shine.

One rush with the long section of her staff, held horizontal, takes the other two in their stomachs. She's hit then too, with live prods on her back and shoulders, but they might as well be fingers tapping her. Her staff isn't elektric like Skøl weaponry, but it looks as if it carries a strange unbalancing force. Using their own momentum, she flips the sailors back over the railing like a pair of synchronized circus tumblers. They fall into the sea.

I'm not the only witness – two younger sailors have been watching. They turn to run for the already overcrowded launch.

The woman strides on, pausing only to send a few barrels and crates of goods overboard. Future salvage.

All around, her companions are dispatching sailors or supplies with similar ease.

Toothsea's captain and pilot are pinned by the sinking far deck, trying to protect the launch from two pirates with blades. They aren't doing too badly until the woman with her two-sectioned staff joins her fellows. The weapon is an extra arm she commands entirely. She's taller than I realized, I see as she squares up to the captain. And her staff has double the reach of even a long cutlass. She moves faster and hits harder than she should too, blurring with the speed of it sometimes. Or perhaps that's just the strange mist, still drifting and pooling around both ships. *Wait. How is it cold enough for mist?*

The crew have the launch in the water and some of those who went overboard alive are trying to get in. I can't see the whole of it from my angle. The two pirates with blades and the woman with her two-sectioned staff board from above, then – much screaming and hacking. More screaming. Burbling and pleading and finally, only three pirates stand in the launch. The woman with her long stave is still, leaning on it, finally breathing hard.

Some of the other pirates start chucking plundered cargo down into it.

Caruq quivers at my side and turns his muzzle to look up at me. The smell of blood is strong.

Churning black water. I think I can hear the gulping of *Toothsea Tear*, the squealing as it swallows more water (as the water swallows it).

I realize abruptly – the screaming is over and the only language I can hear now is Crozoni. The Skøl are no more, and still, I go unnoticed.

I promise not to swim.

My old promise, the one I made for the gods' favour, bubbles up as we lurch lower.

I loved swimming. The calm of being under. In another world, leaving this one behind – muffled and distant and so, so small. When you're in the ocean you remember your smallness. It can lift you (it could lift a hundred of you like nothing, a thousand, thousand thousand). All your trials take on a new colour. That's how I remember it (though I know when you lose something the memories grow crooked).

Still, I watch. The ship, my illusion of solid ground, vanishing by inches. Blood running free. Flame edging from rigging to sails.

An odd motion draws my eyes to the water between the pirates' enormous outrigger and the sinking *Toothsea*, a new rope of ripples, pairs of vortices like tiny whirlpools marking the passage of some huge fish. I imagine it down there, munching on *Toothsea*'s lately live crew. I can't see the twinkle of the elektric creatures any more.

Over the top of it all, like a sheet of smudged glass, lies the promise I pledged to uphold.

The tall woman with the two-sectioned staff (of all the pirates, of course it's her) comes clambering up round the side of the wheelhouse and—

'What in the name...?' Her voice trails off into the mayhem music of her own making, the splintering, bubbling wail of it. She has a young voice, one I recognize (with a jolt like ice to bare skin). She's the woman from outside Selflowers, the one with the eyepatch who was walking out with the ugly Crozoni man.

She doesn't look like a killer. She's round-cheeked as Mora. Her Xan part shows in her darker skin – though it's lighter than mine – and her eyes, which she wipes some blood out of (not her own). They're purple, wide set, bright. Neither in need of patching. I can see her clearly, even in the gloom, because she's part-lit, not just by the fires behind, but also by the phosphorescent orange light glowing off something on her staff.

Her eyes take in my hands (one on Caruq's collar, one on Cinbar's head) before they lock on mine. I read her indecision. To kill me or keep me?

"You were in Shipway," she shouts over the din, in Crozoni. "Why are you crossing my path again?" Her southern accent comes out stronger than I remember.

I feel my own question rising... Break my promise, or take my chances with her and that death-staff?

She looks down at the water, just before *Toothsea Tear*'s wood screams again, lurching anew with an abrupt judder, sinking several feet in an instant. In the light of the flaming sails, and the light still pouring from the lanterns on the outrigger, I see the vortices of the huge fish again. It must have turned abruptly, its wake upsetting the already fast-foundering tall ship.

And so my choice is made. I'm falling into the water.

The sea takes me in its throat.

29

MORA

wait for her

"What's good to eat in this town?" Daruunlis asks when I visit him bearing my letters early the next morning. I've dated them with yesterday's date – Sevenmonth the seventh. He turns, gesturing for me to follow him into his room.

"The Lugger does a good lunch," I tell him.

"That the place you want those delivered?" He tilts an eyebrow at the letters in my hand, but doesn't try to take them. "Convenient."

"Yes, but the cooking is good. Gracie's sauces…" I sigh. "And Renny's pastry is to die for."

"Pastry doesn't agree with me."

"Oh." *What should he try?* Suddenly I'm down in the bustle of the market, surrounded by the barrow-sellers calling, distracted by delicious drifting smells. "You might like our northern apples. They're around on the barrows... What about battered fish? I know a place by the docks for that. There's a bakery in Opal Alley... It's not in the nicest part of town, but the cheese bread is lovely when it's fresh... Nezza might like their biscuits. You could pick some up if you're passing. They do lavender ones... Oh, and I know a shop – I haven't been there, mind, but I hear first-rate reports ... it's in the Mermens, that's the nicest bit of town, over towards the main gates. They do orange ice. It's new..."

When I tail off, he's smiling at me. I'm missing Portcaye like anything, but it's a kind of comfort to describe these places to him.

"I like the sound of the orange ice. Nezza would like that."

"She might but it would melt before you get it back here."

"Then we'll have to take her there." He winks at me.

"What?"

"I mentioned to Sting she needs new shoes fitting. And I volunteered to take you both to buy some."

"But she doesn't need..." I'm sputtering. Joy rearing up in me – I can go out!?

"His mood is easy right now," Daruunlis explains. "His mind's full of expedition planning. He can't wait to get out of this backwater. Good thing I found that map, isn't it?" He's grinning.

I grin back.

"Little girls' feet grow so fast, and she'll need a woman's

help choosing her new ones. But we have to take a guard. And be back directly after lunch for Nezza's treatment."

"Oh." I deflate. It's Fiveday. I've been pushing the thought of Nezza's next round firmly to the back of my mind. Now the day is here.

Daruunlis's jaw clenches. "She will endure. Her cuts will heal. When we get to Hunger Canyons, we will end this."

"How, exactly?"

He looks at the door and lowers his voice, though we're speaking Crozoni as always.

"I can't tell you that. But Sting will meet his desire. Cutting up a child will be his last concern. He wants to find the amber skulls. He will get his wish. He will see the limits of his precious science. Now – shall we?"

I look down at the letters in my hand.

"Stick them in your shoes, or down your top – somewhere hidden," he reminds me.

"I will. This one's for – for my father." I almost said Zako's name. In a few days Zako will be safe – I can't jeopardize that.

"You've family who lived?" His interest feels genuine.

"Just him… And this one's for Kit – for when he comes back. We'll be gone."

Gone, gone, gone. The word echoes in my ears but the thought doesn't make me as miserable as it did last night. After over thirty days in the Castle Hotel, I'm going out.

*

Out. Sun. Shade. Air. Away from the carpeted corridors, fussy wallpaper and formal frippery of the Castle Hotel. Away from cages of small, sinless creatures and collections of the dead. Just standing outside in the light, without a roof over me, it's enough.

Nezza sticks like she's glued to Daruunlis. I notice her casting wary glances at the sky, as if she's worried some giant bird will grab her in its talons.

We're escorted by a familiar guard – the one with the eyes like ice. Also the only one who's ever thawed to me at all, sparing the odd kind word or nod. Kindnesses from anyone in the Castle Hotel are vanishingly rare. Now I don't know if he's here to protect us or make sure we don't run away.

Anyway, it's Nezza, not the guard with the pretty eyes, who attracts stares. A girl with Crozoni curls in hair too light and muddy-violet eyes. A big brown birthmark on her otherwise pale neck. People whisper to each other as they pass. *Did you see that. I thought it was impossible. A half-breed. Is she? Incredible. There's definitely Skøl in her. How irresponsible…* They look at the guard and wonder if he's the Skøl father.

I lift my chin. Nezza doesn't notice. She spends most of the walk peppering Daruunlis with questions as she drags on his arm. He manages to answer most of them. Sometimes he defers to me. It's not his town, after all.

At the Lugger, it smells like something toasting, like fragrant herbs relaxing in a bed of potatoes, like wood polish and wine vinegar and stale ale. The day isn't hot yet. Light angles in from the windows casting everything familiar, warm.

Gracie shrieks when she sees me. I find myself returning her wide smile and rushing over.

Renny emerges from the kitchen and then they're both hugging me at once. The guard stands back, eyeing the Lugger's drinks offerings with longing, for all that it's still mid-morning.

"What's the occasion?" Renny says to me, nodding vaguely to my companions. Her eyes are drawn to Nezza – like all the people we passed on the street – but her look isn't unkind.

"This is Daruunlis." I begin the introductions. "And this is Nezza," I say.

"Hello, Nezza," Gracie says. "What lovely eyes you have."

"Thank you," Nezza says primly.

"And this is Gracie and Renny," I tell them.

"And you?" They look at the guard.

"Name's Wist," he says gruffly. "I'm just the guard."

They look at me again, afraid the guard means trouble.

"We were hoping for a bite to eat here, and then we have to buy some clothes and shoes for Nezza … we're travelling south. I wanted to see Ruzi before he heads west."

"Of course," Gracie says. "Ruzi's in the blue room." She smiles at Nezza. "Choose the best table in the house and I'll bring you a big slice of yesterday's apple cake."

Nezza bolts up to find a table on the mezzanine.

Wist looks concerned by the thought of me going up the main stairs alone.

"You should try the red ale," I tell him. "And the apple cake. I won't be long."

He relaxes, seeming reassured. "Half an hour enough?" he asks quietly, surprising me.

"Yes. Thank you." It's not very long, but it's more than I thought I'd have. He sits at the bar.

I climb the stairs as fast as I can up to the guest wing.

Zako's not in Kit's room, though the door is unlocked. I enter and pause for a moment. *Kit's things. Kit's space. Kit's room's smell.* I take the letter I wrote him from my shoe and leave it on a corner of his desk. Then I take the scroll with Spinda's messy Xan writing out from my top and place it carefully in one of Kit's desk drawers. It's safest here, I think, away from the Castle Hotel.

I pull the door closed and head to the corridor with the guest rooms.

I give a musical rap, but Ruzi opens the door slowly. As soon as he sees it's me though, it's flying open all the way. "Mora!" he says, not just for my ears, pulling me into a hug even as he's shutting the door behind me. He looks the same – his hair perhaps a little longer, his skin browner from the summer sun. Are there more wrinkles round his eyes or is it my imagination?

Zako bursts from behind the bed and pounces into our hug.

I shriek a bit like Gracie. "You got me!" I laugh, holding his head to look at him. "Have you *grown more* in just a month?"

They're full of their plans for Vester Shells, out in the Crozon Isles, where Zako will assume a new name – Ancour Lander.

Their new owners, ostensibly, will be Missus Scarlet's old school friend and her husband. She's already lined up work for Ruzi with a cabinetmaker.

It's not making musical instruments, but at least it's working with his hands. And he'll take his guitar, look for places to play there, like he does in the Lugger.

I tell them I'm drawing insects for Sting's scientific records and looking after his young charge. I don't mention amber skulls and Sting's quest for immortality. It'll just worry Ruzi. He's already looking at me sideways.

"You sure you're all right?" he asks me softly.

"You know me." I smile. "I've had worse."

He blinks. "Watch you don't compare the todays to the yesterdays too much. Now's the only time to live, Mora. Does no good to wallow in the could-a-bins like me. Trust me. It's no way to live."

"I trust you," I tell him.

Zako's looking at us. "Are you looking forward to Vester Shells, Ancour?" I test out his new name. "You'll get to meet other children your age. You'll be able to go out. A kid your age should have friends."

"What, like you do?" He pulls a silly face at me. He's not trying to be mean.

"I have friends," I say, thinking of Renny and Gracie downstairs. They're Kit's friends, really.

"Kit's her friend," Ruzi says, taking my side for once. He must be feeling sentimental.

"No," Zako scoffs. "She's in love with him."

"So what if I am?" I counter. "Friends can be in love."

"Friends are different."

"All right, Mister Twelve-year-old Know-it-all," I concede, ruffling his hair to annoy him.

"I'm nearly thirteen."

"And you're eighteen," Ruzi butts in. "Happy belated!"

"Thanks, Ruzi." I pull the ribbon of my necklace out to show them. "I got your gift. I love it."

"Things will get better for you soon, my girl – I've a feeling in my bones." He gives me a wet-eyed look. "Eighteen already," he murmurs sentimentally.

Too soon it's time to hug them goodbye. We still have to buy a few supplies and be back at the Castle Hotel by the end of Sting's lunch, in time for Nezza's treatment. I squeeze Zako till he squirms and then attack Ruzi just as hard.

"Shall I come and see you out?" Ruzi asks.

"No, stay with Zako," I tell him.

"We'll write," Zako promises.

I walk away, shutting the door quietly behind me. *Is this the last time I'll ever see them?*

*

Wist spots me the moment I come down the stairs, but I can see he's nearly finished a full pint. An empty plate sits beside him.

I can hear Nezza and Daruunlis laughing loudly up on the mezzanine. I've looked after Nezza for four weeks and never made her laugh. Except once when I spilled a scalding cup of fikka over my lap. She cackled, then. This isn't a mean laugh like that, or even a sweet tinkling giggle, but a proper belly laugh.

When I reach them, she has her head flung back, her mouth still has a child's gumminess, teeth small, sharp, gappy. Daruunlis has been pulling faces, narrating some tale, but I exchange a quick glance with him. He's spotted it too. A strange glint in her top row of teeth. Her milk teeth still haven't fallen out, but she's got at least one of her first permanent molars growing in behind them.

It's coming in amber.

"All right," I say. "Who's ready to buy beautiful shoes?"

My heart is pounding. If Sting finds out, what might he do? Carve her open to check her skull? Even Daruunlis, usually so careful to keep his expressions in check, looks worried.

"Why is this happening?" I hiss at him as we leave. "I thought the butterfly treatments were nonsense."

"It's nothing to do with that medicine," he says with total confidence. "That's all you need to know."

"No, it bloody isn't!"

But he won't tell me more.

I push the panic down. We take Nezza to buy shoes and then for orange ice, amber crushing amber.

Wist leans on a wall over the road, keeping us in his sights but not close enough to listen to us. He doesn't want any orange ice.

His loss. It's delicious. Crackling cold and rich and blissfully distracting. I let my senses focus purely on the moment, the sensation in my mouth, the spreading numbness from the cold, the sweet and fresh and sour of the orange mingling in my mouth, pushing back against the heat of the day. I feel like a dragon of old, in reverse, breathing ice instead of fire. I wish I could have had it with Kit, like we planned.

They crush it with orange syrup, he told me. *Gracie won't shut up about it. Come there with me. I'll buy you one*. And he winked at me and assured me they'd sell to us, even a fancy place in the Mermens. He said the weather suited me.

"Does the Sciencemaster ever check your teeth, Nezza?" I ask her quietly.

"No."

"Well … don't … don't laugh in front of him. Or smile too much."

"Why?"

"It's … not polite for young ladies to show the insides of their mouths."

"Okay." She shrugs.

I tell myself she shouldn't have a problem with not

smiling at Sting. She's sullen as a stone around him. Worse than she is with me.

"This is important, Nezza." Daruunlis backs me up, softly, and I swallow down my lump of fear.

Wist peels off as we enter the foyer of the Castle Hotel. After being outside it's doubly awful to come back to this place.

The antiseptic but vaguely musty smell coming off the tiles leading on to the carpet here reminds me of the clinic where I stayed after Venor broke my hip.

I fancy I can hear the soft rattling of the spotted devils in their cages up in Sting's laboratory on the fifth floor. Of course I can't. Just like I can't smell that awful liquid he uses to pickle his dead specimens. Like squashed ants, rotting, burning-sharp and vinegar-sour. Wet copper and blood. Bone dust and misery. Underneath it all, that sweet awfulness. All that effort preserving dead things, and the decay perseveres.

"Nezza!" Sting is passing through the foyer. "Come along now. Time for your treatment."

Her shoulders hunch as she looks up at him and leans closer to Daruunlis. I want to catch her hand and pull her away, but my wants might as well be mist.

"You are so brave, *Ruahee*," Daruunlis tells her softly. I take her new boots up to our shared rooms, thread the laces and wait for her.

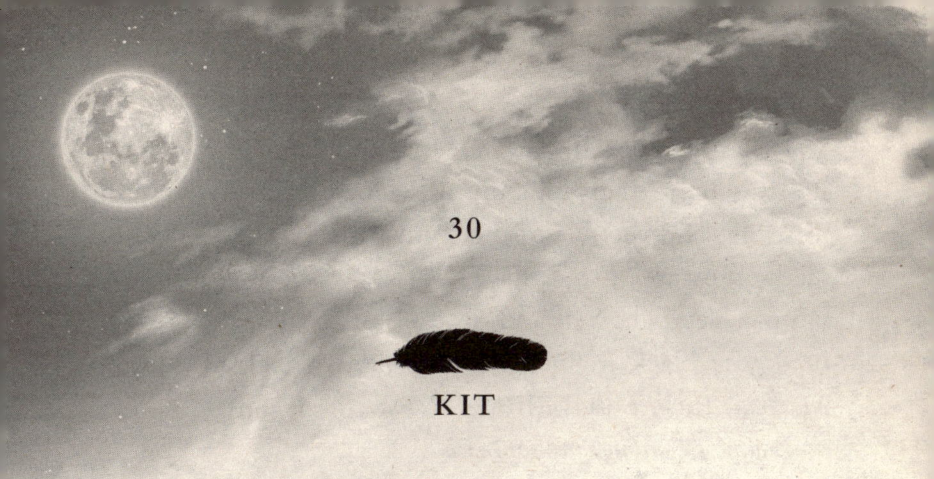

30

KIT

everything else

The salty water is warm as piss. This isn't my choice, but that's a kind of relief.

I sink under the swell, my promise still intact, the water soft as the hand of a goddess, wrapping around my body, pulling me to her breast. Soft like a shroud. I promised not to swim.

Did I promise to drown?

Damned if you do. Dead if you don't.

It's not as dark as it could be down here. The glowing underwater fish with their alluring lights are back, winking like mirrors as I hold my breath and sink. I disturb a shoal of finger-length, grey-green minnows that shatters in every direction, away, away.

I cast my thoughts about to try and will myself to focus on something that isn't about swimming or breathing or dying.

I see my father, like he was then. And my mother, like she was more than half my life ago. I open my mouth to speak, and the salt of the water fills it. The lights I'm seeing now aren't the fish. They're sparks going off in my brain. I need air. Salt and dead ghosts swim black in the not-quite-black water. *Terna, Kalqitlan*, says Dad's ghost. *Mazban, Ruahee*, says Mum's. *Reinac.*

Swim. Be strong, my soul. Live.

The gods know you don't break the spirit of the faith.

So I do as they say. I swim.

One movement trips into another and I break my promise to the gods, driving my sluggish, air-starved limbs as fast as they'll go, sweeping my arms in strong arcs, pushing back against the pressure and weight of all this water trying to bury me.

I feel like a boy again. I think I *am* a boy, until I break the surface, suck in a great lungful of sea air and let my chin rest over the waves. I can feel the water running through my beard.

I'm losing time. How fast is the time going?

Because I need more of it. I need to get back to Mora for a start. I focus on the air (sweet, salty, warm). But a new sea of confusion descends. I feel strong, if anything, stronger than I did just minutes ago, but I'm shot through with more kinds of terror than I can count.

I broke my promise to the gods. Now I will be punished. Somehow nothing feels real.

Half of me is still convinced I'm twelve years old again.

Fresh-inked, fresh-pledged to honour the gods, fresh through the ritual, my father's big hand round the back of my neck, steering me home.

I start to cough, trying to orient myself in the churn that the still-sinking *Toothsea Tear* is making, a froth of splintered wood and ash-overlain bubbles, smelling like a scrapheap on fire. Somewhere, wool burns. The other ship, the pirate outrigger, stands nearly still in its calmer waters. Used to the light of the lanterns now, I see its sail is folded down. I spot the launch, neatly stacked full of salvage, bobbing mid hubbub.

I take it all in with an odd detachment. I broke my promise.

I broke faith with the gods.

Pirates call to each other. Relaxed. High on their recent exertions. They paddle small vessels, hooking and grabbing what they can of *Toothsea*'s remaining floating cargo with long poles, attaching floats here and there and ushering trailing bouquets of soggy goods over to their outrigs. Caruq? I suddenly remember him. No sign of him. Mum? Dad? Them neither. No ghosts, old or new-made – unless I'm one. Suppose I could be.

I hear a noise like wavesong. Then all the noises grow muffled. I can't hear anything from my right ear. Has the water got into it? I swing out an arm to turn, still treading water, and I touch her eye.

The eye of the goddess. There she is, her head – and eye – half in, half out of the ocean, water still running down the glassy black mirror of it, big as a wagon wheel – bigger. A mirror ringed all round with rainbows, like the most beautiful pearl in the world. The source of the not-noise.

I know her right away. Macotl. The mother serpent. The main goddess. The biggest and the best one, and I'm poking her in the fucking eye.

It's not soft or wet. It doesn't have a feeling the way it doesn't have a sound. The eyes of the goddess take in everything, give out nothing.

My hand looks like Dad's hand. *No. I'm not twelve. I'm twenty.*

"Sorry. Sorry," I croak, spluttering water. My voice is deep – a man's voice. I'm falling back in time, back into the confusion. Then the pain begins.

The lightning is all over (inside me, on me, around me) like a promise vitrified and breaking. Broken. Bits of shattered promise sharp as fish scale arc through my veins, opening them, emptying them.

I scream in my man's voice and all the bits of broken promise fly out and start cutting up the world. Then other sounds come roaring back (everything is rushing, time speeding) and still, the pain is sharp.

Finally, it's receding. And so is everything else.

31

MORA

the headline

Like the greenest girl, I thought it was hot and sticky in the Castle Hotel, back in Portcaye. Now I know heat. Now I know air so warm and wet it might as well be fikka I'm breathing. I've ridden a summer storm at sea, seen whales that wouldn't fit in the biggest town square and now, perhaps, I have an inkling of how small my world has been.

Whales aren't like odd seals or big fish. Daruunlis says they weigh forty tons. They aren't like Sculpin's drawings. No. They're something all their own.

Now I've seen a wrecked ship. We're sailing right through it. Split boards slick with ragleaf-fuel rainbows the sea hasn't washed off. Other detritus gently bobbing. We've been delayed for days by poor weather, but the crew reckon we're nearly to Shipway harbour. Two more days. Sting is champing at the bit. We're cutting it close if he's to complete his experiments in time for the rendezvous with Lovemore.

"Is that a body? Try and hook it!" one sailor calls. I see a flash of pale, bloated skin, but it's gone before they can salvage it.

Unnervingly, we aren't very near the coast. It's not obvious what caused the wreck. No rocky shore scuppered it, not this far out.

I think of the last pod of whales we passed. Their size, their power. The threat of their big barnacled bodies, rolling and smacking their tails as they rode our wake. Did whales wreck that boat?

Or was it pirates?

Daruunlis joins me at the side of the boat. For all the long days of our journey, we haven't found much time to talk alone. All he's told me is Nezza's aunt will meet us at Hunger Canyons and spirit Nezza away.

"How will she know when to meet us?" I asked.

"I've sent her messages … telegrams," he said, though he still had that slippery-fish look about him.

Now I speak to him in soft Crozoni. "You told Nezza we didn't have to worry about pirates. Was that true or were you just saying it?"

"We don't have to worry about pirates."

She doesn't see the wreck or the body at least. She'd have to leave the windowless, airless cabin we share below decks for that. She'd rather stay there. I've tried to get her to come out, but she always resists.

"I don't want to go out," she'll say sullenly. Window or no, she'd rather be drawing or curled up in her hammock chatting nonsense to Minty.

She's been sheltered and secluded her whole life, closeted indoors. That's why being cooped up in the Castle Hotel didn't faze her. Why that day we went out into Portcaye she glued herself to Daruunlis like a limpet. Maybe it's hard to miss what you've never had.

Despite the threat of whales and monsters and pirates, despite the close confines, I can see why people choose a life on board. The ship cutting through a new piece of ocean every minute. There's no ground, or the ground's ever changing. Change is constant everywhere, but here you really feel it.

We sail into Shipway harbour one fine afternoon. It's the ninth of Eightmonth – twenty-six days after we left.

Three thousand miles south of Portcaye. It might be another world. A dry wind blows the smell of cut grasses and ragleaf fuel burning.

The sea's a dark bottle-green and the rocks in the harbour are crusted in barnacles looking like mouths. Everywhere near the tideline, thousands of mouths are singing a chorus not made for human ears. Singing or screaming.

The gulls here laugh as maniacally as they do everywhere else, but they're absolutely enormous.

Moments after we disembark, Sting is arranging the next stage of our journey.

"You – accompany me," he tells one of the guards. "The rest of you, escort the party straight to the station. Don't forget the luggage."

Wist secures a carriage and starts piling the cramped cages of spotted devils into the passenger cabin, while one of his colleagues hefts luggage up to the roof rack. Another carriage is secured. There's a lot of luggage. Nezza and I are trying to travel light, but Sting is a stickler for fresh, neat clothing. We have too many changes of clothes and too few personal items. And Sting had to bring his whole laboratory. All the spotted devils under different butterfly-medicine regimes, several cases of potions and paraphernalia he couldn't part with. Crates of butterflies, eggs and larvae. Hiramlan's bones are here somewhere, and the toys from his ruined coffin. Mister Cob's silverprinting equipment and materials aren't lightweight either.

"I will rejoin you at the Shipway train station before the train embarks," Sting tells Glor. "I must discuss *Dominion* with the old Master Engineer here before we travel on to Ridmouth." Sting's heart doesn't lie in shipbuilding, but as Lovemore's Sciencemaster General he's still expected to oversee *Dominion* since it's to be such a major scientific advancement.

"What do you know about *Dominion*?" I ask Daruunlis. They seem to be putting an awful lot of stock in a single ship. Curious.

"Not much." His lips twist. "I've heard Sting say it's to herald the beginning of a new generation of tall ship. Bigger, faster, more lethal. A ship with weapons to gild Lovemore's already golden reputation for brutal suppression." He frowns. "I'm sure he's keeping something up his sleeve though. He looks far too pleased with himself."

I shuffle along with everyone walking behind the carriages. My legs feel wobbly on dry land after so long pitching up and down. I suppose the station can't be far, or Glor would have insisted on taking a carriage too.

The town is lively, full of children – and down by the waterfront I'm astonished to see some metal frames, swings dangling off them. A small public playground. I didn't think the Skøl went in for frivolous fun for the masses.

We trudge past the Harbour-master's office. A fancy old Crozoni building with a square bell tower. Only three of its four decorative finials are in place. A fat gull perches where the fourth would be, dwarfed by the real finials, despite its impressive size.

A SAILOR'S LIFE IS GOLDEN, one sign says. JOIN THE MERCHANT NAVY. A girl nearby is selling papers, calling out news in a sweet, clear voice. A divine smell of grilling corn drifts by. Nezza pulls on my arm.

"I want some! Can we get some?" she says, followed immediately by, "We're getting some!" to Minty as I reach for my saggy pouch of coin and Minty chitters from where she's wearing him in a pocket sling strung round her neck.

Daruunlis is looking over at the paper-seller, a strange

interest rippling his default-bored mask. "What was the ship your fella was sailing on called?" Daruunlis asks me as the corn's handed over. I got one for him too.

"*Toothsea Tear*," I tell him. Then I see the headline.

32

MORA

he's going

Toothsea Tear wreckage found

My mind combs back through the words of the girl calling the news from the general hubbub. *Tear as in paper, not tear as in cry*, is my mind's first, absurd thought.

"*TOOTHSEA TEAR* … DROWNED. PROVISIONS AND TRADE GOODS WORTH TWO HUNDRED THOUSAND KRUNAN LOST WITH THIRTY CREW AND FIVE PASSENGERS! LATEST VICTIMS OF THE PIRATE SCOURGE! READ ABOUT IT HERE! ALL ON BOARD ARE PRESUMED DROWNED…"

No. No. The word loses meaning as it flies around my head. *No, Kit isn't drowned.*

"ROSCLAW VOWS TO TACKLE THE PIRATE

SCOURGE, AS *TOOTHSEA TEAR* FAMILIES DEMAND COMPENSATION! ROSCLAW INSISTS LOVEMORE FAILS TO PROTECT US!"

A hand circles the top of my arm. Daruunlis's bony fingers trying to move me on. No.

My legs have stopped in front of the paper-seller.

"Are the passengers named in there?" I ask her.

She shakes her head. "Harbour-masters has a list of the drowned."

The rest of our group has continued after the carriages. But there's still a guard behind Nezza, Daruunlis and I. Wist, I realize, the one with the ice-blue eyes. He's expressionless now.

"No," I hiss at Daruunlis as he tries to pull me away again. "Stop it. I need to know—"

"I'll try and find out for you."

Wist walks over to us. "What's the hold up?" His eyes flick to me and pause, registering my distress. His forehead furrows. "What's going on?"

I'm not going to cry here, but something's choking me, running down the back of my throat.

"Mora, what's the matter?" Nezza's high voice is pitched with the same concern I see on Wist's face.

I can't bring myself to speak. Daruunlis, from the other side of the guard, says something to Nezza I can't hear. He turns to me, his voice growing harsh. "If he's lost, he's lost. If he's not, he's not. There's nothing you can do about it."

His angry voice moves me. I stumble on, my heart twisting. *If he's lost, he's lost.*

Now I can't hear anything. Just a shrieking, circling panic. All the barnacle-lined rocks hissing and screaming.

How many times in my eighteen years have I wanted to give in to grief? I can't count. Lately, my griefs have sunk – not away, but deeper down. It's been a while since one of them slid to the surface to slap its ten-ton tail. Now I'm underwater with them all. *Did I neglect you? Did you need to send a new emissary? No.*

The more mystery you fathom, the more mystery lies below. Is that one of Ruzi's sayings? I can't remember.

I don't break down. It's never been allowed. I can't scratch and squall until I look as raw on the outside as I feel underneath. And this feeling is so new I won't call it grief. I won't weep. I can't breathe. I don't know how my feet arrived here on the platform of the Shipway train station, when my heart is plummeting, sinking, lost at sea.

"He's on the list. Kalqitlan," Daruunlis says.

I look away from him, like if I don't see him, he won't be here with his news.

"I'm sorry," he says softly.

Don't be, I think. *There's been some mistake.* "He can't be the only person with that name," I say calmly.

"He was registered as a passenger. His fare was purchased by a Golden Reedstone."

Goldie. Were the Reedstones on that boat too?

I don't care. I can feel tears threatening again but I won't allow them.

"Take your time," he says. He hands me a newspaper. "I'll stay with Nezza."

I try to read the report of *Toothsea Tear*'s disappearance.

A pirate attack. No survivors this time, though others have been lucky. They quote the survivor of a similar attack last year. *Their ship is like a demon. It sails under some strange magic. Goes where the winds don't take it…*

On the train I don't remember boarding, I share a small cabin with Nezza. She dangles her feet off the top bunk as she brushes Minty's fur, then lies down to sleep before I can nag her. I shut her out, shut myself out and stare at the purple-black nothing out the window. The bruise this train trundles through, loud and uncaring. Good to have another noise beside the ringing panic in my ears.

I pray. I know this isn't what prayer should be. You shouldn't be angry when you pray, should you? You shouldn't show the gods and the ghosts your whole hand. Thea knows. Thea the Bringer, Crozoni goddess of bounty. The gods know. The ancestors know. They know when you're desperate and begging you'll take any tiny sliver and give everything in return. Eternal faith, love, devotion. Praying shouldn't feel like this.

Kit drowned. Kit gone. Kit promising me he'd be back. *I'll be back before you know it… Mor, look at me. The job's less than eight weeks, travel and all.*

Daruunlis comes, bearing a drink. Not fikka – some

other infusion, heavily honeyed, to help me sleep. I take a sip. He looks at Nezza sleeping. He leaves.

Tears overflow. My nose is going like a tap but I'm trying to be quiet. I sob into a blanket.

Outside there's nothing but the hot bruise. Inside I sense others on the train – dimly bumping or shouting. Nezza cries out and sits up in her high bunk abruptly, her head hitting the train roof. She lies back down again, still asleep. "No, I don't want to!" she cries, but when I stand to look at her, she's asleep again. I think I hear someone else crying, but it might be my ears ringing. My own echo.

At some point the only sound is the train, this great iron, untiring creature rushing through the night. I leave the cabin, the door gliding smoothly in contrast to my stiff arms and legs. I walk back down the carriage, even as the train carries me forward fifty times faster. Back I go into the past while life carries on as it pleases. *Now's the only time to live, Mora. Does no good to wallow in the could-a-bins like me.* Ruzi's words float up in my head.

The door between this carriage and the one behind is heavy, but not locked. I get it open a crack and it rips out of my hand to fly full wide. I stand unmoored, letting the noise and the wind rush around me like water. The *thump thump thump* a blur, as if the monstrous heart caged in this vast iron creature beats as fast as Minty's, huge and immortal.

I feel heavy enough to fall. I could join them. Ma and Pa. Enca and Eben and Char. Our cousins. Our friends.

I'll-be-back-before-you-know-it Kit. Of course he got on that boat to come back. He kept his promise to me. He was coming back to me.

Nezza in her bunk floats up in my mind. Asleep. Who's ever promised her anything? I pull the ribbon of my necklace and feel the glass lozenge of the pendant Ruzi sent for me, press it into my ribs. Beneath it, my heart thumps wetly, sodden as a sponge.

When I draw my timepiece, stone heavy, from my pocket, it's stopped. The hands point to just before midnight. How long ago was that? The poles holding up the telegraph lines fly past, lonely black sentinels in the low, rolling landscape, watching the sleepers pass beneath the train, oblivious, bearing its great iron violence and sleeping still. The noise is deafening, tunnelling under my ribs where it lulls and lulls and I rock on my feet imagining someone is rocking me.

I must be iron too.

To go on without Kit, I will be iron. He wouldn't want me to give up. I can't help it if I feel life wrapping around me like chains. I'll do my time.

The view mesmerizes, until a flash of lightning in the distance snaps me back just as a man's thick arm covered in pale hair snakes around my waist, twists me away from the door then releases me. It's one of the guards. It's Wist.

He pulls the door shut, scooping in the wind and the noise, the great iron heartbeat, before he barks a stern one-word warning. "Dangerous!"

I must look a fright. His expression turns soft, about to say more. Then he shakes his head. "Get to your bunk."

I stumble back to the narrow cabin where Nezza still sleeps and lie down on the space below hers.

The rush and roar feels distant. The ringing in my ears is sinking. I'm drifting, not into sleep, but somewhere else.

Kit's here. He sees me sitting in the shadows. I stand. I've been so worried about him and now all anxiety is drifting away like mist, leaving anger. How dare he worry me like that? Cold fury floods me.

"There you are!" he says.

"Where have you been*?" I shoot back.*

He holds out a hand, strangely formal. "Walk with me?"

My anger drains. We pass the houses and the fish market, shut for the night, then duck through the small door inside the southern gates one at a time to follow the path to the sea. It's shorter than usual, like we're moving impossibly fast, forward along an iron line. Everywhere is deserted. We might be the only people in the world, but I barely notice.

We sit beside one of the bonfire sites, already stacked with fresh wood. I feel strange and self-conscious. Kit heaps sand into a small collapsing mound over a flat piece of driftwood, like something at the bottom of an enormous sand timer.

"Shall I light the fire?"

I don't want him to. "You won't see the stars with a fire going." It's easier to feel we belong when it's dark.

"See you though, won't I?" He has a box of matches in his

pocket, and the breeze is gentle. The fire takes after a few tries. I poke it with a stick until he reaches out to fold a hand around mine. The contact takes up most of my brain now, but I still feel him looking at me.

I look at the firelight flickering over his face.

"You're still alive," I say. "Aren't you?"

"Still alive." His expression says more than his few words. I feel myself igniting like the stack of firewood, low in my belly. His fingers stroke the top of my arm. I run mine down his left forearm, spinning the beads wrapped around his wrist.

Alive, alive, alive, *pulses the sea up the shore.*

He hauls me easily into his lap. Then his mouth is near my cheek, soft stubble-framed lips caressing my neck, near my jaw, light but possessive.

His scent, his thighs and hard chest and the warmth pouring out of him are all turning me weak. Desire leaps, burning between us like invisible flames as our mouths meet. I have to be closer to him. I want to say something clever about being alive and proving it, but then I'd have to break from the kiss. My thoughts are dissolving on the track between my brain and mouth.

"What are we… What shall we…?" I finally manage.

His arms fit perfectly snug around me, our hearts knocking a fervid rhythm together.

His lips brush the edge of my ear as he breathes – "I want whatever you want."

A slow burn spreads through me.

"You. Now." I tell him, before I lose my nerve.

"Done," he whispers back as he draws me closer. His fingers tangle in my hair, tugging it gently. I tilt my head to meet his kiss.

I help him out of his shirt, fumble with his belt. I hardly notice my own layers coming off. I forget to feel self-conscious about my clothes, abandon them tangled with his in a pile in the sand. Lying there beside him, his hands, so warm, still learning parts of me they haven't touched before.

I didn't expect this measured control. I completely abandon myself to his touch, clinging to his arms, his shoulders, his head, all my pointless self-doubt crumpling, quietly drowning. I've never felt so vulnerable or so desperately alive.

The weight of his body against mine, the warmth. A thousand thrills like water arcing up my spine.

There's something important I should ask him – but later.

"I love you." He says it like the answer to a question. But that isn't my question.

He's so open already, like this, like a letter I could read all the words of him. Read him with a touch. Turn him over and examine all his sides. I could taste him. Later. Now desire overrides, climbing, clambering between us, desperate. His touch. His skin under mine. He draws me closer, higher, higher.

His voice is thick with emotion, a whisper near my ear. He's too careful. It should be obvious how much I want every part of him, but still he hesitates, as if I'll break.

"I need you," I tell him. He understands. I gasp. A fullness, our feelings meeting and amplifying like two waves adding together.

"Are you okay?"

The sounds I'm making should say as much. I cling to him

tighter, here where I want him, giving and taking. Feelings rise between us, raising me like the tide. They're strange and new, old and familiar at the same time.

Later, we're in the ocean. "Are you supposed to swim?" I murmur. For some reason I feel worried, but I'm not sure why.

"I wasn't, but … that doesn't matter now," he says.

I relax, boneless as a jellyfish. It's still dark but it's summer. It's so warm, as if the noon sun has heated it. He's warmer still beside me, like a furnace.

The fire's down to low embers. It's simple. All the long days and nights I spent without him, wondering how this would feel, to be with him and have nothing but want between us. Not a scrap of clothing, not a task, not an argument, not a place we have to be. Not a question.

All those fears I had. What were they? I don't try to remember. He rolls to look at me. Gods, his eyes. I could float on my back in them. The sun is hovering on the horizon, like it's rising or setting. It must be rising. Or it's stopped like my timepiece.

I don't feel tired.

I trace some fingers lightly down his face, his shoulder.

I felt his new scar earlier and now I see it. It's down his right arm and passes on to his back, a chaotic unfurling of fern leaves or silver fronds of moss, branch over branch. It's shiny like frost. It mars his vocifer tattoo, but somehow it fits.

"What's this?" I ask him.

"Goddess burned me."

"When?"

My own question upsets something in me. I feel oddly thrown.

He doesn't answer.

"Are you okay?"

"Never been better." He gathers me into his arms.

Back on the sand, we lie chest to chest. Out here by the water we're exposed, but I feel completely secure with him – safe in a way I haven't felt before.

Do we sleep? A rattling sound. His belt buckle? No, it's something rhythmic. The sea breaking like a fist on the rocks. Broken glass filling the sea, tinkling against the stones of the shore. A thundering noise, a train thrusting forward.

I sit up, groggy, trying to brush the sand from my clothes. I'm wearing clothes again.

"I'm coming for you," Kit says. "I'll get you out. Wait for me."

"No, wait." I hold his hand. "I want you to know—"

"I know," he says. "But don't tell me now. Tell me when we're together."

"We're together now."

I can't see him properly. He's going.

33

KIT

numb for ever

Endweek, Eightmonth 7th. Still at Sea.

"Did you break his pretty nose?" A man's voice, speaking Crozoni.

"Wasn't me." A woman. Something hard touches my face, tilts it. "No. It's just a bruise."

I know that voice. The woman with the two-sectioned staff. My heart pounds as I try to pry my eyes open. They're gummed shut.

"My, my," says the man. "He's still a toothsome one."

"Calm down, Dell Garen." The woman (smirk in her voice).

"You wouldn't say no though, would you? Catch of the day." His voice is mocking.

I squeeze my eyelids together and finally pull them open, curling away from the foot in my side.

"… morning, stranger. Wakey-wakey," says the woman.

The sun's coming up with a weird wobble and the world shimmers like it's wet. Must be my eyes. I'm aboard the pirate outrigger. My clothes are damp.

The shreds of my mind wave around like the tentacles of blind, underwater creatures, trying to snare meaning.

My clothes are in tatters, charred and torn, one sleeve completely gone. There's a dull ache behind my eyes, a searing one down my right arm, and the woman is in front of me. Tall, angry, barefoot.

She's leaning on her staff and eating something (fruit? A bun?). It disappears too fast for me to know. She rubs her hands on her trousers.

"Welcome back." The southern flavour in her accent is charming, but her tone is flat (I feel distinctly unwelcome).

She sticks a hand out and I give her my left one. She hauls me effortlessly up until I'm sitting. Her palm is soft, skin cool, uncalloused, unblistered. Not the hand I'd expect for someone who uses a staff like I've seen her using it. After last night, I'd expect at the very least a blister or two.

"I – where are we?" I wring a few drips from my shirtfront. My throat is hoarse, voice crackly. I'm still coming back to myself, memories trying to reassemble but ending up like a locking mechanism, clogged with sand.

I know I'll be … twenty-one this year. I know my

name. Kalqitlan. I know I was on *Toothsea Tear*, a Skøl trader bound for Portcaye. For Mora. The thought of her sends a shiver down to my toes. Worry and anticipation.

Beyond the ship I can only see sky and sea. I feel heavy, stuck, small (a bug on display), pinned between the big, deep ocean and the bigger, deeper vault above us.

"This is *Three Sisters*," the woman says, with more than a hint of proprietary pride.

Three Sisters is nothing like a regular tall ship. No heavy dark wood, no right angles or forest of masts trailing clouds of red sails. No rowdy crew of pallid brickheads who think you're mud on their boots.

Old *Toothsea Tear* didn't stand a chance. Must have sailed ten times ten thousand miles only for these people to punch a hole in it and watch it burn down in an hour.

Three Sisters is gorgeous though, light like we're floating on air. The woman's simple, stark beauty matches it. A heron's beauty (still, sleek, waiting to strike).

She's painted pink-orange in the morning glow. I think for a disorientating second she's behind me as well as in front of me. These gluey eyes are playing tricks on me. My neck on the right side is sore like my arm. I don't want to turn round.

Snap, snap. The pretty, printed awning stretched half over us flaps in a warm breeze. Crozoni cloth on a Xan outrigger of yore (a ship from a storybook, magnified).

The float we're riding is big as a house. Steps lead down a hole to its dark insides. Behind that access a mast juts out at a jaunty angle, its single huge sail hanging cupped like a hand round a warm wind dragging us along.

The woman folds herself down to sit in front of me, draping her smooth two-sectioned staff like a pet over her crossed legs. I think of Caruq and *Toothsea*'s little barrel dog, Cinbar.

"My hound," I say. "The hounds—" And even as the words tumble out, I know, somehow, that they're nearby, aboard.

"They're here," she confirms, rapping her knuckles on the main section of her staff. It's about as tall as her, straight and off-white. I focus on it to try and avoid thinking of the strange new assaults breaching my senses, cracking them open like eggs.

Her staff. Breathe. In and out. I imagine a flicker of flame and blow it out, see its last puff of smoke curling away. Both the long and short sections of her staff are made of an oddly grained wood. The smaller piece is about half a foot long, attached to the top by a silver chain. It flew loose when she was using it as a weapon. Now it's secured to the main piece by an amber-coloured clasp, part-buried in the wood at the top of the longer section, shaped like a letter C.

The amber clasp must be what I saw glowing last night. It must be that clasp she drove (variously) into throats, cheeks, eyes and chests of *Toothsea Tear* crew. It seems absurd, here, in the light of the morning with the whole thing gleaming, freshly cleaned. Did this heron woman really kill all those seasoned sailors? I swallow down a wave of something – stomach acid and seawater – that threatened at the back of my throat.

"What's a specimen like you doing on a Skøl trade ship?" Her tone is light. The word *Skøl* sends reverberations though me. *The Cull*, I think, like an echo of fizzing guns. One-in-ten. *Eyes like cold blue water.*

"Not many get the privilege," says the man, still behind me. His voice sounds different to the man in Shipway, but then he walks in front of us, and it's him. His voice in town was a put-on, like her eyepatch.

He's glowing in the sunrise and his amber eyes have odd dark flecks, like tarnished copper coins. His square head and neck look angry, his broad chest boxy. He wears his hair longer than most Crozoni, but he still frowns down at me with that superior look Crozoni face muscles seem to favour. A natural scowl. A short sword swings from a scabbard at his hip. I recall seeing him last night, plunging it into people.

"What's happening?" I try again.

"Let's start easy." The woman ignores my question. "I'm Pony." She gestures at the man. "This is Dell Garen. And you are?"

"Kalqitlan," I tell them.

"You're from up north."

Is that a question? "Portcaye."

"You're a long way from home, Kalqitlan." Dell Garen's tone is impatient.

"I have to get back there. I promised my friend." I feel panic rising at the thought of breaking another promise. "She's in trouble. Her boss is dangerous. I have to help her."

"Well, Portcaye isn't on the route, Kalqitlan. And you're in no state to ride to anyone's rescue. You just took a few bad knocks." She gestures at my face, my arm. I look down at it. It's red, raw and weeping.

"You remember what happened?" Dell Garen asks. "The lightning?"

I broke my promise. I touched her eye. "I don't remember."

"We saw it," the woman, Pony, says. "Clear as day."

"I don't remember," I insist.

"You fell beside the hull in its death throes. Should have dragged you down with it."

"Then the lightning show started," Dell Garen says.

"Underwater lightning." Pony shakes her head. "Only lasted a few moments. Ten minutes later he finds you floating on your back, peaceful as a babe."

"Thought you were dead," Dell Garen offers in a dry tone. "But worth checking for valuables." I don't like his expression. "You're welcome," he adds, when I only stare back at him. He has to fill the silences. I know his type. Full of hot air.

I make a show of patting my pockets, though I know they're empty. "Did you find any?"

"No."

My papers are gone, then.

"Seems you came empty-handed. Except for the hounds."

Dell Garen folds his thick arms and moves so he's standing at Pony's back, beside the sun, not blocking it. All the way to the eastern horizon is ocean. How far are we from land? I can't see his face properly in the pink glow, the disc of orange breaching the horizon is too dazzling. Half a circle, half over, half under the world.

I scrub my good hand down the side of my face, feigning more tiredness than I feel, and look around. We're alone on this raised platform crowning the central body of the boat. I know there's more crew down inside though. I don't know how I know it, but I do.

I look down, and somehow, through the boat, I can see Caruq and Cinbar, huddled together. It's not seeing them, exactly, more like sensing them. And on the float to my left there are several other creatures, bigger than dogs, bigger than people. What a wretchedly disorientating amount of information I seem to have flying at me. Besides Pony and Dell Garen, I know there are fourteen other pirates on *Three Sisters* – spread unevenly across the three floats. I feel their lives.

One thing is clear. Something has changed me.

I feel life. Everywhere, uncountable, winking away in all directions like stars. Clustering here, flitting there. I hear life, but it's not a sound.

It's like my arm's fallen asleep and I'm wriggling my fingers and it's waking up, tingling. A dead limb, returned.

A pinched nerve, released. A sense I never knew was there, dormant, now rising. It's prickling now the sensation's flooding back. I can feel it rushing over me like the hot blood returning.

A new plane of feeling I never knew I was missing and now I know if it goes away, I'll feel numb for ever.

34

KIT

faintly glowing

“Horses!” I blurt, realizing what those other big animals are on the float to the left. “You’ve got horses.”

Pony and Dell Garen swap a wide-eyed glance.

“When did you see that?” Pony asks.

I’m still reeling, so I just look at her.

“You can sense them, can’t you?” Pony says slowly. “How many horses are there?”

“Six horses,” I say. “Fourteen people. Seventeen including us. Two hounds. One rat. Several mice.”

“A rat! A rat on *Sisters*?” Dell Garen’s scowl deepens.

“You always lived in the north, Kalqitlan?” Pony asks. I nod. “You’re not some long-lost cousin I never heard of?”

I don’t understand her question, so I don’t answer. “Where’s the rat?” Dell Garen wants to know.

“Near the horses.”

"Must've come from that tall ship. Bloody infested, they are." He shakes his head at Pony. "Told you we should get a cat."

She's still sitting opposite, focused on me. "Do you have an amber ancestor? An Alit-fel in your family?"

I shake my head. "What's an amber ancestor? Alit-fel?" *God-cursed?*

She leans closer, her head tilts to mine. Her eyes are bloodshot and there's a faint scar on the side of her nose.

"Did you … break a sacred promise to the gods?"

I take a breath. Blow out an imaginary candle even as I see flame engulfing a ship, the ocean and the fire scrapping over it like hounds at a carcass. I see myself fall. I see myself swim.

"Yes," I tell her. "I promised I wouldn't swim. More than … eight years ago. But then I had to."

"You must have really loved to swim." She purses her lips. Her eyes are sad.

I blink and look away.

"So, we're in a bit of a predicament, here, Kalqitlan-of-the-north," she says. "You need help. Luckily, I know who might give it."

It's nice, the way she says my name, adds a little extra. Dell Garen scowls anew.

"Wait. *He* is in a predicament. We're not. Why is he our predicament?" Dell Garen hisses.

"You fished him out. Now you want to throw him back?"

"You want to take him with us? To see *her*?"

"No. But what else can we do?"

They both turn and look at me.

She rights her staff and uses it to bounce to her feet. Dell Garen reaches a hand down to me. "Up with you," he says.

The sun is a full circle above the horizon now, but the sky is still more pink and orange than blue and grey. Pony and Dell Garen still glow with it. I try to dredge more sense from my uncooperative skull, but I'm distracted by life.

I feel everything that wakes with the sun and slumbers in the deep.

Birds, fish and other things, large creatures. Tiny creatures, shining away and away into the distance. Trees, forests, plants, seaweeds, calm and rooted, or holding fast. Everything alive is glowing, but not with light.

I don't see them, but I *know.* As if everything is unfolding in another reality, just next to this one, just underneath it.

"Let's get you cleaned up before we make any rash decisions," Pony says. "Take him to the guest room."

"Come on," Dell Garen tells me, leading me down some worn wooden steps inside the boat.

It smells like sea and sun, even down here. We reach a chamber strung with half a dozen hammocks holding patterned cloth blankets, suspended at intervals. "Men sleep in here," he informs me. The room is empty. "We rise early," he answers my non-question.

He passes me a cleanish shirt and some trousers like his.

"Do you want to wrap that arm up or leave it to the air?"

"Leave it."

"Follow me."

We head down further into the guts of the ship. I try to focus on the clothes he's given me (they're an odd southern style), not on the fact we're indoors, out of the pretty morning sunrise and yet he's still faintly glowing.

35

KIT

without delay

What they call the guest room has no window, and its door locks from the outside. Locks don't faze me. When I want to get out I will. I'm content to be here for now. My head needs to settle.

It's not like being ill. I've no dizziness or fever. I don't feel tired or nauseous or weak. The pain in my arm and hand from touching the goddess, that pain has already dimmed. But everything is fucking weird.

I strip the remains of my shirt off. I can't see the damage over my back, though I feel it there. If it looks anything like my arm, it's not pretty. Or maybe it *is* pretty, in a horrible sort of way. The lightning strike, if that's what it was, has left a patterned mark down the arm, like whirls of moss or fern branches, a splash of red frost.

But the red weeping is already stopping, replaced by

a tightness, like the whole thing's drying out, starting to heal. Salt water does that, but not this fast.

I strip off my damp trousers and put on the dry clothes. I'm not cold, but it's nice not to see the mess of my arm.

I sit on the bunk trying to settle my new sense. I'm able, a few hours later, to sense someone coming (two someones – no, four) before they're anywhere near the door. It's Pony and Dell Garen, with Caruq and Cinbar.

Pony leaves the door open. She still carries her staff. She's also got a bowl of porridge. Dell Garen hovers behind her as she steps inside.

I know things about them both.

I know that Pony wants me to trust her. Her glow is still hard to read but I feel that. And there's something different about her. Some quality to her glow none of the other people on this boat have. I don't know if it's good or bad.

Dell Garen's glow is just plain worried.

"You're healing fast." Pony squints at my wounded arm, patting Caruq, pain-free.

"Yes." I've been quick to heal ever since the ritual I did when I was twelve, but this is even faster.

"Got you this." She passes me the porridge.

"Thank you." My stomach's flat to my spine but I don't feel hungry. I put the bowl on the bed. Pony flicks a meaningful thumb at Cinbar.

"She'll have it if you don't. We have fed her – she's eaten way more than this other one."

Her glow still looks hungry. "She's welcome to it,"

I say, putting it on the floor and petting the wiry fur on her shoulders. "That good, Cinbar?"

"Kalqitlan," Pony says. "We're heading to Hunger Canyons. Have you heard of it?"

I nod. "I've just … come from there. A few days ago."

"Didn't she find you? I'm sure she would have tried to. The old bird."

"Yes." I nod, thinking of the woman I met in the night. "I met her. She invited me into a cave. Think she wanted me to stay."

"Why didn't you?"

I look at her round face. "Would you have?"

"I'm not invited."

"So I gathered. I'm not interested in joining something like that." *Pure Xan blood only.*

She looks at Dell Garen, brows raised. He shrugs.

"Well, it's important you see her now," says Pony. "Urgently."

I try to remember what the old woman said – she did mention my promise, said something about how if I struggled, I had to find her.

"*Three Sisters* can't get you all the way." Dell Garen pats the wooden doorway. "But you can take one of the horses overland. Get there in time."

"In time for what?"

Pony steps closer. "Look, Kalqitlan, when you made that promise, all those years ago, did they tell you what would happen if you broke it?"

"No."

"Well, they should have. It's not good."

"How not good?"

"Usually the instant your promise dies, so do you. Almost every time, that's what happens."

"Hmm…" I give them a hopeful gesture. "So, if I broke it and didn't die, that's good?"

"No." Pony shakes her head. "It's worse if you don't die."

"Oh." *Worse than a quick death, perfect.*

"Your only hope is to complete a counter-ritual to beg a place with Naqramaree. If he won't accept you, you'll end up serving Seff. Do you understand? I don't want to scare you, but well – I'd be scared. If you fall into this damnation, you won't come out again. You have … a matter of days."

I sense she believes what she's telling me, but do I believe it?

"The crone you met," she says, "she serves Naqramaree. She knows how to carry out the ritual that could save you. She's gone through this herself and she lived. We just have to get you to her without delay."

36

MORA

protest

It's midweek, the tenth of Eightmonth. Five more days until Sting's rendezvous with Lovemore and we've arrived in Ridmouth – a small settlement with an empty feel. The red soil surroundings look fit to swallow it down in one gulp. Sprigs of low scrub stick up like patchy fur on a mangy fox.

I've left my cap off and tied my hair with a ribbon. It's too hot for those awful bonnets. Sting is too occupied with other things to scold me. We pass along the sleepy thoroughfare. Just one road, flanked by low houses and simple structures. The heat gives a hazy wobble to the rocks in the distance.

I'm trying to take in the town, but I keep flashing back to that dream. Kit. The ways he made me feel. I didn't know to imagine some of those things, so how did I dream them? It felt so real.

I watch a bird on a high thermal. A bird of prey. A vocifer? My eyes fill with new tears.

Nezza is unimpressed with Ridmouth. She sticks by Daruunlis, scuffing her feet. She'll ruin her new shoes.

This grief is not like my other griefs. This loss is playing havoc with my memory.

I saw them kill Char, my little brother, in the Cull. There was a time those images would draw themselves over my waking mind, like a projection from one of Sting's lantern slides, impossibly captivating. Memories I couldn't look away from.

They don't fade, but the appalling feeling becomes, I suppose, somehow less of a shock. I hate that it does, but there it is.

I didn't see Kit die. I cling to that hope still – that the papers are wrong. Surely I would know.

There's a bad smell to Ridmouth, but I only half register it. We're to stay one night at a rarely used branders outpost – a single-storey complex of thirteen rooms. It's a far cry from the Castle Hotel, but it seems to be the only place for strangers to stay in this tiny town.

A Skøl man, dressed in a tidy suit, is waiting for Sting in the common room at the front of the accommodation. "Welcome, Sciencemaster General." He bows.

"Mister Henslag," Sting greets him. "I understand all is going to plan?"

"Smooth as clockwork. *Dominion* is nearly ready…"

"Good," says Sting. He nods at the guards. "I will come to see it for myself now."

They depart. All my curiosity about Lovemore's ship, like all my care, is muffled deep, under heavy wool.

Nezza and I leave our luggage in the small room we're to share and go to feed and water the caged creatures stacked in the common room. Then Nezza draws in one of Sculpin's old books while I sit with my hands idle, hiding in memories. A familiar voice from outside, distant but approaching, pierces my fog.

"… Sacrifice, please. It was all a misunderstanding. It's not worth…" the voice is saying.

Sweet and musical, with an undercurrent of steel. *Goldie?* I sit up with a start. *Are the Reedstones here?* They should have been on that ship with Kit. I didn't ask Daruunlis to check the passenger list for them.

Sting, I can tell, is furious. "Trespassing … restricted … entering. Refusing to cooperate … certain obstruction … criminal damage … besmirched the family name…" I don't catch everything he's saying – his voice is muffled. But they're getting closer.

I get up to stand by the window.

"I'm telling you it's a terrible mix-up. Brack has got the wrong end—"

"Mix-up! Rubbish. I know one of your asinine schemes when I see it. Where's that brother of yours? Don't tell me he isn't involved too. I won't believe it."

"He's in Shipway town."

My heart beats faster, fear transforming to hope. If the Reedstones weren't on the boat, is there a chance that Kit wasn't either? Is he with Goldie, or Glister? Alive?

"I've half a mind to take you back and let you suffer the consequences of your perfidy in that cell. But for the memory of my father..."

I squash my nose to the window. Sting is there, berating Goldie. No Kit. But he might still be in town, or with Glister.

"You stink," snaps Sting. "When you're clean I'll decide what to do with you."

The guard at the door stands aside as Sting and Goldie enter. They pause outside the archway to the common room. Nezza is staring over the top of her book, round-eyed.

Goldie's eyes widen too when she sees me. Never have I seen her so dishevelled. Grease and tangles mar her silken hair. The skin on her face is red and blotchy, her eyelid creases black with old make-up and her hands are filthy with browny-orange dirt.

"I mean, what in the world did you think you were doing?" Sting is still lecturing. "You could have jeopardized one of the most expensive projects in history. The valves are delicate."

"I'm telling you, I was just curious, Sacrifice. I certainly wasn't going to sabotage anything! The accusations are false."

Sting huffs – unconvinced. "Enough," he snaps. "You

were intercepted in a restricted area and that is enough to warrant your arrest. Since I have been forced to vouch for your character – against my better judgement – you will stay with me until I can deal properly with this." He turns to the guard by the door, one of the surliest.

"No one leaves. Especially not her!" He points at Goldie, then his eyes land on me.

"Dezil! Show my cousin to the facilities and find her a place to sleep."

The guard behind him mutters something about all the rooms being spoken for.

He looks down his nose at Goldie. "You can stay with the children since you want to act like one. Go and wash." He looks back at me. "Where is your cap? Unkempt! Fix your appearance!" He shakes his head as he stalks away in the direction of his room at the back of the building. I can hear him muttering to himself, "Slovenly! Lackwit!"

"Mora?" Goldie whispers. "What are you doing here? Where's Kit?"

My breath catches. "He wasn't with you? Is he with Glister?" I whisper.

"No – he left us over a week ago, heading back your way. And you've come here!" Her teeth are still white and dazzling.

"He's dead." I push the words past the stone in my throat, admitting it aloud for the first time. Some new part of me fractures. I'm glass, cracking all over.

"What?" Goldie whispers. The smile drops off her face. A stone dropping into a pond. No. The reverse. The ripples disappear, back in time. The stone flies up to lodge deeper in my throat. The pond lies instantly flat, a shining, undisturbed sheet.

She wraps her arms around me, around the timepiece she gifted me that's nestled in my pocket, frozen. I haven't bothered to wind it since before the train.

Her cheek is warm.

She reeks like someone who's been sitting in a jail cell unwashed for days. They shaved Kit's hair when he went to jail. Of course she gets to keep hers.

Goldie Reedstone isn't my friend. I've plenty to blame her for. But now I cling to her like she might slow the cracks arrowing through me. She holds me too, just as tightly, and my tears flow.

When I come back to myself, Nezza is trying to draw and watch us. "Wait here," I tell her. I show Goldie the washroom and dig out some clean clothes.

"Were you trying to sabotage Lovemore's ship, then?" I ask later. She's pulling Nezza's brush through her wet hair in our tiny room.

She meets my eyes and nods. "It was a mistake. I should have run immediately. I might have gotten word to Clem. He still has no idea of the capabilities of this ship." She rubs her eyes. "Now I'm trapped here with no way of getting word out."

"Who's Clem?" I ask.

"Our contact in Shipway. He's County Shipway magistrate in fact, but he's working against Lovemore. He thought there was more to her new ship than weapons. He asked us to investigate. We didn't even know where the ship was – we thought it was still in pieces. Then we heard Lovemore herself was coming and asked Kit to take a message to Clem, to send people here to help. Kit took our message, and Clem sent us a man … but he wanted us to abandon the whole investigation. Said it wasn't safe. I couldn't just leave! I sent Glister and Blithe back to Shipway to reason with Clem. And then I found out what makes the ship so special and—" She stops speaking abruptly.

"And then you got yourself locked up."

"Yes. A terrible error of judgement."

"Why didn't Glister come and get you?"

"They didn't tell him." Her shoulders droop. "They kept me for days and told no one. Because I know how she plans to *reveal* her precious *Dominion* to the people." Her fists are balled at her sides, but she doesn't look particularly fierce, just anguished.

"What's so special about the ship?"

"I have to get word to Glister … to Clem."

"We're not allowed to leave here either," I remind her softly. She's used to moving freely through this world. Her cousin might have greased the right palms to get her out of jail in a heartbeat, but she's stuck with him now as surely as one of his stolen artefacts.

"I know," she says. "But her ship, Mora... Can you imagine why they've named it *Dominion*?"

"Tell me."

"Because it will give her dominion over everything. Land and sea. And air."

"*Air?*"

"It's no tall ship. And it's here, in the big building at the edge of town. Right under our noses. I've seen the blueprints in the office. Its weapons capability..." She resumes brushing her hair, swearing and tugging at a tangle, ripping out several strands. "I've seen the thing practically fully built. The roof opens and they'll inflate the balloon and float it out. They can fly it, full of vicious guards, anywhere. Lovemore will be able to put down any rally, any opposition, anything she defines as a threat – from a position of total dominance. It changes everything. Clem's planning a rally in Shipway town – it's no secret. Eightmonth the eighteenth. A festival in the street with children. But that's not what Lovemore is going to call it. I saw the telegrams. They described this as a riot-in-the-making that needs to be quelled. DOMINION *WILL TEACH THEM MANNERS*. She actually wrote that."

"But she can't just attack her own people?"

"Her branders attack ordinary people all the time. She's High Governor. She's never had power she didn't use. Temper Wilforn has her rattled and she lies like she breathes. She'll say she's done it for the greater good.

By then it'll be too late. The *Evening Gazette* will print whatever bollocks she tells them to. Quelling unrest or violent opposition or keeping the peace. I can see the headline: Dominion *Tempers Terrorists*. The truth doesn't matter to any of them. Clem has *no idea* this is coming for him."

She throws the hairbrush down and stifles a sob of rage.

We leave so early it's still cold as night. A convoy of three quick narrow boats, equipped with ragleaf-hungry engines turning propellors – no, they're waterwheels – on their backs, send us smoothly upstream at a pace.

We go against the flow. I gaze at the bridge suspended over the river. We leave it behind. A red iron web, ten times the size of any of our stone bridges in County Portcaye. *Kit must have liked it*, I think. *Kalqitlan*.

Mister Cob, Daruunlis and four of the guards are riding the narrow boat directly in front of ours, while Sting, his assistants and a pair of guards lead in the front boat.

I'm riding the cramped, rearmost of the three with a lot of the luggage, as well as Goldie, Nezza, Wist and a second guard.

I haven't talked to Wist about what happened on the train. I wasn't going to fall, or jump, if that's what he thought. That door would have been hard for me to close though.

Water travel doesn't agree with Goldie, but when she's feeling well enough, we play I spy with Nezza. Nezza trails her fingers in the water.

Night is falling as we reach Hunger Canyons, lanterns firing up. Beyond the river bend, bare, red-banded rock and packed dirt unroll. The land's rucked up like a thick blanket some giant hand has scrunched into hills and furrows. A red sea frozen in time.

The town occupies the flatter bank. Holes in the rock on the opposite side loom. I spot a few silhouettes in some, watching the sunset. A cave system. People living like the ancients.

There are rope bridges – no, bridges of vines – suspended over the river. Like and unlike the Skøl rail bridge downstream. Something tells me they're far older.

As the luggage and equipment is unloaded, I take in the town of Hunger Canyons. Its raw simplicity evokes deprivation, poverty and want. Goldie said that Kit came here. I wonder what he made of this last refuge for his people. When I scan the middle distance, I'm shocked to see horses grazing in the twilight. Are those donkeys?

I'm wobbly from the water, but doing better than Goldie, who's pale and miserable. Sting sets a relentless pace. Now we're close, he can taste his glory.

"Find me some workers at the old dig, yonder," he tells Daruunlis. "At least half a dozen, used to excavation – bones or clay."

After a terse negotiation, Daruunlis engages the services of a handful of Hunger Canyons men and bids them use some kine to port over luggage and some camp tents and tools from an older dig after us. That other dig, I realize, is where they found Hiramlan's grave.

Sting has the map to the Burial Circle folded in one of his notebooks. He opens it and the man leading the workers leans over with his lantern. It's full-dark now. It gets dark earlier, this far south.

"This is our ultimate destination – see those chimney rocks..." Sting points to some prominent rock formations in the distance that correspond with landmarks on the map. "Procure and bring the essentials – I will pay..." He bargains for camp comforts like containers of water and ragleaf fuel, food and a cook. The cook is Crozoni like the rest of the labourers.

In fact, there are fewer Xan around than I was expecting, given the reputation of this place.

"Let us tarry no longer!" Sting announces, and sooner than I imagined we're proceeding through and beyond the dimly lit town after him.

We pass ramshackle houses, built of materials worn by the elements, then past the fenced-in horses and other four-hoofed creatures in what seems to be a communal corral.

"Is the Burial Circle *really* here?" I whisper to Daruunlis as the space between us and the rest of our party widens. Nezza is behind, talking to Goldie about spotted devils. Part of me wonders if this is all one of Daruunlis's tricks.

"It's here." Daruunlis has been tight-lipped ever since we embarked on this mission. Now excitement ripples through him. "I didn't lie about that, I promise you. Though Sting may have to reevaluate some of his … hypotheses."

The lanterns bob ahead of us as we walk for about an hour. When we stop, the thick sprays of stars are partly hidden by wispy clouds, and the odd rock formations Sting called chimneys loom over us like waves. Smaller rocks with similar shapes dot the landscape, though the night makes it hard to see. The whole scene reminds me of a huge splash, frozen in time.

"How did these rocks end up here like this?" I ask Daruunlis. The amber bones lie between them, according to his map. They looked closer together when we were far away. They're separated by about twenty yards and so oddly weathered it looks almost as if they have heads sitting on necks.

"Different layers of rock. Underneath it weathers easily – up top it's more resistant."

"They look like they should tip over."

"Well…" He gives me a little smile. "You look like *you're* about to tip over, but you don't."

"What's that supposed to mean?"

"That you're strong."

A compliment from Daruunlis? I've pushed myself beyond

feeling. The grief, the exhaustion. But his words wash some of the numbness away.

"We dig at dawn," Sting informs everyone, eyes bright with anticipation. I'm half surprised he hasn't ordered us to work through the night. "High Governor Clarion Lovemore herself, our patron, will join us in four days!"

The guards and the local recruits work on setting up tents for everyone, close to the location. Tall, standing canvas set-ups. They don't strike me as particularly watertight, but then we aren't expecting rain. We eat camp food hauled upriver – tins of leaf-wrapped grain, beans in sweet sauce, potatoes baked in coals – and some river fish with delicate pink flesh caught locally.

"Have you had enough?" I ask Nezza. She nods and yawns.

"I'm sleepy," she tells me. A rare admission.

When I come back from taking our dishes and utensils to the cook-cum-cleaner, she's curled up on her side, already asleep, out here, on the soil.

She shifts in my arms as I carry her to the tent we're sharing with Goldie. She weighs a ton, but doesn't properly wake up, just buries her snuffling face into my neck and murmurs something about me being soft. Nonsense. *I'm iron, now, Nezza. I'm hard, like you.*

When I put her on her pallet and tuck a blanket around her, she pretends to stay asleep. Goldie sits outside, staring up at the sky, but I'm too exhausted.

Half an hour after I collapse under a blanket, Nezza's

sniffing. Perhaps she's heard my quiet crying. What a pair we make. "Goodnight, Mora," she whispers into the darkness.

"Night, lovely," I say, daring to use an endearment on her like Daruunlis does. She doesn't protest.

37

KIT

lend her speed

Firstday, Eightmonth 8th. Still at Sea.
Two of Pony's pirates are adjusting the sail trim to keep us on course, though the wind continues in our favour. We clip along at a pace. I follow Pony and Dell Garen over to the starboard float, where they're collecting something from the hold. A sort of tuber, like potatoes but yellower.

"So, what was it like, being favoured by the gods – before … you broke your promise?" Pony asks.

"I've healed from some bad injuries in the past," I tell them. "But I was never sure it was down to the promise."

"What sort of injuries?" Dell Garen asks.

"Falling from a height. Arrow in my side."

"What do their guns do to you?" Skøland's elektric guns kill most people with one (even indirect) shot.

"They burn me, but … they don't knock me out."

"Sounds like a gods' favour. There hasn't been someone like you in a century," Pony tells me as we work. "The Ralkalit Rites – that's the promise ritual you did – has been forbidden for years. You might be unique."

"The crone is like me, you said."

"Yes, but she's over a hundred. I mean, you're unique in our generation, in many generations, and we'd be fools not to help you. You could be another…" She stutters then carries on. "You could tip the balance in our struggle against the Skøl. We can't do much more than irritate them and disrupt a bit of their trade – they have the advantage of numbers. The old crone stays out of politics. But you…" She looks at Dell Garen, but his frown only deepens.

"He could be worse than her," he says.

"We already know he's not a purist like she is," Pony counters. "This girl you're after saving, Mora … she's not Xan, is she?"

"She's Crozoni."

"Well, there you go. He could help." They talk over me as if I'm not here.

"Power like that changes a person. He could turn around and piss on us."

"He wouldn't, would you?" Pony looks at me. "We'll get you to the old bird. It's the least we can do after we made you break your promise." The sack of potatoes is full, but we stand in the hold, contemplating each other. The two of them glow more, on that spirit plane, when they're near each other. It's quietly mesmerizing.

As if she knows what I'm looking at, Pony asks. "Can you read us?"

"You glow. In my mind … it's hard to translate."

I wave a hand to indicate, beyond. What I see in my mind's eye is near impossible to describe.

"Can you tell what we're feeling?"

"Sometimes."

I don't say that I can see plain as day how the quality of Dell Garen's glow intensifies around her. How hers is calmer when she's near him.

"My oldest sister could see life glowing," Pony says. "Crimona. And she could tell people's feelings."

"I thought you said no one in our generation—"

"I did." She waves a hand as if to swipe away my confusion. "Crimona and me, and our other sister, Jafalla – we inherited echoes of power. From our mother who inherited them from her mother. Jafalla was the strongest. And our mother's favourite. Ma told her all the secrets."

"What happened to your sisters?"

"The invasion happened. Crimona died right away. Jaffy … suffered longer." Dell Garen puts a hand on her back. "I'm the last sister standing," she says, keeping a tight rein on her emotions.

"I'm sorry."

"Mist is my best trick," she tells me with a sigh, holding up one hand. I watch as she draws moisture from the air around us to form a small cloud that hovers a few inches over it. The air grows cold and begins to smell pleasantly herbal, even down here, surrounded by tubers and dirt.

"So, was that you – all that mist around the boats?" I think of the clouds of billowing, unearthly fog that sprang out of nowhere when they attacked *Toothsea Tear.* She doesn't consider that strong? And I've seen the way she fights, heron-quick – that's like a gods' favour, surely. Waving that staff around and having palms soft as butter. "You heal yourself too, don't you?"

She frowns. "Yes. But not like you. Not the Ralkalit way. I have to focus on it. My great-grandmother, Spinda, made and broke the Ralkalit promise, became an Alit-fel in service to Naqramaree. To the outside world, she died years ago. But she lives, in Hunger Canyons."

So, that old woman back in Hunger Canyons is Pony's kin. "How old is she?"

"Oh, I've stopped counting. Over a hundred and twenty at least."

"And what exactly does the ritual entail?"

She shrugs. "She won't have the likes of me in her confidence."

"She's your family."

"Not in her eyes. She only bothers with pure Xan and I'm half Crozoni. Half rot. Would you eat a half-rotten apple?"

I don't say anything. *Depends how rotten* … but also, "Who is to say you're rotten at all?" My head is throbbing.

Dell Garen clears his throat. "Exactly," he says into the

prickly silence. "If your Crozoni half's rotten, then what am I? Whole rotten?"

Pony waves a hand dismissively. "You're whole. You don't count."

He hides his wounded feeling away, but I can see it in his glow, on the other plane.

Thirday, Eightmonth 10th. Approaching Ridmouth.

The travel is a blur. Partly because Pony's false mist creeps along with us, partly because I am transforming in ways I don't understand.

I blank out. Lose time. I wrestle a kind of control over my new sense, even as it drives a wedge between me and my ordinary senses. It's as if a layer of glass (or ice, something cold) stands between me and the world.

At my temples the bone has gone soft, as if parts of my skull are gone. When I stretch, my bones crackle like kindling. My reflection shows a hunger I don't feel. *It's not real*, I tell myself, over and over. I try to sleep, but my new sense won't let me.

It wanders out like a thousand hands reaching from my skull, arcing towards life and heat and power and light, sifting and sieving sensations through desperate fingers. Creatures, plants, storm clouds, lightning, hot springs. I sieve people from animals. Animals from insects. Big ones from small ones. Everywhere I look, the more I see.

Night four of no sleep. I sit cross-legged in my

floating room. My thousand hands reach out. A bright glow catches my attention. It's bigger than a whale and shining like something alive, but it's not. It's in a town, I realize. Then I recognize a human life there with a start. Goldie Reedstone. I'm sure it's her. This town must be Ridmouth. I can't find Glister or Blithe. And Goldie glows like she's … trapped and frustrated. I can't communicate with her. She doesn't know I can see her. *What has happened to her?*

I reach past her, around her, back across the distance between us, my many hands still sifting through lives until they snag, incredibly, on another person I know. I'd recognize her anywhere. She's moving fast, like she's on a ship under full sail. But then no, she's on the land. She's on a train.

Mora. How can she be here? Her glow is miserable.

I try to reach her, somehow let her know I sense her, but I can't. She's moving, so I move with her. I'll be damned if I lose her.

Eventually, her glow seems to shine brighter on one side – like the shutters on a lit room opening into the night.

I fall into her glow. She's dreaming herself back in Portcaye, sitting on the steps in Opal Alley.

When she wakes up, I'm flung back into myself. Gods. I thought I was in love before. This is more. I need to see her again. Immediately. To feel her in my arms, in my blood. But I'm back in my real body, in the real world.

This crackling, cursed body with its sideways perception that feels like it's not even mine.

I reach out desperately with my mind and all its hands and find her familiar glow. Sad. But closed. It's closed like a flower curled up against the night.

Only then do I clock, *I'm not alone.* Spinda is here.

I nearly start out of my skin. My thoughts are private. Somehow, without meaning to, I've thrown my own shutters wide. I've left myself open to ambush by this woman. She slices through the waters of my mind like a crocodile.

The crone I met in Hunger Canyons. Pony's great-grandmother. Spinda's in my mind, like a live haunting, though her body's elsewhere.

She looks up, like she's… Is she reading a book?

"Ah," she says. I hear a book snap shut but I can't see it. "You're back. I have been waiting." Is that a smirk? Does she know where I was?

I tilt my head. My dream head, my real one.

"Your powers grow. This is good and bad."

"Where did Mora go?" I ask.

"She is awake," says Spinda. "That's why you lost her. It is hard to do this with the conscious mind. It wants always to reject what it does not understand, which is most things."

I study her expression and her glow.

"It's a good sign you sense life so keenly."

"Is it?"

"Well. It's not a guarantee, but it might help with

Naqramaree. And your … friend. She has a memory that looks like one of Naqramaree's blessings. Odd, that."

"Odd because she's Crozoni?" I guess.

She nods.

"Perhaps the gods care less for such things."

Her glow is too tricky. I can't understand it. But she reads me like her invisible book.

"There is much you don't understand. The important thing is to offer yourself to Naqramaree. To do that, you must be swift. Seff wants you too. His claws tug at you. You must resist. Come to the Amber Altar, or Naqramaree won't be able to hear your plea over the din. Tell those pirates to hurry. And tell my great-granddaughter that the grave robber is heading upriver tomorrow with the girl." Her gaze meets mine. "We will help unite them at long last. That, above all else, will lend her speed."

38

KIT

a big roof

Fourday, Eightmonth 11th. Passing Ridmouth.

"Have you heard of the Amber Altar?" I ask Pony the next morning. Altars make me think of sacrifice.

"Yes, of course. It's … the sacred site. Spinda will take you there. It's in the caves beyond Hunger Canyons, so I've never seen it." She doesn't hide her bitterness. "How did you hear of it?"

"I saw your granny – great-granny. Last night. In a manner of speaking. She wanted me to tell you to hurry up. That the grave robber is going upriver with the girl."

She snaps her head round to me. "He's already on the river with her? Good. Is she well?"

"Who is the girl?"

"My niece."

"And the grave robber – I suppose that's Sacrifice Sting?"

She sounds like her normal self, but on the spirit plane she's glowing with excitement, anger, love, bloodlust. Her niece means a lot to her.

"What did Spinda tell you?" She studies my face. "Let me guess, she was deliberately cryptic and not at all reassuring. Did she scare you? I don't think she knows how scary she is."

My mind goes unbidden back to Pony attacking *Toothsea Tear. Maybe that runs in the family too, Pony.* I don't say it. When she's calmer, I ask, "Is the altar really made of amber?"

"It's not true amber. It's like this—" She taps the piece of amber at the top of her staff. "It's indestructible. Sacred. We call it honeybone."

Honeybone.

"This is the bone of an Alit-fel. One who broke their promise and was cursed to serve Naqramaree or Seff. Which one I don't know. Your bones will look like this too. They're probably changing right now."

"Honeybone." I hear myself echo softly. So, it's changing me down to the bones, this curse.

"That's one reason why the Amber Altar is so special. It was made from a lot of ordinarily indestructible Alit-fel skeletons – moulded together, melted and reformed. They say Kol-Koldia – the greatest Alit-fel who ever lived, the caller of True Prophecies – herself made it over a thousand years ago."

When I look blank, she shakes her head. "What did they teach you up there?"

"I went to a Crozoni school. My parents thought I'd be better off without the old ways."

"But they put you through the Ralkalit Rites!"

"My dad was desperate. He was dying. About to leave me all alone."

Her brows pinch together sympathetically.

"He didn't want me dying of the same thing," I tell her. "My mum had already passed away – heart troubles." My words lodge in my throat. I gesture at her staff. "Can I see it?"

Pony nods, bobbing the top of her staff so it nods along.

What I thought was a clasp of brittle stone is a hyoid bone, partially sunk into the wood, hugged by it, like a wooden throat.

"This is indestructible?"

"Yes."

That would explain why Pony managed to drive it so ably through so many throats back on the sinking *Toothsea Tear.* How fitting, a throat bone, tearing out people's throats.

It's cool to touch and something about it hums.

"It sings," I murmur.

"The honeybone? Or the staff?"

"I'm not sure."

"This part's from whalebone." Pony indicates the main piece of her staff. "Is it singing?"

I can't tell. But I do hear a sound, low and plaintive.

Pony looks worried.

"Is singing a bad sign?" I ask.

"They say the Alit-fel in Seff's service can hear the dead," she explains. "If he has his eye on you, then … well, we need to hurry."

She twists her staff out of my hands gently.

"You haven't eaten in days," she says. "How are you feeling?"

"Been better."

"You look a fright," she confirms with a sympathetic grimace. "It's not far now. You'll have to ride for the last part."

"A horse?"

"Yes, Kalqitlan, a horse. One of the ones over there." She points to the float where the stables are.

"I've only ridden kine. Horses are easier, aren't they?"

The noise she makes is not particularly reassuring.

We reach the Red River estuary only a few hours after Mora and her companions (I've been keeping my mind's eye on her glow) left Ridmouth on their small boats, heading upriver.

Skøl tall ships can't go much past the river mouth – they float too low in the water and this river is shallow and sediment filled. Oden told me that when he was taking me upriver on *Clara* – only ten or eleven days ago. Feels longer.

Pony calls her mist, thick as soup for privacy, and the three huge floats of *Sisters* carry us lightly upriver – another advantage Pony's craft has over its Skøl counterparts.

She steers us ably. "Pirate instincts," she tells me. Says she doesn't see through the mist, just remembers the river and the route that well.

I see hints of the suspension bridge, reduced by the fog to looming grey shapes.

The awful smell of that Ridmouth factory doesn't penetrate the clean, minty mist, and I can't see it either. But I can more than sense it. I feel as if my head is about to burst. In the other plane, there's something there. It's not alive, but its glow is dazzling.

"What is that?" I breathe. "That *glow*."

She glances at me. "Gods, you see that too?"

"What is it?"

"They say copper shines to those who see beyond. The gods love it. And one of the buildings in Ridmouth has a copper roof. That's what you're sensing."

"It's more than shining. It's blinding."

"It's a big roof."

39

MORA

bad news

Humming. A papery scraping as something brushes my face, bristly like Kit's stubble. My head tilts on its own, searching for his lips. Wait. That's not right. I snap my face away. The thing follows. I'm awake. It's dry and brittle. Alive.

Buzzing. Is some huge Badlands mosquito here to drink our blood? Nezza's dark shape sleeps, her breaths barely audible. Goldie's out for the count too. The buzz hasn't woken either of them. Where is it coming from?

It's more than one. Not mosquitos, I decide with relief, dragging myself from the tent into the moonlit cold, tamping down the familiar protests of my sore hip and exhausted body. It's bees. *Night bees?* Are the bees of the south nocturnal, then?

My eyes are puffy. When they finally focus, I can see the bees are swarming away behind the tent. I stumble after them and there, not twenty yards distant, in the shadow of one of the mushroom rocks, I spot Daruunlis. He's not alone.

She's there. Glistening, dark in the dark. My feet keep carrying me towards them. Spinda, my ghost. She's not light and ethereal like she was in my dream – she's a black, quivering cluster. *Oh, Thea's wounds. She's made of bees.*

My body shudders as if mirroring the swarming, unnatural tremors running through the woman-shaped cloud. I thought in my eighteen years I'd experienced most forms of horror and revulsion, but no. Look! Here's a new one.

You've always liked bees, I scold myself. Bees have never hurt me.

Once I was stung by a wasp that flew down my shirt.

It stung because it was trapped. You scared it more than it scared you, Pa said.

My rational side says run. My wild side says scream. *Come now*, I tell myself sternly, *you are flesh and blood. She's just a ghost made of bees.*

Daruunlis is right next to her. He doesn't look afraid. I edge closer. The air grows colder.

"I can't leave Nezza. Where the hell is Pony? She should be close by now." I hear him as I approach. He sounds rather blasé for someone speaking to a ghost.

The "mouth" of the cluster of bees moves. I don't hear her with my ears. The buzzing fills them. But somehow, I know what she's saying.

"She will come," the bee-woman says, in Xan, which I don't speak, but again, from this ghost, I understand it. "First, the boy needs your help. Seff's Circle draws him. If Seff claims him … he will become like Seff's other servants, sleeping through the ages, living by draining the lives of others. Naqramaree must choose him, fight for him. You must find the boy – he is near. Bring him to me. He borrows time already—"

"Who?" I find my courage, stepping beside them.

Daruunlis turns to me, his shoulders relaxing. His wicked grin flashes.

"Do you want the good news or the bad news?"

40

KIT

ravenous

Fourday, Eightmonth 11th. Approaching Hunger Canyons. Evening.

Three Sisters sails on. That ungodly noise its engine made the night they attacked *Toothsea Tear* – that was just for effect. Under its power, our journey is faster, smoother and quieter than when I came here with Oden and *Clara.*

It must still be Fourday when we reach the river's narrowing. Big stones clutter the edges and the water begins to run faster. White and grey in the fading light. Night is falling. The moon rose a while ago, but now it's not a flat scythe in the blue. Its edges are throwing light out into a darkening sky, brighter by the minute.

Pony turns to me, telescoping her spyglass back to a small baton – the size of one of the Skøl's pocket guns instead of something longer than her arm. "We're coming up on it."

More than ever I feel like I drowned in that roiling sea, between *Toothsea Tear* and *Three Sisters*. Was it even me who survived the swim and the lightning, who Dell Garen hooked out of the water? Or am I still in the sea with her, with the goddess, and none of this is real?

A pull I've been feeling for hours intensifies when the boat stops. *Keep moving that way.* A compulsion. It's like having Spinda in my head, amplified. It's not her. I think it might be blocking her.

"Seff's Circle, perhaps," Pony says, when I point out the direction to her. "Your body wants to go there – he draws you. It's part of your … transformation." It's all I can do not to plunge into the water and start to swim (look where that got me last time).

I almost forget Caruq in my daze, but when I force myself below decks to reassure him, he backs away from me, whimpering. Never done that in his life.

"He senses something off with you," Dell Garen says bluntly, giving me a wary look.

The two horses, saddled and bridled, splash delicately into the water. Pony and I follow them. I clamber up on to the saddle of mine there in the water while we're submerged. It wades, burdened with me, up the bank after Pony and her mount. Pony waves at Dell Garen and the handful of her crew who gathered on deck to see us off.

From *Sisters'* mid-river vantage, the bank looked like a small, flat edge before a sheer wall. Now I see an incline threading up the canyon wall, its base hidden artfully by some tufts of sagebrush. Pony spurs her horse up, into the lead.

"Is this natural?" I call to her.

"They built it."

"Who?"

"Spinda's people."

Something about it doesn't seem built at all. We all drip river water down the dry incline. I don't know much about horseflesh. Both of these seem sturdy, but the poor creature carrying me is fretful.

"The mares sense your change," she observes. "They're afraid."

"I'll not hurt them."

"You'll not be you by tomorrow. Especially if Seff claims you."

We ride, my mount following her stablemate nose to tail. I cling with my legs and loop the reins around my wrists. I'm drying already, but don't feel cold. Or hot. Sensations like that have fallen away. No hunger or exhaustion. Pain signals are working fine though. Pounding head – check. Aching jaw – check. My ribs feel like someone with hooves kicked them when I wasn't looking.

Behind the pain, still that pull. To Seff's Circle, it would seem. We're going in the right direction. My sense of the spirit plane is merging with this one, my true vision and the extra sense growing into each other like tangling roots.

Mora's there too – she's so close. I'm still following her glow as she travels with her company. It includes the little girl, Nezza, the Sciencemaster, and – a bit surprisingly – Goldie Reedstone.

I return my focus to Pony and the matter of swaying in time with my horse so I'm not jolted to pieces. In the dark, the mounted pirate ahead of us looks like granite on granite. An old Xan waymarker, stone statue in the starlight.

I tip my banging head back to the sky. Gods, the sky in this place (more stars than not). My view is narrow – we've ridden into a canyon and the walls slice a rectangle. Back in front, the honeybone clasp of Pony's staff glows. I can hear its sad singing, wordless but insistent.

My mind drifts to another night-time ride – a moonlit one, with Mora, last winter. The smell of her in the cold, the shape of her fit so perfectly into me.

Something above us on the canyon wall sends down a rain of gravel. I hear a snarl. Pony's horse snorts and takes off. Mine plunges after, but hers is much faster.

Through the battery of hoofbeats on dry earth, smashing underbrush, spraying stones, I strain to hear Pony's voice. She's trying to wrangle her horse back under control. I can't see the glow of her honeybone clasp any longer – they're gone from ordinary view.

On the spirit plane, I watch Pony, still clamped to her plunging horse, grow more distant.

Mine has chosen a different path – or no path at all

(hard to tell in this murk). I cling for dear life as she leaps a dry gap like a crack in the world. She shakes her head, attempting an abrupt turn before rearing up, her front hoofs kicking the air. There's a lot of stars, but their light is worlds away. I slip off her rump like a sack of sand. My head bounces on a rock, right in the soft part of my temple.

Fuck me, that hurts. Sleep's left me by the wayside for five days, so it doesn't come to coddle me now. My body's a dead weight, prone and stunned.

My mind floats across that spirit plane. Blood and something sweet coats my tongue. I glimpse Pony and her mount, star-distant. Slowly, I reel my senses in, searching. There! The creature that spooked our horses. They were already flighty (my fault), but this thing (a jackal? A desert fox? A wolf?) plunged them into a deep panic.

It chose my mount (slower than Pony's) to keep pace with. Now that she's dumped me off her backside, it's chosen me.

I see in the real world now. Two shining eyes meet mine. A mountain lion. Tall as a wolf, but stocky. Jaw like a bear trap. Each paw could deal my head a blow to match the one it just took from that rock.

A fucking lion. Fuck's. Sake.

It got what it wanted, scaring the horses, unseating a juicy human. But now it sees me (really sees me) and it's scared shitless.

At first it doesn't move. Only a tense quivering in its legs tell me it's just managed to stop itself leaping for me. We regard each other with an awful kind of mutual fascination.

It recovers first, flattening its ears and then leaping away in great, springy bounds. *Too late*, I think. Damage done. My horse is gone – off perpendicular to the way Pony's mount carried her. And I'm alone.

The pull from Seff's Circle calls me onwards, without sound, like one of those impossible songs from the old Xan tales, singing the starveling boy to his doom. I can't control it. It drags me to my feet. I start walking, ravenous.

41

MORA

her authority

So, the Spinda of Sting's legend – my ghost – is alive. She can walk in dreams – and take over bees so she doesn't have to enter a guarded camp in the flesh. Daruunlis works for her.

And Spinda's not the only one who's not dead.

Kit. I push down my elation. *Don't get your hopes up.* But they're long gone, up into the universe, dancing down the Haymaker's Way.

Taking care not to wake Nezza and Goldie, I swap my sleep dress quickly for a plain baggy blouse, a woollen top against the cold and a pair of trousers. As I change, I try to swallow what I've learned. Pony Dewilder, Nezza's aunt, is a pirate. I've seen her *Wanted* poster, back in Portcaye. She's the one who attacked Kit's boat – but she also fished him out of the wreck and brought him upriver. What's more, she and her crew are the pirates who killed Nezza's father, Mister Sculpin.

I pull on my brown boots, not the pinching black shoes from my uniform, and hear Daruunlis's words in my head – *She wanted Nezza back. She wanted vengeance for what he did to Jafalla.*

Back outside, I find Daruunlis carrying a line of rope over one shoulder, and Spinda's bees, waiting for us to follow them.

They've broken from their uncanny Spinda-ish shape – for that I'm grateful. They form a squashed, sideways teardrop that swarms along with a low buzz. I didn't know bees could go this fast. We jog to keep pace. I'm winded already. My hip gives me the usual trouble, but I'm flying. Kit is near. Alive.

"This mess has the gods' handiwork all over it. Wish they would keep their bloody oars out," Daruunlis grumbles good-naturedly.

"Is Kit in a lot of trouble, then?" I gasp.

"You've read Dewilder's book." Daruunlis isn't struggling for breath, though I'm huffing and puffing. "He broke the Ralkalit promise. Naqramaree and Seff will play tug of war with his soul. Seff keeps his servants in eternal undeath. Naqramaree offers a Greater Life." He is breathing a little harder now.

"What is eternal undeath?"

"It's not living."

"That's not –" I puff – "an answer."

His face is grim. "Let's just get him to the altar."

Out of nowhere, another sound grows over the buzzing. Drumming, rhythmic. Tinkling. A pale horse, saddled and bridled but riderless, is flying like my hopes down the path towards us.

Horses. I saw some when we arrived in the field by Hunger Canyons. The Skøl haven't killed the horses here, like they haven't killed the people. They've got donkeys too. But they were fenced in, near the town, and this one is free, running us down.

I start to step aside, but the beautiful creature has seen us and slows. It comes right up to me and drops its nose to my neck like it's looking for comfort. It's lathered all over with sweat, eyes rolling white. I croon encouragement. Soft words, soft sounds. *Pretty, my pretty. Don't worry.* I murmur, barely words.

"I know this horse. It's one of Pony's," Daruunlis says. "She must have given it to Kalqitlan to ride." His eyes scan the way the horse took, but there's nothing moving except Spinda's possessed bees.

I focus on leading Pony's horse through the wastelands.

Kit is crawling when we find him.

Sticky blood coats the left side of his head and a prickly crown of spinifex is tangled in his hair. His cut isn't serious – or not that I can see. The blood is thin and pale, half ichor. He's thin, I realize, with my arm around him. More gaunt than Daruunlis. But he's alive.

"Mora," he croaks, lifting a quavery hand to my face, like he thinks I'm some mirage.

The bees buzz around us. He cradles the side of my face in one hand, but he's looking away, distracted by something I can't see.

Daruunlis spares us a few moments before he tells Kit, "We have to gag you, I'm afraid. Spinda's orders. She says you'll become frantic, drawn to Seff."

Kit nods. He's in a bad state – he can barely speak. "Wait." He forces out the word. Then he groans and his fingers leave me to clutch his temples, his jaw. They search out his ribs, near his heart. He's rigid with pain. I hold him until he unfreezes. He takes a deep breath and blows it out slowly.

"The gag is in case you make a noise," I tell him. Daruunlis told me he might fight us involuntarily. "Sting is nearby with his guards. We have to get you to Spinda and the Amber Altar. Do you understand?"

"Pony's horse…" He tries to say something else. I gesture to the horse beside us, but it's like he can't see it.

"We have her, don't worry, she's here," Daruunlis says softly. "We'll ride her."

"She's here?" Kit says, still confused. His eyes dart everywhere but the horse.

"Pony shouldn't have let him come alone," Daruunlis mutters to me. "He's delirious,"

"Pony didn't let me…" He forces out more words but then he starts shaking and moaning.

Daruunlis holds out the gag.

"All right," Kit whispers, moving his head closer in consent.

We get him on his feet. I soothe the mare while Daruunlis wrestles Kit up to perch on her quivering back. He clings there, looking nauseous. Daruunlis climbs behind him and ties Kit's torso to his own with the rope he brought. I reach up to help secure it.

"Tighter," Daruunlis says. "He's going to fight."

"Mmm-mmm," Kit says through the gag. *I won't fight.*

"You won't be you, soon," Daruunlis says. "We need to head away from Seff's Burial Circle."

The bees lead me. I lead the mare.

When we change heading, Kit goes frantic as predicted. He kicks and jerks, trying to twist his tied arms to pick at the ropes binding him. I lead the horse as fast as I can, taking short, frequent gasps of air. We approach the settlement of Hunger Canyons.

"Follow them!" Daruunlis calls my attention back to the bees. They're not going into the town proper, but up to a large rock standing near the paddock.

Daruunlis may be slim, but he's strong as wire, holding Kit in place. Kit is kicking, anguished noises escaping muffled through his gag. He sounds like he's choking. I can't bear it.

Then we see her, looming out of the light pouring from behind the standing rock. Spinda. Some part of the stone has been shifted aside to reveal a yawning entrance, into the red rock and steeply down – a tunnel. On the threshold, Spinda waits for us. She's real. Flesh covering amber bone, amber marrow. *Does her blood come amber?* She's wearing a grey-green hooded robe, the hood thrown back. She smiles.

I tell myself I never believed she was a ghost.

Her teeth are a cloudy amber. Three Xan women clad in similar styled but darker robes flank her. They're each a decade my senior, sturdy and strong-looking, ready to help us manhandle Kit down the tunnel sloping away behind them. Spinda looks maybe fifty or sixty – but if Dewilder's text was true, she's lived for close to a century and a quarter.

"Spinda." Daruunlis greets her with a formal clasp of his hands near his sternum after he slips heavily off the horse, dragging Kit down with him. I hold one of Kit's arms.

"Well done," Spinda says, reaching to lay a hand on Kit's forehead. It seems to relax him, his breathing sounds less ragged, though his eyes are still staring, wide with pain. The three women circle us, unbinding the rope anchoring Kit to Daruunlis.

They remove his gag, and he slumps against me. He weighs too little. It's easy to hold him up. "Come, bring him inside. We don't have much time."

Daruunlis steps back. Spinda's already ushering her helpers and Kit inside the tunnel. One tries to untangle me from him.

"No," I protest breathlessly. "I'm coming with you."

Kit finds my fingers and grips them. He glares at Spinda then turns to Daruunlis. "Pony," he manages to say.

Spinda leaves her lips set in a straight line and turns to Daruunlis as well.

"Our pirate is in some difficulty. Her mount carried her towards the copperhead wastes. She is alone. You must go to her if she is to save the girl."

"Pony was with him?" Daruunlis sputters, then softer, "He tried to tell us."

"Take one of the horses," Spinda orders. "The bees will guide you. Her ship waits before the narrows. Now go. We must begin."

Her violet gaze swings to me.

"Not you. You are not permitted beyond the river."

"I need her," Kit says haltingly, as if it takes a great effort. He plants his boots against the women's urgings.

"There is no time," Spinda snaps at him.

"Then –" he groans in pain– "yield."

Spinda considers me for half a second. "You may enter," she says.

One of the darker-robed women starts to protest, but Spinda silences her with a raised hand.

I'm allowed. The shocked women bow to her authority.

42

KIT

she leaves me

Fucking hell. My head, my chest, my jaw. My hands. Gods, my hands are being ripped apart, joint by joint. They feel like ribbons of flesh being combed with some torture device. Like they shouldn't be capable of feeling. The nerves should be gone. The tunnel I'm walking down (or more accurately, being dragged along) seems to ripple around us like the gut of a great red worm. But the air is cool and fresh, and the walls are lit with yellow glows at irregular intervals. I'm still trying to figure out what they are – not elektric lights and not lanterns or candles – when we stop.

"Here. Up here." Finally. More strange lights spring to life and I see the space is large. A cavernous room, shelves hewn from its rock walls filled with items. Ordinary ones (like spools of thread and bowls), ones I can't identify (odd sculptures and sacks of leaves), and ones I can identify but would rather not (a solitary amber skull sits in one high niche).

Soft hands help me to a big, flickering, glassy orange slab. This must be the Amber Altar.

"Lie down," Spinda says.

Arms lift and lay me on the surface. As soon as I touch it, something wails across my senses, all of them. A predator diving, a scavenger about to feast. *Gods. What kind of altar is this? What sacrifice does it demand?*

I sink into its bed, warm, rippling. Soft as boneless flesh. The thing's screaming like a moon slung round a planet, crying. It's crackling, not like fire, but like something huge straining against something huger. A bed for a sea, not a person. How does this poky cave hold the infinite? I should be terrified, but I can't hold fast to any feeling, even terror.

"You must tell Naqramaree you offer yourself," the crone instructs me. "Repeat these words."

I obey.

"*By the grace of eternal Macotl, by the truth of Naqramaree and the mercy of Seff, great lords, forgive my break. Naqramaree, I will be true…*"

The pain recedes. I float above myself. Mora's fingers clasp mine. The three attendants in linen robes are wafting scented smoke about the room and chanting another prayer. I'm drenched in sweat. The room grows hot as an oven.

I'm on the Amber Altar that Pony said was made of melted bones. I see myself from above, and from this remove, the strange, impossible sound and motion of the altar is no more. I can watch the women stripping off my clothes and my bracelet of beads and covering me with a rough-spun brown cloth. Am I dead? No. It's some part of the ceremony. All my ribs stick out. Oh boy, I've looked better. Really let myself go.

Spinda is removing her thick robe, changing her clothes. Her attendants fetch a ceremonial robe hung with discs of copper that chime against each other. I see her naked back from this vantage. It's adorned with a bird tattoo like mine – but her bird is different. It's the one we watched together by the river. A Butterfly Bird. The ink seems to move, as if it wants to dance away.

I've left myself behind. What's real and what's not? Mora's holding one of my ravaged hands. They look normal, not shredded. But I can't feel anything.

"It's melting," Mora gasps. I feel her worry and wish I could soothe it.

Time flows like a river, up and down. There's a river underneath us. A water one. I can feel it too. Spinda's soft fingers rest on my neck, feeling my pulse.

A strange hunger – Seff's hunger – is in me again, but it's muted.

"Pray louder, Kalqitlan," she tells me. "Naqramaree must hear you."

I close my eyes and chant. "*By the grace … by the truth*

… great lords… Naqramaree, in sunlight. In rain. Heavens and beyond, be my keeper. Naqramaree. I wait to hear you."

"What's happening to him?" Mora's words come to me stretched and distorted, pliable as warm beeswax.

"Seff still calls him. He does not concede easily. What people do not realize about Seff is … he is full of love. He will open his arms to anyone. Naqramaree is choosy. Kit must draw him."

Blackness. Constellations swimming through it. Then fire all around, not flame. *Blow it out with me, come on.* I can't blow this one out, Dad. I don't want to. I blow on it and it only feeds on my breath. It grows. I want it to consume everything.

I open my eyes. Mora is watching me. I'm back in my body again. The Amber Altar knows me now. Its roar is down to a flicker. Behind Mora, a flue open to the sky. We're under a natural chimney. Stars wheel back and forth with haywire time. The Haymaker's Way looks like those underwater creatures. Life (life, pulsing), glowing everywhere at once. Far away and right here next to me, inside me.

I hear buzzing.

Stars detach from the Haymaker's Way and rain down the flue, landing on me, covering me in tiny sparks of light. Something beautiful alights on every inch of me. I close my eyes. *Naqramaree.* He hears me. He is kind. Bees drink my tears.

I wanted to live. I want that still. To atone? No. To live. Living is more than atonement.

"I thought I lost you…" Mora. Her voice sounds like home. Crozoni with the accent of the north. "… and I never got a chance to say so many things to you. Well. I won't say them now either. You must come back to me. You must wake up and be well and then I'll tell you everything." She has a kind voice. She sounds softer than she is. I like that about her – she's never what anyone expects.

I don't need to open my eyes to see her face. Lovely, in a wide-mouthed, wide-eyed way. I love it. She's molten glass. She's wildflowers. A shady pine forest, frustration and fear. And something else, buried like a seam of copper, buried like something secret and glowing, a treasure, not a corpse.

Did I sleep? The old bird is cutting me. Honey. Blood. My blood? Thin yellow stuff trickles down my arms. The cuts seal.

Spinda tells Mora about the bees. "Naqramaree loves bees. He loves memories. Bees and memory fly together. Sweetness and pain. Honey and sting. Night. Day."

The shining creatures still cover me, a moving blanket.

We will hear you. Come home and be weighed. Two voices. Naqramaree? Seff? When they leave, they leave gently. The stars still cover me. I am wax. I am an altar.

"What are they doing?" Mora asks.

"It's a good sign. The gods will let him enter for the final trial."

"So, he'll be saved?"

A whirring and clanking. One of Spinda's assistants

brushes bees off my forehead. She drapes a damp cloth there. I'm hot but the others are cold.

Out the flue, day begins to find its feet.

Papery clouds. A scent trickles behind the sweet smoke and the smell of thin blood and old sweat – both mine. Orange blossom. Over the chimney, small birds wheel and dart. Their songs pierce the low buzzing of the bees.

"We can only pray now," Spinda says. "Pray that it is Naqramaree who takes him."

"Can I do nothing to help?" Mora pleads. "Let me do something."

"You may bring flowers. Their scent will do him good." She looks up the flue, then sends one of the other women to show Mora the way through the caves.

Mora leaves. She leaves me.

43

MORA

my charge

The sun rising over the desert beyond the Badlands is one of the most beautiful things I've seen in all my eighteen years. The golden band of air above the horizon merging into deep-blue sky, everything backlit like a slice of the world rising up the great celestial stage. *Curtains!* I think of the stage that used to be part of the old Town Hall in Portcaye. Now it's one of their Life Registry buildings. I hate how they ruined that place. Now that hate, like that stage, feels insignificant.

This time yesterday I thought Kit was dead. He's been returned to me, in mortal danger, but not dead. It's one of the ancestors' own miracles. I feel like I haven't stopped praying for days.

Spinda's people have made this place so beautiful. Flowers and trees, water, crops. I recognize prayer grass growing in shiny clumps. Homes. A Xan community. A sanctuary away from those who would belittle, hurt and murder them.

I gather armfuls of dew-covered flowers. The woman who led me here called them asters. Some are mature, with layered rings of petals framing brown-eyed centres dusted with pollen. Some are heavy closed buds the size of my fist.

I go back and forth from the sacred cavern to the open air beyond the caves, glad for the task. Petals stick to my dewy shoes.

The sharp green scent of their torn stems is comforting. The leaves are grey-green, with fuzzy undersides. My palms blister. I love them. My proof of life, his life, still there.

It feels different inside the red rock walls, knowing what's beyond. In the ceremonial cave, the resonance in the air goes under your skin. It's not wind or bells, not touch or sound, but some cousin to all those things, reverberating there.

"That'll do," Spinda tells me as I place the last blooms in the final few pitchers. The attendants have gone.

Kit is still silent, eyes closed and unresponsive, half sunk in the honeybone. A few bees linger, but most have flown. I love the way his breath rises and falls.

I kiss his clammy cheek.

Spinda pats the pallet beside her.

"It's beautiful," I tell her as I sit, gesturing to the cavern's exit. "I had no idea."

"That's … the idea," she says. "It has been the effort of more than one lifetime. And our plans are great. No one must know of it. Beauty draws invaders like locusts. If they know it is here, they will come to strip and ravage."

Her words seem to hang in that oddly ringing air around us.

"I'm sorry about Hiramlan," I blurt. "Sorry for disturbing his remains."

"Hiramlan." She says his name very gently. "He was not conceived in love, much less pleasure… I loved him though. Even before he was born. His father's sins were not his. He was there in my womb when I underwent these rites. When Naqramaree sealed my fate and changed me, he was new-conceived. Together we went into the Altar of Souls. Together we changed."

I think of his small bones, part white, part amber. "His bones changed before he … even developed bones? Before he was born?"

She nods.

"Sting thinks the change happened when you tried to resurrect him."

"If that man had a year of life for every wrong thing he thought, he'd be as old as the rocks. No, my boy did not change then. He was beyond. I failed to bring him back. But I had to try. Sometimes impossible things happen if you believe…" She tilts her head to look out the flue at the cloudless sky.

"What was he like?"

"Trouble. He was wild. With eyes like yours. He loved to sing. And such a quick imagination. He was beginning to learn his share of Naqramaree's blessings. All my children and their children have inherited a share, passed down in my blood. I should never have left him – but I was young. I tried to support too many. I left Hiramlan here and went north to the aid of a group in need."

Xan being persecuted, by my people, I think, *the Crozoni invaders.*

"He drowned. An accident in the river. They tried to revive him, but … he swallowed the water, he breathed it. I might have saved him, not with any extra ritual, just … my healing. But I wasn't here. I will be here for every other child of this community if they need me. We must first protect our own."

"Why was he buried outside your sanctuary?" I gesture to the east, the lands Spinda and her people have guarded and gardened so carefully. I think of what I saw there, past the small field of sagebrush and the canebrake of high, stiff grasses, like the shore of some other world. A beautiful oasis, face-sized flowers and water-fat trees. Paths winding through wild plants, inviting homes raised from the rock and earth, flourishing fields and trickling streams.

I know Hiramlan's coffin came from an old Hunger Canyons graveyard across the river.

"The elders decreed it. Better for me, they said, to have him apart. No blood but pure Xan blood, east beyond the caves. The Crozoni did not want to live here, then. They visited to trade. They knew only what we showed them, and so we have kept it. Hiramlan's father ... well, father is not the right word..." Her voice tails off again.

"He was Crozoni?" I ask, and she nods.

"But that is not why ... that did not matter to me."

I think of how it must have been for her, here, a hundred years ago, when the Crozoni invasion of Makaia was fresh. How did she feel, six years ago, when the Crozoni began to seek refuge in Hunger Canyons, fleeing the Skøl?

I watch Kit's chest rising and falling. Exhaustion fills me up like a bowl. "Have you never been tempted to change the rules?"

"Lately? I am tempted every day," Spinda admits. "We wanted safety. We still offer those with Crozoni blood the sanctuary they offered us. The desert. The red earth. The wild horses. But perhaps we are too rigid."

I sense an old anger behind her words, but I don't think she is angry with me.

"Thank you for allowing me to be here. For letting me see your garden beyond."

"I did it for his sake." She gestures at Kit.

"And I thank you for everything you've done for him."

She nods and we fall silent.

"We have Hiramlan's remains," I whisper. "He's at the camp. Will you take him back? And if you do, will he be buried outside again?"

She doesn't answer. She stares at the Amber Altar like one lost in a fire.

"You were only twenty-six when he died," I say. "Surely you are the eldest of elders now. A grandmother. A great-grandmother. Surely you can decide?"

"I can," she says eventually. "And how old are you, girl, to sway my decision?"

"Eighteen," I tell her, a little indignant, which makes her laugh.

"For you it is a different world," she murmurs, not unkindly. "Should we take in a people who raped and dispossessed us, to build an alliance against a new menace? Where will that lead?"

"I wasn't talking about…" I start to say.

"And yet…" she sighs. "You are not wrong. We must listen to the children."

Kit stirs. His eyelids flutter but don't open.

Spinda nods at him and stands. "It is time. The honeybone will take him and I must help."

"Take him where? What more must he do?"

"A final test. He will go to the crossroads of the gods. He must convince Naqramaree to accept him."

The three attendants return, as if called. Spinda pours her energy into Kit. I can't see it, but somehow, it's clear that's what she's doing. He even starts to look less thin. She chants in Xan. She sings. The three women join in, arms waving in their dark robes. I understand little more than the occasional name. Naqramaree, Seff, Macotl – Kalqitlan. The chant fills me from my knees to my throat. Their voices blend with the hum of the bees echoing up the natural chimney. The part-molten altar melts further. It does look like honey.

I kiss Kit's sleeping forehead. His sweaty hair sticks to my lips. I hold his hand.

The honeybone feels hot. It's not sticky. It rolls off me like oil off water but it absorbs Kit gently while he sleeps. I can't help thinking of bugs in amber, suffocating.

It swallows him. Everything not him is left outside the box. His blanket, a film of dust and dirt, some thorns that were hidden in his hair. I see why they removed his bracelet and clothes earlier – this sinking would have torn them from him.

The amber grows hard and slightly opaque – Kit is just a shape now, drifting behind frosted glass. I press my nose to the outside. His eyes are closed.

Spinda looks depleted. Twenty years older. "I went through the same," she says. "I stayed there three days."

"Three days!"

"Though it felt longer on the other side. But –" she holds up a hand to stop my next exclamation – "he is more loving than I was. His promise was older. He may solve it sooner. I will lend him what strength I can. He could live many years, heal thousands. I have always hoped…" She draws a long, shaky breath. "Another would come. Long have I served Naqramaree here alone."

I'm still kneeling beside the altar. She touches my shoulder. "You must go to the girl now. The only grandchild of little Raqmalis… She needs you."

"Nezza?"

"Yes. I fear she is in grave danger."

"From Sting?" I ask, but Spinda doesn't answer.

"She reminds me of him," she whispers instead. "Hiramlan. He would have liked her. He didn't like everyone. He was … her great-grandfather's older brother."

Understanding hits me like a slap. Who Nezza is to this woman. Why her little teeth are growing in amber. Why her cuts heal. Why her beloved Minty lives unnaturally long. It has nothing to do with butterflies or Sting. She has inherited powers from Spinda, her great-great-grandmother.

Nezza heals herself. I recall the words from Lume Dewilder's preface … *my devoted wife Raqmalis, who, in joining her life with mine, was forced to leave so much behind.* Jafalla's mother. Nezza's grandmother.

I stand up. "Raqmalis wasn't welcome here – because she married a Crozoni man. Even though she was your granddaughter," I whisper.

She looks at me with her old eyes but doesn't deny it. Then she wipes a hand over her forehead. "I never meant to hurt them."

"Just to … exile them? To leave Nezza in the hands of those … scientists!"

"I have been trying to help her. To make amends. But the gods sent this urgent trial. I am weakened. *You* must keep Nezza safe until I regain my strength. I will pray to Naqramaree for his favour in this."

I'm loath to leave Kit. I just got him back from the dead and now he's … what? Stuck at a crossroads for three days, arguing with gods?

But Spinda says Nezza's in grave danger. I touch the Amber Altar one last time, and go to look after my charge.

44

KIT

alone

Time and day unknown. Warm weeping. The honeybone lays against me like a cat, soft, breathing, heavy.

The altar takes me. It's not a place, but I leave all places. It's not bones or air. It's not here in this cavern or now in this world. I can't see the women's faces, the cave or the bees, the birds or the stars.

I'm lost. Nothing. Nowhere.

Everything, I realize, everything in my life has been leading to this moment. Everything was practice for this. And I'm failing.

"I am with you," Spinda says, back in the world. "But you must pass this test alone."

45

MORA

try blood

I've only been gone half a night and one day, but I leave that sacred sanctuary a different person.

I go by the tunnel we came in through. It's still lit by warm yellow light, shining right out of the rock walls, though it's not as bright as it was when we arrived in the night. Outside the sun is setting. A trio of amber Glass Butterflies flutter around each other above a patch of prickly greenery thriving in the hard ground. It's quiet – Sting's dig too distant for any sounds of it to reach me. There's only the chatter of small birds and the crackle of plants spreading themselves in the waning heat. Tendrils of some wild bean weave through the other vegetation, going to seed. Their pods are black, dried and twisted on the outside and white on the inside, full of small black dots. I can hear them going *snap*, popping open to fling their seeds as I hurry past, back to Nezza.

If she's in danger, Daruunlis and Pony's plan must have failed.

Sting's armed guards are patrolling the camp perimeter, but they know me and wave me through. The dig is a hive of activity, though the mood feels sinister. The hired men have located a circle of graves between the two big rocks, yards from where the canvas tents are pitched.

I scan the bodies. Twelve graves. All adult-sized, at least. No more children. They've all been interred without a marker or headstone, not a coffin or even a shroud between them. Just bodies sunken in the soil, now exposed by Sting's work. The men are still digging – the perimeter of the circle within it – looking for another body.

The twelve they've found lie spaced evenly, like the picture in Lume Dewilder's book, except here they are full bodies and not just skulls. Some have decomposed down to the bones. Some still have hair and leathery skin, remarkably well-preserved. Glor and Hunter are helping to expose them. I can't see Sting. He must be in his big tent.

With a wave of relief, I find Nezza, cross-legged – and crosser-tempered, in the entrance of our tent. She's trying to weave desert daisies into a chain.

"Where were you *all* day?"

"I went for a walk and got lost," I tell her lamely, but she doesn't question my story.

"Daruunlis is gone too. He told me we'd see the honeybees but he hasn't come back."

I glance at the guards. "I know where the honeybees are. Will you come with me?"

"No. I'm waiting for Daruunlis. You'll get us lost." Nezza doesn't bother to whisper.

"I won't. Please, Nezza—"

"Everything all right?" One of the older guards casts his wide shadow over us, a dark patch in the dark dusk. His elektric gun is holstered but I can see the glint of gold at its end. Obvious and awful.

"Mora wants me to go with her, and I want to rest," Nezza tells him.

"You rest," I say quickly. "Maybe we'll try and stretch your legs later."

I find Goldie at the northernmost edge of the camp, pacing restlessly under the watchful gaze of two guards.

"For my safety," Goldie explains with a wry twist of her mouth. She's been trying to charm them. It hasn't worked. These men are hard as nails.

We head back towards the camp centre, staying out of earshot of the guards patrolling. "If these are the rewards of *science*, I'm glad I chose a different career," Goldie tells me, grimacing at the unholy scene.

"We need to get Nezza away," I tell her.

She looks at me closely. "What's happened?"

"Kit's not dead," I blurt. "He's been ill. But I think he can be saved. He's here – over the river in the caves..."

I fill her in on the parts I think she might believe.

"And this old healer thinks Nezza is in grave danger?"

"Yes. I fear it too. Sting has been experimenting on her. He believes his … medicine has given her special abilities. It's hard to explain, but he's completely wrong…"

Goldie snorts in an un-Goldie-like way. "I can well believe that. He's been completely wrong for years."

"You!" Sting snaps, appearing suddenly. "Where have you been? Get a brush and help clean that one." He points at one of the corpses Glor is brushing red soil off. "Don't just stand around gawking. You too, cousin. Make yourself useful for once!" He turns back to the workers. "Keep digging! We still haven't found Spinda and she will be the most powerful. Keep searching!"

I help brush dry red dirt off some leg bones until nightfall. In the dark the exposed amber glows eerily.

Nezza manages a little food for dinner.

"Are you feeling better?" I ask her. She sniffs.

"Will Daruunlis come soon?"

"Soon."

We'll rest tonight, I tell myself, watching Minty tuck himself in around Nezza's neck. *Tomorrow, we'll escape.*

My sleep is fitful, and I dream of bees and of Nezza, drowning.

Daruunlis stumbles back into camp – from the direction of Hunger Canyons – at first light, filthy, looking like he hasn't slept in days.

Sting has been up before dawn, stirring everyone out of bed, and I notice I'm not the only one groaning with fatigue. "Up and out! Time is wasting. Today we must finish the dig. The High Governor will be here in two more days!"

It's already the thirteenth. Lovemore's ship flies on the fifteenth. She's coming here. And then, Goldie is convinced, she'll flap over to Shipway town to cast gloom and doom over her political opponents. I still can't believe she has a ship that flies. How would such a thing even work? It sounds like magic.

Sting is glaring at Daruunlis. "What do you think this is?" His hairy cheeks quiver. "A holiday? Where have you been?"

"My apologies, Sciencemaster." Daruunlis dips his head. "I had word a relation was sick."

"You have to fulfil your duties here. It is of absolutely no interest to me whether every damn makkie in your blasted clan drops dead. Don't disappear again without my express leave."

"Of course, Sciencemaster."

Sting jabs a finger into the shoulder of the most convenient guard. It's Wist. "I want tighter security. Tell your fellows. We must be protected from the creatures of the night – desert wolves and mountain lions prowl these parts. And – mark me – not one member of my personal party comes or goes *from this moment* without my prior consent."

"Yes, Sciencemaster."

I catch Daruunlis's eye and I know he's thinking the same thing. *How will we sneak Nezza away now?*

Sting is driving everyone hard, still searching for the skull he saw Spinda brandishing in Lume Dewilder's book. "And there should be a thirteenth grave – much newer than the others!"

Daruunlis bites his lip. Sting's so sure we'll find Spinda buried here. What will he do when he doesn't?

Sting is down on his knees beside another grave. He even has Nezza out here with a trowel. Minty sleeps in his sling across her chest while she piles dirt into little mounds.

"What news of Pony?" I whisper to Daruunlis as I brush dust out of the eye sockets of a corpse.

"Took me a while to find her. She was lost in the wastes, bloody miles away. No water. Could have died. But she'll recover. I took her back to her ship – they're still moored before the narrows. I had to return the long way, so they wouldn't spot me riding a horse up here from nowhere. She means to rescue Nezza soon. She'll ride to Hunger Canyons then come up here on the quiet. We just have to stay alert for her. She'll wait for dark."

"Tonight?"

He nods.

Sting is walking around, pushing us hard. "Look there! Work faster!" He has eyes only for the dig, but the guards remain vigilant.

The landscape is rocky but exposed, with few places to hide.

"Where are you, Spinda?" Sting mutters, rubbing a sweaty shirtsleeve over his forehead. "You would not be decayed to this extent after only six years." He whips round to Daruunlis. "Where the hell is she?"

Daruunlis holds his chin and looks around. "Maybe the stories are wrong. It's hard to be sure with these unwritten tales. I have never, as you know, met anybody who knew how to find this place."

Sting groans with frustration. "So she may, in fact, *not* be here?" He runs a hand covered in dirt through his already dusty hair. "We cannot keep digging in vain," he decides. "Spinda's remains or no, Lovemore will be here tomorrow and we must recreate the ritual. We will adjust the layout of the elektrical circuit."

He waves Glor over. "Start wiring up the skulls, now." Glor rushes to obey. "Hunter!" He summons his other assistant. "Fetch Dewilder's book from my tent. The blue one."

She brings it while Sting orders the hired Crozoni workers to move the ragleaf-fuel generators they've hauled up here inside the circle of corpses. He pulls out a notebook and, looking at the thin paper version in his precious book, redraws the elektric schematic so it has eleven circling skulls leading to a twelfth central one.

"Leave this one out," Sting says, standing over the

largest of the most decomposed corpses. It's nothing but a gleaming amber skeleton.

His heavy hand falls on my shoulder and I jump. "Don't neglect to make sketches of this for posterity. Draw the set-up – and those bodies from different angles. I will be the first of the Skøl race to be irradiated through this process – but not the last!"

I nod mutely and see Glor giving him an uneasy look. Sting imagines himself in the history books already. Why else experiment on himself? He believes he's paving the way for the likes of Lovemore to undergo the same. I recall Daruunlis's damning judgement of his character – *I never met someone more afraid of death. Not Sculpin. Not their precious High Governor. Every person has a fear bigger than death. He has none…*

This quest has always been personal for Sting.

"Go to the tent, quickly," I say to Nezza. "Wait there for me. Promise me, Nezza."

I breathe a little easier when she obeys without questioning for once. I have a feeling Sting is about to realize the limits of his science – and I want her out of his sight.

The assistants wire eleven skulls up in a chain, while Sting places the twelfth skull near the centre of the circle. I watch his thick fingers twisting wire between the jawbone and the top piece of the skull to hold them together, Glor looping it round with a spool of copper wire.

My sketchbook is full of death and desecration. Here a copper wire wrapped around a leathery-skinned skull.

Here another, suspended between two amber nodes. Here one adorns the central skull. A thin, perverse crown.

The dust goes up my nose, down my throat, sticks to the pages of my sketchbook until they look a pale orange instead of white. This book would give a seasoned death doctor nightmares, but it still doesn't capture the full horror. The scent of hot grease from the generators can't mask the cloud of sweat and desperation Sting exudes. My hands, my face, my neck, my very heart all feel caked in squalor. My dread is visceral.

"That should do it," Glor mutters, twisting the wire tighter on the central lone skull. He points back down the line of copper. "The flow of elektricity will mimic the lightning described in the Xan histories. It will pass like so." His finger roughly traces a path in the air through the eleven other skulls. "Each in turn. The unique properties of the amber will amplify and transform it from raw elektricity into a concentrated, life-giving force." His voice cracks with excitement. He sounds so much like Sting. "That force, concentrated into the final skull, will irradiate the bearer, giving them great power—"

"Hurry!"

Sting is standing in the centre of the circle, holding the twelfth skull between his two palms. Hunter stands beside the generators which are humming, already primed.

The rest of Sting's party – plus several of the hired help from Hunger Canyons, are gathered around to witness his moment of triumph.

Mister Cob has set up his apparatus. He stands poised to capture a silverprint of the scene. Goldie hovers near him, eyes fixed on the circle.

"Now, we make history for all of Skøland!" Sting announces. "Now, we transform elektricity to transform *life*!"

Sting raises the skull in his hands to eye level. He stares into its sockets for a moment, before shouting, "Start the power!"

Hunter opens the flow of power, sending elektricity into the array. The elektric current crackles.

Sting yelps abruptly and drops the twelfth skull. He stoops to pick it up again.

"Is it working?" Glor calls, examining one of the skulls in the array. "They're not glowing."

"Wait," Sting says, gritting his teeth, still holding the central skull. "Wait…"

But it won't work – it can't. Mister Cob's hand hovers over part of his equipment, then falls to his side. He exchanges a look with Goldie.

"Switch it off!" Sting shouts. "Check the connections!"

"It – it should work," stammers Glor.

"Try it again," snaps Sting. "Bring more wires. Look at that skull! Remove the skin to expose the amber – the wires must sit *directly* on the amber!" Sting's helpers bustle around, reinforcing the wires. Glor and Hunter painstakingly remove large sections of leathery skin off the skulls of the more well-preserved, so that the elektrical connections sit flush against bone.

"The configuration may need adjusting." Sting consults Dewilder's illustration – the one of lightning striking the central skull held aloft by Spinda. His assistants hurry to do as he says.

"Again!" Sting holds the skull higher, aloft between his two hands, and this time Glor flicks the power switch, sending elektricity pouring through the eleven circling skulls. Some of the mummified flesh starts to burn with a woody smell.

"It's heating up," Sting says. "I feel a vibration. Continue. We must give it time."

He holds the skull while the generators run and run.

We wait. Sting grips the skull and stares at his fingers. The silence is eerily calm, broken only by the crackle and whirr of the generators and the small noises Cob makes taking silverprints.

"Damn it!" Sting finally grunts. In a rage, he drops the skull and then kicks it with the toe of his boot. The lower jaw, still wired to the upper, snaps shut with the same sound Lovemore made banging Hiramlan's bones against the marble bench back in the Castle Hotel. That sound bounces back and forth in the air between the two big chimney rocks, a slow, portentous knelling.

"We must be missing something." Sting gestures to Daruunlis and opens the Dewilder translation. Daruunlis stands at his elbow. Everyone else, Cob, the hired workers, even the guards, seem to be using this opportunity to eat, drink or relieve themselves.

"This list of requirements." Sting has found the page he wants. "The sacred promise, the ingesting of a creature beloved by the Xan gods, the letting of blood, the singing of sacred incantations and lightning strike..." He hands the translation to Hunter and takes the original Dewilder out of his armpit, flipping to the image of Spinda drawing the knife across her palm.

"Is there something in the blood, perhaps the blood of one who has ingested the butterflies that interacts with the forces flowing through the skulls? What does this text say, here?"

I cast my mind back weeks, recalling when I stood in that room outside Cob's darkspace, the smell of paints overlaying that Castle Hotel staleness. I read this caption in Crozoni:

> Inside Seff's Burial Circle, one with the blood of an Alit-fel in service to Naqramaree can rouse and wield the power of Seff's eternal undead.

That passage was the second time I realized the translation didn't match – and the first time it really gave me pause. Does Daruunlis remember all the parts he – or Jafalla – changed?

Hunter's already flipping through the translation, trying to find the page.

"Within Seff's Burial Circle..." Daruunlis begins. His eyes scan the text, and I see his throat bob. He knows he – or perhaps Jafalla – deliberately botched this. I doubt he remembers how. I edge closer to peer around his elbow.

"… the blood of an Alit-fel can rouse and wield the power of life, healing and preservation of youth." I say softly, recalling the exact words I read in the translation back in the Castle Hotel.

Daruunlis shoots me a grateful look and clears his throat. "Indeed," he confirms.

"Very good.," Sting decides. "We must try blood."

46

KIT

their place

Time is a different beast in this nowhere place, gathering and gathering before the start of a race, ready to explode. I must figure this out. I am alone, but for one feathery strand. Spinda's strength. It clings to me.

Macotl is all around. Seff and Naqramaree within her coils.

Mercy. Comfort. Do not fear me. *That is Seff. I know him now.* To serve Naqramaree is to channel his power. That path is steep and dangerous. *Not just for the servant, he means. Also the people they care for.*

Seff's pull on me is not cruel. He seeks to spare me. At the end, everything dwindles, and if my servants have little, it is only because I have little. *Lord of the Gods of Endings, thin and worn. Accustomed to giving everything away.*

In the end we are all equal.

Naqramaree. Charm and desire. *He is strong and well fed*

and fresh and better … because he is the Lord of the Gods of Beginnings. At the beginning, always, everything is new laid before our feet. *Unending glut.*

Spring and winter. They exist together. But Naqramaree, with his plenty, is picky, while Seff has less to give, yet more to care for. No one wants to end.

But endings have their place.

47

MORA

he promises

"Now!" The Sciencemaster General's voice rings from the centre of the circle again, this time edged with pain as he drags one of his scalpels across his palm and squeezes blood on to the twelfth skull. Glor and Hunter begin the flow of elektricity.

Red smears the cloudy amber. I can smell the metallic tang of it. I think I can even hear it, faintly fizzing against the bone.

Sting doesn't believe in the mental, immeasurable ingredients, only physical ones he can count. Songs and promises aren't scientific. But butterflies or elektricity – even blood – those are things he knows the weight of.

"I feel the vibrations more acutely. A throbbing sensation," Sting declares from the circle. His blood drips, thick and obscene, but it seems to add little more than pain and frustration to his experiment.

He winces once more and steps off. Glor hurries to bandage his hand.

"The power could be insufficient," Sting says. He scours the clear skies with a scowl and wipes his bandaged palm over his face.

"We may have underestimated the amount required. An elektrical storm would deliver many orders of magnitude more … but we cannot wait!"

"Would fresh butterflies make a difference? Taken while you stand within the circle?" Glor suggests. Sting appears to consider this. I imagine him holding that skull with one hand and shovelling butterflies down with the other. A shudder climbs up my spine.

"We can add power," Sting decides. "More generators! Pull some off the paddle boats. I want half a dozen more at least. Get them here. We will pay – the cost is no object!"

Sting moves back to the array where he checks and double-checks the set-up while his assistants and the hired men rush to find and attach more generators.

Hours of activity later and the extra power has been attached. They are ready to try again.

Sting removes the bandage from his cut palm and resumes standing in the circle with the skull. He grimaces. Beads of sweat break out on his forehead. He struggles not to cry out as he reopens the cut across his palm and smears more blood over the dried blood already crusted on the otherwise gleaming skull.

Still, his experiment fails.

The day is far from young. "We *must* have something to show the High Governor tomorrow!" Sting announces to no one and everyone. He flexes his injured hand ruefully. "The power is simply not enough," he mutters.

"Perhaps if there were enough blood to anoint each skull..." Hunter says slowly.

Sting clicks the fingers of his uninjured hand. "Blood ... blood..." he mutters. He grabs the book again, flicks to the image of Spinda with the knife.

"You all have young eyes." He looks up at Hunter and Glor, then sweeps his gaze over Daruunlis and even me. "What do you think this is? Red earth or blood?"

"It could be blood," says Hunter.

"A substantial volume of blood," Glor agrees.

The original, though faded, shows what I have to agree is a patently bloody scene. "I think it could be ... wet earth, after a rainfall," I say, clutching at straws. I'm afraid for Nezza. Whatever danger is here, it will be directed at her – I am sure of it.

"Yes. That fits with a lightning storm." Daruunlis backs me up.

Glor is shaking his head. "It's blood. We could use the girl's."

"Yes!" Hunter chimes in. "She's had the butterfly treatment."

What? I could throttle them. My heart thuds hard.

"That may have given her blood the required quality," Glor goes on.

I cast a panicked look at Daruunlis. His violet eyes are hard and wide, gazing back at me without an answer – or not one I want to hear.

Nezza's just another creature in a cage to them. They don't even see her as a person. They know nothing of her ancestry or inheritance and they don't care to learn. They think *they* made her strong. Spinda's warning is clear as day now.

Nezza's still in our tent with Goldie, but Sting gives the canvas a long, thoughtful stare.

"It won't work." Daruunlis draws his attention away. "If the blood of a vigorous man does not, a girl's will give thin magic. But I have another idea. Give me leave to consult the elders who remain in the caves. Their expertise will help us—"

"No! No more input from primitive theoreticians! No more sneaking off. You are to stay here, in this camp." Sting looks up at the sky. It's grey. No sign of the moon that was out in the daytime yesterday. "Maybe we'll get a storm, yet," he says hopefully.

A light rain sweeps over us soon after – weak and short-lived, nothing near the fierce sky-shattering tempest he craves.

"We can't continue running the elektricity in this wet," Glor says gently. Sundown's come quickly, further dampening Sting's already low spirits.

"Be sure to wipe off all the water! We will try again first thing tomorrow!" he orders, retreating to the big tent with his equipment and butterflies and caged spotted devils.

"We have to get Nezza away from here," I hiss at Daruunlis, catching his arm. "Sting's thinking of using her blood – in *substantial volume*."

"I share your fear," Daruunlis murmurs. "Pony is sure to come tonight. But she's weak and the camp is guarded."

"Then *we* must get Nezza out."

He nods. "I'll come to your tent when it's dark enough," he promises.

48

KIT

he steers

Seff lets his servants sleep. They wake rarely, like when his brother calls. To channel Naqramaree is ferocious joy, where Seff is the kindness of inevitability. One holds tight, the other lets go.

Who would you serve? *a god's voice asks, and I feel like I did when my fingers touched Macotl's eye. Everything mixing, life and death, no endings, no beginnings.*

I am not … selfless enough for Seff's service, *I plead. Because I want to live.*

Naqramaree answers: You have love, and many memories.

And I would gather more in your service, *I pray.* I would make more in your name. I would help people.

They murmur together. Breath and drowning.

Paths converge here like lines in a palm. I stand at the crossing of lifeline and heart line and I think I hear Mora's voice pleading for help.

Then he is all around, lifting me, accepting.

I belong, *I think. Even here. Every place, every moment, a crossroads.*

Naqramaree's big hand is round the back of my neck. I have only to walk where he steers.

49

MORA

it's mine

In the dead of night, Daruunlis parts the entrance to the tent I share with Nezza and ducks in, a dark shadow.

"Let's go," he breathes. We wake Nezza, and Daruunlis whispers instructions to her as I tie her shoes. She has Minty secured in his carry pouch, asleep. Goldie watches us from the shadows. I've asked her to stay behind to stage a distraction – but only if we need it.

Nezza doesn't argue or make a noise, for which I'm grateful. Daruunlis exits first and we follow, crouching low, sticking to shadows near the tents.

"Going somewhere?" The guard with the loud breathing has seen me and Nezza. How did I not hear him coming? At least Daruunlis is ahead, still undiscovered.

"Nezza needs to relieve herself," I whisper. "She was scared to go alone."

"Latrine ditch is that way." He speaks at an ordinary volume.

I nod, but my eyes catch on the Burial Circle. The bones there, softly glowing, create a watery, waving impression – like a desert mirage in the deep of night.

Another guard – the big, surly one, great – comes round one of the tents and spots Daruunlis. He hauls him over to us by the arm.

"Has morning come early?" he quips. "Everyone up and about already?"

Another guard appears – Wist. Three guards to three of us. Our odds are plummeting.

"It's a wonderful night for stargazing," Daruunlis says. "Do you see the deer?" He points up, tracing a constellation. "She drinks from the river of stars."

"Not here for stars," says the surly one, just as Wist asks, "Where's the deer?"

Before Daruunlis can point it out again, the loud-breathing guard interrupts.

"Enough. Back to your tents before you wake everyone. Piss in a pot. And no stargazing." He gives Daruunlis a scowl.

The surly guard leads Daruunlis away. Wist meets my eyes, then looks awkwardly up at the stars. He lets his colleague escort Nezza and I back by our elbows.

Daruunlis is out of sight in the dark cluster of tents. I part the entrance flap of ours just as Goldie jumps out, knocking me over and shrieking, "Snake! Snake in the tent!"

Nezza screams with her.

A distraction – and an opportunity. I find my feet and grab Nezza's hand to pull her away, just as someone else seizes her opposite arm.

"Enough!" It's Sting. *How did he get here so quickly?* Our earlier disturbance must have woken him.

"Cousin, control yourself! Nezza, stop. Nezza Sculpin! Every snake we could possibly encounter in these sands is harmless."

Goldie ignores him, shrieking, "It'll kill us in our sleep!"

Nezza's terror is real and I'm doing my best to pretend. Unfortunately, Sting has no fear of snakes. He gives Nezza a shake. "Calm down!" His barked command carries over every other voice. "Guards, search the tent."

They do and, of course, find nothing.

"Whatever you're playing at, cousin, enough of it," Sting says. "You two," he addresses the guards, "keep an extra close watch on this tent tonight." He gives Goldie a mean sneer. "No. More. Noise."

It's over. We file back through the canvas flaps to the musty smell of fabric and failure.

Nezza whines about the snake but she settles back to sleep relatively quickly.

"You were very convincing," I whisper to Goldie.

Her sigh floats past me in the darkness. "I can't even help one little girl escape my own cousin. If only I could have got word to Clem about that ship. It'll be fully operational tomorrow. Lovemore could fly it over that rally in Shipway and murder fifty children like Nezza in a heartbeat."

We've both failed miserably. I slip in and out of wakefulness the rest of the night, praying for Pony and her pirates to come. But when dawn breaks cold on the fifteenth, Sting's tight ship sails on.

Lovemore comes today.

Sting's barked instructions rouse us. He's wearing a grey suit, clean and pressed like his hair. Looks like he hasn't slept a wink though. "Everyone must look their best today," he reminds us, with a glare at Glor's untucked shirt and bleary eyes.

I get Nezza dressed and tidied. Well, apart from Minty, who she insists on wearing in his grubby sling, strapped diagonally across her smartest blouse.

The cook has come down with a fever. Indeed, the hired help have become very scarce.

Goldie helps put some fikka and toast together, but remains firmly on Sting's bad side.

"Under no circumstances are you to show your face when Lovemore arrives," he tells her.

"Naturally," Goldie snaps. Then under her breath, perfectly loud enough for Sting to hear, "Why didn't he leave me in Ridmouth jail? I'd have had more freedom!"

"Freedom? You viper... What do I care for your freedom? Do you have any idea what you were jeopardizing, committing criminal damage ... forget bringing our family into disrepute. You could have set the High Governor back weeks!"

"I wish I had! She's going to use that ship to crush anyone who naysays her. And you know it."

He grinds his jaw, red spreading up his cheeks past the edge of his mutton chops. "There, then! You admit it. You were deliberately trying to sabotage years of progress!"

Goldie doesn't flinch.

"You're a silly girl playing at politics you don't understand," he rails.

"Oh, I understand very well what Lovemore is capable of. As do you. The difference is that I don't condone any of it, and you line up to help her. You are a monster, just like her."

"Get out of my *sight*!" Sting screams the last word.

She starts storming off in the direction of the town.

"Oh, no!" Sting snaps. "Put her in my tent," he orders the nearest guard. "Chain her to the cot if you must."

Goldie lashes out at the guard dragging her away.

Sting turns to another guard – Wist. "Help him!"

Goldie consents to walk so she won't be dragged further.

"*Stay* like a good girl," Sting sneers as she passes him. "If you want to be a bitch, you'll get tied up like one."

Goldie's eyes widen, meeting mine. Mister Cob abandons his silverprinting equipment, with an angry glance at Sting, and follows after her. We watch until they reach the tent. Goldie ducks inside, followed by Mister Cob and Wist. The first guard stands outside.

Sting turns on his heel.

"Nezza!" he calls angrily. The altercation with Goldie has left him in a foul rage. "Come. It is time." He marches up to where I'm standing with Nezza and takes her wrist to pull her behind him.

"I don't want to," Nezza whispers.

"Stop," I say, pulling on her other arm.

Sting strikes my arm, viciously hard. He'll hurt Nezza if we tussle, so I release her just as he pushes me back with a hand near my neck. I fall to a knee, my bad hip misbalancing. Then I feel Daruunlis's hand on my shoulder.

"Wait," he says, squaring up to Sting.

He's taller than the scientist. Sting is heavier.

"Stop," Daruunlis says, his voice louder. "The girl's blood will not wake the powers you desire. You have read the book. It takes an Alit-fel in service to Naqramaree. She is neither."

Sting gives a scornful laugh. "Alit-fel is just a silly title. Naqramaree? A thought! A dream of savages. Myths and gods have no impact on *science*!"

"You are right," Daruunlis placates him. "Such things are not science. But harming a child, that is not science either."

Sting's fury only grows. "I made this girl. She would be dead already, culled, if I wasn't paying for her life and her upkeep. Her blood will work. She has undergone the butterfly treatment. She heals herself." Glor and Hunter stand near him, nodding.

He drags Nezza towards the circle though she clings to me and cries out wordlessly.

"Wait! There is more." Daruunlis rushes after Sting, and the scientist pauses.

"What?"

"The butterfly treatment does nothing," Daruunlis tells him. "The child heals because she is the great-great granddaughter of an Alit-fel. She has Spinda's blood. Only that. I have not been honest with you, Sciencemaster. Let me explain."

Sting drops Nezza's arm. His whole face goes an unnatural shade of red as Daruunlis confesses – first to the mistranslation of *Butterfly Bird* and *Glass Butterfly*.

"In my language, as you know, *bird* and *glass* are spelled the same way. But bird is *mash*, and glass, *mahsh* – they sound different. Amber Glass Butterflies are not Spinda's emblem. That is the Butterfly Bird. Jafalla felt it best to make that simple swap. She did not want this place discovered."

"No!" Sting spits loudly, jaw quivering. "Desperate drivel! Deliberate obfuscation!"

Glor and Hunter are exchanging looks.

"Spinda carries the image of a Butterfly Bird inked on her skin. She still lives," Daruunlis says. "She did not die in the Cull. And only Seff's servants sleep in this circle. Spinda serves Naqramaree."

Sting goes still, his jaw hard. "Lies," he whispers. "I couldn't be – be tricked by common makkies."

"We lied to protect everyone. Some secrets should not be learned. But give me time. I will bring Spinda here to you. She can answer your questions. She is the embodiment of all this."

Sting appears to think for a moment. Then his mouth twists into a sneer as his confidence reasserts itself. It's never let him down before.

"Oh, no." He waggles a finger in Daruunlis's face. "I see what you're doing and it won't work! You seek to throw me off! I made that girl heal. I made that rat live for years. Now you come with these fairy stories. A great, ageless healer, a stone's throw away. Very convenient. Your plotting is transparent. Muddying the waters because I'm right! The butterfly treatments *have* made her blood special! It will work. You will keep me from nothing," he chokes out. "The glory of this discovery will be mine. For Skøland. Today."

"Hear me out. Please." Daruunlis's voice has grown desperate. "Minty lives because Nezza sustains him with the powers she inherited as a descendant of Spinda. Because she loves him."

Nezza's latched on to my side. I can feel her breathing, fast and unsteady. She's shaking too. She looks down at Minty in his sling, then up at me, quizzical.

I can see one of Sting's eyes twitching.

Glor and Hunter are shuffling, open-mouthed.

"More lies," Sting says, but his conviction is faltering.

"I can confirm the mistranslation," I say, my voice trembling as I draw Sting's glare. I move Nezza behind me with one arm. "I've read the original in my language." I have to pause to draw a breath. "And your translation. They're different. You were wrong about—"

I don't see his slap coming. It whips my head to the side with a *crack*.

Daruunlis draws in a sharp breath.

"Enough!" Sting growls. One of his big red hands bunches in the high, ruffly collar of my white blouse and drags me away from Nezza. "You're lying to save her."

"This girl?" I touch my cheek, hot from the slap, and think of the contemptuous way those guards dealt with us last night. Like we were obstacles, not people. I give Nezza a look like the surly guard – dead behind the eyes. "What do I care about her? Who is she to me?"

Nezza's face falls. Gods, does she believe me? Daft child.

"The girl's none of my concern, but I want you to hear the truth," I go on. "Spinda lives. I've met her. She's over a hundred and twenty, and she looks younger than you. I can take you to her. She's in the caves, across the river."

We must at least stall him until Pony and the pirates arrive. I'll promise anything to buy Nezza time.

"In the caves!" Sting snorts with laughter. "You propose we follow you to your troglodyte friends so they can set upon us? Perfidious slut!"

"What if they're telling the truth?" Glor pipes up.

"Poppycock!" Sting declares. He lunges for Nezza and resumes dragging her into the circle.

"Let me go, please." She squirms bravely in his grip. "I don't want to." Her voice comes out clear but quavery. "I'm scared," she admits.

"Shh. Buck up," he tells her. "You will lend me some blood and we will have done." He raises his head and his already booming voice. "Does anyone else presume to tell the Sciencemaster General what is science and what is not?"

Glor and Hunter stand gormlessly shaking their heads.

In the silence, I weave my fingers together and pray to the ancestors. To Thea the Bringer. No. To Naqramaree. *Please, Naqramaree,* I plead. *Send Nezza's pirate aunt and her ship of pirate fellows. Please let Kit come back, please accept him as your own. Let Spinda come. This child needs help and we are not enough…*

Mister Cob comes out of the tent where Goldie's still trapped. The guard outside puts a hand across his chest, then lets him pass. Wist is still inside too.

"Well?" snaps Sting, shoving Nezza into the circle and breathing hard. "Today we repeat the procedure with this chit's blood. And if she is Spinda's kin, her blood may be just what we need." His hand is still clamped firmly around one of Nezza's thin arms.

He needs a result to prove his years of work have not been wasted. He's already imagined his long, long life stretching out like a cat in the sun. He's banked on Lovemore's gratitude and admiration. He can't bear to see his balance fall now, or to fail so personally.

"You cannot do this!" Daruunlis steps up to Sting and tries to peel his fingers off Nezza's arm.

"Desist!" Sting orders, but he drops Nezza's arm. "Seize him!" he instructs two nearby guards.

"Run, Nezza," I cry, but another guard catches her swiftly, tossing her to me.

"Don't try it," he says.

Sting's full attention is back on Daruunlis. "I'll have you strung up for treason before the month is out," he threatens.

"Don't hurt him!" Nezza pleads.

Daruunlis is pinned between two massive guards. "I trusted you." Sting pokes a finger into his translator's chest. "I treated you like a Skøl man. I kept you out of repay labour and still you thank me by sticking your knife in my back." He leans closer and lowers his voice, his tone mocking. "You know … I have a secret too." He laughs. "I wonder if it would interest you to hear it now, when you can do less than nothing about it?" His head swivels like a hairy snake to Nezza. "Her mother did not die of that fever…" His voice trails off.

Daruunlis goes stiff.

"She was indeed very ill for a time. Ill enough to have died. But she lived."

Nezza gives a slight hiccupping gasp.

"Shhh. Not a word," he snaps.

Daruunlis says nothing, but his posture relaxes, his bored look taking over like a reflex.

"Sculpin wished his experiment to be raised without her savage mother's influence. What was her name again?"

"Jafalla Sc-Sculpin," Nezza whispers.

"Not Sculpin." Sting shakes his head at her. "Dewilder. They weren't married. She never took his name. I warned him not to give you his. Put you up above your station. No. Look at the state of you. Your mother was a common whore. Already a mutt by savage standards. You are a mutt's mutt. Her influence would have ruined you for polite society."

Nezza's muddy-violet eyes fill with angry tears. Minty starts to wake in his grubby sling. Her best blouse is untucked, already stained with red dirt, and her hair is escaping in hundreds of wisps from the two plaits I tied it in this morning.

"You said Mother was a scientist's daughter," she says in a slightly louder voice.

Sting laughs again, high-pitched. "Well, she is a repayer now. She has been helping us with our *Dominion*. At the gas processing works, I believe."

Daruunlis watches like a hawk. Now his mind moves fast as one. "She's been in Ridmouth? All this time?" His voice drops to a murmur. "Under copper ... too dazzling. Spinda didn't know. It masked her sight."

"Over five years she's been there," Sting muses. "Such labour is not good for the lungs..."

Daruunlis lurches, jerking his arms so suddenly that the guards at his sides are surprised. One loses hold of his left arm. He throws himself into a swing at Sting, his fist connecting under the scientist's jaw, snapping his teeth together and knocking his head back.

The thud of the punch echoes. Sting staggers but doesn't fall. He cradles his face as the guards get Daruunlis back under control. The translator's mask of calm boredom is shattered, his rage clear as day. His eyes are twinkling, his pupils tiny black spots.

Sting licks his split lip and spits blood, but if anything, he's pleased. He's got a rise out of Daruunlis.

"The brute will out. The mark of your race. A treason trial would take too much effort and cost," Sting says. "More than you're worth."

He opens his neat case of scalpels and selects one before advancing on Nezza beside me.

"Your blood will be just the thing. Stop snivelling for once in your life."

"She's six years old. You can't—" I step in front of her.

"Out of my way!"

"It's my job to look after her—"

"Wait your turn," Sting cuts me off again in a deranged sing-song. "Maybe you will bleed too."

Sting is not interested in fine detail or truth now. He doesn't care that I haven't ingested his butterfly elixir and don't have amber bones. He's desperate.

"Please—"

"Shut. Your. Filthy. Mouth!" His jaw grinds audibly.

And over his screeching, a low rumble of hooves. Two horses, three riders are approaching from the wastes to the southwest.

Sting lets go of Nezza's wrist and watches them. "What's this now?" he asks the nearest guard. Then louder, "What's *this*?"

"I don't know, Sciencemaster General," one of the guards responds, unholstering his gun and moving to the edge of the circle of graves.

Daruunlis squints out into the wastes. The riders are churning up red dust, coming fast.

Nezza cowers further into my side. I put an arm around her.

"What now, weasel?" Sting grabs Daruunlis's chin. "A new plot? A miniature army summoned to your rescue?"

I can see the newcomers well enough now. Their horses are handsome and healthy. A dappled grey, I think, beneath the red dust caked on it, and a chestnut brown. The first carries two women easily, the second a man.

"Jafalla?" Daruunlis's neck jerks forward. "Jafalla. Jafalla. *Ruahee*, Jafalla." *Is that his desperate imagining?*

Jafalla Dewilder? Could it really be her, moments after we learned she's not dead?

Nezza whispers, "Is it her?"

Only I hear her through Daruunlis's continued calls.

"Shut up!" Sting orders, slashing Daruunlis across his chest with the scalpel. Nezza screams.

"Guards!" Sting calls, gesturing to the thundering horses, now within range. "Shoot them!"

The guards start shooting. The pretty chestnut stumbles, keeping its feet, but throwing the man. A Crozoni man, stocky and strong. He rolls in the red dirt before nimbly regaining his feet. He draws a short sword as he runs towards us. The dappled grey with the two women is ahead of him, nearly upon us.

Sting drags Nezza out of my grip. He holds a scalpel to her neck.

"No. Let her go," I sob, but there's another guard restraining me. I strike at him wildly, jabbing an elbow back at him, but he's a wall of unfeeling muscle. I can't free myself.

Daruunlis has been bent, clutching the wound across his chest. Now he straightens and goes very still.

"Sacrifice," he says, his voice slow, low and full of friendship. "Mister Sting, please. She's a child with no part and no fault here. Stop now. We can fix this."

The grey horse has slowed. It stops, blowing hard. The women slip off its back, the younger dropping a long stick – some kind of blunt weapon – to the ground. The older isn't carrying a weapon, not one I can see. They both raise their hands in surrender. The man further behind puts down his sword at the same time, following the lead of the women.

"Benezza," chokes out the older woman. "Baby."

Nezza whimpers in Sting's grip.

Gods alive, I think. *It really is Jafalla.* And now I see the young woman from Sculpin's old sketchbooks, older, unwell, her cheeks less round, her expression pure wrath.

And the two with her, who are they? The younger woman wears a long coat of thin material, cinched round the waist, dark trousers tucked into high boots, a patterned blouse. Her coat tails billow. This must be Pony. Her eyes, like her sister's, are murderously locked on Sting. I see how she could be a pirate, although her resemblance to the image on her wanted poster is passing at best.

"Not one more step!" Sting orders. "I'll cut her throat!" He gestures to the available guards. They bind Jafalla and the pair of pirates immobile with rope and cruel twists of wire left over from the skull array.

"Please." Jafalla starts to say something, but Sting silences her with a furious gesture.

"Gag them!" he orders.

"Mum?" Nezza's voice comes out small, but only half a question. She's stopped crying but her nose is dripping.

I watch as Minty scurries out of his sling, edging around Sting's hand still holding the scalpel to Nezza's neck. He perches on Nezza's shoulder. His thin tongue flits out to her teary cheek. Then his sharp white teeth plunge into Sting's hand.

Sting drops the scalpel, roars and flings Minty through the air, losing his grip on his hostage, who wrenches away from him.

Daruunlis sees an opening. He explodes away from the

guards flanking him, grabbing the elektric gun of one and pointing the barrel towards Sting. He's slim but incredibly scrappy. Still – he has no time to pull the trigger, no time even for half a word. The other guard still has his gun. He lifts it and shoots Daruunlis in the back.

Nezza's scream goes through my bones. I'm reminded, awfully, of the happy shriek she gave when Daruunlis surprised her in the kitchen at the Castle Hotel, all those weeks ago.

I want to live with you, she told him a few days later. Children know who loves them and who doesn't. Better, I think, than adults.

The guard holding me tightens his grip as I reach out a hand to hold one of Nezza's. Minty's found his way back to her shoulder. Daruunlis pushes himself up on one elbow, then collapses. I see his chest moving. He still lives.

"Drag him there!" Sting indicates the centre of the array, near the stack of generators. "And engage it!"

Glor and Hunter power the generators until everything elektric hums. A smoky smell drifts anew from the corpses. Not the smell of burning flesh. More like perfumed wood. The prisoners huddle, the guards watching them closely. Nezza presses closer to me, trembling.

We can do nothing but witness. Only the guards and the assistants and Mister Cob remain. He's not making any silverprints of this mess.

Sting picks up the scalpel and crouches beside the prone form of Daruunlis. Only Jafalla breaks this quiet, trying to talk around her gag, her eyes snapping from Sting to Daruunlis to Nezza. I can't tell what she's trying to say.

"He's going to hurt him," cries Nezza. "Let me go to him!" I pull her back. He's not really going to do it. I can't believe he'd just—

"Look at me," I tell her, moving my one free hand to her cheek, forcing her head on to my shoulder. Jafalla's muffled screams pierce her gag and then all I hear is sobbing. Some of it's mine.

50

KIT

start to run

Firstday, Eightmonth 15th. The Caverns.
I tumble back with a sensation of falling. That feeling of going off a cliff as you drift off to sleep. I'm inside the Amber Altar again, back in Spinda's cave. The Doorway to Worlds. Naqramaree's Altar. The Altar of Kol-Koldia. The Altar of Souls. In the gods' memory, in its thousand years, it has collected many names.

I breathe. The false flames that threatened to burn me up to cinders are gone.

I kneel.

Through the layer of honeybone, inches thick, the cave is distorted. Parts of it shine that shouldn't.

Naqramaree speaks to me and I hear her voice in his. Mora's voice, urgent and afraid.

Please, Naqramaree … let Kit wake up… This child needs help … please…

The altar returns me like a song ending, the notes crashing down. It shatters and reforms as I swim out. It doesn't break. Liquid bone peels off quick as mercury, sticking to itself. I sprawl on the rock of the cavern floor, letting the sensations strike (old senses and new ones), quick and sharp as a beak snatching fish from the river, soft and welcome as waves in the clear shallows. Cold on my knees, dust and blank stone on my palms.

Sweet, ordinary air hugs my skin, earthy and grassy. Macotl's teeth. It's as if my whole life I've been ill without knowing, and suddenly I'm cured. It's the limb and the senses amplified ten times. The gods' curse to feel what they feel.

I am back, an Alit-fel in service to Naqramaree, Lord of the Gods of Beginnings. Seff released me with his blessing. There is no pain. I'm a vessel full of memories, maps and healing. Incredible, indescribable knowledge.

Piles of fat orange flowers are everywhere, several propped in clay vases, wilting. I touch one as I stand, sending amber petals snowing to the red stone floor. A seasoning of black pollen follows. The pupil at the centre stares into me, now fringed with a few thin, clinging lashes. I'm naked.

I find the rough-spun cloth they used to cover me when I was on the altar, wrap it around my waist and secure it with a knot on one side.

Spinda is here. I sense her now, though her power ebbs low. She lies in the shadows on a palette set into a niche in one wall. I lean over her and touch her forehead. She has given me every feather of her strength. I cannot return it now, but she recovers as she sleeps.

I send my sight up and out, a bird escaping the flue. I see what Mora saw to the east – why they call Spinda *Builder.* I see the paradise she has built here, stretching into the desert (four further oases are joined with tunnels to the central hub). We sit at the palm and those are its long fingers. An echo of the convergence and crossroads I felt in the honeybone, in that place beyond all places.

Inside the tunnels, copper wires. They shine in the other plane so that from above, with all my senses, I see a fan of fancy feathers. Like that strutting bird's tail, the Butterfly Bird. Moss green, emerald, blue and gold and copper, growing into the red and white and grey of the Badlands like bright patches of lichen.

A hundred years of work with the energy of an Alit-fel poured into it.

I look away. No more distractions. Mora called out to me. I must find her.

My mind with its thousand reaching hands travels effortlessly now, out towards the town of Hunger Canyons and beyond. I was wading in the shallows trying to use these powers on Pony's boat, searching and filtering glows of life. Now I swim the open ocean effortlessly. Mora, I will know anywhere. I must see her –

There.

No. I realize what's wrong. I start to run.

51

MORA

No One Special

"What have you done?" Mister Cob whispers, his words lost behind the Sciencemaster's next instructions.

"Cover that rubbish!" Sting sneers at his translator's dead body as a guard finds a blanket and throws it over.

He turns to the guards nearest Nezza and me. "Tie them – arms in front. Legs together!" Then looks at his assistants. "More fuel in! Bring me the beakers!" His sanity is in tatters.

"But should we—" Glor briefly locates his backbone before his voice tapers away.

"Are we … hasty, Sciencemaster?" Hunter chimes in, only to shrivel under the Sciencemaster's glare.

"We?" he says softly, a strained shudder to his voice. "There is no *we*." He looks between her and Glor. "I am the master. You are the students. Who is in charge here?"

"You, Sciencemaster." They can't submit fast enough.

"Don't forget it again."

His craven students scurry to do his bidding while his guards bind us. Mister Cob is stumbling to the latrine ditch. This is the Skøl way. Power can do any evil it wants. People will look away. Puke in a ditch but do nothing to stop the evil confronting them. Become the evil.

When we're immobilized near the centre of the circle, Sting calls, "We're ready. Put the power on. I see clearly now. The text mentioned *sacrificial promises*. A blood sacrifice fits. The savages are a violent race."

I think of the image in *Sacred Secrets*. The blood everywhere, pooling around the central figure.

Beside me, Nezza doesn't scream, though I know she has a great set of lungs. She grits her teeth and winces, scrunching her eyes closed as he slices along her forearm.

"It's just a drop of blood. No need to dramatize." His tone is back to being kindly and calm. A scientist's detachment. The anger of moments ago swept away. We might as well be a pair of spotted devils. I try to be as quiet as Nezza when he cuts me, but I whimper.

"Nezza," I whisper to her between Sting's trips to his glass vials, trying to make her look at me and not at the blanket covering what used to be Daruunlis. "You must heal yourself as he cuts you. You must do it right away. Don't let too much blood fall. Are you listening to me, Nezza? Heal yourself."

"I'm trying," Nezza whispers back.

Try harder! I want to snap, looking at the state of her wounds. "Please keep trying," I tell her instead.

Sting carefully collects blood in his spouted jars. My own he pours into the ground. Hers, they divide between the central amber skull and the eleven surrounding. All the while, elektricity flows and Sting returns at periods to raise the central, fizzing skull. Nezza's blood wets the amber bone. Still, the life-altering radiation refuses to show.

Nezza tries using her powers to stem her bleeding. That unnatural cold I recognize from Kit's time in the caves blooms beside me. She smells like mint. I'm amazed I can smell anything other than the iron tang of blood and soil.

"Are you helping me? Focus on yourself, Nezza," I whisper as the air around us grows colder. She's struggling.

"Mum?" she sniffs, her big eyes turned on Jafalla.

But Jafalla is focused like a predator on Sting. If looks could kill. Then I hear a strange, sharp sound. Sting grunts and reels, his head snapping back like it did when Daruunlis struck him.

Is his ghost here?

No. Jafalla's mouth curls around the gag. It's her, somehow, I realize. She's forced Sting to relive his punch to the face.

"W-what?" Sting is looking around, baffled. Glor and Hunter didn't see it happen. Now they peer at him.

They all look confused. Sting shakes his head to clear it. He passes his scalpel and beaker to Glor. "I – I must have tripped. You carry on. More blood." He sits beside the lone skull and rests his head down between his knees.

Nezza is shaking beside me, colder than ever. Glor takes more blood. Hunter hurries with the beakers.

"You're so brave. You can't be brave if you're not scared. You're strong, Nezza. You can do anything," I whisper.

Despite the cold I begin to feel feverish, needles of warm sensation prickling through me, bringing with them a strange need to sleep. The fog is like a blanket. Is it real, or is my vision misting over?

Stay awake, says a voice that sounds like Daruunlis. He's dead though.

Now Minty is fading. A tuft of his fur wafts past me on the cold air of a gathering storm. It's falling out in clumps.

"I can't do it," Nezza cries, her blood welling. It's getting dark awfully quick. The clouds are heavy, ominous. The breeze is only growing higher. Now the pages of Dewilder's book are fluttering madly. I think it might rain. A thunderstorm coming, like Sting wanted. Too late.

Sting stands, holding his jaw. His bottom lip's fat and bloody. I see new blood on his shirtsleeves, as if old cuts on his arms have reopened.

You're killing us, I try to say, but these cold lips and clenched jaw can't form words.

What a road to take on the way to a long, healthy, life – draining the blood of a six-year-old.

"You're a bad man," Nezza's high-pitched voice declares. "And a cack scientist."

Then I'm floating along the Red River, bumping down the rapids. My heart is a bird, not a sponge. It's not ragged and dripping. I've hit my head a few times. My hands are numb. Either I'm still dreaming, or Kit is coming through the mist towards us.

He's topless and he's riding a donkey. I've had worse dreams. I've never seen a donkey run so fast in my life. It's a fierce little thing with a bray like a war cry. They make a glorious sight.

Nezza squints through the sudden darkness of the impossibly huge rain cloud hanging over us and says, "Isn't that your Mister No-one-special?"

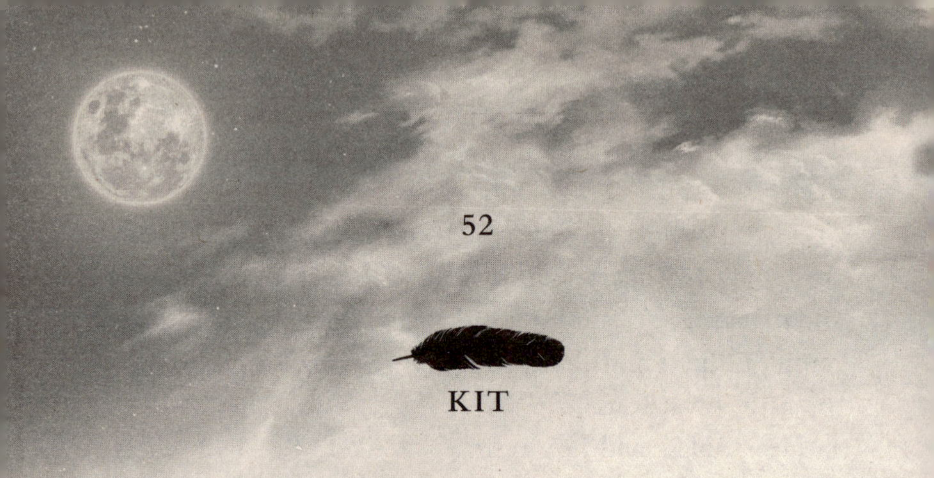

52

KIT

damages

Several minutes earlier… Firstday, Eightmonth 15th. Leaving the Caverns.

This power I have now is more than something extra. I feel I've sloughed off my old skin. It couldn't contain what I am now. What I know. Nothing can hold me back now.

First, I must save Mora. I'm beside her, in the spirit plane, though she's still a few miles away as the crow flies. She's at the circle of Alit-fel. The ones that serve Seff. The undead – neither alive nor dead.

There are twelve buried there, some for a very long time indeed. Aunties and uncles, I should call them – it's more polite. They're glowing like embers left to smoulder under the ashes of the world. Seff's servants to the end.

I might have been one of them had he not let me go.

Mora's glow, I sense, is guttering. I feel her numbness, though within she still carries that bright hope of hers.

The small girl with her is suffering too. Children glow brighter on the spirit plane, but Nezza glows with a different quality, like her aunt. Sting is there too, of course. He must be stopped.

I'm already running back the way we took through these twisting cave passages. The yellow lights in the walls are dim, near extinguished. Spinda's power feeds them no longer. I don't need them to remember the way, even if I'm in two places at once. I'm here, in Spinda's tunnels, and I am also there, hovering close to Mora.

I know what to do next. Naqramaree wills it, and I am his servant.

I begin to gather a storm.

His blessing of knowledge oils my memory. I know how the God of Storms does this, like I know how to stir a pot of stew. What's he cooking with this storm? I feel he will reveal his reasons in good time.

I run without shoes. No matter. The earth gives me strength and the air for miles crackles with it. I push my vision on that spirit plane out further. Downriver, I sense the beautiful pirate craft, *Three Sisters*, still anchored before the Red River narrows. No mist hides it.

A twinge of concern pricks me just as my mind's fingers snag on another cluster of lives further downriver. I know immediately what it must be. Lovemore's secret ship, her *Dominion*, is coming this way, loosely following the river, moving incredibly fast. It casts a great black shadow in this world and the other, shimmering with menace, with Clarion Lovemore's sinister purpose. It was made with pain and designed to bring more. The Reedstones failed to stop it.

Now *Sisters* and all aboard her are in danger. Lovemore's *Dominion* will make mincemeat of them.

I'm out of Spinda's tunnel, but I don't pause. The field of horses and donkeys and those other long-necked hoofed things is near. I destroy the gate holding them, reducing it to splinters with a word and a gesture (Naqramaree's memories) and call the closest creature over. It's easy to mount, even without a saddle (we've both fewer clothes than I'd like).

I serve a god now, and in his house he holds a stock of knowledge and skill like a thousand jars of honey. I have his tools and the confidence to wield them. I pour strength from the earth into my mount's hooves and haunches and solid chest, and it lets out a monstrous call as it thunders along.

I'm no longer a terrible horseman. Mora will love this. *Mora.*

You're so brave, she's telling Nezza. *You can't be brave if you're not scared.*

I concentrate on *Sisters. Dominion* will reduce it to splinters.

The pirates should have someone on lookout, should know this threat approaches. Why isn't Pony shrouding *Sisters* safely under mist?

I search the craft for her and find my answer. She's not aboard. So, where is she? I check again. Fourteen crew remain. Caruq and Cinbar are still there. *Oh.* I pause. Cinbar's glow is bright. I don't have time to count the pups inside her (Caruq, you dog). No Dell Garen. And two horses missing.

I set my mind's hands trawling again. There! Pony is near Mora – very near the circle of undead. She's trussed up and gagged, furious and desperate. And she *is* calling mist – to the circle. Dell Garen is bound beside her, injured and groggy. And a third, another woman. Not one of the crew I've seen before, though her glow is like Pony's and Nezza's – strangely intense. She's hurt too, conscious, and utterly consumed with the kind of rage that burns all sense from anyone.

The two big rocks looming over them look more like giant figures from a game board than mushrooms. One's thinner than the other, one wider. *Seff*, I realize, *and Naqramaree.*

I sift quickly through the others in Sting's camp and find Goldie sitting in a tent with one other, yards from Mora, yards from a child bleeding to death. She's captive. She can't see what's happening.

I move instinctively with my mount's rhythm as it hurtles along, but Pony's ship is still an easy target, bright and obvious, waiting on the river in broad daylight.

If she can't hide it, I must. How to call mist from afar? This memory is weak, but it serves. I must cling to the short mane of my snorting mount as we gain the mushroom rocks. I must urge the mist over Pony's boat some four miles away, as the crow flies. And I must continue to conjure the storm over Mora and Nezza in the sacred Burial Circle. Naqramaree still compels this last. He says I will need it.

The effort makes me sweat, but soon, thick tentacles of fog rise, a million tiny droplets cluster and crawl over *Three Sisters*, a low, heavy mist, flowing down the river and up it.

Part of me still watches over Mora, slumped beside her young charge in the circle of Alit-fel.

Sting's servants have dug Seff's from their beds.

The aunties and uncles lie still, their red clay blankets rucked up. The place looks like a charnel ground. *Even the undead cannot rest.*

In the other plane, wires glow. Copper wires are wrapped around the heads of the aunties and uncles – some touching honeybone directly, others on mummified flesh and hair. More wires link it all up to a small mountain of generators.

My mount is faster than its paddock-mates, if only because our glows are connected and I'm pouring energy and intent over it like syrup. The whole herd gallops after us.

Mora sees me. We're coming up fast, stirring red dust. The towers of the storm I've gathered above us rise from flattened bases to deeper, darker stacks. It's midday, but the sun has been banished to a pale dot. The shade is so deep, some of the exposed bones of Seff's Alit-fel glow softly.

Sting and his crew have dared this twelvefold insult to all the gods. And Macotl's coils. They will pay.

Five of Sting's men stand out in the swirling fog, watching us approach. They swing their guns our way. Armed guards.

"Fire!" Sting orders. I lock eyes with the nearest. His eyes are grey and grim. He fires.

I swallow the energy like a snack. The four others fire on me. They don't miss. The animals behind me skid and slow, scared by the whipcrack, elektric noises.

I focus on defending myself and my mount, but I can't help experimenting with my new, weird abilities. I find if I am careful, I can pluck and drain more than the energy of the shot. I can reach back along the fizzing, flashing path to suck the whole gun dry, like pulling up a weed. My first try leaves the roots underground. Then I get the knack. In moments, I'm reaching through the guns and sucking the energy from their bearers. Long, long roots tear from the earth. Satisfying.

The men go pale as great white radishes who've never seen the sun. First one, already crouched low to avoid the mist, crumples into sleep. I turn to the others and repeat.

Two more guards join the fray, but I've soon knocked them out like the others. Only one guard remains. He's emerging from a tent. I see Goldie ducking out after him. Better late than never.

Sting is hopping up and down screaming things like, "Shoot him! Fire, man! What are you waiting for?"

The lone guard looks at me. He has pretty eyes. He holds his fire. His glow lacks the murderous tinge of his lately conscious fellows. He drops his gun and raises his hands.

My mount stops outside the circle and I slide off. Now I see how short and scraggly it is. It throws back its head to give that terrifying cry again. A braying hee-haw. It's a donkey, not a horse.

I'm already at the centre of the circle where Mora and Nezza sit slumped against each other. Mora's unconscious.

"She's hurt really bad!" The words rip a sob out of Nezza.

Sting and his helpers are frozen mere paces away, speechless, watching me, the whites of their eyes bright in the gloom. The Sciencemaster General holds a bloody scalpel as if it's a pen and he's merely been taking notes.

Mora's blood has been watering this already-red wasteland. I kneel and wrap one arm around her, one around Nezza. The girl gives a small hiccup of relief. She's been bled too, but her wounds are less severe.

I trickle energy into them both. Naqramaree's health.

"Minty?" Nezza whispers, adjusting the folds of her outfit until a small rodent nose twitches out. Her pet. I remember him. I see now, on the spirit plane, how she's been keeping him healthy, keeping him here.

"Minty's fine," I assure her.

"She's getting warmer." Nezza brushes some of Mora's hair off her forehead and sniffs.

Goldie is finally making herself useful. She's over by Pony and her two companions, tugging at their bindings and trying to remove their gags.

"Benezza!" The woman with Pony and Dell Garen has her gag out now, though she's still tied up.

Nezza hears her. "She's my mum," she tells me, like she can't believe it.

Sting has dropped his scalpel. His eyes twitch up to my mountainous clouds and the thunderous, molten light within, waiting to leap to the ground, charging fathoms of air with the promise of a great elektric storm.

Mora's glow flares. "Mora," I murmur in her ear. "Come on, sweetheart. This way." She's reviving.

Her eyelids flutter. "I'll tell you when you wake up," she says, still confused. I pour more strength into her, but there are limits to my healing capabilities. I'm not sure what's best. I think she needs water. She has lost a lot of blood.

I call rain. Behind it, the elektricity gathers still, coiling its haunches like a mountain lion the size of a sign in the stars, ready to split worlds. My skin feels tight all over. (*Hold*, I tell the haunches of lightning. *Hold*.) Warm, lush rain falls, not like rain but in great cataracts, a white waterfall, a chain to anchor the clouds to the world. We're immediately drenched.

I tilt Mora's head back and catch palmfuls to pour into

her mouth. She swallows then sputters then wakes fully.

Nezza has run to her mum. The woman's wearing black. Beside her, Nezza is so red she might be a rock in the landscape. She looks like she's been rolling around a slaughterhouse. But it's not all blood. The rain has turned the red soil to mud that paints her clothes. Tears and rain.

There's an older man helping Goldie now. I think he's the silverprinter they told me about. They free Dell Garen from his restraints and he turns immediately to work on Pony's bindings. Nezza's mum's legs are still bound, but they're sawing through the ropes and wires.

On the other side of the circle, Sting and his assistants watch me. They watch the sticky blood wash off in the rain and the cuts on Mora's soft skin stitching together. I feel Sting's chest churning with a mix of fear, awe and envy. I meet his eyes. There's a swelling around his jaw, part-hidden in his wide sideburn. It's going blue. His bottom lip is badly split and bleeding, like someone punched him in the face, repeatedly. I'm jealous of that person, but not as jealous as Sting is of me.

I see how he sees me (barefoot savage in a skirt, drenched, static crackling across my skin). I look away. I will deal with him in good time. Life before death.

Goldie turns to him. She retrieves the gun of a fallen guard and points it towards Sting and his assistants. "Stay back!" she orders them. That gun's drained, but only Goldie can see the dial telling her that. She's bluffing.

Nezza darts back over to me. She tugs at my hand.

"Can you save him?" She points to a black blanket next to the mound of generators. It's lumped over something. Her muddy fingers dig into my forearm. She blinks, her eyelashes soaked with rain or tears or both. "Please."

In the spirit plane, nothing glows under the blanket. There is no life left to save.

The old spotted devil wrapped around her neck gives a sad chirrup as Nezza pulls me away from Mora, over to the blanket. She folds some of the woollen weave back, and I see a man's body, face first in the dirt. This circle's only fresh corpse.

I look back at Mora, swaying to a stand, at Sting, still surveying his handiwork without a wrinkle in his conscience.

These Skøl like to pay for their lives. Life's a kind of coin to people like Sacrifice Sting. Well, today he will pay with his currency. This man's life is on his bill. This girl's pain.

Today he pays the damages.

53

KIT

the chant

Firstday, Eightmonth 15th. Seff's Burial Circle. Around Noon. I go to Mora, slip my arm around her. She leans into me, then tips her head back, open-mouthed to catch more rain. I want to catch her mouth with mine, but I must be practical. I stroke her cheek.

I shake my head and focus. Nezza's still kneeling beside the dead man. She's pulled the blanket back up, leaving the back of his head and shoulders exposed. She's trying to turn him over. Mora and I move to help her. He's not a heavy corpse, but with my new powers, I'm not sure I'm a proper judge of the weight of things.

His eyes are closed, his throat open. A small cut mars one of his prominent cheekbones, another the bridge of his nose. The front of his shirt and his chest bear a gash, blood still wet. Rain starts to wash it.

I know this man. He helped. He held me on that horse when I would have leaped off to crawl here and insert myself like a thirteenth hour into this eternal clock of the damned.

Rain drips from the ends of his hair and pools pink in the dark hollow between his collarbones.

"He did it for me," Nezza says in a small voice. "He'd be fine if it wasn't for me."

"That's not true," Mora tells her. "He knew what he was doing, Nezza. This is *not* your fault."

Mora keeps telling her things like that, even as the girl begins stitching the gash in the dead man's throat with her power, touching his skin near his torn throat with her fingertips. The effort makes her shine on the other plane with a deep, pearly quality.

"You don't have to do this, Nezza." Mora sets a hand on Nezza's outstretched arm.

"Leave her be." The woman Nezza said was her mother, finally freed of her bindings, lurches over to join us, kneeling in the mud beside the little girl.

"They had her locked away in Ridmouth," Mora whispers to me. "Jafalla Dewilder. Pony's sister. I think Daruunlis and she..."

Jafalla gives Mora a sharp look (in her glow, shock, distress) then turns back to the body.

I touch the woman's shoulder to lend her strength. Her bones feel rather prominent.

Rain washes down as Nezza doggedly closes Daruunlis's

wounds. He's still dead, and when she's finished, so is her pet.

"Minty," whispers Mora.

The animal looks smaller, wet and slumped against the little girl's neck, partly obscuring a dark birthmark. Nezza knows he's gone. She tucks his body into a little pouch she has strung across her. She couldn't keep feeding her pet's life and heal Daruunlis's dead flesh at the same time. Even now, she's exhausted.

Ease, I tell the rain, and it slows to a fine drizzle.

I feel Mora stiffen beside me as a wave of dread ripples through my guts. Something bad is here.

"Lovemore," Mora whispers. I don't need my spirit senses to see it any longer. To the southwest across the wasteland, partly hidden behind one of the tall rock formations, *Dominion* is coming.

Sting spots it at the same time.

"High Governor!" He has a loud, flat voice that reverberates unpleasantly. He glances at Goldie, still training a gun on him, then runs away from Seff's Circle in the direction of *Dominion*, flapping his arms up and down. His two assistants hasten after.

I step to the edge of the circle with Mora, pushing my dripping hair from my eyes. The great blot approaches.

"It's really … *flying*," Mora whispers as Goldie comes to stand on the other side of her.

I saw the ship in my mind, but this is different. Now it's clear what those endless yards of black sails they were piling on to the wagon in Shipway became. A bulging, oval balloon – floating fast this way – with a box of lives strung underneath it. It is a ship, but not like any before it. *An airship.*

Lovemore and her sack of spiders.

"It's armed," Goldie says, shielding her eyes from the rain. "With terrible weapons. It's built to be offensive. And she means to use it."

The balloon looms larger and closer. It's huge.

Goldie looks round Mora to give me a small smile. "I'm glad you're not dead. Mora was devastated."

I smile. "I'll make it up to her."

Goldie stares at my mouth, then at one of the nearby corpses. "Your … teeth…" she stammers.

I widen my smile, looking back at the approaching airship. Lovemore is responsible for this – and for so much more. She and her Sciencemaster General can both pay.

And not the Reedstone way. Jail cells and lawyers and due process. Naqramaree fights fire with fire.

I call my weapon (lightning) with one raised arm and a prayer to the right quarter. I think of the old Xan name for a curved sword. I've been holding it back, though it's there, gathered in this heavy churn above us. It's ready.

"What are you doing?" Goldie asks.

I send a great bolt of lightning to strike *Dominion*, imagining it as a sword, slicing through the balloon. The noise is immense.

"That." I point my arm at the white fizzes crackling over the black sail, as Mora and Goldie recover from the bone-shuddering thunder.

But the airship sails on, unharmed.

"It's a robust build," Goldie laments. "It's designed to withstand storms and lightning and – as I discovered – a certain degree of sabotage."

That apocalyptic bolt of lightning would have sliced right through one of Lovemore's tall ships, reduced it to a plume of fire and ash. But her airship is impervious. I don't try to hit it again.

"They're landing it!" Mora cries.

It drops until the dangling box of lives touches the red soil about a hundred yards away.

A small clattering noise draws my attention to the old man standing over a metal contraption. He's trying to shield it with a blanket, making silverprints, despite the rain.

Sting and his assistants are closing the gap to the landed airship.

"We can't just let them … get away! We have to try to stop them!" Goldie says.

"They're not running away," I tell her. Not Sting, anyway. Others in his party might have more confused intentions. He will stay to see this through.

The balloon-like sail stays inflated, but the wooden ship is now firmly earthbound. A doorway opens in its side, before a gangplank is pushed down to the ground. Several guards disembark, encircling a woman I recognize even from this distance. Lovemore.

I think of how I drew energy from Sting's guards and their guns. I can make short work of Lovemore's protectors too, even this many. I pick her out on the spirit plane. Her glow is dim, her soul scuffed over with years of ugly living.

She and her party begin towards us.

"What is the meaning of all this?" With my enhanced senses, I can hear her ask as she takes in the Burial Circle, her gaze catching on the dug-up bones, still slightly glowing in the gloom. Sting and his assistants have reached her. His glow is still lurid with desire and greed. The power he sought so long was here. He still believes he can claim it for the glory of Skøland.

"Stay back!" I shout, loud as I can – which is now, actually, really loud. "You are not welcome here."

Lovemore, Sting and their party turn to me. I know they will not heed me, but they've been warned.

Mora squeezes my hand tighter. Her fingers feel cold. *Ease further*, I tell the rain. And miles away I let go of the fog shrouding Pony's ship. *Enough.*

Noise and distractions drop away.

I sense that others are coming from Spinda's community, down the tunnels linking each splotch-of-lichen settlement in the desert to her garden beside the caves. Perhaps they've seen my unnatural storm building over their sacred site.

Another stream of people approaches from the town of Hunger Canyons on this side of the river.

Jafalla comes to touch my shoulder. She looks into my eyes with frightening intensity. "I know what you can do. You can do as she did. Spinda. You can raise the undead, and they can raise *him*," she tells me in Xan. "They can save Daruunlis."

"Jafalla," Pony says softly, having followed her sister to stand with us. "It's cruel. Spinda regretted her attempt."

"Only because it didn't work."

"Exactly."

"Her boy had been dead three days. Daruunlis has only just … gone. He won't be far."

"Raise the undead?" I interrupt. Jafalla's deep eyes hold mine.

"Seff's servants. Together, he and Naqramaree can do this. You can ask them."

Her thin hands flutter towards me and I feel a sudden pain as she slashes a scalpel down my bare arm. The one with the scar like frosted ferns.

"What the hell?" Mora snaps, plucking the scalpel from her.

I shunt the pain aside. It's already dull.

"I'm sorry," Jafalla says, speaking Crozoni now for Mora's benefit. My blood drops on the ground. "We need your blood – to wake Seff's servants. But we need more."

I take the scalpel from Mora and cut my other forearm.

My strange, pale blood streams out, light coloured (light in the air), glowing in the grey.

We watch the Burial Circle, looking at the decomposed corpses of Seff's Alit-fel.

"It will work," Jafalla says simply, and then she turns back to me and takes my hands. She begins to chant. My mind turns Naqramaree's memories like a waterwheel. *This can be done.*

"*Seff, release them, Seff, we beg you.*" Jafalla drops one of my hands and holds her free hand out to Nezza.

"Is it working?" the girl asks as she slips her small fingers into her mother's hand. Jafalla nods but doesn't stop chanting. Mora takes my other hand, then the free one of Nezza's. We form a tight circle of four.

Jafalla looks at Nezza with a kind of wonder. They are both so determined. I can't fail them. I watch my blood flowing all by itself in tiny little rivers along the ground, and join the chant.

54

MORA

and fall

It's working. Kit's glowing blood is streaming unnaturally away from the puddle they've made – in twelve directions.

Jafalla ends the chant and we drop hands. She claps twice. "They need energy." She looks up at the storm. "Lightning."

Kit blinks. A tiny pause. He draws his other hand out of mine and tilts his chin back. Stepping away from us, closer to the pile of generators near Daruunlis's body, he raises his arms with a close-lipped smile. It's not like him at all.

A crack like the world's fiercest whip and a seam of lightning brighter than any I've ever seen strikes Kit. It's louder than when he hit Lovemore's airship. The air, the ground, all the space inside my body, everything is quaking. It's all happening at once, too fast. The generators clustered only yards away from him are vibrating.

He remains standing, unmoved, unburnt, channelling lighting. The pile of generators full of ragleaf fuel beside him explode.

I throw my arms uselessly over my head. Such a blast should be strong enough to kill everyone in this circle of death thrice over. But we are unscathed. Kit contains the damage. He directs all the broken, twisted pieces of metal and ceramic, and the heat of the fire and exploding fuel *away*. Away from each one of us, away from Daruunlis's dead body. He's surrounded us with individual tornadoes of protection. The noise drops away – or I've gone deaf. The light endures.

I try to look at Kit through my streaming eyes. It's too bright. His arms are still raised. The strike hasn't come and gone in a flash. It's still striking. Him. A continual, blinding gush of energy pouring from the sky. He's connected to the lightning and now, I see through slitted, watering eyes, he's sending its energy on, through himself, into the amber-boned corpses circling us.

Am I seeing things? I meet Goldie's shocked squint. Jafalla has both arms locked around Nezza as if they're standing at a precipice. Outside the circle, Mister Cob and the only conscious guard, Wist, have abandoned the silverprinting equipment and are simply gawping.

The light and shadow are incredible, but I'm pretty sure a silverprint wouldn't capture this. The rock formations around the Burial Circle cast columns of intense, dancing shadows. Keeping their distance, Sting and Lovemore and their coterie stand deathly still even as their shadows flicker. Their watching faces look whiter, reflecting the unending lightning.

No time to think of them. The dead – the undead – are rising.

A corpse shifts. A knee jerks. Fingers twitch. I see one's neck tilt up. A leathery hand wipes a leathery forehead, dislodging a copper crown. I spin as I watch them, one, then another, rolling, getting their bony knees under them. Squatting. Dripping mud and dust, rain and Nezza's blood. Standing on skeletal feet. Unseeing eye sockets stare at Kit. Jaws grin with amber teeth. *It's not grinning*, I tell myself. *It's got no lips*.

They are, somehow, not terrifying, but pitiful. Goldie is trembling and whimpering.

I look at the little white faces of Sting and Lovemore, their mouths open black holes. This is what Sting's elektric array was mimicking. His motley pile of elektric generators, his few gallons of ragleaf fuel, his stolen blood and worthless hypotheses. *Sting will meet his desire*, Daruunlis told me back in Portcaye. His hypotheses are proving more reliable.

Immense power courses through Kit. He's dark surrounded by light, beset by it. He's not moving, not showing any signs of letting the lightning go.

"It is enough," Jafalla shouts at him. But he doesn't stop.

I fight my way towards him, like walking into a violent windstorm or wading through an elektric sea, the waves up to my neck. I'm floundering. As well as the lightning covering him, flowing through him, there's his own invisible whirlwind circling. I can't reach him. I push. It's too strong. I must be stronger. I finally push through. It's admitting me.

"Don't touch him." Jafalla is trying to lunge after me but the swirling forces are too strong for her. "He will kill you."

I twist away from her, close my eyes, and fall.

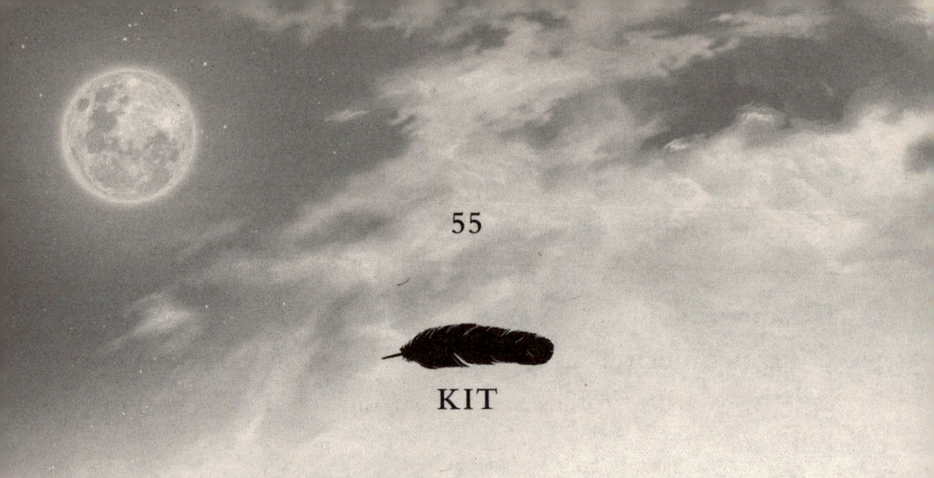

55

KIT

joking

Firstday, Eightmonth 15th. Seff's Burial Circle. Early Afternoon.

Crack. The power goes right to my head, lights me up all over with a gushing sensation. I'm a giant, lightning in my veins instead of blood, lightning filling all the room in my heart.

Crack. Everything throbs like one enormous heartbeat, or a million heartbeats at once. The twelve bright souls in service to Seff awaken.

Twelve fiery wills gaze into mine. Buried sensation and bare confusion. I read their glows and feel I know them already. Naqramaree's memories.

All around, they rise from their undug graves. Some stand. I help them. *Enough.* I think I hear my mother's voice. I mustn't add to this fire. I must be like water. Direct them, not control.

How? I am alone and away, surrounded by a storm. I'm enormous but I'm tiny, a speck holding two worlds together. The joining of the gods' domains. Here I stand at the centre (beginning and end).

Until I'm not alone. Mora is inside the storm, beside me. *Mora*. If I don't release these chains of lightning, she'll get hurt.

So I drop them.

Her hands reach for me. I hold her. The world shrinks to this circuit of my arms with her inside them, safe. My bare toes are coated in red, my feet bracketing her muddy shoes.

The aunties and uncles can help us. My weird blood, combined with Jafalla's pleas to Seff and Naqramaree worked. Now the gods' energy moves them. They are full of a wild sadness.

"You must ask them to save Daruunlis," Jafalla instructs, breaking into my private circuit with Mora, letting in the world. "They will listen to you. Be very polite."

"I wouldn't dare be otherwise," I tell her. I feel their minds still. I can enter them like I entered Mora's dream, when she was asleep.

Please come, I bid the two nearest. *Come to Daruunlis, if you will. He was a good man. We would like to call him back from the gods.*

One is all bones, no skin, glowing bright as a lantern. The second auntie is more preserved. Her skin sags into dark moons under her non-eyes. She has some lashes and brows still, round the dark, ragged holes. More hair is attached to her head in two plaits. She has no clothes, or they've rotted around her. Her breasts droop like her cheeks, deeply wrinkled leather pouches.

"Please bring him back," Jafalla whispers in Xan, but she's not talking to me. She's asking the more-preserved auntie. The woman puts a light hand on the back of Nezza's head and nods. Nezza's plaits are messier than hers.

I feel the skeleton agree as well. Yes. These two are willing. *We need at least one more*, I urge a third, and he joins them. The three begin, arranging Daruunlis's body, joining their hands around him, starting Seff's work on the spirit plane.

I turn to Seff's other Alit-fel.

Nine wills left. Five of them feel quite … vengeful. I look over to where Sting and Lovemore and their guards and assistants have unfrozen. If they fly off, they might live. *Dominion* squats not far behind them, bloated, still and sinister. But they're not running. They're arranging a phalanx of guards some fifty yards outside our circle, getting ready to advance and attack. Only two of the crew are running back to *Dominion*. To ready its state-of-the-art weapons, I guess from their glows.

They truly believe they can defeat *this*.

There's a likely slew of villains, I suggest, gently, speaking in turn to each mind of the five vengeful Alit-fel. They're communicating among themselves as well. Let them have vengeance if they desire it.

The five set off with one will, their bodies in various states of decay, their bones shining like their souls.

Goldie is cowering outside of the circle with Cob, whose silverprinting equipment has fallen into the mud. *They're friendly,* I mention to one of the aunties who's started draining Sting's unconscious guards. The guard with ice-blue eyes watches Lovemore's party, seemingly oblivious to any personal danger he might be in.

The two crew members have reached *Dominion,* but the vengeful five move fast, with unnatural speed. They are nearly upon Lovemore's group.

"Stop right there!" Lovemore's voice reaches us.

Then Sting's, to his guards, with unbending arrogance, "What are you waiting for? Fire!"

On the spirit plane, the anger of the Alit-fel turns to delicious anticipation. Weapon ports on the side of *Dominion* facing us open.

The storm-shaded vista sparkles briefly with the guards' elektric fire. Then a hugely powerful pulse of fire and elektricity shoots towards us from *Dominion* – they're aiming for the Burial Circle. They don't dare fire too close to Lovemore. I use the air and my intent to catch the ball of fire and lob it away into the wilderness.

"Gods alive," Mora whispers, her head turning from

Lovemore's group to me, to the conflagration burning redly in the distance. Over at the scene of confrontation between my quintet of vengeful kin and Lovemore's guards, the guards are dropping like flies.

"You are men of muscle with the greatest weapons of the age!" Sting's rousing words reach us, drifting across the charged landscape.

"Fire, idiot!" he shouts. "Don't crumble like a cretinous kine! Useless fool."

Another pulse comes at us from *Dominion*, and another. I redirect them, losing count, until *Dominion*'s firepower is spent.

Mora stands beside me still. The heavy, soothing beat of her heart thuds through her skin. One of her arms hugs my hips. We watch as the first ragged skeletons – two of the five – break through the guard, drawn to Sting's booming voice. They eat the distance with ease, creatures of elsewhere. They glow in the real plane as well as the spirit one.

"They're beautiful though, aren't they?" she whispers. The beauty of things strikes her differently to most people.

Sting wouldn't recognize beauty if it smacked him in the face. "Away!" he cries. "Begone, foul omens!"

Lovemore's few surviving guards surround her and her sailors, ushering them back in the direction of *Dominion*. Sting's assistants hurry after. One of her party hesitates, eyes on the Alit-fel.

"Please," begs Mora. "That girl, Lovemore's attendant. She only waves a fan. She's not evil. Or … I don't think so."

"We can spare her," I reassure her, though I'm far from certain Seff's undead will heed my request.

As you wish, one of the uncles tells me. The girl slumps in the mud and the guard I spared earlier runs towards her.

The two Alit-fel chasing Sting nearly have him. They're magnificent. Landmarks on the march, urging the whole world ahead of them. If we could see the stars now, I think they would be wheeling, pell-mell.

Bony fingers dig into Sting's shoulders. They grip his ribs, his neck as he struggles in vain to fend them off.

"You will regret this!" he shouts, loud as he can.

But this is what he wanted. Their eternal life. Their undying undeath.

"I must inform you," he chokes out before his voice gives way to a gurgle. A moment later it reaches us for the last time (the same tone, but thinner). "I am no common man to be killed by brutes. I carry Skøland's future—"

This is Makaia, I think.

A hand of hardest bone crushes his voice box.

The two Alit-fel take turns draining him to the end, pushing his prone body back and forth between them, sucking the life from him like I sucked it from the guards and their guns. His face grows as cadaverous as his assailants. The rest of him must too, beneath his formal clothes. He can't believe, right up to the end, that some bunch of upstarts, even undead ones, would subject a man of his status to this indignity. When he collapses, empty,

Mora releases an anxious giggle and then covers her mouth with her free hand.

The three undead who went after Lovemore and company reach them as they gain the ship.

"She's getting away," Mora says, outraged, as Lovemore runs up the gangplank, followed by two nimble sailors. She disappears through the black hole of the opening.

Don't let them leave in that vessel, I say into the minds of the aunties and uncles. I'm not sure how to convey the risk of the airship to them. *They wish to float away and do evil*, I explain.

The sailors who boarded with Lovemore kick the plank down from above, trapping their fellows below.

On the other plane I see Lovemore's dim glow retreating further into the ship – she's ordering the two who fired the weapons on us to fly it away.

The entrance is shrinking, but it's not closed. One of Seff's Alit-fel leaps up and into it, arms first (unnaturally agile), an impossible leap for a normal person. She pulls herself over the edge. She's inside. The glows of the four crew in there with her snuff out like candles one by one.

On the ground more screaming and pleading. "Hunter and Glor are dead," Mora says softly. Her glow is tinged with pity.

Then the auntie's there at the ship's opening, jumping down, dragging the still-live Lovemore behind her into the mud. Her companions join her. One wraps his bony fingers around Lovemore's neck.

"Let me go," she's shrieking, "I will pay whatever you wish."

Deep down though, her emotions are muted. Perhaps seeing this manifestation of her fantasies of long life, she would rather not dream. Her glow drains like water into the life-parched skeletons. It doesn't take long. *Larger than life*, the Skøl liked to call her. Not really.

Lovemore is dead. Everyone in her party with her except the young attendant Mora wanted to spare.

Very little time has passed.

We turn back to the Alit-fel near Daruunlis. I see they've moved his body closer to the thinner of the looming mushroom-shaped rocks (the one that makes me think of Seff).

Pony, Jafalla and Nezza watch over him, oblivious to the fates of Sting and Lovemore.

The guard I spared is with Lovemore's attendant now, locked arm in arm, stumbling towards town.

My storm cloud still hangs over us, dark and gloomy. *Will they need more lightning for this task?* I don't know. I bid it wait.

Come, one of the aunties near Daruunlis tells me. *Bring more. More are needed.* For their ritual, they mean. Human presence is enough. Our will to help one another.

"Come quickly, we need you," Jafalla calls, waving me and Mora over.

We need you. Please. A sudden memory flows through me. Not mine. Spinda's. I see what she did here – how they helped her as she tried to re-tether her small son's soul to his body.

"Come and help!" Nezza takes up the call, running over to first one then another of the nearby Alit-fel.

Mora cups her hands in front of her mouth and shouts to the fleeing guard and the attendant. "Wist! Wait! Fan-lady!"

"She's called Mercy," Nezza tells her.

"Mercy! Wist!" Mora screams.

The guard and the attendant turn to look.

"We need your help!" I shout. They look at each other, hesitating only a moment, then hurry over.

The big skeleton cradles Daruunlis's lifeless body like a baby and stands. Next to him, the preserved auntie takes one of Daruunlis's drooping hands and holds it in hers. With her other hand she touches the base of the big rock towering beside them. The shorter skeleton holds Daruunlis's other hand, and one of Nezza's. Nezza holds Jafalla's hand – and so, on we go in a line. Pony, Dell Garen, Goldie, a couple of aunties and uncles, Cob, Mora, Mercy, Wist and me. I stretch my free hand out to touch the rock formation at the other side of the circle, the wider one. I can't possibly reach it. But reality … bends. In the spirit realm, and in this one. The rock moves until I can touch it. A spark of something like lightning (but not) travels through our joined hands. I feel its echoes running like tremors from my hand to Wist's.

The Alit-fel at the other end of the line start making a

noise like singing. Hard for a skeleton to sing, but the most preserved auntie isn't half bad.

Jafalla joins them like she knows the tune.

The rock at the far end seems to move in the spirit plane too now. I blink and it's Seff, a giant Seff, swishing his tail. A crown of enormous feathers round his head. Do the others see it? I think only the other Alit-fel do, as if Seff appears only in the spirit realm. My hand on the rock formation beside me grows warm. When I look up, it's Naqramaree. His attention is locked on the other towering rock – on Seff.

Then they move. A dance like a flight of birds, circling around us, faster and faster. But only in the spirit plane. In the world, everything is still – impossibly so.

Something unseen builds around us. The thicker it coils, the lighter everything feels. A work of grace. A miracle of Macotl.

Now I see Daruunlis, his glow distant but growing. Then he's back, in his battered body. I recognize his glow before he coughs, tries to sit up and puts his fingers through the ribs of the skeleton cradling him and shrieks. The big skeleton puts him down. His knees buckle.

It is done.

Seff and Naqramaree are gone, the huge rock formations at either end of our chain of people nothing but rocks again. I go to take Mora's hand as we all separate. I can still feel the heat in my palms, like the friction of a rope ripped out of them, without the pain.

Daruunlis's eyes track Jafalla like she's the ghost. We all know it's him, not her, back from the dead.

"Daruunlis," Jafalla says.

"*Ruahee*," he says. *My soul*.

"You came back." Nezza kneels beside him, her glow dazzling. "I fixed your throat!" Her voice, high and laden, cuts through all the others, though it isn't loud. They're all hugging each other.

"Thank you," Daruunlis's muffled voice says. I think he's crying.

Mora's crying and hugging me.

It's too dark.

I let the storm clouds go. A few hailstones, soft, perfectly round like small peas furred in snow, fall down. The wind drops away and the clouds melt like spun sugar in the sun.

Jafalla takes the well-preserved auntie's hands.

"Thank you. Thank you," she says, stretching up to kiss a dark leathery cheek.

Then she turns to her daughter. Takes one of her small hands. "They told me you died."

"They told me *you* died."

"I only found out you lived when I met Pony after I escaped. I came as soon as I healed enough to ride. I would have… I would have done anything to escape earlier if I'd known."

"You would?"

"I sometimes dreamed you and … I still never

dreamed you'd be so … incredibly brave. And clever. And gorgeous."

I enjoy how the sun warms everyone, shining right through Mora's baggy blouse. Around the edges of her, I can see her shape as a darker shadow, the curve of her waist and hips.

She brushes her thumb over my lower lip. I catch her hand and hold it, stroking her inner wrist gently. There's no feeling of Sting's violence there. It's all gone.

I remember her looking at my lips like this, before, when she kissed me in a cool pine wood. It felt like falling to pieces and being remade. I kiss her and I remember her arms around me and there they are.

The inevitable interruption comes too soon.

"Mora…" Nezza pulls on Mora's trailing blouse. "Is he your true love, then?"

Mora laughs.

I raise an eyebrow at her, and she laughs more.

"Of course!" she says eventually. "Nezza, this is Kit."

"Was he dead too?"

"No. I was wrong about that…" Mora starts to explain.

Later, she peers up at Pony. "So … you're the pirate aunt. I've seen your wanted poster. Impressive list of felonies."

"Oh, thank you. What am I fetching these days?"

"Ten thousand Krunan."

Pony exchanges a look with Dell Garen. He stifles a laugh. "No," he says softly, "that's insulting."

"It must be an old one," Pony says, turning back to Mora. "You saw it up north?"

I leave them talking and drift over to one of the aunties. She sees me coming and gestures between Wist and Mercy. *They love.*

I notice the peculiar intensity of their glows. They have that same look as Dell Garen and Pony when they're near each other, but less … uncertain. The auntie regards me affectionately. We don't exactly know each other but I feel it too – a kinship.

I check the glows of the Alit-fel. The angry five over by *Dominion* are pleased with themselves, communicating with each other like old friends.

Mora's over by the tents, releasing Sting's captive spotted devils and butterflies. She looks like a ragged shepherdess with some very unbiddable lambs. The devils scarper as the butterflies tip and tilt through the rain-wet air.

Now she's back by my side, taking my hand. "I'm not sure … what to do with them," I confess, gesturing to the distant skeletons.

"Well, I'm not surprised," a voice says. I turn, and there she is. Spinda, coming up behind us. Her glow is brighter. She's not back to her full self, but she's stronger. "You don't have to know everything on your first day."

Firstday, Eightmonth 15th. Near Hunger Canyons. Late Afternoon.

Spinda finds the crate with her boy's remains. His things. Hiramlan. She sees his skull, in pieces.

"Where will you bury him?" Mora asks.

"I will have him near me on the sunrise side, near the flowers. As I wanted, before."

Outside the tent, the people I sensed earlier are arriving from the town of Hunger Canyons and the Xan territory further east. Xan and Crozoni, and a mixture of the two. Spinda is touched to see so many people, here to help.

I recognize the three women who tended to me at the Amber Altar. Then I see Neema, Jevlan and their children.

"Mora, wasn't it?" Neema comes up to us, seeing our joined hands. Her baby is asleep in a sling. Mora greets her.

"We will spend the day with the Alit-fel beyond the caves," Spinda announces. Her helpers (there are far more than three) gather the undead and lead them back to the caves.

We will sit with them and sing. We will eat – they will not. The thought of food sets my stomach growling. I haven't eaten in days. As Naqramaree's servant, I don't need food. I can draw energy from elsewhere. But I still like food.

"When the lightning that filled them is spent, Seff's servants will sleep," Spinda tells me. "Then we will bring them back to the circle to rest. And I hope you will stay, after," she offers. "The community needs you. I won't last for ever and there's much I can teach you."

"I'm not the only one worth teaching. What about your great-granddaughters..."

"They'd like to teach me a thing or two," she says, clicking her tongue. "And maybe they're right."

"You had your reasons."

"My reasons," she echoes. "I have been a collector of reasons. I've plucked the ones that suited me and let the others lie."

I nod.

"I promised I would protect our people, all our children. I can't keep that promise. I am old enough to realize that. I need you – we all do."

She looks at me with an old woman's wiliness. She's not so different to Missus Scarlet, I think. Women don't grow old without knowing how to get what they want.

"I'll come back," I assure her. "And we'll figure out a way ahead ... together. All together."

"Is that a promise?"

"You must be joking."

56

MORA

my blessings

The public mood greeting the news of Lovemore's untimely demise is jubilant. A rather sensational end for a sensational woman. At the very least, people say, she was an embodiment of the Skøl spirit. There's a period of official mourning, but it's not closely observed.

Long Live Temper Wilforn, New Leader of the Golden World! proclaims the *Evening Gazette*. Without Lovemore, he sweeps to victory as High Governor of the Council of Magistrates.

The papers still insist on their version of events. Clarion Lovemore was misled, the verdict goes, by the real villain of the piece – the fraudulent Sciencemaster General, Sacrifice Sting.

The technology behind the first passenger-carrying airship to be launched for the glory of Skøland, Lovemore's precious *Dominion*, proved catastrophically unsound. The ship failed on its first short test flight, crashing close to a million Krunan worth of parts and labour, including advanced weaponry, into the Badlands, right on top of Sacrifice Sting's misguided anthropological dig – another dud.

Many good people, Lovemore's guards and attendants included, were simply exploded to smithereens. Never to be seen again. Not a body part recovered. Nothing of the ship was left to salvage either – or so the official reports go, corroborated by respectable witnesses to the destruction who miraculously survived it: Golden Reedstone and Mister Praiseworth Cob – the Sciencemaster General's cousin and long-serving silverprinter.

Several Makaians in the area were also thought to have been killed.

The people of Hunger Canyons might tell a different tale. Of invaders and grave robbers reaping the fruits of their sowing. Of a hundred-year thunderstorm sent by the gods, of skeletons wreaking vengeance, of a weaponized airship abandoned, then sailing into the Badlands to be hidden. But such tales are rarely told and never believed.

The pursuit of air travel is no longer a Skøl priority.

"*Birds and bugs are built to fly. Humans are not!*" the new High Governor has quipped.

And as regards Sting's experimentation on extending life – Wilforn is not a believer.

"Under my leadership, we will focus our efforts on living the best lives we can – not on drawing out the lifetimes of the few!" says Temper Wilforn. He still heads a regime where life must be paid for and the whole world impoverished for it. The Reedstones insist he feels the system is antiquated, inequitable and due for an overhaul. Let's see.

Kit and I are back in Portcaye, all garish greens and blues – just for a while. It's been a month since the dust settled, but some things still feel tender and new.

I remember everything and it's like I've never seen this place before. Moss growing between the cobbles with a green like no other. Lightning-white gulls splintering the blue. Bees fat and loud as feelings. The River Rin sounds like a drum full of dry seeds rolling down the world.

With Lovemore gone, will the world really change so much we might belong here – Portcaye, in all its loud colour? One day? I don't know.

The Lugger's almost-home smell hasn't changed. Kit takes my hand, and I can feel the ghost of my long-healed blisters from picking asters in the Badlands stretching the skin of my palm taut. His slow pulse and my faster one strum a rhythm.

I can't help indulging in memories of our voyage here. Pony brought us, on her beautiful ship. It's so much faster than a Skøl tall ship, though that's not why I saw rather less of the voyage back than I did on the journey south. Kit and I spent a lot of time in our shared cabin.

"You praying to Naqramaree, *again*?" Dell Garen would ask us with a smirk.

"I'm very devout," Kit would say, setting my pulse racing, or "Some things need adoration," or "Worship's good for spiritual growth. You should try it."

Dell Garen shut up after a while.

This intimacy with Kit is less intense than it was in that first shared dream, less effortless. But it's better. It might take some practice, but spiritual growth is no hardship.

Blithe has prepared immaculate new paperwork for us. But who needs paperwork with pirate friends? We're going to visit Ruzi and Zako in the Crozon Isles. My ancestral homelands. We'll see how they like it there. We might travel with them to Hunger Canyons. Zako would love to see Caruq and Cinbar – and their pups have arrived. Spinda told me in a dream. She's looking after them – well, Jafalla and Daruunlis and Nezza are, back in Spinda's sanctuary. Spinda wants Kit to go back, and he's said he will – one day.

Kit is still learning what he can do, and what he must do, as a servant of Naqramaree. I couldn't shoulder such a burden. But I know Kit can.

I miss Nezza. Incredibly. All those weeks I felt the care of her like a chore. Now she's three thousand miles away, safe with her mother, and my heart's not giving up that work. Worrying about her. Wondering how she is. The wages of this labour are more than coin and meal and bed.

When we left, I gave her my most precious possession – lock picks aside. She strung the green-glass pendant on its black ribbon around her neck and then strung her skinny arms around mine, my first and last hug from her. I thought of how she used to have Minty dangling around her in his sling and my heart was going like a spotted devil's. Galloping like Kit on a donkey.

When will love stop sneaking up on me? When will I be able to hold on to it for good?

Today, I think. *Tomorrow.*

I take a deep breath and count my blessings.

epilogue

KIT

your mother

Fiveday, Ninemonth 16th. The Lugger, Portcaye.
Mora left Spinda's letter to Hiramlan in my drawer. Today I unroll the brittle old paper.

With Naqramaree's memories I sense how her heart felt to pour out these words. Unbearable. How her hand trembled. I hear my mother's voice when I read it.

I wear the gods' memories like armour. I'm fireproof. But inside I'm just me, and no armour defends a thing like this.

My child, Hiramlan, dearest of my soul,

Forgive my going and my late coming. Forgive my weakness in begging your return. Your mother there beyond, Macotl, our mother, loves you too dearly to part with you. I know because I feel what she feels.

We lay your bones on the sundown side. The elders will it. But in my soul, I stay with you. The best part of me will go always with you, through making and unmaking and beyond.

I miss you. What is left of me will look after your friends here, I promise.

You were joy, my love.

My little one. Go with the gods and be well until we can sing together again.

Your mother

acknowledgements

Thank you for reading this far 🙏 Special thanks if you read *These Stolen Lives* and had kind things to say; reader support makes all the difference to a writer starting out.

I am very thankful for: the moral support of my brilliant agent, Kemi Ogunsanwo, who has buoyed me up throughout, as well as her colleagues at the Seventh Agency; the editorial support of my incisive and empathetic editors at Scholastic – Julia Sanderson and Genevieve Herr; the cheerful support of the wider publishing team including Jamie Gregory, Wendy Shakespeare, Kiran Khanom, Ellen Thompson, Mollie Schofield, Camilla Chetty, Olivia Towers, Harriet Dunlea and Susila Baybars; the mutual support of the *2024 debut group* – more than fifty people, all absolute gems; and the practical support of the GLL Literary Foundation.

Huge love and gratitude to my family and brilliant friends. Especially my lovely mum and dad, my brother, sister-in-law and nephews, Melinda and Des, and JiaJia. Extra special thanks to my partner and sons 🥰 Mark, Jonah and Milo. Love you always.

A final reflection and acknowledgement: it has been emotionally bruising to dream up a dystopian fantasy for a young audience about fictional, historical supremacists in 2024 and 2025. Many days I feel plunged neck-deep in moral dysfunction that is more appalling than any dystopia I could imagine.

At some point there are no words, even for people whose livelihoods are all about words. I simply wish to acknowledge this context, because we do not write in a bubble, no matter how comforting a bubble would be. And while we're here, I wish to acknowledge the Universal Declaration of Human Rights, which is a total banger and very inspiring. It turns seventy-seven in December of 2025, and more people really need to read it and take it to heart.

Collectively, I hope we can work to dream up a world where all people, especially all young people, are treasured and nurtured.

June 2025

Read how Mora's story started in...

When Mora finds out that twelve-year-old Zako is to be put to death by the dangerous new Skøl Governor, she and her friend Kit conspire to smuggle him to safety. But their plan draws them into a dark mystery – and to a heart-pounding mission at the Life Registry itself.

"A striking, thought-provoking YA dystopia"
– *Guardian*

"An intricately crafted world with characters who live and breathe beyond the pages"
- Aisha Bushby, author of *A Pocketful of Stars*